# IN THE DARK TOWER

Inside each globe was a dark shape. Each was black, its skin leathery. Each had two legs, two arms, and a tail, but was no bregil. And no human, either. The necks were long and sinuous, supporting narrow, wedge-shaped heads.

Were these the creatures that had built this place? Were they the ones that had written the ancient books in Laird Douganan's workshop? The prehuman race of man's legends?

"Tanafres! Tanafres!" It was Teletha; she was with Peyto. "You've been staring at these things for nearly an hour!"

Yan knew that they didn't understand. So he told them. "This is it," he said. "Before us is the juncture of seasons unspent, of aeons beyond mortal knowledge. This is the Well of Time, the heart of the magic we seek!"

HEREIN

# TIMESPELL

## FIRST CHRONICLE OF AELWYN

A Tale from the Life of a Man in his Youth and
but Newly Come into his Art

## Robert N. Charrette

HarperPrism
*An Imprint of* HarperPaperbacks

This is a work of fiction. The characters, incidents, and dialogues are products of the author's imagination and are not to be construed as real. Any resemblance to actual events or persons, living or dead, is entirely coincidental.

HarperPaperbacks    *A Division of* HarperCollins*Publishers*
      10 East 53rd Street, New York, N.Y. 10022

Copyright © 1996 by Robert N. Charrette
All rights reserved. No part of this book may be used or reproduced in any manner whatsoever without written permission of the publisher, except in the case of brief quotations embodied in critical articles and reviews. For information address HarperCollins*Publishers*,
10 East 53rd Street, New York, N.Y. 10022.

Cover art by Jean Francois Podevin

First printing: March 1996

Printed in the United States of America

HarperPrism is an imprint of HarperPaperbacks.
HarperPaperbacks, HarperPrism, and colophon are trademarks of HarperCollins*Publishers*.

❖ 10 9 8 7 6 5 4 3 2 1

For PRH, the road from Hawkmoor to the Sixth World was a long one, but a lot of it ran through here. Thanks for the help, ideas, and, of course, the fellowship. The mistakes are the sole responsibility of the author.

# PROLOGUE

YAN TANAFRES' HEART RACED as he bowed his head to accept the benediction of Bishop Colym Danashev. He wanted to smile, but he kept his expression solemn. The old prelate's own face was all grim dignity; doubtless he would disapprove of levity, or any show of joy for that matter, on this occasion. Bishop Colym didn't approve of magic, or magicians.

"Do you come willingly to place yourself in the light of Horesh and submit yourself to the scrutiny of the gods?"

The question was posed in Nitallan, the language of Church, scholars, and educated men. Yan gave his affirmation in the same language. "*Assentar.*"

Certainly he had come here willingly, as far as it went. Yan didn't have much use for the Triadic Church. Not that he didn't believe in the gods; no sane man could deny their existence. It was rather the Church hierarchy and their dogmatic beliefs that he found unpalatable. He didn't see the world as the Church saw the world. This ritual was theirs, not his. The ceremony was a formality, the last step in his long journey of learning. He was here out of political necessity, not religious. Imperial law said that he must be certified by the Triadic Church, so he had submitted himself to the Church's scrutiny in order to be here today. One had to obey the laws if one was to practice magecraft within the boundaries of the Coronal Empire.

Yan understood the importance of ritual—what magician did not?—but though this ceremony was for him, it didn't really involve him. And a good thing, too. His mind was flitting over everything: the clear morning sky above him, the cries of the birds wheeling over the nearby harbor, the chill sea breeze cutting through the thin white linen of his ritual robe. He seemed adrift in time within his own mind, his plans for the future mixing with memories of the past. Were he supposed to take an active role in this ritual, he would have ruined it.

Bishop Colym seemed oblivious to Yan's lack of presence. The prelate accepted a thurible from an acolyte and shook it thrice over Yan's bowed head. Clouds of incense rose to the heavens, but enough billowed out to fill Yan's nose with the heavy, cloying scent. The blessing completed, the bishop turned and led the way into the cathedral, where he would celebrate the morning mass.

A quartet of acolytes fell in behind the bishop while the six concelebrating priests, each garbed in the colors of his or her order, formed up around the kneeling Yan. An arm clad in gray reached out and motioned Yan to rise.

Gray was the color of the Einthofites, priests devoted to the god of learning. They were the vigilant guardians of the Church. Ever alert for signs of the taint of the old dark magic, they would only certify those they considered competently trained and morally correct, and without their certification no one could obtain an Imperial license to practice magic.

Yan looked up into the face of Fra Shain. The priest had been Yan's chief examiner and the Einthofite's approval was the important part, not this fancy dress display. The smile on the man's face was friendly and it told Yan what he wanted to know.

Yan had been judged morally correct. Whatever that meant. And why shouldn't he have been? He gave his honor to the gods as was appropriate for any man, and he had never had enough concern for Triadic doctrine to have ever been tempted by any heresy. The questioning had all been just another formality.

Rising to his feet, Yan entered the cathedral, surrounded by the priests. The morning-cool shadows of the cathedral steps gave way to the deeper chill of the nave. Ahead of them, the bishop began the chant of greeting, singing as he advanced across the cathedral floor toward the sanctuary. Yan and his priestly escort emerged from the nave and entered a pool of variegated light that the morning sun cast through the great window in the eastern wall. The colors were brilliant, amazing, almost magical. There were so many of them, shades and tints and strong clear primaries. He smiled to see them.

Most of the children born in his year were long past their apprenticeships. He knew his dalliance in childhood was not really a fault in him, though he had found it hard to believe on the long dark nights when he had struggled over some point of arcane theory. Another flaw in his integration of heart and mind, he supposed. His mind knew that a mage's path was different from an ordinary man's. Longer, certainly. He hadn't let that deter him because the call to magic was too strong. And now he was almost free to follow that call.

The bishop reached the edge of the sanctuary, bowing before stepping up and continuing on toward the altar. Three banks of candles burned on the plain altar, sparking light from the veins of mineral crisscrossing the dark green stone. Malachite, Yan observed, with veins of quartz and flecks of mica. He knew that there would be other inclusions that he could not identify from a distance. There would have to be, if the stone was suitable to serve as an altar.

The bishop bowed before the altar, holding his bow as the acolytes separated, moving around him in their stiff formal gaits. They continued on to their assigned places along the sides of the sanctuary. The priests escorting Yan stopped at the edge of the sanctuary. Fra Shain nodded once to Yan, signaling him to kneel. He did; at once the cold of the stone floor flowed up through the worthless barrier of his linen gown and into his knees. One by one, the priests left him. As each passed, he or she spoke words of blessing from the deity to whom that priest was especially devoted. A green-clad priest of the martial deity Vehr abjured him to bear sufferings with a glad heart, for the betterment they brought to those who understood that suffering preceded enlightenment. That was a sentiment Yan had heard often enough from his master. Did the Vehrite know how cold the cathedral floor was? Probably.

Bishop Colym took the holy mirror from the altar, raising it to catch the light from the main window and send beams flashing around the cathedral. Shafts of light illuminated the bright paintings on the vaulted ceiling and in the arcaded walls, bringing the new day to frozen scenes from Triadic scripture, and incidentally gifting the worshipers gathered in the church with momentary blindness.

Prepared, Yan had bowed his head to shield his eyes. He had no need for the reminder of his earthly mortality, just as he had no eye for the splendor of the paintings or for the sparse crowd. He searched the sanctuary for what he knew had to be there, distressed that it was not immediately visible. Then Fra Shain reentered the sanctuary from a doorway to Yan's left. The priest carried a fat velvet pillow upon which lay what Yan had sought.

Upon that cushion lay the real end to Yan's long apprenticeship: his *claviarm*, the amulet whose construction was the last work of an apprentice magician. Under the guidance of his master, he had painstakingly constructed the talisman of only the finest materials, or at least the finest he could afford. Nine months it had taken him to make it, nine months in which he had feared he'd slip and destroy some component, or that his workmanship would be insufficient for the task and it wouldn't work. But in the end he had completed the *claviarm*, and though it was far cruder than his master's, Gan Tidoni had praised Yan's craftsmanship.

Besides being the culmination of his apprenticeship, the *claviarm* was a magician's most basic tool. With it in his grasp, Yan could more easily focus the power of magic and wield the energies of sorcery. Not that he'd had any real chance to do so. Upon finishing the *claviarm*, Gan Tidoni had guided him through the bonding ritual; and then taken away the *claviarm* pending Yan's approval by the Church. Yan had barely tasted the power, but the brief touch had been enough to tell him that he had been right to pursue the path he had selected on his choosing day. Soon his *claviarm* would be returned to him. He would be able to taste the magic whenever he wanted. Soon he would be practicing the art he had studied so long and struggled so hard to learn.

Fra Shain paced across the sanctuary with excruciating slowness, carrying Yan's *claviarm* to the altar and laying it before the mirror the bishop had placed upright in its stand. Overhead in the south tower, the cathedral bells started to toll. Within the sanctuary, the mass began.

Yan's mind refused to focus on the ritual. He realized that he had paid scant attention to the people in the cathedral. There had been a few persons scattered about, but he didn't remember seeing any familiar faces or shapes among the gathered shadows, save for the stout form of Gan Tidoni. Yan wanted to know who had come to this mass, who had come to observe the new magician receive his *claviarm.* Yan wanted to look around him, but that wouldn't do. The bishop was facing him, intoning the Creed of Belief. Yan could not look around without the bishop seeing, and disapproving. He feared that it was not yet too late for Bishop Colym to withhold the Church's certification.

The mass continued. Yan's knees felt dead, pressed to total compaction against the stone. Experimentally, he tried wiggling his toes.

Two of the priests approached the altar, Fra Shain and the Vehrite. The Einthofite again took up the pillow, while the Vehrite took up another object that had lain unseen on the stone, a long two-handed sword. The bishop took his place between the two lesser priests and the three of them approached Yan, stopping halfway between him and the altar.

Yan felt a buzz in his head, a strange sense of *over there*, and found his eyes drawn to the *claviarm.* He realized that he was experiencing what Gan Tidoni had told him he would: the mage's bond with his *claviarm.* This was what his master had meant when he said that Yan would know the *claviarm* and the *claviarm* would know him. It felt . . . right.

He missed much of what the bishop said next.

" . . . and behold on my other hand the symbol of the might of our heavenly lords and ladies, warders of this world we call Aelwyn. As the sword of justice smote the unbelievers in ancient times, so too will it smite those who are so deluded as to follow in such wicked paths."

With the *claviarm* so near, Yan's mystical senses were enhanced, and he realized with a shock that an aura of power limned all three of the priests. He had no time to consider the revelation before the bishop stepped up to him and laid his palm on Yan's forehead.

"Do you renounce the dark path?"

As much as the mysteries of magic had always attracted him, Yan had never felt drawn to the power reputedly offered by the forbidden dark magics. What loss was it to give up something you didn't need?

"*Assentar.*"

The bishop's hand lingered on his head for a moment as the old prelate glowered at him. Was the man's expression a trifle grimmer than it had been before? How could you tell? Bishop Colym's habitual expression was a frown.

"In you, I sense no taint of the deceivers," the bishop said in the common tongue as he took his hand away. He reached back and took the *claviarm* from the pillow. Turning again to Yan, the bishop held out the *claviarm* to Yan.

"Receive by my hand this talisman of your own making. Your life, too, is of your own making, and you shall gather in only what you have cast forth. Remember always who grants you the power you will wield through this talisman."

Yan reached up to take the *claviarm* from the bishop. As his fingers touched the chain, a jolt hit him like the shock of touching metal in winter. This too was expected, and he controlled his impulse to flinch. Gan Tidoni had warned him of this common phenomenon, resulting from the reunion of magician and *claviarm.*

With a slow, reverent motion, Yan slipped the chain

over his head and settled the *claviarm* on his chest. Everything was all right. In fact, more right than it had ever been. With the *claviarm* hanging around his neck, he was, at last, a mage.


When Yan stood again on the steps of the cathedral, Alys his mother and Dancie his sister rushed forward to greet him. Dav Tanafres, his father, trudged up the stairs behind them, wobbling slightly as he put his weight on his wooden foot. Dav's face was scrunched into a tight ball of disapproval, as always. In the midst of the cheerful reunion with the feminine side of his family, Yan noticed that neither his brother nor any of his brother's family was present.

"Where's Fal?"

His mother looked down suddenly and his sister looked to their father.

"Still ain't got no sense." Dav hawked and spit on the steps. "It's the middle of the week, boy. Shop's got to stay open. Can't just shut things down and hare off to the city when it ain't no holiday. *Some* people understand about responsibility." Dav cast a venomous glance at the well-dressed man standing a few yards away from the family group. "You've had your fling. Don't say I agree with her about everything, but I gotta say Alys was right to say we can't fault you for wanting to try. But your contract's up and you're all done here now, aren't you, boy?"

"I've just begun, Father."

Dav's mouth hardened, making the bristle of his stubble stand out. "Don't be talking stupid. You ain't too old to learn an honest trade. I was older than you when I put up the sword and took up the craft. There's room for another in the shop."

"Yan is not going to be a shoemaker, Dav," Alys told her husband. "He's too smart for that."

Dav spun on her. "You saying I'm stupid, woman?"

"I ain't saying that."

"Shoemaking's an honest trade. Good enough for me. Good enough for Fal. Good enough to put a roof over your ungrateful head, woman." Alys cringed under the lash of her husband's tongue and started to sob. He raised his hand. "I ought to knock some sense into you."

Without thinking, Yan stepped between them. Dav's narrowed eyes stared into Yan's.

"You're not big enough to stop me from thrashing you, boy."

"But you're too smart to try, Father."

To Yan's surprise, Dav's eyes darted down to the amulet on Yan's breast. The old man's mouth twitched as Dav gave Yan the eye, the same evaluating eye that he gave customers while deciding how much to charge. Unsettled, Yan stood his ground more from uncertainty than from any conviction. Dav Tanafres had an uncanny ability to sense fear in others and his usual response was to strike out at it.

Yan thought for a moment about what he'd do if his father struck him. Most people would expect him to use sorcery on his father, but there wasn't anything he could do in that regard. Gan Tidoni had not taught him any spells suitable to fighting. Besides, it would be unethical. If his father resorted to violence, fists and feet would decide the issue. It had been years since his last beating, but Yan remembered the punishment he'd taken from his father. Though Yan was older now, bigger and stronger, he doubted he was a match for his ex-soldier father, even if he could bring himself to strike the man. Old lessons, learned far too well.

Dav's eyes flicked to the *claviarm* again. Slowly, he lowered his arm. "Ain't nobody says I'm stupid."

"No one did," Yan said. In a gap in his mother's sobbing, he heard his sister sigh in relief.

"Good thing, too." Dav tugged at his jerkin, settling the garment back into place. "Well, we seen you get your magic thing. Time to go home. Got a lot of work that needs doing. You got work, boy?"

"I've got expectations."

"My roof's only good for them as can earn their keep."

"Dav," Alys said plaintively.

"Man's got to be practical, Alys. I don't want no argument."

"But, Dav."

Dav's anger flared again, but a sideways glance at his white-robed son cooled him down. "You want to talk about this, Alys, we talk about it at home, not out in the street where any gossip can hear. You understand, Alys?"

"Yes, Dav."

"Good." Dav turned to Yan "I made you an offer, boy, and you turned me down. I done what a man ought to do. Now, I'm only gonna tell you once. I paid all I'm gonna pay to feed you. You made your choice and now you can live with it. Ain't many that gets a second choosing day. Fewer still that throw it away. We're quits now, boy. There ain't no place for you under my roof no more. You understand?"

Yan nodded.

"Good enough." Dav stretched out his arm and herded Alys and Dancie down the steps. He didn't look back, but Dancie did. Her eyes were full of tears.

Yan felt frustrated and angry. He didn't know what to do. Then he remembered that someone was waiting to speak to him, and felt ashamed that his former teacher had witnessed his family reunion. Trying not to be obvious, Yan looked to see how his master had taken the scene.

Gan Hebrim Tidoni leaned on a staff, looking out over the city as if nothing of interest was occurring nearby. Yan knew better, but was relieved that the gan had elected to be polite.

Gan Tidoni's appearance gave no clue to his profession. The staff he bore was not carved with arcane sigils, nor was it begemmed as a ritual staff might be. It was just a simple walking stick suited to a man of his age and girth. His *claviarm* was concealed beneath ordinary clothes. He wore a velvet doublet with the upper and lower sleeves slitted to show the fine white linen beneath, and the cuffs and collars of his shirt bore a single loop of lace trim, the absolute minimum demanded by fashion. Tidoni's trousers bore a stripe of satin to set off the cloth-covered buttons along the side, and were tucked into boots of fine tandra hide that were part of Dav's payment for Yan's apprenticeship. The bulging purse at Tidoni's waist, like the belt that supported it and all rest of the leatherwork worn by the gan, was part of that payment. There was no mistaking Hebrim Tidoni for anything other than the gentleman he was, a far better master than a shoemaker's son deserved.

Yan bowed to him. "I'm sorry, Gan Tidoni."

The gan regarded him for a moment before softly asking, "For yourself or for them?"

"Both, I guess."

"Understandable."

There was an awkward silence while Yan struggled unsuccessfully to guess what the gan was thinking. Taking a deep breath to calm himself, Yan felt the unaccustomed weight of the *claviarm* on his chest. That, at least, was a positive thing.

"I wear my *claviarm,* Master."

The distant expression on the old mage's face disappeared as he smiled with pride. "Did you doubt that you would?"

To anyone else, Yan would have lied. "Perhaps a little."

"Unnecessarily. You lack confidence in your abilities, but it is a failing that will pass in time. Mark my words, Aelwyn will take note of your passage. You have talent, Yan."

"I only know what you have taught me."

The gan's eyes twinkled. "Not true."

"I meant that I would know nothing of magic if not for you."

"Also not true."

The teasing answers that were no answers annoyed Yan, just as they had throughout his apprenticeship. "I am apprenticed no longer. Why do you play with me?"

"Play? I only hold longer than I should to my role as teacher. As one ages, one finds it increasingly difficult to become accustomed to changes in one's life. But youth, now, youth is made of changes and I see that you feel you are ready for changes now. The old ways no longer suit you, even if you have not found new ways to replace them. So accept my apology, young mage. I did not mean to diminish your accomplishments."

"Accomplishments? I am an untried initiate. You still mock me, my master."

"Master no longer, as you yourself have said."

"But I had thought you would teach me still. There is much I don't know, much I would learn. I am ready for the inner secrets, Gan Tidoni."

"Are you? Well, so am I," the gan replied. "You can teach them to me when you find them."

Taken aback, Yan didn't know what to make of the gan's indulgent smile.

"Your apprenticeship is finished, although I will continue to guide you where I can, for as long as you wish my guidance. However, if you expect a continual parade of secrets opened to your eyes, you will be disappointed. In these latter days, the magic is weaker

than it once was and many secrets are lost to us. Of
those that remain, I know very little. One of the two
great mysteries I have already shared with you, the key
to your own magic." Tidoni pointed a chubby finger at
Yan's *claviarm*. "But, as I have said, there is another
great secret."

Yan waited as the gan paused. The moment grew
longer, stretching Yan's patience beyond its limit. "And
that is?"

"It is a mystery that is also a duty, a duty that I, as
your teacher, am bound to share with you. It is also
something that, as one mage to another, I am pleased
to share. Do you know why?"

"No, Master Tidoni."

"Master no longer, remember?" The gan admon-
ished him with a wagging finger and a smile. "We are
fellow seekers now."

"You're speaking in riddles again."

Gan Tidoni chuckled. "Another riddle, yes. But life
itself is a riddle, is it not?"

"One that can be puzzled out in time," Yan said con-
fidently.

"As, we may hope, this great secret will be. Perhaps
you, my former pupil, will be the one to find the
answer."

"I must needs know the question."

"Perhaps. If it were a question, that would be so. But
this secret is a truth, though still a riddle."

"And what might this secret, this truth, this riddle
be, then?"

"I will tell you," Tidoni said, then paused. The
silence stretched out again, driving Yan to distraction.
The gan seemed to lose himself in thought, leaving
Yan's curiosity to nibble, then gnaw at him. Just as Yan
felt he was about to burst, Tidoni gathered himself and
said, "I will tell you in the words my master told me.

The way of magic is now as it ever was, as it was when I held my first *claviarm*. On that day, my master said to me, 'True magic must be mastered alone. The great wizards learned, but they were never taught.'"

The gan's voice trailed away as he spoke, leaving the last words almost a whisper.

"You are a great wizard, Master Tidoni. Will you share what you have learned with me?"

"To a pup like you it may seem that I am a great wizard, but as you travel across the face of the world, you will find that there are many greater than I." Hebrim Tidoni smiled sadly. Then he met Yan's gaze and the smile quickened to a truer life. "Now you, my boy, *you* have potential."

Tidoni slapped him on the back. "But today is your *Akchepthio claviarorum*, and it is a time of celebration. Today is for rejoicing. Tomorrow you may ponder the depths of philosophy and magic. Today, as he who brought you to this day, I lay upon you one last command."

"And what might that be?"

"Come with me now to the Clever Cony. Goodwife Dybella has set aside a side of bacon and the best of the day's eggs. Her daughter will have churned a fine butter and added honey to savor it. Such a condiment lathered onto the day's new bread would raise a hunger in even a well-fed man."

The gan's talk of food certainly woke hunger in Yan, causing his empty belly to cry out in protest of his as yet unbroken fast. They spoke no more of magic that day, but Yan thought of it often, pondering what real magic might be and what made a magician great. He found he had no real answers, but in his mind he listened over and over again to Gan Tidoni's words declaring his potential and wondered what that potential might be.

# 1

THE SOUND OF ANGRY SHOUTING woke Yan from his sleep. For a moment he was confused, thinking the hoarse, harsh clamor part of one of his father's rages. He hauled in a deep breath. The astringent scent of the chemicals softened by the fragrance of fresh spring herbs told him that he was in his apartment above the Anchor and Plow, not in the house where he had grown up. The noise was not his father, could not be his father. More than likely, whatever was going on had nothing to do with him.

But the racket went on, coming no closer and going no farther away. Yan turned his eyes to the tiny window and saw that the night's stars were beginning to fade into the predawn light. It was much too early for such nonsense.

He flung back his coverlet and scurried across the room to dig through the pile of clothes for his gown. By the time he had tugged it on, the only warm part of him was his head, snug in his coif. He shivered as he fastened the buttons on the gown's front, his *claviarm* a chill weight against his chest. The cold air was fine for sleeping, but moving around in it unprotected was too much to ask of a person first thing in the morning.

He ran his hand through his hair, doffing his coif and massaging his scalp simultaneously. Yawning, he walked to the window and stuck his head out. The noise seemed to be coming from the street, where some kind of argument was in progress. The sound working its way around the Anchor and Plow was distorted; he could make out none of the words comprising the outraged yelling. The crack of a whip and the cry of horses were clear enough. It might be a teamsters' dispute though it was too early an hour for the ore wagons from the mountains to be rolling into Talinfad. Curious, he padded across the small bedchamber and ducked through the arch into the larger chamber that was his workroom. Remembering that folk expected wizards to maintain decorum, he stopped at the door. He formed the symbols of calling in his mind, focusing the spell on his discarded linen coif. The cap leapt from the floor and flew to his waiting hand. Tugging it on, he went down the stairs.

From the amount of noise pouring in from the street, Yan could tell that the window shutters in the main room were open. Whenever he had returned at dawn from all-night collecting trips, they had always been closed. He understood the unusual circumstance when he caught a flash of skirts disappearing into the back room. Goodwife Kavarin was a kindly woman, but she loved gossip. Obviously she had been drawn to this source of potentially interesting tales, and, equally obviously, she did not want to be caught gathering her day's wares.

Through the open window Yan could see the cause of the problem. A cart carrying firewood had overturned in the street outside. Such an accident was not surprising, considering the condition of the winter-rutted road;

however, the teamsters usually worked together to clear such obstructions with no more than a few curses and harsh jokes about the competence of the driver of the overturned vehicle. The tumbled load filled the street and a rancorous argument was under way. Yan stopped by the entrance to the back room.

"What's toward, Goodwife?"

"Dunno, Master Tanafres."

She said no more but busied herself in the kitchen alcove. More likely, she didn't have all the details yet and was reluctant to risk her reputation as a well-informed woman. Yan made his way to the window to see for himself. Heavy footsteps on the stairs behind him said that his landlord, Goodman Ness, had finally roused himself to investigate the disturbance on his doorstep.

The street outside the Plow and Anchor was completely blocked by the overturned cart and its spilled load. The cart horse, its broken traces dangling, stood sleepily by the building opposite. Yan envied the animal's ability to ignore the yelling humans in the street. The carter's young helper built haphazard piles of bundled sticks by the side of the road, while his master engaged in argument with the driver of a vehicle that wished to pass.

And what a vehicle it was, under its layers of travel dust. In daylight, and cleaned, the shiny lacquer and gilt trim of the body would dazzle, the elegant lines impress with their subtle form. The coach body was big enough to carry four, though Yan could not tell how many sat within, for the curtains were drawn on the windows. Two footmen clung to the back, ominous shapes in their wide-brimmed hats and enveloping cloaks. A third cloaked man sat beside the argumentative driver; the glint of weapon hilts at the cloaked man's belt suggested that he and the other two were guards as well as servants. Six horses, matched beasts, well harnessed and plumed, stood fretting in their traces and blowing steam. A postilion rider sat his seat on the left lead animal and stared sullenly ahead.

A heraldic device was painted on the door of the coach. Between the dust and the uncertain light Yan could not be sure of the colors, but the charges were plain enough: the main field was dark and bore a portcullis; the upper left corner of the shield shape was replaced with a light-colored canton in which a dark bird spread its wings. The Imperial rapenar?

Pennons bearing the sign of the portcullis, but not the bird, fluttered from short posts at the corners of the coach. Yan didn't recognize the heraldry, but knew that its presence, even if the bird was not the Imperial rapenar, marked the owner as a person of import. Though what someone of import would be doing traveling at such an hour, Yan could not guess.

Goodman Ness flung open the door and momentarily stilled the quarrel. Yan's landlord seemed oblivious to the reaction among the coach's guards, but Yan noticed how the two at the back reached under their cloaks, relaxing only when it was clear that Goodman Ness was no threat to whomever they guarded. The argument soon became a three-way round as the vituperative driver upbraided Goodman Ness for his shoddy care of the road before his house. The three men rapidly became more interested in slandering each other's ancestry than in settling who should clear the road.

A gentle, barely heard rap from within the coach stilled the driver's tongue, halting him in mid-insult. Goodman Ness and the carter followed the driver's glance as he looked toward the coach. A hand, slender and delicate, thrust through the curtains of the coach's windows. Before the heavy cloth fell back, Yan had a fleeting impression of a pale, slim face and dark eyes.

The hand simply pointed at the wreck in the road, then vanished within. That single gesture sent the footmen to leaping from the back of the coach. One of them insisted that the coach driver step down as well, and with an aggrieved glance at his hidden passenger, the driver swung reluctantly down from his perch. His dark-cloaked companion stayed aboard, standing now with one boot on the footboard and the other on the seat to better survey the area around the coach. The guard's hand rested on a pistol butt.

One of the guards took the carter by the shoulder and the other grabbed Goodman Ness. They led their charges to the overturned cart, lining up along its side. The five men gripped the cart and heaved upright again. Once they had it back on its wheels, they rolled it over to one side of the street. Yan noticed the carter grinning behind his hand and grunting, though he didn't apply his full strength to the effort of righting the cart. He let his newfound helpers take the burden, a small enough victory for the man and the best he could hope to achieve against his betters.

The coachmen remounted and the driver shook the reins, adding his voice to the postilion rider's command for the horses to be on their way. Wood cracked as the horses and coach crunched over the bundles remaining in the way. As the coach passed, the driver lashed out with his whip, striking the carter across the shoulder.

"Be thankful you got no more for hindering."

The carter snarled and made to catch the whip, but Goodman Ness, showing uncharacteristic wisdom, restrained the man. The guard on the near side laughed as the coach rumbled down the road toward Bar Gate.

The carter shook off the restraining hand.

"Come on, boy, we'd best clear this street before some other fancy rattletrap costs us more." He turned on Goodman Ness. "You should pay for this."

"I'll not pay for anything."

"If the road was in better shape–"

"The road? If you knew how to drive better–"

"How to drive? Why you fat son of a–"

"Don't you call–"

Sighing, Yan turned away from the window.

The smell of fresh bread was a welcome distraction from the new argument. Yan walked into the back room and sat at the table, a privilege granted only to long-term boarders. He snatched a roll from the tumble on the table and instantly regretted his impulsiveness. He dropped it and sucked his burned fingers.

"They're still quite hot, good sir," Goodwife Kavarin said needlessly.

"I'd noticed."

"It's early even for you, Master Tanafres. Be you wanting your breakfast?"

"Might as well. I think I'll not find sleep again after that racket."

"Still, an early start means a full day."

She nattered on, talking of small things: the quality of the day's milk, the look of the morning sky, the prospects for the spring's weather, and other such homey things. And when she had exhausted those topics, she moved on to the gossip that she favored. The houses lining the road to Bar Gate made a cozy neighborhood, but it was not one to which Yan felt attached. Who had said what about whom and who had seen who with whom held little interest for him. What did he care whose son had gotten caught snatching a pie from Toby Baker's tables? He tried to think about other things, but his mind stayed stubbornly unfocused. His landlady's chattering was too distracting to allow him to think and too boring to listen to. Abruptly he realized that she had stopped talking and was looking at him expectantly. She must have asked a question.

"I said, do you think you'll have it ready?"

"Have what ready?"

"Goody Bestillio's salve, of course. She said she'd be by to get it today."

Yan sighed. He had forgotten to make the salve. It was only an hour's work to grind the herbs and mix the paste, but somehow he hadn't gotten around to it in the last week. "When did she say she'd come?"

"Afore noon."

"I'll have it ready."

Salves and ointments and the occasional potion had become his stock in trade. He might as well be an apothecary. What good was all his knowledge when he was reduced to making herbal remedies for housewives?

A year ago there had seemed so many possibilities. Gan Tidoni's gift had allowed him to buy equipment and supplies and to rent his flat here. He had been so proud the day he'd hung out his sign. He had painted it himself, so that he could add a glamour to it. Though smaller than the sign for the Anchor and Plow from which it hung, the sign attracted the eye. "Tanafres, scholar and thaumaturge," it said. "Tanafres, scribbler and herbalist" would have been more appropriate.

Had it truly been a year since his *Akchepthio claviarorum*?

It had. A long, frustrating year. He'd waited all that first spring, and summer, for a summons from the dochay's palace. Dochay Komat Junivall was said to be a patron of the arts, including those arcane. Did he not retain Gan Tidoni? But no summons had come. Not from the dochay, nor from any of the nobles of his court. Finally, Yan had decided that if the court wouldn't come looking for him, he would go looking for them. He had swallowed his pride and asked his old master for an introduction. He still smarted to remember that first humiliating interview.

Gan Tidoni had brought him to a posh residence in the shadow of the dochay's palace, the home of the Lady Evenara Shessandini, dowager thley of Choriam and a most influential woman of the court.

"I am very busy these days, madame," Gan Tidoni had told her. "The dochay has so many demands. Perhaps you will allow me to suggest a colleague most suited to meeting your own needs."

"Another mage?" Lady Evenara sounded at once delighted, thrilled, and suspicious. "How generous of you, Gan Tidoni. What is the name of this sage gentleman?"

"He is Yan Tanafres, a native of these parts."

The gan had nodded his head at Yan and Yan had bowed to the dowager thley. The lady had looked him up and down with a sour stare. Though Yan had worn his best clothes, she had made him feel like a pigboy come fresh from the slopping.

"Tanafres? I have never heard of him," she had said as though he wasn't there. "Has he university credentials?"

"Nothing so formal, madame. Yet you need have no fear on that account, for he was my student."

"Oh. Well, I'm sure he is well taught, my dear Gan, but a lady of my quality must have the master and not the student. He could not possibly match your expertise."

"But, madame . . . "

"Now, now, my dear mage. I have my reputation to consider."


"You'll do your name no good with such shoddiness, young man," Goody Bestillio chided him. The old woman's expression was pained, as much from her condition as from the aggravation of a wasted trip from inside the gate. "A man who does not keep his promises is no man before the Lord Einthof and the light of Horesh."

"I'm sorry, Goody Bestillio," Yan said sincerely, though he was more sorry for the aggravation she was causing him. "I must ask you to come back. I will have your salve ready at noon."

"Noon? Last week, you said this morning. I ache terribly, young man. If you can't provide me with relief, I will have to look elsewhere."

That was not what Yan wanted. He needed the old woman's business. Like Goodwife Kavarin, with whom she was friends, Goody Bestillio was a gossip and one of his only regular clients inside the town. Her words could win or lose him customers. He drew himself up and spoke in a deep and, he hoped, authoritative voice. "The stars require that the salve be made at a certain time for maximum potency. You do wish the magic to work, don't you?"

"Oh. Why of course. The stars, you say."

"Indeed, they rule all. The best magic is made only under the right configurations."

The old woman nodded knowingly. "That's just what Ollem the Wise says."

Yan knew that. He also knew that Goody Bestillio was a devotee of the quack astrologer. That was why he had chosen those words. He hated sounding like the charlatan, but Goody Bestillio, like Ollem the Wise, didn't understand the real influence of the stars and Yan couldn't explain it to them. Not that it mattered. Beyond being a convenient excuse, the stars had nothing to do with the efficacy of the medicinal salve he sold to the goodwife.

A few more meaningless assurances mollified Goody Bestillio and she took her leave. Yan dropped his forced smile and huffed in relief when her bulky shape cleared the doorway. Almost immediately, he heard her crackly old voice start up a conversation. He couldn't see to whom she was talking, but it didn't matter; she was complaining. It seemed complaints made better conversation than assurances. He could hope her praise would be as quick once she had her medicine, but somehow he doubted it. He pushed back the stool and stood. What could he do? Goody Bestillio's voice followed him as he walked across the room. At least the woman had more to gripe about than his service; her grousing had shifted to how she had been wakened early this morning and how that had aggravated her condition. Trying to expel Goody Bestillio's complaints from his mind, he started up the stairs.

"Not going to make your reputation that way."

Had it been any other voice, Yan would have been stung by the words. He turned to see his sister leaning in the doorway, shaking her head. Dancie's mouth was set in a frown of disapproval, but her eyes belied the expression. They danced with mischief.

"What are you doing here?"

They met in the middle of the common room and embraced.

"I'm running away to Essarin to find a cozy harem."

"Does Father know?"

"Poppa knows I'm out." She slapped the leather satchel slung at her side. Her merry attitude vanished. "Deliveries, of course. Sends his daughter, hoping she'll get paid where his crabby face would scare away the customer. Doesn't know I've come to see you, of course. He'd tan me if he knew."

"Tanning's not allowed to his guild."

"No laws against the kind of tanning he'd do."

It was an old joke between them, a joke intended to hide the pain and never really doing a very good job of it. But the joke, like the pain, was something they shared. They smiled sadly at one another, each unwilling to say more on the subject

Dancie looked around the empty common room. "How's business?"

"I'm expecting a call from His Grace any day now."
Her expression told him she no longer believed that.
Well, he didn't either. More seriously, he said, "How
has it ever been? I'm getting by."

"Poppa puts me to work when he says we're just getting by." She started edging back toward the door.
"Maybe you haven't got time for a visit, what with getting that salve done and all."

"Yes, I do have to make the salve, but I can talk
while I work." He caught her arm. "Come on upstairs.
I promise I won't put you to work."

She looked hesitant for a moment, and perhaps a little
bit frightened, then she nodded. Yan led her up the
narrow stairs to the garret for which he paid entirely
too much rent. She hesitated in the doorway when he
threw open the door. Her eyes darted about the clutter
on the long table that filled most of the chamber,
roamed over the packets, bundles, and sacks dangling
from pegs on the rafters, and lingered long on the crystal
and its stand of twisted bronze rod.

"It's safe," he told her, smiling to reassure her.

He stepped past her and started about his work.
Dancie wandered the workroom while he selected
sprigs from the bunches of herbs hanging in the
rafters. She was short enough that she didn't have to
duck as he did to avoid the beams. She looked and
sniffed, but never poked, and for that he was grateful.
She wouldn't know what could be safely handled and
what could not, and he would rather not have to
scold her away from those things she shouldn't touch.
Her curiosity was a shy beast and he had no wish to
frighten it away.

He bound the herbs together and spelled them to
enhance their potency before tossing them into his
bronze mortar. While he ground them, he asked after
the family. She talked mostly about Fal's children and

shifted to other inhabitants of their village without saying much about their parents.

"Maize flour?" she asked as he sprinkled the yellow powder into the mortar.

"It makes a good paste to hold the herbs," he told her as he added fragrant oils.

The mixing done, Yan scraped the last of the salve from the mortar and transferred it to a small crock. With brisk efficiency he wrapped a scrap of linen over the mouth and secured it with a leather thong. Dancie sniffed at the jar.

"This is magic?"

"Not really. Good medicine, though. Any medical doctor could do as much."

"You sound unhappy."

"Shouldn't I be? I make herbal remedies for folk who are too cultivated to go to a hedge witch and too poor to go to a doctor. Sometimes I can help them and sometimes I can't, but it certainly doesn't use my real skills. The complaints people bring to me don't need true magic, so I concoct simple herbal remedies and apply simple natural philosophy to remedy their problems. I use what I know about the natural world. It's not what I thought being a mage would be."

"What about your, what do you call them?"

"Experiments."

"Yeah, them. Aren't they what mages do?"

"In part. But they're not going well either."

"Maybe you should take up an honest trade. Shoemaking, perhaps?"

"Never," he said with exaggerated vehemence. They laughed together. "Besides, I have an honest trade. At least it's honest enough, as long as I don't have to pretend I'm doing real magic when I'm not."

"So you're a magician who doesn't do magic?" She looked confused. "Doesn't make much sense. I didn't really mean you should make shoes like Poppa. I just meant, I don't know, I think I meant you maybe ought to have a good trade."

"One that the Church approves of?"

She nodded.

"I have that, too." He pointed to a stack of papers. "That's where most of my meager income comes from."

"You make paper?"

He almost laughed but caught himself when he realized that he would embarrass her. "No. I write on it. People come to me and tell me what they want written and I write what they say. I read them letters they bring to me as well. I do a lot of scribal work for Gan Lym."

Dancie looked at the writing with an expression of wonder. "An educated man's job. Guess Poppa didn't waste all his money."

"He didn't waste any of it. And being a scribe is not an educated man's job, it's just a way to scrape by. It's a waste of my education."

"At least you're out of the house."

That was true. "Your choosing day is coming soon."

Dancie crossed to the window and stared out, hugging herself. "Who'd look after Momma if I left?"

"Does it help to stay?"

"I don't know." She was quiet for a while and he waited patiently. "But I have to. I'm not like you, Yan. You can do so much. But I'm not smart and I don't have any magic."

What could he say? "I want to help."

"There's nothing you can do. I'll be all right. Momma'll be all right, too. It hasn't been so bad since you left."

He knew she lied, but wouldn't contradict her.

"Here. Give me the satchel."

She handed it over and he took out his father's

handiwork. The goods were well made, as always. He took each in turn, handling it, learning its shape. As he had done before when Dancie brought the goods to the town, he surreptitiously cast the spells that would bind each part, strengthening the construction. He added a glamour to hide the flaws. Small magics, but while he was doing them, he didn't have to think about anything but the magic.

# 2

GOODMAN NESS CLUMPED DOWN the stairs in front of Yan, grumbling under his breath as he always did. Ness's own rules didn't allow unaccompanied strangers upstairs in his inn, so when no one else was available, the innkeeper had to carry messages himself. Ness disliked acting as messenger even more than having Yan as a boarder.

Since it was just after noon, there were several people in the common room finishing up their midday repasts. All but one were familiar to Yan as regular patrons. That one stood by the door, a battered pack festooned with the products of a tinker's craft by his feet and a sullen expression on his hollow-cheeked, weather-beaten face. Dust covered his rustic clothes and dried mud caked his rough-made boots. The man wore a Triadic amulet, a triangle of hornleaf twigs and yellow twine, prominently on his chest.

"This man says there is a sick man in his village," Ness said, pointing to the rustic with a thumb before departing for the back room.

"Cursed, more like," the man said once Ness had passed out of earshot.

That would explain why a magician was being sought instead of a doctor or a priest. However, most of the victims of "curses" Yan had dealt with would have been better served by a member of either of those two professions. Still, Yan was intrigued, and he invited the man to sit at the table where he usually talked to his customers. The man followed, dragging his pack along. When they were both seated, Yan smiled at him in a friendly manner. "Now, Goodman, why do you say the man is cursed?"

"I mislike talking of this," the man said, his eyes shifting uneasily across the small crowd.

Yan saw that several of the patrons had heard his question and were listening. Curses were good fodder for the rumormongers. Moving his hand on the table in apparently mindless activity, Yan traced the runes of the privacy spell he had previously placed on the table and activated it. The listeners would only hear a soft mumble. "You may speak freely to me," he told the rustic.

"What have you done?" the man asked suspiciously.

Interesting that he could spot the magic. Perhaps he was a sensitive. "Nothing much, just assured us of some privacy."

The man's face scrunched down into an expression that seemed equal parts of distaste and disapproval. "I wouldn't have come, but Dav insisted and I owed him the favor."

"Dav is the one you say is cursed?"

The man looked at Yan like he was an idiot. "Dav's the innkeeper."

"He sent you, then."

A curt nod.

"Why did he send you to me if he thinks the man is sick? I think you know well enough that I'm neither a doctor of medicine nor a healer priest."

"Not to you special. That's your sign out front, ain't it?"

"Yes."

"You magic it yourself?"

So the man had recognized that as well. He had to be a sensitive. If he thought the sick man was cursed, maybe there truly was a curse in operation. "Yes."

"Then you'll be what Dav wants."

"So you have seen this sick man and have come looking for a mage."

"*I* ain't looking. I don't want nothing to do with this. Like I said, it's something I owe Dav." The man paused for a moment, then continued with a sour face. "Dav said he'd pay good silver for help."

Silver was something Yan couldn't easily turn down. More importantly, if the man in question really was cursed, there would be a need for Yan's magical skills. "Have you seen something that makes you think this sick man is suffering from something more than an ordinary illness?"

The man's eyes shifted down to the table. Without looking at Yan, he said, "I ain't seen nothing."

His attitude said otherwise. "If I am to be of any use to this, man I need to know more. If you could tell me something about the, ah, sickness, I can be better prepared to help him."

"Look, I said I'd come and find somebody. That's all. I done what I said and now I'm quit of it."

The man stood and shouldered his pack. He was clearly not going to carry this tale of the sick, or cursed, man any farther.

"Wait," Yan called after the man as he headed for the door. "I'll need to get my tools."

The man ignored him and stepped into the street. Yan hurried to the doorway, annoyed at the man's churlish manner. He was surprised to find that the man was heading down the road toward Bar Gate.

"If you won't take me there, you have to tell me where this man is."

"Crampton," the man called without looking back. "Crampton-by-Drivvaner Stream. Everyone knows it."

Yan had never heard of it.

But Goodman Ness had, and he knew the roads to get there.

Yan gathered a selection of his herbs, powders, and oils and placed them in his travel bag along with his ritual tools. He wasn't sure what he would need, or whether he would need anything at all, but he was excited at the chance to deal with an actual magical phenomenon. He was sure he would prove equal to the task.

So he set off briskly on Camnor Road. The village he had grown up in was along that road and Yan thought about visiting his family, but not for long. He kept on walking. There were still daylight hours for working and his father would be there. Besides, Dancie would not be back yet from her errands to Talinfad, and that would reduce his welcome by half. He didn't even look down the lane that led to his family's house. A couple of miles farther on he passed beyond the lands he knew, and a few miles farther still he found the crossroads that Goodman Ness had described as the turnoff that would take him to Crampton.

The sun was kissing the upper reaches of the western mountains when he reached what had to be the village he sought. The odd dozen of buildings that made up Crampton-by-Drivvaner Stream stood at the confluence of its identifying stream and a trio of smaller waterways. The convergence offered a convenient point to bridge the waters and so a bridge had been built and Crampton had grown up around it.

Most of the structures were simple thatched dwellings clustered around a thin-spired chapel. Upstream on

Drivvaner stood a mill, one of two multistoried structures. The second stood near the bridge and a weathered sign hung from a stanchion by the door. Yan could not discern what was on the sign, but its presence proclaimed the building as the village's inn.

The narrow track winding up from the main highway to Crampton split beyond the bridge into tracks narrower still that led deeper into the hill country. The bridge was a choke point to travel and an opportunity for a travelers' inn, though to judge from its state of repair, the volume of traffic was never high.

As he approached the inn a dog ran out, barking. He quieted the animal with a word and a smile. He peered in through a window. This inn was smaller than the Anchor and Plow, and gloomier. To dispel the growing chill of the late spring evening, a low fire was set in the fireplace. There was no bar in the common room, only a trio of hard-used tables and their attendant stools. An archway at the back obviously led to the kitchen and another, darker one sheltered a stairway.

The sign retained enough of the peeling paint to show a hornleaf tree. At least that's what the letters beneath the picture said the tree was. Yan wouldn't have guessed from the rendering.

As he opened it, the door hit a bell that jangled brazenly. A burly man, wiping his hands on a cloth, appeared in response to the summons. The man was much of a type with Goodman Ness, though sparser of hair. He squinted for a moment at Yan, who stood silhouetted against the outside. Taking obvious note of Yan's bag, the innkeeper stretched his arms wide and put on a smile. His words, though a customary greeting, seemed buoyed by a true enthusiasm.

"Welcome, traveler. Night comes on and there is no finer place for you to break your journey."

"I thank you, innkeeper, but I am not a traveler in need of rest. I come in response to a summons. You are Dav?"

Suddenly serious, the innkeeper nodded, his eyes darting again over Yan's bag and staff. "You are a wiseman?"

"I am Yan Tanafres, a magician."

"You're certified?"

"Yes."

"Horesh shine upon us." Dav made the sign of the Triad. "Rea," he called back to the kitchen. "Bring ale. We have a guest." He gestured to a table. "You must be tired and thirsty, Master Magician."

"Your messenger said you had a sick man here, suggesting that he was cursed."

Dav's jovial manner vanished and he made the sign of the Triad again. "For a man of few words, Galon oft says too much."

"He said enough to bring me here. Your guest—He is a guest? —Ah—whatever his affliction may be, it would be best that I see him soon."

A slim girl, presumably the Rea whom Dav had called, emerged from the kitchen bearing a stoup of ale. Her skin coloring and hair matched Dav's, so she was likely a daughter. She was young and pretty, in a country way.

Yan shook his head when she offered the ale. "Perhaps later."

"I've never met a mage before."

She sipped the ale herself, running her eyes up and down him in an evaluating way. She smiled invitingly. He gave her a half smile in return, realizing that there might be compensations beyond the silver after he had done his business here. Her eyes dwelt on him while Dav lit a candle from the fire and placed it in a lantern. The innkeeper gave no sign of noticing the byplay.

Though there was still light outside, the common

room was already well into its night and the stairway to the upper story darker still. The innkeeper led Yan up the rickety stairs. Yan noticed a sour smell when they reached the landing. Someone had indeed been sick in this house. The stench grew stronger as they walked down the narrow corridor toward the far end. Dav opened the door without knocking, unleashing a fresh reek of vomit and waste.

In the light of Dav's lantern, Yan could see an old man lying on the bed that nearly filled the room. The coverlet lay half off the bed, apparently tossed free by thrashing, for the sheet was wrapped around the man's body tight as a shroud. One arm was outflung, its hand curled into a claw. The man might have been a corpse, but a hollow rasping sound that came at irregular intervals told Yan that the man still breathed.

Cursed or not, the man was far gone.

Yan put down his bag, walked to the window, and started to throw open the shutters. This late there wouldn't be light for long, and he could use all he could get.

"Please, Master Tanafres, refrain. His cries will be heard in the street."

"Without more light I can do nothing."

"Candles?"

"Time for those later. Sunlight is better."

The innkeeper subsided into a gloomy stare.

Yan looked the man over. No wounds or obvious signs of injury were apparent. Reluctant to examine the man with his magical senses, Yan settled for questioning the innkeeper on the sick man's physical reactions as he made a cursory physical inspection. He was unsurprised by the man's fever. What the innkeeper said and what Yan learned from his examination were all consistent with ordinary illness. Some of the symptoms Yan could treat, but an ordinary illness this advanced was beyond

Yan's skill with medicine, perhaps even beyond the art of a proper doctor.

"Has the village priest seen him?"

"Nay." Yan's hard glance made the innkeeper take a step back. "Good Master Tanafres, he made me swear not to involve the Church. Besides, our priest knows nothing of the healing arts. She is of Baaliff."

That was odd. Why would the man want to avoid the Church? Yan nodded his head at the sick man. "Whatever I can do for him will not bring him back to full health. A healer is his best hope."

"Pray, sir. Do what you can, but do not ask me to break my oath."

"I swore no oath. Send someone to the city in my name. There are healers at the temple."

"It is late, sir. No one from the village will travel into the darkness."

Yan knew that sort of attitude well enough. Mostly it was superstitious fear that kept country folk from venturing beyond their familiar surroundings at night. Occasionally there was a reasonable expectation of danger, but Yan had heard no recent talk of bandits or supernatural infestations. "In the morning, then. Your friend Galon made it to Talinfad in time for me to reach your village. A youngster fleet of foot should be able to return with a priest within the day. If someone can spare a horse, this man's chances of survival will be greatly improved."

"I will try to find someone."

"If you do not, this man's death will be to your credit."

"Say not so, sir. I sent for you, did I not? I have done all that could be reasonably expected. I would have called a priest had he not forbidden me to do so. Horesh knows I've done what I could."

There was little point in bothering the innkeeper further. By his lights, he had done what he could.

"Innkeeper, did this man tell you his name?"

"No, Master. Though his dress was ragged, I knew him for a gentleman by his speech. I thought he wished to be unknown, and so did not question him."

Perhaps the innkeeper dreamed of reward. "So you served him."

"Good food and ale, sir," Dav said quickly. "Nothing foul or spoiled. I ate of the same stew and drank of the same keg. So did Rea and several folk of the village. None of us took ill. By V'Delma's healing heart, he did not take ill from being under my roof."

"I meant nothing of the sort. I thought to ask of what he may have said or done. Tell me how he came here."

For a moment Dav gathered his thoughts, perhaps seeking to put the best light on things. "The stranger arrived last night, hale and whole. Not even a sign of chill despite his coming in soaked from the rain. He ate and drank like any man hungry from a day's travel. He spoke little and the folk in the common room spoke little to him. It's their way around here, and he was a stranger, after all.

"In the morning when I sent Rea to wake him as he had asked, she came back screaming and weeping and in such a state as I could get no sense from her. I came to the room myself and found him as you see him now, an enfeebled, white-haired old man. When last I had seen him as he went up the stairs for the night, he had walked with the strength of a man in his prime and his hair had been as dark as the night.

"I was shocked and frightened by the way he thrashed and raved. Fearing greatly for my own well-being, I went to his side. I thought that if he had some sort of plague, I must needs get him out of the inn before others were affected."

"You might have been affected yourself."

"I knew that," Dav said bluntly. "But if he died in that bed of some plague, my business would die, too."

"So you thought to spirit him out and say nothing."

"To my shame, I did think that, but as I reached the bedside, he suddenly sat up and spoke to me in a clear-headed way. He told me to fetch a wiseman. When I said I would call the priest, he forbade me under pain of becoming as he was. Having seen the change that had come over him, I feared that greatly. So I spoke to Galon and sent him off and returned to inform this man. 'Good,' he said, then warned me to touch not his goods. He had protected them, he said. Then he fell asleep again. Since then he has not spoken in words that I could understand."

"But he has spoken?"

"He has made noises that sounded like they might be speech, though I could make no sense of them. Other noises he has made as well, that were not speech at all." The innkeeper shivered.

Despite having had contact with the man, the innkeeper had not become ill, suggesting that this afflic-tion was not contagious. Its dramatic effects strongly suggested magic, though Yan knew of no curse that operated in such a fashion. Curses were usually slower in their effect. Yan considered the possibility that the man might be possessed by a wasting spirit, but he sensed none of the malignancy that seeped into the world in such cases. He remained curiously reluctant to use his magical senses.

He told himself that he was just being prudent. If this man was under a curse, it might be transmitted magically in the blending of auras needed to under-stand the nature of the curse. He wanted to know as much as possible before risking that. Knowing who or what the man was would make reading the man's aura, and avoiding contracting the curse, easier.

"Perhaps in his goods there is something to identify him."

"His goods are where he left them, Master. I swear I have touched nothing."

"That is good. There may be some clue among his goods to tell us something about him."

Yan looked about the room. In one corner lay a rolled blanket, a hat, a sack, and a traveler's staff. On the stool by the bed lay a pile of clothes. Yan felt for magic protecting the sick man's goods and found nothing configured into a ward. However, something in each grouping contained arcane energy. The staff was obvious, but whatever lay in the pile on the stool was not immediately visible.

Turning his attention first to the corner, Yan looked over the mundane items. The blanket was just a traveler's roll with nothing stuffed inside. The sack held a few sundries common to travelers and a set of damp clothes smelling of mildew. They would be what the man had worn in the rain. The hat, though damp, had not been stuffed away and remained unaffected by the mildew. Its bedraggled feather hung forlorn, worn and listless as its owner.

The staff looked ordinary, but Yan knew better; he had sensed the magic in it. There were no embellishments save narrow bronze bands around each end. The wood itself was dark and had an oily sheen. The staff was surprisingly light when he lifted it, and resisted his attempt to flex it. Whatever else the strange wood was, it was strong. Without further study he could not unravel the spell bound into it, only sense that the magic was related to combat. It appeared that the staff was the only weapon the traveler had carried with him, so Yan was not surprised by the nature of the spell.

A combat spell on a staff was unusual. Most persons who wanted enchanted weapons wanted swords. What sort of traveler would carry an enchanted staff? A mage might, but this staff didn't have the feel of Gan Tidoni's staff.

Yan turned his attention to the man's other goods. The pile overflowing the stool by the bed was haphazard, as though made in haste. Poking from beneath a linen shirt was the silver-studded hilt of a fine dagger, rich enough to confirm the innkeeper's assumption that the traveler was a man of means. The dagger was not the source of the magic Yan had sensed. As he lifted the shirt to get a better look at the dagger, something dislodged from the folds of the garment and fell rattling to the floor. The innkeeper gasped and made the protective sign of the Triad. He smiled sheepishly when Yan glanced at him.

Yan bent to examine the object on the floor and saw at once that it held the magic he had sensed in the pile. It was a silver disk studded with flecks of gemstone and covered with tiny engraved sigils. In the center of the disk a glass dome covered some dark object. It was a *claviarm*. But whose? Yan had not sensed a link to the man in the bed.

Did this *claviarm* belong to the traveler, or had he taken it from a mage?

Focusing his concentration, Yan viewed the talisman with his arcane senses. The amulet was active, pulsing the way a *claviarm* should when near its maker. The amulet wasn't Yan's and nothing about the innkeeper suggested that he was a magician, so the man in the bed had to be a mage.

Something was definitely wrong if the *claviarm*'s maker had removed it and set it aside. The likelihood of malefic magic had just increased a hundredfold.

Yan examined the rest of the traveler's belongings and found nothing to give a clue to his identity or profession, nothing to suggest what might be wrong with him. Having cleared away the objects from the seat, Yan sat on the stool and stared at the man.

For a time there was nothing to disturb the room
save the sound of the man's raspy breathing. Then,
with a long moan, the traveler began to toss about,
twisting, writhing, and babbling strange, half-mumbled
words. Dav suddenly remembered that he had business
about the inn, and left Yan alone with the mage. If
mage he was.

Reluctant to disturb what he didn't understand, Yan
sat by the bed, listening to the man's ravings. They
were so disjointed that they made no sense at all. Even
the words that were not mumbled were, as often as not,
in a language unknown to Yan. Then there were the
hissings, sibilant sounds that seemed out of place in a
human throat. No surprise that Galon had thought this
man cursed. It was a wonder that the innkeeper had
not broken his promise to the traveler and fetched a
priest, in fear that the mage was possessed of a demon.

Yan was startled when the man suddenly turned his
face to him. The traveler's eyes were a deep clear gray.

"Good greeting to you, brother in the Art." Yan said
nothing, but the man continued on as if he had. "I had
hoped the man here would have sense to summon a
mage. I knew you when you came, but for so long I
was unable to do anything about it. What is your
name?"

Finally finding his voice, Yan replied, "I am Yan
Tanafres."

"And your master?"

"Hebrim Tidoni."

The man's brow furrowed as though he was searching his memory, seeking a face to put to the name.
"Will he come if you call?"

"If the matter is of import."

"Import? Oh, yes. Can you not tell? Can you not
feel it?"

Yan feared that the man was about to lapse into

delirium again and did not want to lose this opportunity to learn something of him. "What is your name, Master? Perhaps Gan Tidoni has heard of you and will come for the honor of your name."

The man smiled, but his eyes were sad. "I am beyond names now."

"I need some way to address you."

"Call me Adain," he said at last.

"That is a saü name, and you are merin."

Again the bittersweet smile. "Yet it is mine."

Even conscious, the man was enigmatic. But he was ill as well, and there might be no time for the word games that elder mages loved so well. "By Einthof, I mean you no harm. I only want to help you, and I cannot do that if you conceal things from me. How came you here? Where are you bound? What is more important, how have you come to be in this condition?"

Adain rolled his head over to face the window. He said nothing. Outside, night was gathering among the thatched roofs of Crampton.

"I must know more about you in order to help you."

"Being beyond names, I am beyond help."

"Do you have any idea what has happened to you?"

The man turned his head back and lifted a palsied hand, staring at the blue veins pulsing on its surface. "I see. I feel. The why, perhaps, I begin to understand. The how?" He shook his head. "It no longer matters."

His hand dropped to the bed and he sighed deeply. This time Yan left him to his silence. Clearly, Adain would talk if he wanted to and would not respond to Yan's urgings. Finally, Adain spoke again and his voice seemed to come from far away.

"There are great powers stirring in the depths of the world."

"What are you talking about? Are you foreseeing?"

"A shift in the wellspring of magic is upon us."
Adain paused. "Any true mage would feel it."

"I have felt nothing like what you are talking about."

Adain's head snapped around and he pinned Yan
with a piercing stare. "I mistrust your lack of sensitivity."

"You have been ill. Perhaps we should speak of this
when you are better."

"Unlikely."

Unsure of whether Adain meant to conceal his secret
upon regaining his health, or if he kenned that he would
not rise from the bed again, Yan said, "You have come
to your senses after a time of wandering. That is a good
sign. Tomorrow you will see things differently."

"No," Adain said flatly. "The wheel of the universe
turns and we all have our place upon it. All in its order,
each in his place. Our wheels have intersected. I have
come here, and you have come to me. I go, and you
must go. That is the order that is, the order that shall
be. You must share this burden with me."

Adain closed his eyes and lapsed into silence. Yan
wanted to ask again what the mage meant, but couldn't
find the words for his questions. After a few minutes,
Adain began to toss his limbs about, flailing them as if
fighting off some foe who beset him. He shouted something in a guttural tongue, then gasped and fell slack.
His breathing deepened and he was still.

Yan found Adain's more regular breathing encouraging; Adain sounded far better, healthier, than when
Yan had first entered the room. The relapse into delirium
was worrisome. This was a perplexing situation. Yan
stayed by Adain's bed for another hour, waiting in vain
for the mage to return to lucidity, but the mage lay still,
as insensate and unmoving as a corpse. Only Adain's
slow, steady breathing showed him to be still alive.
Through the window Yan could hear the hunting calls
of night birds and the shrill cries of the bats. The

insects were silent, hiding from their hunters. They knew Death was nearby.

Yan himself was tired, this long day begun before he was ready with the altercation in the street outside the Plow and Anchor. Whatever had brought Adain to this point was strong, too strong for a tired young mage. In the morning, perhaps, things would look different.

Retiring to the room Dav had prepared for him, Yan took Adain's *claviarm*. Some of what the mage had mumbled in his delirium had sounded suspiciously like spells, though Yan had felt no magical energies, perhaps because Adain was not in contact with his *claviarm*. If Adain were to take up his *claviarm* in his delirium . . . A mage in the grip of irrationality could wreak much harm, better for all in the inn that Yan guard the *claviarm*.

Despite his exhaustion, Yan lay awake for some time, listening to the sounds of the night outside. Once he heard a sharp cry as an owl pounced on a mouse. Hunters and hunted, he thought. One of the oldest wheels within the wheel of the universe. At some point he drifted off into sleep.

In the morning he woke to the smell of smoke that carried with it the sharp tang of searing flesh. Breakfast was his first thought, but duty bade him to check on Adain. He found the mage's room empty and his mouth went dry. He raced down the stairs, following his nose around the inn. In the field behind the building he saw the source of the smoke, a bonfire. A dark, human shape was charring within the flames. Protruding from the mass, as yet unconsumed by the growing fire, was Adain's dark walking staff. The villagers were burning the mage and his possessions.

Yan could only hope the man had been dead before they kindled the flame.

# 3

THE MORNING HOSPITALITY of the inn was less friendly than it had been the evening before. Breakfast was served without conversation and was poor fare. He was not wanted. Even through his melancholy, Yan could see it. It was as though Dav blamed him for Adain's death, and Yan was tempted to agree. Last night he had felt too tired to attempt a dangerous magical work. He had told himself that there would be time; that he could overcome his fear of this curse, if curse it was, once he understood more. He had lied to himself, and Adain had paid the price.

When he finished his breakfast, he looked up to find Dav watching him from the kitchen doorway. Once noticed, the innkeeper approached.

"There's still the matter of the room, Master Tanafres," he said solemnly.

"You can deduct my lodgings from my fee."

"*His* room." The innkeeper was sweating. "It needs be cleansed. It needs to have the curse taken off it."

"I don't think there's any residue."

"I'll pay good silver. Three kartes."

"All right."

Yan agreed to Dav's request more to relieve his own guilt than for any good it might do. Ritual cleansings were easy enough, but Yan had no consolation for Adain's spirit. Thus, he was relieved to find no psychic residues from the dead mage. It was as if the man had never been in the room. Yan was vaguely surprised as well; shouldn't there have been something? Well, it didn't matter. While he chanted the spells and spread the powders, he noticed that a small group of villagers had gathered outside, watching him through the window. He wasn't used to an audience but he put them out of his mind and concentrated on the ritual. When he was finished and his ritual implements packed away, he was confident that he had done something right on this trip. If Adain's ghost walked, it would not be from this room.

Tired from his short night and recent exertion, Yan returned to his room. The bed he had left rumpled had been made up, his hat and staff laid upon it. Money lay on the brim of his hat, silver against black. Three kartes, one missing two ceins. The deduction for his lodging, no doubt, and more than his stay had been worth. Nevertheless, the silver was more than he had seen for a task in the whole year since his *Akchepthio claviarorum*. It was also far more than he felt he had earned. But earned or not, he needed it.

He scooped up the oblong wafers of metal and tucked them into his belt pouch.

Common wisdom said that such a sum was enough for a man to live on for months. But a mage's expenses were uncommon. Though the money might pay Yan's rent at the Anchor and Plow for a triple fortnight, Yan knew it wouldn't last him that long. He took up his hat and staff, accepting the obvious suggestion that he be on his way.

Outside, the small clump of villagers remained. Still watching to make sure the mage left, he guessed. Yan noted a new figure among them, a slim form in the yellow and blue of a Triadic priest. The stocky, bald-headed innkeeper stood next to the priest, talking earnestly. Yan caught the flash of light on metal as money changed hands between the innkeeper and the priest. Yan had no doubt that the room would soon be exorcised. Practical man, that Dav, not the sort to take chances. Likely the innkeeper would hire a guiltcatcher too, if he could find one who would dare to take on the accumulated wrongdoing of a mage's life.

Well, Yan's business in Crampton-by-Drivvaner Stream was finished. He settled his hat on his head, took a firmer grip on his staff, and set out. He felt the villagers' eyes on his back as he left the settlement.

He tried to tell himself that their animosity was not directed at him personally. It was just that he was a mage. He found no comfort in that thought. Instead, it made him think about the people he had met on his way to Crampton. They had been reserved in his presence. At the time, he had taken such reactions as typical villagers' reaction to strangers and had taken the awkward politeness of those who spoke with him as untutored respect for a man of learning. Now, he saw those reactions differently. There had been a wariness about those folk, almost a fear. Now, he remembered crabbed hands covertly making the triangle as a ward against evil. What had they thought of him? Did they think he was a dark mage? Were they so uneducated that they thought there still were dark mages?

Yan found it unsettling that people who knew him not at all might fear him simply because he had chosen to study magic. The people of Outgate where he lived weren't like that. They knew he was not evil. Didn't they?

But these strangers saw only his profession and not his person.

They were so ignorant.

Fearful.

But was he any better?

He prided himself on his learning, but he had done nothing for Adain. What good had his learning been? What help his understanding of magic? He had feared the strange thing happening to Adain as much as the villagers had.

Wryly, he realized that he should not find such fear in himself surprising. He had been born in one of the villages around Talinfad, and raised as one of the commons he thought so little of now. He had opened his mind and learned.

Why couldn't they?

Still, he had to admit that the mage Adain had frightened him; not by what he was, though Yan felt a certain disquiet about the strangeness clustered about Adain; nor by his ravings, though they were disturbing, but by what he had said when he was lucid. Dire predictions of great changes were common enough among streetside prophets and moneygrubbing charlatans, but rare among those who could actually touch true magic. It made one wonder.

The weight of Adain's *claviarm* lay heavy in Yan's belt pouch, almost as heavy as the weight of Adain's words in his mind. *Any true mage would feel it.* Yan hadn't felt anything. He didn't even know what Adain had meant by *the wellspring of magic.*

So what kind of a mage did that make Yan?

Was he a mage at all? Or was he just some sort of bumbling artificer of limited skill?

No. He *was* a mage. Or at least well on his way to being one. He had worked too hard, studied too long to let a madman's ravings unsettle him. Hadn't Gan

Tidoni said he had potential? Hadn't even the mistrustful
Adain addressed him as brother in the Art?

But what if they were wrong? What if they weren't
seeing him clearly, as he hadn't understood the reactions of ordinary folk? For a year Yan had struggled to
make a name for himself as a mage, struggled to learn
more of the secrets Gan Tidoni had said he must learn
for himself. For a year, he had failed.

Maybe he really wasn't a *mage*? Maybe he was just a
dabbler in the Art, doomed never to touch its inner
secrets. He thought of Ollem the Wise and pictured his
own face beneath the turban that the old charlatan
affected.

Yan was haunted by that image all the way back to
Talinfad. Anxious, he passed by the Anchor and Plow
and headed through Bar Gate for Gan Tidoni's town
house. He wanted to talk with his old master, wanted to
hear what Gan Tidoni would say about his fears, about
what Adain had said. When he arrived Olvon, Tidoni's
manservant, answered the door.

"The master is away," Olvon said in his bored, tired
voice.

"But I must see him now," Yan insisted.

"He will see you at *his* convenience. I will tell him
you called."

"Tell him. Tell him as soon as he returns that it is
most urgent. Tell him that it's a matter of the Art."

"I will tell him," Olvon said blandly.

Frustrated, Yan returned to the Plow and Anchor. It
was three days before an invitation to visit arrived,
three days in which Yan's experiments stood idle while
he wrestled with his fears.

Yan hurried to the town house and told Tidoni the
whole tale of his trip to Crampton. He stuck to the
facts, leaving out his feelings and thoughts. He felt
somewhat guilty about them now that he was in the

presence of his old master. His fears seemed foolish. As he concluded his story, he pulled Adain's *claviarm* from his pouch.

"This was his."

The gan took it from his hand and held it up so that the light from the window reflected on the bright metal. Placing his spectacles on his nose, he watched the amulet twist on its chain for a few moments, then gathered it up and examined it closely.

"Fine. Very fine. Classical style. Note the rendition of the sigil for the Sickle. Earth affinity," he mumbled as he tilted the *claviarm* so that light reflected from every part. "Yes, definitely Earth, but more than that, too. Most unusual. I think these sigils indicate an astral aspect. Yes, I think they do. That would accord with the black diamond within the crystal."

Yan leaned forward. "Do you recognize it, Gan Tidoni? Did you know Adain?"

"No to your first question, but there is no reason I should. A mage may have many different *claviarms* in his life. It is but a tool of focus. Even if I knew the man, I might never have seen this amulet." The gan sat back in his chair, returning his spectacles to the case on his belt. "Adain? I don't recall any mage by that name. You say this Adain was not a saü, despite his name."

"Yes."

"Hunh. I'd say this *claviarm* was not of saü magical tradition. This mage was a man of mystery even before his mysterious affliction. I wonder where he was headed."

"The innkeeper told me that he asked about the road conditions between the village and Talinfad. I think it likely that he was headed here. Perhaps to see you."

"An unwarranted assumption. Talinfad is a port. The city would be the destination of any traveler in these parts who sought a ship. If he did seek a ship, his destination could have been anywhere." Gan Tidoni ran a finger absently around the edge of the *claviarm*. "I wonder where he started his journey."

"What does it matter where he came from or where he was going?" To Yan, all the speculation about Adain's travel plans seemed unimportant. The mage had carried a dire message. If they were to ponder anything, that seemed more important. "Adain said that there are great powers stirring. He said that a shift in the wellspring of magic is upon us."

"So you said. Are you sure that he was not simply raving?"

"No," Yan admitted. "But there was a *truth* to his words. I can't explain it."

"Were you observing his aura when he spoke these words? Truth sense is notoriously unreliable when dealing with disturbed minds."

Yan looked away. "I wasn't reading him. "

"You weren't?"

Yan knew he should have been. "I said I wasn't."

"I wasn't criticizing. Merely trying to ascertain all of the facts."

Yan had heard the tone Gan Tidoni had used. It had been criticism. Justified criticism. That made it hurt all the more.

Tidoni touched his lower lip with the index finger of his right hand. "And he appeared calm when he spoke of momentous things? Rational?"

"He did. He was. I was the one who was not calm."

"And so you didn't trust yourself to contact him astrally. That was wise. If he was cursed, you might have succumbed to the same twisted magic."

"But I wasn't really wise; I was afraid. I didn't do what I should have done."

"If we all always did what we should do, this world

would be a far happier place and there would be few to listen to the message of blissful union with Horesh in the afterlife. No one would want to go."

Platitudes were not what Yan had in mind. "But I didn't do justice to your teaching."

"And what would be such justice?" He didn't wait for Yan to answer. "You went when you were called and faced something you had never faced before. Suddenly all your learning was no longer theoretical. You hesitated. Understandably so. Do you think you're the first mage ever to stumble like that? Put it out of your mind. If you have described the man's affliction accurately, and from past experience I have no reason to doubt your observations, Adain would have died whether you interfered or not."

"Then you know what happened to Adain?"

"The physical you have told me; concerning the magical I can only make suppositions. I cannot be sure, but I feel confident that you, with your current understanding of the Art, would have been unable to help the man. Any magic that could wither a mage so quickly would have to be powerful indeed, more powerful than anything you have dealt with previously. You were out of your depth, Yan.

"But you should have known that. There is more to your agitation, isn't there?"

Trust Gan Tidoni to know. There was more, but it was more of the same. Everything about the trip to Crampton, everything Adain had said seemed to undermine Yan's confidence in his abilities and his calling as a mage. This seemed to be the time to ask the question he really wanted to ask.

"The portents Adain spoke about, Master. Do you feel them?"

Gan Tidoni sat quietly for several moments, considering something. Finally, he said, "No.

"But then I haven't been looking for any portents either. Foretelling was never my strength."

*Any true mage would feel it*, Adain had said. Gan Tidoni had not answered at once. Yan knew Tidoni was a true mage, he had seen evidence enough during his apprenticeship. As if confessing a crime, Yan said, "I don't feel anything either."

"I thought as much," Gan Tidoni said, immediately ripping away Yan's tiny feeling of restored confidence.

*The wheel of the universe turns and we all have our place upon it*, Adain had said *All in its order, each in his place.* And what was Yan's place? Was he a practitioner who could not feel what any true mage would? What was his fault? Or did the fault lie in magic itself?

If magic were simply the imposition of the trained will upon the universe, he should be a success. He was trained. He had the will. All his life he had wanted to be a respected mage. When Gan Tidoni accepted him on his choosing day, he knew his heart's desire had been fulfilled. Had he been pursuing a dream with no real meaning for him?

Yan had not felt the stirrings of which Adain had spoken, and Gan Tidoni was unsurprised by Yan's failure. Where was all of Yan's great potential now? What had he done to lose it? Was his lack of perception a sign that he could never achieve true mastery of the Art?

Maybe it was only inexperience, a matter to be resolved with time and perseverance.

Or maybe he had taken a wrong turn on the road of life and should never have taken up the Art.

Gan Tidoni's hand on his shoulder snapped him out of his self-pitying stupor. "You are worrying too much over what are most likely the ravings of an illness-blighted mind."

He wished he could find a way to believe it was so. "Perhaps you are right."

"You have trusted me in the past. Trust me in this. You are a young man and your life still lies before you. The path of a mage is not an easy one, and it is not one open to all. You have crossed the threshold, a considerable accomplishment in itself. To turn away now would be a waste of a wonderful gift. I can assure you that if you abandon the Art now, your spirit would curdle within you. You will become embittered and hateful." Tidoni chuckled in a deliberate attempt to lighten the mood. "There are worse lives. You could have been a worker in the mines."

The very thought of being enclosed in the earth made Yan shudder. He was thankful he was not a miner. But not being a miner had no bearing on what he was. "It's a poor enough life here, even for those who are not ore delvers."

"Then perhaps here is not where your life is best led." The gan waited a moment for Yan to respond and, when he did not, said, "You must find your own way to greater magic and a better life. I ask only that you think clearly about your choices. Make decisions that are the best that you can make."

But Yan was not really listening. The mention of mines had brought a new thought to him. Talinfad was one of the cities of the Iron League of Merom, a cooperative of the island's city-states that had built their wealth on the most plentiful resource of Merom: iron. And iron, as every apprentice learned, was inimical to the workings of magic. Here on Merom, iron was everywhere.

Maybe the fault was not in him, but in the land.

Maybe he would find true magic elsewhere.

Just the thought of somewhere else was attractive. Yan found he didn't really care where. Anywhere. Anywhere had to be better.

"I think you're right, Gan Tidoni. I think that I

would do better elsewhere. Somewhere other than Talinfad, most especially somewhere other than Merom."

Gan Tidoni's eyebrows drew down over his eyes. "Are you suggesting that your problems come from the land?"

"Why shouldn't it be so? There's so much iron here. Iron is the antithetical metal, the corrupter of magic."

"Other mages practice here," Gan Tidoni said quietly.

"Aren't you always telling me that all mages are different? Maybe that's what makes me different. Maybe it's the iron. Maybe I'm more sensitive to the iron."

Frowning, Tidoni said, "It's not the iron or the magic. They are natural. Problems can only arise when you try to change the natural condition. Make it what it should not be. There are no problems when all is in its natural order. All problems, like all solutions, ultimately come from within."

Yan didn't want to hear it. The thought that the ground beneath him might be the problem sparked his mind with new thoughts, new dreams. It was liberating. Surely, it would be easier for him to practice his craft elsewhere in the empire.

Perhaps Sharhumrin. Yes, Sharhumrin, the capital city and the heart of the Coronal Empire, the greatest city in the world. The great Imperial academy was there. The city thronged with scholars. There he would find others to study with, others with whom he could share the results of his researches, others who would understand. The capital would be a wonderful place, free of the ingrown provincialism of Talinfad, free of the unenlightened biases of Merom. In Sharhumrin, his talents would be appreciated and put to far better use than writing out wills leaving a single cow to the heir of a farm. Better still, no one there would know he was a shoemaker's son.

"I said, you seem to be too distracted to continue our conversation." Gan Tidoni sounded annoyed.

Well, let him be annoyed. He was always telling Yan to find his own way, and now that Yan had found an answer, the old mage didn't want to hear it. Yan had a lot of thinking to do. "Maybe I should go back to the Anchor and Plow."

"Perhaps that is for the best. Go home and get some rest. We can talk again when your head is clearer."

Yan walked back to the Anchor and Plow, rolling thoughts over and over in his mind. Leaving Merom sounded so right. But . . .

Was he running away?

What if he was? Did it matter? What was there in Talinfad for him, anyway? He'd spent a year trying to get noticed and he'd gotten nowhere. A year trying to develop his magic in a land whose bones were hostile to magic. He could hardly do worse elsewhere.

The rest of the week went slowly, all the more slowly for the failure of his latest experiment and the lack of callers. Each night Yan lay awake, thinking about how the silver he had gotten from Crampton was draining away. How he could do no more than simple magics. How the people on the street looked at him and how even the regular patrons of the inn said little more than the minimal pleasantries to him. In short, thinking about how unhappy he was. But more importantly, thinking about how he could see that, as long as he remained where he was, nothing would change.

During the days, when he wasn't botching a procedure, he paced the garret, ducking beams. The confined space of the garret irritated him. He couldn't stand upright and walk even half the width of the floor. It was so cramped. It began to seem a metaphor for his life in Merom.

It would be better in Sharhumrin.

But he wasn't in Sharhumrin. He was in Outgate, in Talinfad, on Merom. Really, what was so bad about that? He had been born on Merom, in a village within sight of Talinfad's cathedral spires. He'd been born in a shoemaker's house in a little village. He'd gotten out of that. He had his own rooms now, here in an inn in Outgate. His own, as long as he paid the rent. He'd come a long way.

The silver from Crampton was the most money he'd had at once since Gan Tidoni's gift on the day of his *Akchepthio claviarorum.* The sum was a fortune for him. Enough even to buy the copy of Arkyn's *Properties of Fire* he'd coveted in Master Corbelone's shop. But then the money would be gone and he'd be poor again.

With no prospect of more.

With no chance to get out.

At midweek, he returned from a collecting trip in the middle of the afternoon to find his alembic cracked, its contents boiled away. Heedlessly of anyone below, he threw the useless glass out the window; his gatherings for the day followed in short order. Yan spent the remainder of the day staring at the distant mountains. Night came and his stomach was too upset to go down to supper. He continued to stare out the window, running all the arguments over again in his head. When Arsha rose to join the other two moons, he took off his clothes and got into bed. He found himself still awake, still worrying, when the cathedral's morning bells tolled. He knew then that he would have to leave.

But that presented its own problems. The silver was enough for a book, but not enough to ensure passage to Sharhumrin, nor to open doors when he got there. He had no money put by, having invested it all in glassware, bronze work, books, and those magical materials he couldn't gather himself. Although his workroom was

nowhere near as well equipped as Gan Tidoni's, he had
managed to acquire a substantial inventory.

Minus one alembic.

There was no point in staying.

After breaking his fast, he walked down to the customs house and learned that there was a ship bound for
Sharhumrin due to sail in a day or two: *Mannar's Grace*
out of Offat. The harbormaster was not expecting any
others sailing the direct route for weeks.

Weeks!

Yan hurried back to the Anchor and Plow and set to
work disposing of all but those few things he would
carry with him. The herbs and powders went to Gentla
the Apothecary in return for a draft on a merchant
house in Sharhumrin. Not immediate cash, but funds
Yan would need once he reached his destination. For
the bronze and the glass he received less than he had
hoped; each of the craftsmen had despaired of reselling
the specialized pieces and offered only prices suitable
for scrap. Wondering if they were taking advantage of
him, Yan agreed. He needed the cash.

The books were the hardest, but Master Corbelone
gave him a fair price. Yan even parted with his copy of
Arkyn's *Principles*. In Sharhumrin, he would be able to
acquire another. He could even make do with one of
those new printed copies if he had to.

It was near to dark when he reached his family's
house on Leather Lane. The still evening air was
allowing the stink from the tannery to drift up toward
the village. Most of the shops had their shutters down,
closed for the day, but his father's shutters were still
up, shoes still standing in rows on the counter. A light
within said that he still worked. Yan walked around
the back, preferring to enter the family room rather
than the shop.

Before he reached the door, he could hear the

sounds of conversation. He recognized the voices of his mother Alys, Dancie, and Fal's wife Sonia. The women were talking village gossip, the same sort of things they always talked of. Yan announced himself as he stepped through the doorway and reached up to touch the rusty piece of iron nailed to the frame.

His timing could have been better. His mother looked up from her work and smiled, dropping the vegetables she was cleaning in order to hug him. Yan smiled back but, at that moment, his father entered from shop. Alys halted just outside of Yan's reach, her eyes warily going to her husband. Dav said nothing, but Alys shifted her course away from Yan as though heading for something in the aumbry behind him.

Dav Tanafres stared at Yan with narrowed eyes.

"What are you doing here?"

"I will be traveling soon. I've come to say good-bye."

"Say it then and be on your way," his father said gruffly. He pulled the tall-backed chair away from the wall and set it by the table before slumping down into it. "It's been a long day and I'm hungry. Not enough food for another."

"That's all right. I wasn't planning on staying." Yan's stomach growled in protest. He hadn't had any food since breakfast. He'd been too busy. "I just came to say good-bye."

His father stared at him in stony silence.

"Where are you going?" Fal asked.

Yan had barely noticed his older brother's presence. Fal looked good, healthy, but older. Lines from squinting at his work were already etched around his eyes. Yan gave him a smile. "To Sharhumrin."

"Have you found a patron?" Dancie asked eagerly, though it earned her a scowl from her father.

"I will."

"Ain't yet, though." His father harrumphed. "Fits."

Dancie shook her head, and his mother smiled sadly under a furrowed brow. She looked older than Yan knew her to be.

"Well, woman, where's the food?" Dav demanded.

Alys and Dancie jumped to get it while Fal and his family took their places at the table.

Excluded from the gathering, Yan stood at the edge of the light from the lamp in the center of the table. "Well, I have to be going."

"Be careful on the road," his mother said worriedly as she placed the stewpot on the floor by the table.

"He's a mighty magician," his father snapped. "What's he got to worry about? Let him go. You've got a family to feed."

She started to ladle stew into the bowls. Dav got his first, and tucked into it noisily.

Always first. Always *his* way.

"Good-bye, everyone," Yan said softly.

He stepped outside. For all the tannery stink, the air seemed cleaner somehow. He had grown up here, but this was no home for him. After he established himself in Sharhumrin, things would be different. He would see to that.

He started back to Talinfad.

Dancie met him at the end of Leather Lane.

"Does he know you've left the house?" Yan asked.

"I don't care."

"I don't want to be the cause of a beating for you."

"You won't be."

They walked on in silence past the last house of the village and up the hill. On the crest, they embraced. The contact reminded Yan how much his little sister had grown since he had left to be apprenticed to Gan Tidoni.

"When I'm gone there'll be no more sneaking away on your trips to the city."

"No more to visit *you*, you mean," she said with a sly grin.

She had indeed grown. "You pay other calls?"

"I'm not telling. A girl has to have her secrets."

"Be careful, Dancie. Father won't like it if your friend isn't a fine, upstanding craftsman."

"I'm careful."

He hoped so. "I will write to you as soon as I reach the capital."

"But who will read it?"

"You could if you make your choosing properly."

She tossed her head and looked away. Her long, dark hair hid her face. "I don't know."

"Well, if you don't learn to read it yourself, you can have it read to you. There are lots of clerks around Talinfad. Kesem Fanalli in Outgate has a good reputation. Something of a scholar, I hear. Goodwife Kavarin can introduce you."

"I thought you said reading and writing other people's letters wasn't good work for a scholar."

He shrugged. "It's all right for some. Reading and writing is their calling. But for someone like me, someone who has touched the magic, such work seems petty and irrelevant."

"Ear what?"

"Less important. Sort of like putting decoration on work shoes. You can do it, but it doesn't make sense to do it. It's a waste of time."

"You never did like to waste time. 'Cept when it was Poppa's time."

He went for her ribs to tickle her, but she danced away. She was faster than she used to be. They laughed for a moment, then Yan became serious.

"It's time to say good-bye."

"Good journey, you mean."

"Even so."

Smiling, he kissed her on the forehead and started off. Looking back from the next hill, he saw her silhouette still standing in the middle of the road. He waved one last time and she waved back.

He spent his last night in the garret above the Plow and Anchor composing a letter to Gan Tidoni. He tried to marshal his arguments, to lay them out so that they made the sort of sense that the Gan would understand, but every approach he tried seemed lacking. He made a final attempt, sanded the ink dry, folded the paper, and sealed it. It was not perfect, but he hadn't found a way to put into words what he felt.

In the morning, he stood in the street outside Gan Tidoni's town house, still undecided about whether to deliver the letter. People began to notice him standing there and he started to feel very self-conscious, but he still couldn't decide either to leave the letter or go in to speak to Gan Tidoni in person. He cast a spell of seeming over himself so that he would at least be less noticeable. Who really wanted to look closely at a crippled beggar, after all?

He knew that he should go in and speak to his old master. The gan deserved to learn of Yan's decision from Yan himself. But he felt sure that Gan Tidoni would not approve. He'd written the letter so he wouldn't have to face his old master, and now he wasn't even sure he could deliver it.

Maybe he should stay after all.

He thought about the garret at the Anchor and Plow and knew he couldn't face it again. Besides, he had told his family he was leaving.

He looked at the letter in his hand. He could just leave it with Olvon, telling the servant to deliver it after he was safely away. That was the coward's solution, but wasn't the letter itself a coward's way?

Across the street, the door opened. Yan ducked

back into the shadows, hesitant and uncertain. He watched as the gan appeared in the doorway and looked up and down the street. The old mage's brow furrowed as his gaze passed over Yan, but he gave no sign of recognition. After a word to Olvon, Gan Tidoni stepped into the street and started down the road toward Bar Gate.

Yan watched him go.

There was still time to run after him.

Gan Tidoni was soon lost among the morning traffic wending its way into the city.

Yan looked again at the letter in his hand. It really didn't explain his thoughts very well. It wouldn't do what he wanted it to do. The gan wouldn't understand. With a sigh, he tore the paper in half, then in half again and again, until it was a jumble of ragged pieces. A gentle sea breeze wafted by and blew them out of his hand. The scraps tumbled away down the street, taking his words with them.

Dropping his spell, Yan stepped into the road and headed for the docks.

# 4

BY THE TIME YAN REACHED the plaza at wharfside, his hand
was sore from gripping the handles of his work satchel.
He wasn't used to carrying so much in it all at once,
especially not while shouldering the additional burden of
a sack containing the rest of his worldly goods. Having
gotten to the square in good time—the tide would not
turn till almost noon—Yan felt he could relax for a
moment. He set down his satchel and laid the sack
against it. Rubbing his sore hand, he looked around at
the midmorning throng seething across the cobblestones.

Every breath he took was full of the tang of the sea,
of freedom. Indeed, it seemed that the sea surrounded
him. The plaza was Talinfad's fish market. The fishermen, the crabbers, the shrimp trappers, and the mussel
grubbers were all here, as well as the seaweed gatherers,
the kafdenwhal hunters, the beachcombers, and the
shellfish divers. They had gathered all the bounty the
sea offered and spread it here for the citizens of
Talinfad to choose among. Of course, the choicest bits
would be gone by now, unless some boat had put in
late through delay or design.

For every seller there was a handful or more of buyers
and that meant there was little open space in the square
as the city's inhabitants took advantage of the fish market and the purveyors of other goods took advantage of
the market's draw to peddle their own wares. The
resulting crowd was bigger than Yan was used to. He
was also uncomfortably aware of the unfriendly glances
and barely concealed signs of protection aimed in his
direction. Yan had thought the people of Talinfad more
sophisticated. Certainly, the people of Outgate hadn't
reacted toward him this way. Or had they only been
more circumspect?

He was glad he would soon be away from this
provincial backwater.

Yan looked out past the crowds of buyers and sellers
into the harbor. A ship, its broad white sail full of the
seaward breeze, was tacking slowly across the bay
toward the open sea. Could it be? The harbormaster
had said that the captain of *Mannar's Grace* was an
impatient man. Could he have sailed before the tide
turned? The ship was too far away for Yan to make out
decorative details that would identify the vessel, and
the banners and flags she flew meant nothing to him.

He flung his sack over his shoulder, grabbed his
satchel, and hurried toward the water. Maybe if he was
closer he could see. But that ship couldn't be *Mannar's
Grace.* It just couldn't be. He couldn't be stranded here
for *weeks.*

The crowd suddenly was no longer between him
and the water, and Yan's precipitous pace almost took
him right over the edge of the wharf. Shifting his
weight at the last moment, he caught himself against a
piling and avoided plunging into the harbor. He
strained to see something identifying about the departing ship, but the small difference in position availed
him nothing. He still couldn't identify it. He was staring

so intently at the distant ship that only slowly did he realize that another vessel was tied up to the wharf, not fifty yards from him.

Hopefully, Yan looked the ship over. She was a big oceangoing caravel, most of her hidden from view by the high quarterdeck and sterncastle. But Yan could see what he needed to see: standing watch over the sterncastle was a carven figure, her dress painted a deep blue and sparkled with white stars. Yan didn't need to see the sigils carved in each of the flanking lampposts to recognize Mannar, goddess of the air.

He hadn't missed his ship after all.

Yan moved through the throng in the direction of *Mannar's Grace.* Most of the people he passed ignored him, treating him as just another passerby. Those who did notice him, noticed his *claviarm* as well. They didn't smile at him, or nod politely. Was this suspicion and distrust to be his lot? They showed respect to Gan Tidoni. It seemed unfair. After all, Yan had been certified by the Triadic Church and was no dark mage. He was sure that things would be better in Sharhumrin; the Imperial capital had to be a more enlightened place than this provincial town.

A wagon blocked Yan's approach to the ship, but the space beyond it was mostly open. Thinking he'd be able to get a good view, and maybe spot the captain, he walked around past the horses, whispering a hello to each of them as he passed. They, at least, were friendly. He halted on the other side, reluctant to get in the way of the activity around the gangway to *Mannar's Grace.*

He didn't know much about maritime customs, but he knew one didn't board a ship without permission. Arranging for some other member of the crew to summon the captain would cost. Mentally, Yan recounted his money. There was enough, but every unplanned

expenditure cut into his reserves. There was still time
before noon. Perhaps the captain would appear.

A crew of stevedores and seamen were unloading
barrels from a wagon. Judging from the effort they
were expending, the barrels were of considerable
weight. A middle-aged man dressed in clothes suited to
a merchant supervised the operation with fussy dili-
gence. The man's face was etched with worry lines,
which deepened when the workers nearly lost control
of a barrel. If he wasn't the owner of the cargo, he was
responsible for it. He seemed more burdened than the
stevedores.

Reminded of his own burden, Yan put down his luggage. There was still time; he could wait. It would be
best not to get in the workers' way.

Yan noticed that he was not the only observer of the
loading. A half dozen hard-bitten men and one woman,
with swords scabbarded at their sides and wearing buff
coats, stood by the gangway to the ship. Only one of
them had a breast-and-back of russeted metal, but all
had twisted black-and-white cords bound around their
sword arms, showing them to be hired members of the
Guild of the Sword. Occasionally the armored man,
obviously the leader of the mercenaries, spoke to the
merchant. After those brief conversations, the merchant would stop fussing at the porters. But only for a
moment or two.

Finally Yan grew bored with the show and looked
around again. He was still unable to spot anyone likely
to be the vessel's master. What if the captain were
belowdecks, only to emerge when the ship was getting
under way? If so, Yan might not get a chance to
arrange his passage. Yan checked the sun, still time; he
decided to wait some more.

The day was warming rapidly. Even here by the
harbor, the breeze from the city was warm, full of an

early promise of summer heat to come. Yan took off
his hat and fanned himself. His rush across the plaza
and his hike through town had left him thirsty. He
looked about for a water vendor. The first one he saw
was a bregil, cask strapped to his brawny back. Yan
had seen bregil before, usually riding as guards or
porters for the caravans to and from their strongholds
in the mountains. They were not common in Talinfad.
None lived in Outgate. Eyes on the sweaty cask, Yan
could almost taste the cool water within. He waved the
waterseller over.

Reaching into his pouch for the shev he would need
to pay the vendor, Yan found the small coin eluding
his grasp. He tucked his hat against his neck, holding it
there with his chin and using his freed hand to steady
his pouch. He was still fumbling for the coin when the
bregil planted himself in front of Yan. The vendor's
huge, dark eyes and forthright stare seemed to make
Yan even more fumble-fingered. At last, he got a grip
on the coin and held it out to the vendor.

The bregil grinned wide, baring his strong yellow
teeth.

"Fine clear water, sir," he said as he accepted payment. With his tail he grabbed a cup from among those
hanging on his barrel, and held it out while he dipped
the ladle into the cask. His free hand tapped at the
bunch of small pouches hanging at his belt. "Will you
take herbs in it? I have mint, or chazz leaves if you prefer a sharp tang."

"Plain will be fine." Replacing his hat on his head,
Yan accepted the water.

The vendor's eyes fastened on Yan's uncovered
*claviarm.* The bregil's pupils widened, filling even more
of his dark irises than before. His nose quivered and
with it his bifurcate upper lip. He stuck out his arm,
keeping his hand hovering around the cup as Yan

drank. "Busy day, sir. Very busy. I've gotta be moving on, sir. If you're done, sir."

Yan drained the last of the water and the bregil snatched the mug away. He passed it to his tail as he backed away, bobbing his head in place of the bow he could not perform without dumping the contents of his water cask all over himself.

Even bregil.

Depressed, Yan returned his attention to *Mannar's Grace.*

While he had been occupied, a new person had arrived to watch the loading of the ship, a stocky man in a wide-brimmed hat and a salt-stained velvet coat around which was wound a scarlet waistband. A broad black belt held the sash in place and supported a complicated network of straps attached to a short, curved sword in a fancy scabbard. Among the decorative whorls of the scabbard carving, Yan could see the sigils of Mannar.

Yan grabbed his luggage and approached the man.

"Are you the master of this vessel?"

"Aye, sir. Owner and captain." The captain gave Yan a sideways glance, swift and evaluating, but continued to observe the loading as he spoke. "Vik Lorenalli, late of Hellaspor, Learth, and just about every other port on the Danteriff, but most recently out of Offat, where the winters be too cold for a hot-blooded seaman, by Mardian. You'll be seeking passage south."

"I am."

"Passage ain't free, young fella. I've rarely met a boy carrying his worldly goods on his back who had good silver in his pocket. You don't look like a sailor. Are you expecting to work your passage?" The captain didn't give Yan a chance to answer. "Well, forget it. It's still early in the year and I don't want any fumble-fingered,

know-nothing, easy-puking landlubber working my ship.
Not in the kind of seas we're too likely to meet. Give it
time. You'll find a berth later in the season."

Yan was annoyed. "I have money."

That got him another glance from the captain. "Do
you now? And how much do you think it'll cost you to
ride the Lady's *Grace*?"

"Five full pieces of silver."

The captain's mouth froze half-open for the briefest
moment. "Five kartes? You be wanting to sail all the
way to Timedrin?"

"I wish to go to Sharhumrin. That is your destination, isn't it?"

"Oh, aye," Turning to face Yan, the captain grinned.
"The *Grace* will be sailing soon. Off to turn your inheritance into a fortune?"

"What makes you think I've an inheritance?"

"You're a young man and you've enough for passage. You don't look like a thief." Then Captain
Lorenalli's eyes dropped to Yan's *claviarm*, and he
seemed to see it for the first time. His smile vanished as
his mouth drew into a hard line. "Too bad I ain't got
room aboard."

Yan frowned himself. "You seemed ready to take
me on as a passenger a moment ago."

The captain harrumphed. "Did I? Maybe you mis-
understood."

"I think I understand all too well."

"Good, then you'll understand I'm a busy man."

"I understand you're a man interested in money. I
may not have an inheritance, but I can afford to pay
more." Yan hoped the captain wouldn't demand too
much more. He wanted to get off Merom very badly,
but he needed to have something to live on while he
looked for a patron in Sharhumrin.

"How much more?" Lorenalli asked.

Hooked him. But before Yan could reel the captain in, an argument broke out aboard *Mannar's Grace.* Captain Lorenalli took one look at the barrel hanging suspended over the main deck and stormed up the gangway, shouldering the last of the stevedores aside. Yan followed, offering an apology to the stevedore as he pushed his own way past the man. His business with Captain Lorenalli was not concluded, and he was afraid that the captain might use the opportunity to slip away from granting Yan passage.

Once aboard, the captain thrust himself into a knot of sailors arguing about who was responsible for the problem. With all the name-calling and indiscriminate blame-laying, Yan couldn't tell what had set them off. Once Captain Lorenalli got them quieted down, he asked for an explanation.

"The main hatch, Cap'n. She's wedged tight," one of the sailors told him. "If Ab hadn't hammered—"

"You whoreson," shouted the man who was obviously Ab. "You're the one—"

"Batten it all," the captain roared. He heaved at the hatch himself, grunting with strain. His face darkened with the effort. But no matter how hard he tugged, the hatch cover remained in place. "By Baaliff's brazen balls, she's stuck fast."

The barrel suspended above the hatch started down as the men on the line eased off. Deckhands reached out to guide it away from the hatch and back onto the deck.

"Ye lazy spawn of a kafdenwhal," Captain Lorenalli bawled. "Haul that line taut. We ain't got time for this. We're not gonna miss the tide. The hatch'll open and ye can hold her there till then."

The barrel went back up.

The captain ordered two sailors to either side of the hatch and positioned himself on one end. At his

command they heaved in unison, but their combined
strength was insufficient.

"She's still tight, Cap'n," Ab said needlessly.

"Shut up," the captain muttered. The barrel started
to descend again and he roared at the haulers, "Belay
that, you jelly-muscled sods."

The captain's bellowed evaluation of the parentage
of the haulers captured the attention of almost everyone aboard. Ignored by the seamen, Yan bent down
and looked at the hatch. The wood on both sides of the
frame was clearly warped. Splinters on the deck gave
evidence that the cover had been recently forced into
place. The freshly exposed wood had swollen in the
damp air and made a tight fit even tighter. He edged
forward into an empty place next to the coaming, and
laid a hand on the offending wood. He whispered the
words of a restoration spell, stumbling once as he
sought the right form for this application. He repeated
the charm, surer now, and focused his will. Slowly, the
wood shifted back into its shaped form. The spell complete, Yan waited for Captain Lorenalli to pause in his
tirade.

"Perhaps you should try again, Captain."

"What say you?"

"I said that I think the hatch will open now."

Suspiciously, the captain gave the offending cover a
shove with his foot. The wood moved easily. Several of
the sailors made the Triadic sign.

Looking across the hatch at Yan, Captain Lorenalli
shouted his orders to his men. "All right then, you lazy
sons of Mardian. Get this hatch clear and load the belly
of this tub. The tide won't wait."

The captain stalked aft, stopping at the foot of the
companion ladder to the quarterdeck. Yan followed.
Captain Lorenalli stared out over the rail, apparently
watching the seabirds wheel over the waves, but Yan

saw his eyes shift over once. Yan said nothing; the man knew he was there.

Finally the captain spoke. "It was you, wasn't it? You used your magic."

"I did."

"Why'd you do that?"

"I only sought to show you that magic can be useful."

"Aye, I know it can be."

"Well, then why—"

"By Mardian! I know, too, that it brings nothing but trouble." The captain's hands were clenched on the railing, his knuckles paler spots on the dark skin of his hands.

"I won't trouble you anymore," Yan said, turning to go.

The captain's hand snagged his arm. "You'll not leave me owing you, magician. I would have missed the tide had you not done what you did. Will you take this as payment?" The captain held out a pair of kartes. "I'd have lost more if we'd been late in sailing."

Yan looked at them. "I did not do it for money."

"Damn your hide, magician. I'll not sail while in your debt."

"If I sailed with you, we could discuss the matter."

Jaw clenched, Captain Lorenalli nodded, gritting out, "Fair passage paid? Four kartes?"

Yan's earlier offer of five for passage had been designed to impress. The captain's offer of four was still high. "Fair passage you said, Captain. Three kartes."

If the captain had been a bregil, the sound he made would have been called a growl. "But no more magic unless I order it."

"I don't usually work for free."

Captain Lorenalli's jaw worked but he said nothing and stomped up the companion ladder. Yan watched him go and smiled to himself at his victory.

"Smartly done."

Yan turned. The speaker was the leader of the mercenaries. He leaned against the centerline stanchion that supported the quarterdeck, a rakish smile on his rugged face. Yan's luggage sat at the man's feet. The mercenary swept off his hat and flourished it, the fluffy white struth feather fluttering frantically. He replaced his hat, tugging it down to seat it properly, and said, "I thought you'd be wanting these despite having abandoned them on wharfside. Jost Martello at your service. Within the bounds of my bond, of course."

"Of course," Yan replied automatically. Recalling his manners, he introduced himself. Pointedly he added his profession, as custom demanded and the mercenary had failed to do. "I am Yan Tanafres, a magician."

"So I gathered. Our good Captain Lorenalli is not fond of magicians. I was rather surprised that you managed to persuade him to take you aboard."

Yan shrugged. He really didn't care what a common mercenary thought, not even one of the vaunted Sword Guild. Yan dug into his pouch, feeling for a coin to reward the man for bringing his luggage aboard. Although the service was unasked for, Yan was grateful for it. His own preoccupation with convincing the captain might have cost him his goods.

Martello sauntered to the railing beside Yan, pointedly ignoring the offered coin. "Don't get away from home often, do you, young master?"

Yan didn't want to talk to the man. What did he have in common with a mercenary? He tried to think of a polite way to tell the man to mind his own business. He didn't want to offend Martello; warriors were renowned for having short tempers. His thoughts were interrupted by the echoing crack of a whip.

Yan and Martello turned their heads, seeking across

the wharfside plaza for the source of the sound. After
a moment, Yan heard a rumble and clatter resonating
from the main street leading into the plaza. Seconds
later the crowd stirred into motion near that entrance
to the square. The last few citizens scrambled out of
the way as a team of six matched horses cantered into
the open space, pulling a dark coach behind them.
The coachman angled his team directly toward
*Mannar's Grace*. Perforce the coach's passage was
slowed by the throng, despite the shouts of the postilion rider and the liberally cracking whip of the
coachman.

Yan recognized the coach even before he saw the
arms painted on the doors. It was the same one that
had disturbed his sleep on the anniversary of his
*Akchepthio claviarorum.*

As the coach rolled to a stop, one of the footmen
dropped off and hurried forward. He was at the
door as the carriage stopped. Opening the door, he
bowed, one hand still on the handle to prevent the
door from swinging, the other stretched forward to
aid the passenger in debarking. A hand appeared
from the dark interior, a hand as familiar to Yan as
the coach. This time he saw more than the lady's
hand as she stepped delicately into the doorway.
Holding the frame with one hand, she reached out
and laid the other on her footman's arm. As she
stepped down, Yan caught a glimpse of elaborately
patterned stocking and sueded brown shoe beneath
the lady's full skirt. Safely on the cobblestones, she
stood and waited while one of the footmen reached
into the coach and produced a parasol. He opened it
and handed it to her.

She was slender, almost willowy. Her skin was as
pale as the color of new cherrywood, her hair of a midnight hue, sparkling with stars of cut stones tucked

among the elaborate tresses. She stepped out of Yan's
sight, disappearing behind a wall made by the ship's
railing and the still-bustling sailors.

"She's beautiful."

Martello chuckled. "Trouble for you, young master."

Yan felt embarrassed for having spoken aloud, dou-
bly so that he had been overhead by the mercenary.
"What would you know about it?"

"Don't you see the arms on the carriage?"

"I see them."

"But you don't know them."

Yan didn't want to admit his ignorance to this man.

"She's part of the Renumas clan."

That was not a name Yan knew, but he tried to
sound as though he knew it well. "I see."

"As a passenger, you're entitled to be on the quarterdeck."

"Why are you telling me that?"

"The view's better from up there," Martello said
with a wink. "I've got men to square away. Maybe we'll
talk later."

Though unasked for, the mercenary's advice was
welcome. Yan wanted to see more of the lady. He
mounted the companion ladder and found the captain
waiting impatiently at the top. Captain Lorenalli
frowned at him.

"If you move that slowly while we're docked, I
expect you'll be underfoot for the whole voyage."

"I'm sorry, Captain. I'll try not to be in the way."
Martello was right; the view was better from the quarterdeck. As the captain started down the companion
ladder, Yan pointed out the lady and asked, "Captain,
is that lady to travel with us?"

The captain stopped his progress and turned his
head toward the wharf. He grimaced as the lady called
several of his seamen from their work and set them to

unloading her trunks from the carriage. "Would she take such liberties otherwise?"

Yan watched the captain's deferential approach to the lady. He could not hear their exchange of words over the clatter and clamor of the loading, but watching Captain Lorenalli's extravagant gestures and catching the flash of the man's teeth, Yan guessed that the captain kept to himself his distaste over the lady's usurpation of his crew. Preceded by one of her footmen and followed by the other two, the lady boarded *Mannar's Grace* with a grace of her own that Yan thought must rival that of the goddess.

She climbed the companion ladder on the landward side of the ship with a practiced step and took up a place at the railing, leaving her men and the seamen carrying her trunks to tramp past her to the cabin under the sterncastle. Leaning against the rail, she gazed out over Talinfad. Yan looked across the ship and past her, seeking what she seemed so intent upon. By the angle of her head and her seemingly steady gaze, he decided that she was looking at the statue of Casorn surmounting the huge granite block in the center of the wharf plaza.

Was she an art lover? If so, he had an opening with her. He stepped quietly to her side. She did not seem to hear him coming, but she could not avoid noticing him as he leaned on folded arms beside her at the rail.

"It is a fine example of the conciliation art commissioned by the Council of Lords after the Iron League joined the empire, isn't it? The artist was only a minor luminary at the local court, but I think he caught something here. He excelled himself in capturing the pathos of Casorn's burden. I think it far better than the others of the set."

"Oh, I think so too. Especially that horrid thing by Pattiyarm in Learth."

"Most definitely." Yan had never seen the statue at Learth. "Pattiyarm is overrated."

She checked him over with a glance, and if she found him lacking, she showed no sign of it. Holding out her hand, she said, "I am the Lady Selanna Renumas."

He took her fingers upon his own and bent low over her hand, not daring to touch her flesh with his lips. "I am Yan Tanafres, and I am at your service, Lady."

"Are you a scholar of art?"

"A scholar of many things, but always a lover of beauty."

She had the grace to blush though she had no doubt heard the compliment before. "You are far too young to be a sage. Too young as well, I think, to be a teacher, and you do not smell like an artist. At least not like a painter. Are you a sculptor?"

"My efforts are unworthy of your eyes."

"How can you know?"

"My dabbling was unfit for *any* eyes. At least that's what Gan Tidoni always said."

"Tidoni? Dochay Junivall's mage?"

"The very same."

"And how do you know the esteemed Gan Tidoni?"

"I had the honor of being his student, my lady."

Her voice was suddenly guarded. "His student?"

"To his despair, as he told me," he said, hoping humor would return her previous mood.

He was disappointed. She turned her head away, ending their conversation. To avoid standing there at her back and looking stupid, Yan retreated across the deck. He leaned over the railing, watching the waves slap against the ship's hull.

Was he destined for more and more complete shunning? Girls had found him attractive before. Even after he earned his *claviarm*. He could have blamed his failure on his approach or the difference in their stations, but she had been receptive until she learned he was a magician. There seemed to be only one inescapable conclusion.

Yan felt more out of place than the time he had accompanied Gan Tidoni to the dochay's palace. If this was the way of the wider world, perhaps he was better off without it. His practice in Talinfad was not large, nor particularly remunerative, but no one had spit on his shadow. He had exchanged no money with the captain, no bargain would be broken if he left the ship now, no harm done if he returned home to his papers and herbs.

Bits of flotsam passed by, faster than before though he had felt no freshening of the wind. He looked up and saw the headland and its lighthouse nearer than they had been. A look back showed him the wharf plaza of Talinfad, small and growing smaller. It was too late for second thoughts now. The ship had sailed.

It would be a long voyage confined with these people who did not care for him. Well, maybe they didn't dislike him personally. How could they? None of them knew him. But the lady, the captain, and enough of the sailors had made it clear that they disliked magicians. Though he'd never been on one before, he knew a ship was a small place, smaller than Outgate, smaller than the village in which he'd grown up, and too small to be comfortable if he constantly reminded his fellow travelers that he was a magician.

Yan cupped his *claviarm* in his hand. This was the sign that told others what he was. Hiding it wouldn't change what he was, but it might change the way they looked at him. Did he really care so much? He stared at the amulet he had fashioned with his own hands. He knew it by heart, every curve in the metal, every stone, every sigil, as well as every mark made when a tool slipped and every place his skill was not what he wished it to be. He had been proud to finish it, prouder still of what it had meant.

The *claviarm* marked him as a magician.

As an outcast.

He tucked the amulet inside his shirt.

Just for the trip, he told himself. He hung his head, ashamed of himself.

"Never sailed before?" It was Martello again.

"No."

"Falde's got some herbs for the stomach; if you're in need, I could get them for you. The sea'll get rougher once we clear the harbor."

"No, it's not that."

"Glad to hear it, since we'll be sharing the same space," Martello said cheerfully.

"What do you mean?"

"Law of the sea, young master. The Lady Renumas bumps the captain from his cabin. He bumps the passengers to the forecastle, which bumps the ship's officers to the helm cabin and me to the underdeck."

"But I'm a passenger."

"One unwelcome in the forecastle. Nat Gorremo is a richer man than you and has a significantly larger piece of the captain's ear. Soon as he heard you were a magician, he concluded that there was no more space in the forecastle. He was unhappy enough at being moved there when Lady Renumas came aboard. But I said I didn't mind. Underdeck's not so bad as long as we don't get a storm. Besides, from what Gorremo's clerk told me, Mistress Gorremo snores like unto the iron bull at Tradestad."

Yan didn't care about people who snored. "I expected a cabin."

"Be thankful you're not down in the hold."

Given everyone else's reaction to him, Yan wondered

at Martello's friendliness. "Why don't you care? Aren't you afraid of being contaminated by the mage?"

"I, for one, am glad to have you aboard."

Yan thought that odd, until he thought about the mercenary's profession. "Are you expecting danger?"

"It's not like we're headed into the Sea of Storms."

"But you are expecting trouble?"

"There is always danger at sea," Martello said. "We'll be passing through waters where Essarinic privateers sail. They've been active of late, but at least we're not at war. War puts too many of the sallow-skinned bastards out to sea. As it is, we're not likely to see much trouble, it's still early in the season. Not much work for pirates when there's not much trade moving on the Danteriff. Still, it's my business to protect the Chaylenti cargo, so I welcome anything, or anyone, who can make my job easier. I'm a diligent man, but lazy enough at times."

"I can't do your work for you. I don't know any combat spells."

"No? Too bad. Guess you won't be as useful as I thought." Martello helped Yan watch the lighthouse pass by as they cleared the harbor. "Do you play trey?"

"Some."

"Guess you do have some uses after all. Hard to find a good player at sea. Trey doesn't seem to appeal much to oceangoing folks. Wonder why."

Yan had no idea and said so. The rebuff sent Martello away. Yan remained at the railing until night fell. The was little to see, so he took himself down to the underdeck. Martello had placed Yan's gear in one corner and someone had strung up a hammock for him. Yan managed to get into the net without dumping himself to the deck. The gentle swaying soon eased him into sleep.

The days of Yan's first sea voyage swiftly settled

into a pattern. As a passenger, he was privileged to walk the quarterdeck, but the continued chilliness surrounding the other passengers made that uncomfortable. He spent most of his time in the waist, where he got in the way of the sailors. They'd curse him if they didn't realize who he was and mutter under their breath when they did. The sailors' curses were at least honest if not open.

In the mornings, he'd watch Martello drill his three men and one woman. Lady Sarella's guards watched the drills as well. They would call out jibes whenever one of the mercenaries slipped or missed a stroke because of the pitch of the vessel. They especially taunted Falde, the female mercenary, but she ignored them, never even tossing back a curse as her companions routinely did. Yan admired her stoicism.

His afternoons were spent in conversation with Martello, usually with a game of trey before the evening meal. Yan found himself pleasantly surprised that the mercenary could talk about more than just his trade. Martello wasn't a scholar of Gan Tidoni's accomplishments, but he had been to a lot of places and seen a lot of things that Yan had only read about in books. The mercenary had no formal education, but he was a keen observer and his insights often surprised Yan. It also surprised Yan that he was coming to like the man.

Early on the third day, they reached Yawymti's Horn. Legend said that the great rocky spire, taller than the masts of *Mannar's Grace*, was the tip of the demon Yawymti's horn, transmuted to rock when the Sazarn, the great prophet of the Triad, had thrown down the forces of the ancient empire of Mür. Sazarn was supposed to have drowned the demon and the dark mages who had summoned it; hence its horn projecting up from the sea. Yan thought that the spire looked remarkably like the basalt cliffs behind it.

Strange, awe-inspiring even, but ultimately natural, totally a part of the real world.

"Doesn't look like its supposed mate," Martello said.

"What mate?"

"The other demon horn on the mainland. They're both black and spindly, but the other is different. You'll see."

"We'll pass this other horn?"

"We're going to be headed straight for it. The reach between the two horns is the shortest passage to the mainland. Lorenalli will be taking us that way. Ah, see. He's coming to give the orders."

Captain Lorenalli did indeed begin giving orders, and in response seamen swarmed up the ratlines to trim the sails. Before long *Mannar's Grace* shifted her heading, putting Yawymti's Horn directly astern. Catching a fresh breeze, the ship picked up speed. Yan wandered up to the forecastle and looked ahead. There was no land in sight. By midafternoon the Horn had sunk below the horizon behind them and there was nothing to see around them but sea and cloud.

Yan found the openness strange and a little unsettling. He had never liked dark, enclosed places and so he thought that such openness should have been pleasant. Instead, he found himself feeling lost, fearing that he might never see land again. He knew it was unreasonable, but knowing didn't calm him much. He went back to the underdeck and spent the rest of the day there, only coming out after night had fallen.

The next morning Yan awoke to an odd silence. He heard no rush of water against the hull, no shrill of wind in the rigging. By the odor of the morning porridge wafting in from the waist, he knew it was morning, though it was still dark. Curling into the underdeck was the reason for the darkness: fog.

Yan rolled himself out of his hammock and rubbed his face, trying to convince himself to wake up. If they had sailed all night, they should be off the coast of Scothandir, but when he stumbled sleepily out into the waist, he could see nothing but fog. The world seemed to end just beyond the railing of *Mannar's Grace.*

Sailors were gathered in knots around the railing of the ship, staring off into the dim grayness and muttering to each other. One noticed him and made the triangle.

Here in the open, Yan felt uneasy. The fog was so still and everything was so quiet. Extraordinarily quiet. Entirely *too* quiet. He began to fear that the fog was unnatural. Afraid to set off the sailors by going into trance, he did nothing to confirm or deny his fears. He was a first-time sailor, after all.

Just nerves, he told himself.

He looked back to the sterncastle. Captain Lorenalli, barely visible, paced the deck in a fretful manner, but he seemed more frustrated than worried.

Good enough then.

The captain knew the sea; he could do the worrying. Looking for something to fill his empty belly, Yan stumbled to the foot of the mast, where the cook was stirring the morning porridge.

# 5

THE END OF THE DAY WAS DEFINED only by a darkening of
the fog.

The mood aboard *Mannar's Grace* darkened as well.
The Gerremos and their clerk emerged from the forward cabin only to collect the evening meal. Lady
Selanna had hers brought to her. Jost Martello and his
mercenaries stood or sat in a quiet group at the edge of
the underdeck, while the lady's men lounged near her
cabin door, occasionally tossing dice in an indifferent
way as they had all day. The sailors stayed in the waist,
neither gaming nor singing as they had when released
from work in fairer weather. They sat about the deck,
singly or in pairs, and spoke but little. Yan noted that
none but the cook and his assistant ventured below
deck. Captain Lorenalli glowered down on everyone
from his vantage point in the sterncastle.

*Mannar's Grace* sat as still as a model ship on a
retired captain's mantel. They were adrift on a sea of
glass, wound in a wad of cotton wool. The ship's
lanterns glowed sullenly, casting faint illumination into
the shrouded night.

The hours wore on.

Sometime after the cook and his assistant had finished cleaning the dinner vessels and damping down the cooking fire, Nat Gorremo emerged from the forecastle cabin. The fog and night obscured his expression, but the merchant's stiff carriage was easily seen from across the deck. Gorremo marched the length of the main deck and mounted the companion ladder to the quarterdeck. He appeared on his way to another complaint session with the captain. Curious, Yan emerged from the underdeck and stepped to the rail in time to see Gorremo stop short of the companion ladder up to the sterncastle. The merchant gripped the rope railing of the ladder as he looked out to sea, head turning slowly as though he was trying to locate something.

A sound, a distant rumbling like thunder in the mountains back home, came to Yan's ears. He wondered if he was hearing surf. Had a current caught them and begun dragging them toward shore? Would *Mannar's Grace* be driven onto the rocks?

Gradually the sound grew louder.

Loud enough for all on board to hear it.

Sailors roused themselves and moved to the rail, listening.

Yan watched them. They would know if the sound was waves rolling into a distant shore. They would know if the ship was in danger.

The sailors only stared into the fog with haunted eyes.

Whatever the sound was, it didn't seem to be surf. That made sense once he stopped to think about it. If they were headed for a shore, the sound should be coming from only one side. The rumble seemed all around them, but how could one tell in all the clammy grayness?

Yan considered using his magical senses again.

During the day he had tried several times to pierce the mists around them, to no avail. Each time, his trance had been noticed by either the sailors or his fellow travelers. Each time, the muttering among the sailors had gone on longer. As jittery as the darkness had made the sailors, their nervousness seemed multiplied by this strange sound. They glanced with increasing frequency in Yan's direction, which suggested that they might believe that he was responsible for the ship's predicament.

Blame it all on the mage. Hadn't Captain Lorenalli said nothing good would come of magic. Had the captain spoken the thoughts of his crew? Yan imagined that if they decided that he was the cause, they might be inclined to toss him overboard to the charka as the old tales said had been done to Yussof the Mariner. Given that he might stir the superstitious sailors to action, the chance of discerning something didn't seem worth the risk. Besides, he had promised Captain Lorenalli that he wouldn't do any magic without his permission.

The noise grew louder, becoming a rolling rumble with a more complex rhythm. Not thunder and not surf.

"Drums," Martello said. His voice carried all over the deck to judge from the heads that turned in his direction.

Captain Lorenalli was down from the sterncastle in a moment. "Are you sure, Sergeant Martello?"

The mercenary nodded.

"Where away? How many?"

"I can't tell for sure. The sound's coming from somewhere off to port, I think."

Anxious eyes stared into the dark as the sound of drums rolled ever clearer through the fog.

"Trouble?" Yan asked.

Martello and the captain looked at him as if he were a simpleton child.

"Mister Heis," Captain Lorenalli called in a carrying voice that wasn't quite a shout. "Ready the port cannon and bring up the deck guns. Mister Raldry, issue pikes and cutlasses."

Heis gathered some of the crew and disappeared below deck. Raldry came to get the key to the arms store from the captain before following. The unoccupied sailors crowded by the port rail and stared into the fog, fear on their faces. Martello and his mercenaries disappeared into the darker shadows of the underdeck; Yan soon heard them bustling about with their gear.

The activity brought Mistress Gorremo and the clerk out of the forecastle cabin. They joined Gorremo and the lady's men on the quarterdeck. Mistress Gorremo snugged herself against her husband's side.

Yan stepped back into the underdeck and tucked himself under the port companion ladder and tried to use his arcane sight to pierce the fog, but he remained as blinded astrally as he was mundanely. Frustrated, he rejoined the captain at the rail. Two seamen cradling lengths of dark iron hustled past them and up the companion ladder to the quarterdeck. Yan watched as the men settled their burdens into fittings on the rail. Deck guns.

"Cap'n!" Heis shouted as he regained the deck. The sailor reached down and took a small but obviously heavy cask from a fellow still on the ladder. Heis slammed the keg down. Rocking up the lid, he revealed a lumpy black mass. "Look at it, Cap'n. It's all caked as hard as a whore's heart. It'll never burn right."

Captain Lorenalli ground his teeth.

"What wrong?" Yan asked.

"That's our powder, Master Magician. Rather, what

used to be our powder. It's nothing but ballast now.
We've got no cannon if it's a fight."

Martello joined them. "We may have no guns at all.
Our cartridges have taken the damp."

Captain Lorenalli ground his teeth again. "What
about Lady Selanna's men?"

Martello shrugged. "They only carried pistols
aboard that I saw, but I doubt their powder is in any
better shape than ours. If there's trouble, we'll be meeting it at sword's length."

"Run out the guns anyway, Mister Heis. Whoever's
out there won't know we can't fire them."

Heis nodded once and was off. Martello and the
captain began discussing the best disposition of the
men about the ship. The talk was beyond anything with
which Yan was familiar.

Raldry emerged from below deck with an armload
of boarding pikes and began distributing them among
the sailors. He had disappeared below deck again, presumably to retrieve the cutlasses, when one of the
sailors by the rail put up a shout.

"Look there!"

Like everyone else, Yan turned to look where the
seaman pointed. Yan squinted into the fog, seeing
nothing; then he realized that one patch of fog seemed
darker. More sailors began pointing at the darker patch
and shouting excitedly, fearfully.

The dark shape loomed larger, coming closer.

The thundering roll of the drums pounded the night,
louder and louder.

"Mannar's mercy," a sailor gasped, and fainted.

The form in the fog took on shape.

It looked to be a giant charka, the dread man-eating
fish of the island waters, breaking the surface of the sea
in a killing rush. Jaws wide and almost as broad as the
beam of *Mannar's Grace* gaped open, the light of the

ship's lanterns reflecting from gleaming teeth. The beast's eyes burned a fierce and malevolent red. Froth, churned up by its many-rayed fins, sprayed from the monster's sides as it rushed at them.

Sailors scrambled away from the rail, dashing helter-skelter about the deck as the giant fish rushed toward the merchantman. Most screamed in terror, dropping their weapons.

Captain Lorenalli snatched the boarding pike from a sailor racing past him and smacked the man with the haft, dropping the sailor to his knees. "Damn your craven hides! Stand to!"

"That's no monster," Martello said as he stared at the approaching apparition. He shouted, "A warship! She's a warship!"

As soon as the mercenary said it, Yan could see clearly what attacked them. It was not giant fish, but a ship designed to appear as one. The burning eyes were lanterns; the snout, a bizarrely ornamented prow; the churning fins, oars. Their attacker was a warship of the type known as a galleass, equally capable of traveling by sail or oar. The dead calm was no bar to her.

The charka ship flew no flags that might identify her origins. Narrow black streamers fluttering fitfully from bone-white stanchions were the only ensigns she carried. Some ships hoisted painted sails to identify them, but this charka ship's sail was furled and battened down along with her mast. She was rigged for ramming.

The chaos aboard *Mannar's Grace* calmed slightly. Some of the sailors stopped to see if Martello's shout was truth. Captain Lorenalli ordered his men back to the rail.

"Without a wind, she has us," the captain said glumly.

Martello turned to Yan. "Master Tanafres, can you call us a wind?"

"Air is not my expertise, Sergeant Martello. I know a ritual, but it would take some time to set up the equipment."

"No time," said the captain.

"Damn." Martello spit. "No hope then."

"Some, maybe," the captain said. "She's within range for cannon and she hasn't fired. They must want to take us intact. The odds will be long, but if we can cut down enough of their boarders, they may decide us too costly a prize."

"I'm sorry I couldn't have been of more help, Captain," Yan said.

"So am I, Master Magician. But we thought of you too late," the captain said. "A ship doesn't jump to speed like a horse. Even if you called a hurricane at a word, we'd still lie athwart that bastard's bow. My own fault for not having thought of it sooner." He gripped the boarding pike fiercely and stared at the warship that was nearly upon them. The prow of the charka ship seemed aimed at the waist of *Mannar's Grace*, just aft of the forecastle. "They'll not take my ship without a fight."

The captain ran to the rail, shouting for his seamen to join him in repelling boarders. Martello ordered his men into place near the port companion ladder. The lady's bodyguards just clung to the rail and stared.

Aboard the charka ship, Yan could see men rushing forward, struggling up the incline of the fish-shaped head to crowd at the bow. Some of the charka ship's crew wore armor of black plates trimmed in white; others were naked save for breechclouts and paint, white stripes and dark. Their decoration made them look more like animated skeletons than living men. Their voices were raised in a deep, strange chant in a guttural tongue.

Martello's men tried to fire their muskets, but only

one ignited. The weapon roared, belching smoke, and one of the painted men tumbled back from the rail. "Reload and try again," Martello ordered as he drew and fired his pistol. The wheel lock whizzed, spitting sparks, and a moment later the gun banged. Another attacker dropped. The charka ship seemed too close, to be moving too swiftly, but somehow the mercenaries managed to reload their weapons But there was no roar, not one, only the sound of snapping locks as even the priming charges failed to ignite.

Yan didn't know what to do. He wasn't trained to fight and what little he knew of the art was a country boy's unschooled brawling. He knew no sorcery suitable to combat either. His other magics? Nothing seemed suitable, except perhaps . . .

He ran into the underdeck and grabbed his satchel. Unlikely that the captain would refuse permission now. As Yan emerged again into the waist, the charka ship rammed the merchantman.

*Mannar's Grace* shuddered. The deck pitched up on the side of the attacking ship, hurling Yan from his feet. He crashed down and slid along the deck, fetching up against the starboard bulwark. One of Martello's men staggered back with him, flailing. The mercenary hit the railing and pitched overboard.

As the merchantman started to settle back to an even keel, the upper jaw of the charka ship's fish head swung down, snapping lines, and buried its teeth into the *Grace*'s deck as if it were about to bite out a chunk. The vessel shuddered again as if in revulsion at the assault.

The fish head prow was a corvus, a boarding bridge that provided the attackers with a ramp from their ship to *Mannar's Grace*. A tall figure in full armor, his helmet wrought to resemble a skull, led the rush. Panicky sailors thrust boarding pikes at him, but the points

slithered off his armor. He cut them down without
mercy, smashing them to the deck with his double-
handed maul.

Captain Lorenalli engaged the leader, slashing at
the man. The skull-helmeted man blocked the first
attack and countered with a waist-level swing of his
weapon. His weapon of insufficient mass to halt the
maul, the captain was forced to back up to avoid the
blow. The armored man stepped forward, clearing
the end of the corvus. Painted raiders swarmed past
him on either side.

Yan watched in horror as raiders poured onto the
ship. The boarders soon seemed to outnumber the crew
of *Mannar's Grace* by two to one. The melee swelled as
the invaders engaged more of the seamen. Men shouted,
and screamed, and died. One group of painted men
led by a half-armored man split off a handful of sailors
and began forcing them back to the forecastle. The rest
dueled with the force led by the captain of *Mannar's
Grace.* Shouting, Martello led his band forward. The
swords of the mercenaries cut and thrust in economical
movements as they pressed the forwardmost raiders
back. Yan saw two of the boarders fall before Martello's
sword alone. A new wave poured off the corvus and
Martello ordered his band to retreat, calling to Captain
Lorenalli to do likewise.

A retreat would bring the fighting to Yan's feet.
Terrified, he scrambled up the starboard companion
ladder to the quarterdeck. As he neared the top, a
strong hand grabbed him by the arm and hauled him
up. It was one of the lady's bodyguards. The man
pushed Yan behind him and, his rapier to his right
hand, stepped back to block passage of anyone else
attempting to reach the quarterdeck.

Yan stumbled across the quarterdeck, clutching his
satchel to him. Had he left Merom only to find death?

The fighting in the waist was appalling. He could see little now, just weapons rising and falling. But he could hear the screams. He climbed halfway up the companion ladder to the sterncastle deck, shoving his satchel up onto the deck before looking back across the quarterdeck and down into the waist. The fight was still swirling there, men were still fighting and dying there.

The invaders had cut down almost all of the sailors and Captain Lorenalli was nowhere to be seen. Beset by a half dozen raiders, Martello and his band were retreating toward the port companion ladder. Only a trio of wounded sailors continued to fight from the forecastle. The defense of the merchantman was clearly failing.

The last sailors trapped in the forecastle went down under the weapons of the boarders and a commotion rippled through the invaders' ranks. The pressure on Martello's men eased as if the raiders were suddenly reluctant to come to grips.

Martello and his surviving three mercenaries used the respite to scramble up the companion ladder to the quarterdeck. Martello himself was the last up the ladder and he would have been skewered in the back had not one of the lady's guards knelt by the head of the ladder and thrust out with his rapier. The painted man throwing himself at the sergeant's back met the bodyguard's point and jerked back, a surprised look washing over his face before he fell back into his fellows, disrupting their advance. Rather than rush the ladders, the boarders drew back to cluster around their corvus.

No more attackers leapt forward.

"Why have they stopped?" Lady Selanna asked.

"Maybe they want prisoners," Nat Gorremo suggested.

"Should we surrender, then?" Mistress Gorremo asked.

"They'll not treat you gentle, Mistress," Martello said.

"But we'd be alive," she said.

"Doubt it," Falde said. "Watched them gut Raldry when he held up his sword for quarter."

"He was just a seaman," Mistress Gorremo protested. "We can provide ransom."

"You'll provide more than that to them if they lay hands on you," Falde told her.

"The sea would be more kind," Selanna said.

"Do you fancy a swim?" Martello pointed to the waist, where the snout of the charka ship lay buried in the ship's boat. Strakes from the small craft stuck up from the teeth like feathers in a cat's mouth. "Even if we were to take the boat back, it'd be going nowhere. Swimming's the only way off this tub."

"I can swim."

"There are real charka in the waters, Lady. Sharks, too. They'll all be here soon, for there's blood in the water."

Selanna folded her arms across her chest and glared at Martello. He said, "Horesh and His children made the world, not I. I can't change it for myself, nor for you."

Yan could swim, too, but he didn't like the idea of diving into charka-infested waters. Besides, they had no idea of how far or in what direction to swim. It was all too likely that a swimmer, no matter how expert, would exhaust himself, or herself, well before reaching land.

There had to be another way.

He had always thought that magic would hold the solutions he needed in the world, but he was still only barely initiated into the Art's secrets. He knew no spells of flight or transport, and it was too late for a wind even if the raiders gave him time to call one up. His mind raced through the spells he knew but they all became jumbled in his head. There was no time for a ritual spell, and he knew too little of spirits. Sorcery seemed the only hope, but every time he tried to assemble a useful chain of symbologies, he found himself lacking a succinct form. The only spells of which he could conceive were too complex or too powerful for him to cast safely.

He felt sure he was forgetting something. He had his notebooks in his satchel. Maybe he could jog his memory if he flipped through them. Yan looked back over his shoulder for his satchel and saw it lying against the coaming of the sterncastle deck hatch.

The hatch.

He had seen the captain on the sterncastle deck talk through the hatch to the helmsman in the sheltered part of the quarterdeck. Though the hatch was now battened down, covered with canvas and lashed tight, he remembered its construction. Like the hatch he'd repaired to win his passage, it was a latticework set into a frame of heavy timbers. It wouldn't float well with more than one person on it. But covered with canvas and reversed it would be much like the hide and sapling watercraft built by the rangers of Ched. If he strengthened the canvas and bound it to the wood, the hatch would become a boat of sorts—a raft at least. It would be small, but a half dozen people could be crammed onto it.

Someone might survive this affair.

"Sergeant Martello," he called. When the mercenary arrived, he explained his plan. Receiving the mercenary's agreement, Yan climbed the ladder and started his work. He hoped there would be time. Behind him he heard Martello address the passengers.

"We'll need every able hand here, but I think the ladies should go up to the sterncastle deck. These dogs fight like demons, but we may be able to hold them at the companion ladders; but if we can't, we'll have to retreat to the sterncastle. Quickly. I don't want to have to stumble over any of you."

"What about me, Sergeant? I know nothing of swords," Peyto Lennuick, the Gorremo's clerk, asked. The man's hair was white, and he was a veritable scarecrow. He would be of little use in a fight.

"Go with the ladies," Martello said. "But stay near the ladder top. Yell out if you see those dogs in the waist begin to move."

Peyto and the ladies climbed onto the sterncastle deck and Yan set to work.


A stirring among the invaders took Yan's attention from his spells.

One man advanced, stopping halfway between the corvus and the ladders to the quarterdeck. He was one of the unarmored ones, and his body paint was smeared, scarred by runnels of sweat and washed away by splashes of blood. The man raised his bloody sword and shook it at the sky.

"We are *baratani!* You *will* fall before us. Come down to us now and we will give you quick deaths."

"This for you," sneered Bern, the bodyguard who had tugged Yan up the ladder. He cocked his arm up and straightened it suddenly. A knife buried itself in the chest of the painted man. The boarders roared, but held their positions.

The painted man sank slowly to his knees, breathing stentoriously. He looked as though he might collapse at any moment, but he remained steady on his knees for minutes on end.

"*Sadatonee ray verbarasell,*" a voice shouted from among the boarders. "The ritual must go on."

An armored man stepped from among the ranks of the boarders, a long-hafted ax in his hands. He swept the weapon up, then down, decapitating the painted man in a blow. "*Sadatonee ray verbarasell,*" he said as he returned to the ranks without another glance as his fallen comrade.

"What in Horesh's name are they playing at?" Bern sounded incredulous.

Martello shook his head. "It's no game and I doubt the Lord of Light has anything to do with them."

"Anyone know what this *baratani* is that they're calling themselves?" Gorremo asked. "What about you, magician? Know anything about it?"

Yan had never heard the term and said so. No one else had either. Leaving the soldiers to their jobs and the passengers to their speculations, Yan returned to his spells. He was having trouble finding a proper significance for canvas. He'd just figured out something he thought would work when another painted warrior advanced from among the raiders.

"None can withstand *baratani!*" the man shouted. "We call you a second time. Come down. Let us make for you honored deaths." The man spread his arms wide and stared avidly at Bern. For a double dozen of heartbeats the raider stood. Then, with a look of disgust on his face, he lowered his arms to his sides. Turning suddenly, he bent over and pulled aside his breechclout to expose his buttocks to the people on the quarterdeck. He straightened, faced Bern again, and began to walk backward to his companions. As he went, he said, "I am *baratan*. Your refusal shames you more than me."

Gorremo scratched his head. "Does this make any sense to anyone? Magician? Anyone?"

"The speeches have the cadence of ritual," Yan said.

"They're doing magic?"

"None that I know," Yan replied.

"One *baratan*, two *baratani*," Peyto said quietly.

"There are demonically more than two of them, Scribe," Gorremo said acidly.

Peyto's mouth twitched and he said no more. Yan thought silence a good policy and tried to take up his spells again. He completed the bonding of the canvas to the wood just as Peyto tapped him on the shoulder. He looked up, then turned his head to see where the clerk looked. The painted man was again standing between the bulk of the *baratani* and the quarterdeck.

"For the third time we call. We are *baratani!* We are your deaths! Surrender your illusion of life and come down to us."

The survivors on the sterncastle and quarterdeck watched the man go through his gesture of contempt again. This time no one said anything. Martello split his band with a gesture; two to each ladder. Two of the bodyguards joined Martello's pair at the starboard ladder and the other went to the port ladder. Nat Gorremo started one way, then the other, then stopped amidships.

Something arced up from the among the clustered *baratani* in the waist and struck the quarterdeck with a squishy thud. Blood splattered as it hit. The object rolled until Nat Gorremo put out a foot to stop it.

Captain Lorenalli's open eyes stared sightlessly at the sky.

The *baratani* raised a shout and surged forward.

The fighting at the ladders was fierce and brief. The stalemate broke when one of the painted men threw himself onto the point of the boarding pike wielded by the mercenary ranker at Martello's side. The weight of the impaled man dragged the mercenary forward and away from the protection of his comrades' blades. Before he could let go of the pike, a *baratan* grabbed his arm with both hands and pulled him down to the main deck. As the two men tumbled down, several *baratani* forced themselves up the ladder and into the gap in the defenders' ranks. The first raiders to reach the quarterdeck died swiftly, but their companions behind them pressed forward, using the dead bodies as shields. More *baratani* forced their way onto the quarterdeck. Without the advantage of a narrow front offered by the bottleneck at the ladders, the defenders could not hold against the *baratani* numbers. Martello called for retreat. Only Martello, Falde, Nat Gorremo, and Bern made it to the sterncastle deck.

The *baratani* did not rush the sterncastle at once, surprising the survivors with their reluctance. Gorremo speculated that the *baratani* were going to go through their ritual again, but Yan doubted it. He had no time to think about the situation, though, because Martello set Falde and Gorremo at the ladder and came to him.

"You ready yet, Master Magician?"

"The spells are not complete."

"They'll have to do."

Martello called Bern over and the two men set themselves against the hatch and heaved. Yan joined the effort and the three of them managed to tilt the hatch up onto its side. Grunting with the exertion, they wrestled it to the railing.

"Wait," Peyto called, brandishing the rope into which he had been tying knots. "Attach this first. The hatch will float away otherwise."

As soon as the rope was secured, the hatch went over the side. Yan was relieved to see it bob up almost instantly; something of his spells must have worked.

"The ladies first," Martello said.

Lady Selanna nodded to him and stepped to the rail. She looked down, then put a hand to the rope. She grimaced at its roughness. With an imperious gesture she summoned Yan to help her step over the railing. Yan steadied her as she found the rope with her feet and lowered herself to the first knot. She took a deep breath as she gripped the rope. With surprising skill, she lowered herself hand over hand. Yan watched until she stood upon the raft.

Gorremo joined them at the rail. "They're forming up."

"They're coming," Falde called from the ladder.

Martello and Bern rushed to join her as shouts of "Death! Death to you all!" rose from the quarterdeck.

"Go, woman," Gorremo urged, shoving his wife toward the rope.

"I'm afraid," she said. Her voice cracked, revealing how close she was to hysteria. "Let Peyto go."

Without protest the old clerk crawled over the railing and started down, but his strength was insufficient for the task and he lost his grip, falling into the sea with a splash. Mistress Gorremo screamed. "The charka!" She took a step back away from the railing.

"Stupid cow." Gorremo pushed her aside and swung himself over the railing.

A grunt behind him made Yan turn. One of the raiders was crawling through the hatchway to the quarter-deck. Yan yelled a warning to Martello.

"Can't help it," the sergeant shouted back as he thrust forward, cutting a raider on the arm. "You do something about him."

Like what?

This *baratan* was one of those who wore a full harness of plate. His features were concealed within a visored helm wrought to resemble a skull. Two dark plumes nodded over it like a pair of hooded vipers. For a moment Yan thought him the one who had led the charge onto the deck of *Mannar's Grace*, but that warrior had worn no plumes. Neither had he wielded the stained two-handed sword that lay on the deck by the coaming. If this one was as fell a warrior as that first one, they were all doomed.

The armored man struggled to lever himself up onto

the sterncastle deck, hindered by his armor and the
narrow width of the hatchway. He would never be
more vulnerable. Without thinking, Yan rushed him,
intending to kick the *baratan* back below, but the man
saw him coming. Bracing himself with one arm, the
raider snatched up his sword as Yan approached.
Sweeping it at Yan, the *baratan* almost took off his foot.

Yan skipped back out of range, shivering. He nearly
vomited when he realized how close he had come to
being maimed.

The *baratan* laid his sword on the deck and returned
to his struggle to climb through the hatchway.

At the companion ladder, Falde took a boarding
pike to the belly, falling back into Martello. Two
raiders seized their chance and bulled their way past
the dying woman. Martello was bowled over, his sword
skittering away on the deck.

It was all coming apart.

The armored man finally pulled himself onto the
sterncastle deck and heaved himself erect. He retrieved
his sword and advanced on Yan. The *baratan* swished
his sword back and forth before him like a reaper.

Yan backed to the railing, feeling the knotted rope
pressing against his back. Sweat ran in rivulets down
his side. Mistress Gorremo stood paralyzed, a step
closer to the *baratan*. The armored man's sword licked
out, severing her head from her body. Yan gulped air,
looking at his own death as the *baratan* raised his
sword.

Yan threw himself to one side, barely evading the
sword as it whistled down and chopped into the railing where he had been. He glanced down. The hatch
was still near the ship, but the *baratan*'s blow had sev-
ered the rope. There would be no more climbing
down.

More *baratani* swarmed the sterncastle deck.

The armored warrior freed his sword and, raising it, advanced on Yan.

No more time.

He couldn't fight. He had no magic to use.

"Your time." The *baratan*'s voice echoed from within the helm.

No. No.

The sword shifted higher.

"No!" Yan seized his only chance. Vaulting the railing, he dived into the sea.

The water was cold, engulfing him. He was disoriented, and opening his eyes didn't help. Everything was dark. He struck out for what he thought was the surface. Fortunately, it was.

His head broke the surface, his ears immediately filling again with the sounds of the struggle aboard *Mannar's Grace*. He was only a few yards from the hatch. He swam toward it. Lady Selanna sat in the middle of the improvised raft and Nat Gorremo clung to its side. Peyto Lennuick thrashed nearby, obviously making no progress toward the raft. Yan changed course and swam to the clerk. They struggled briefly before Peyto realized that Yan was trying to help and allowed himself to be towed toward the raft.

Above them, Yan could hear the armored *baratan* shouting, "Death! Death to you all!"

"Out of your reach now, you Horesh-forsaken bastard!" Gorremo shook his fist as he shouted. To the lady he said, "That armored bastard won't dare follow us, he'd drown in an instant; his heavy armor would drag him down as surely as Fisé's nets."

The *baratan* disappeared from sight; then in a moment he was back, throwing himself from the sterncastle in an insane leap, screaming, "Death!" The armored man hit the raft on his feet, but the shock of his landing drove one end of the canvas-covered hatch

underwater and spilled Lady Selanna into a sprawl at
his feet. The *baratan* brought his sword down in a one-
handed swing that was as much an attempt to regain
his balance as it was an attack. The great sword swept
down, chopping into Nat Gorremo at the juncture of
his neck and shoulder and killing the man.

Yan heaved himself halfway onto the raft. The
*baratan* wobbled again. Lady Selanna scrambled to her
hands and knees and tried to crawl away. Yan reached
out with one hand, stretching for a grip on the killer's
ankle. He felt himself sliding back into the water, but
his fingers closed on the man's ankle. The *baratan*
swung his sword up again, ready to sever Yan's arm.
Yanking hard, Yan overbalanced the man. Arms
milling, the *baratan* dropped his sword and started to
fall. As the armored man crashed into the sea, his hand
snaked out and his gauntleted fist closed on the Lady
Selanna's skirt. Screaming, she was dragged over the
edge as he sank.

The struggle had propelled the raft further from
*Mannar's Grace*. Apparently released from the unnatural
calm surrounding the *Grace*, the raft drifted away. As
the distance between the raft and the vessel increased,
the sounds of combat muted, became dim, and finally
stopped. For a moment Yan heard a bloodcurdling
roar, like some beast about to gorge on flesh. Then
silence descended, save for the gentle slap of wavelets
against his raft and the harsh breathing of Peyto
Lennuick, his last remaining companion.

In the direction of the captured merchantman, the
fog began to glow like a crucible of molten metal.

# 6

IT WAS ONLY IN AWAKENING that Yan realized he had drifted off to sleep. He had the feeling that someone had awoken him. His brother Fal, perhaps, slapping him on the butt to rouse him for another day in the shop? But no, Fal was safe at home—thanks to whichever merciful god was responsible—and not here with Yan, adrift at sea, riding the swells with a bedraggled clerk, aboard a ship's hatch that Yan had bespelled into a makeshift raft.

The fog still surrounded them, but it was day. Low in the sky, a sullen red ball glowed; the sun had come up, and the strange fog was finally beginning to dissipate, burning away under Horesh's eye. Soon Yan might be able to see what was around them. He feared he would find that terrible charka ship bearing down on them.

The sensation of having been awoken remained, though the phantom memory of Fal had left Yan. There was no one on the raft save Yan and Peyto. He gazed across the raft at his companion. Peyto lay huddled against one edge of the hatch, asleep. His legs were drawn up tight against his body, making a ball of the clerk's lanky form. One arm was cradled under his head, a pillow against the framework of the hatch; the other hung slackly over the edge. The old clerk looked deeply asleep and sounded so, too. He snored.

Yan thought he would have known if Peyto had buffeted him while rolling over in sleep. He was still wondering what had awoken him when the raft was jarred as if struck. Peyto groaned, and Yan looked at him. The clerk was still in his curled position; he had not thumped the framework.

Something in the water, then.

The fog was still with them, so visibility was limited. Yan could only see the surface of the sea for ten or so yards around them. On his first scan, Yan saw nothing disturbing the waters beyond the hatch's rim. Then a flash of movement caught his eye, something cutting across the surface of the water, moving toward them.

A fin.

Yan kicked the clerk in the leg. "Wake up, old man." Peyto just quivered.

The fin was closer now. Yan could see a dark shape just under the surface, broad at the front and tapering to a powerful tail that drove it through the water. Shark.

Scrambling across the raft, Yan grabbed Peyto to pull him away from the edge. The old man flailed wildly at Yan's touch, but Yan managed to heave him up and away from the water just as the shark broke the surface. Yan got a frighteningly close look at the beast's dagger-filled mouth as the jaws snapped closed on empty air.

Too close a call.

Yan was no seaman, but even he knew better than to trail an arm in the water. Yan turned to berate Peyto for such dangerous foolishness. His eyes went wide as he saw the blood flowing from the mangled stump of

Peyto's forearm. Yan's stomach clenched, then heaved.
He turned his head just in time to avoid spraying the
remains of his last meal on the injured man.

He recovered to find Peyto holding both arms
before his face, eyes fixed on the space that his left
hand had occupied. Blood pumped feebly from the
stump. The thump that Yan had felt while awake must
have been the shark's attack or Peyto would have bled
to death by now. He could still bleed to death if Yan
didn't do something. The bleeding had to be stopped.

"Hold it up, man," he told the gray-faced Peyto.
"Keep it above your heart."

Yan tugged off his coat, then his shirt. He burst one
of the shirt's seams, ripping it open for a few inches,
then began tearing strips of linen from the shirt's hem.

His mind raced as he worked; he knew he'd need
something hard and thin to tighten the tourniquet, something like one of the slats that made up the hatch.
Something exactly like that. He remembered noting that
the impact of the armored *baratan* warrior had cracked
some of the wood, despite Yan's strengthening spells. He
looked for the spot and saw that one of the slats had been
snapped through. So much for the strength of his magic.
Still, he was relieved that he'd have what he needed to
help Peyto. His failure to magically strengthen the wood
beyond breakage was unimportant now, or rather, very
important; his earlier failure might be Peyto's salvation.

Taking hold of the slat, Yan prepared to dispel his
magic, but found that the spell had dissipated already.
A glance below the slats told him that the sealing spell
on the canvas still held, but he suspected that the condition was only temporary. After he had seen to Peyto,
he would have to reinforce his spells.

Yan placed his foot where he wanted the stave to
break and tugged on the wood until the slat broke free
with a snap. The sudden lack of resistance sent him

sprawling, to land painfully with his back against the framework of the hatch. Fearfully, he clambered away from the edge.

Gathering his makeshift materials, he returned to Peyto. Yan wrapped a strip of linen around Peyto's arm and inserted the slat into a loop made of the loose ends, twisting it tight. When he was satisfied that the bleeding had stopped, he tied the stick into place. He used more strips to bandage the wound.

Peyto would need a real doctor or a healer soon, because Yan wasn't competent to give the injured man the care he needed. He did what he could, entering trance and extending the calmness to Peyto. Yan drew the clerk into a deep sleep, forcing him into a resting state which would allow him to devote all of his body's resources to dealing with the injury.

By the time Yan emerged into the ordinary world, the sun had completed its work of dissolving the fog. There was no sign of land, but at least Yan saw no sign of the charka ship either. He and Peyto were alone, two men on a flimsy contrivance of wood and canvas in the midst of a broad sea.

Yan set about ensuring that their vessel was as seaworthy as he could make it. Without tools and supplies, his spells were even weaker. They would need to be renewed frequently. He was quite tired by the time he finished. Tired and hungry and thirsty, but most of all thirsty. Yan looked about. All that water and none to drink.

He had fasted before as part of his training, but it hadn't been like this. Then, he had always known that if he really needed them, food and drink were nearby. Out here, a failure of will would bring no relief. Out here, there was no easy out and no comfort.

Evening brought relief from the merciless sun. Yan's skin was tender on his face and hands and on his torso where his tattered shirt failed to shield him. Peyto had suffered less in that regard, having Yan's coat to shade him from the sun. Yan wanted to recover his coat as evening moved into night and the air grew chillier, but he didn't. Peyto needed it more than he did. Chill would only make Peyto's battle to survive the injury harder. Yan snugged the coat tightly around the clerk.

Besides colder air, the night brought stars in a profusion greater than Yan had ever seen. They stretched from horizon to horizon, filling the heavens in their multitude. The moons drifted among them. Mavra, the largest, was close to dark, the light of her crescent shape doing little to dull the sparkling glory. Arsha, the second, was more full, but tiny Heka, completely in her dark phase, was only a hurtling blank spot among the stars.

Here upon the sea, the stars looked brighter, the constellations more defined. The Wheel, the Serpent, and the Sword were easy to spot. He looked for the Plow before remembering that it was below the horizon at this time of year. The Stallion had never had an eye before, nor had the Wheel's spokes ever seemed so solid. The Chalice gleamed high overhead and his own birth sign, the Ghost Lord, hung low, half-obscured by the sea.

It seemed that there were more stars out here. Yan wished he had Gan Tidoni's big telescope. Captain Lorenalli's spyglass would do. But he had neither, only his unaided eyes. And they were filled with such glory that he almost forgot his predicament for a few hours.

By morning he was sure that they were not drifting aimlessly, but moving, slowly and steadily, in a single direction. He suspected that the raft had been caught by a current, and hoped it was bound toward land. Without charts and instruments, his navigational skills were inadequate to tell.

Hunger and thirst were Yan's attentive companions

the second day. Peyto was still unconscious most of the time, which Yan found easier to take. When the clerk was awake, he cried incessantly. Yan used up the rest of his shirt changing the dressing on Peyto's stump. He began to fear that the wound was going bad. The day dragged on in oppressive heat. By evening, Yan was unable to concentrate enough to renew the sealing spell on the canvas.

The skin on his torso and arms was blistered, and peeling in ragged gray strips. Peyto's face and remaining hand were burned and peeling as well. It made the man look like one of the attendants in Boshkieron's painting of the demon court. Yan didn't need a mirror to know his own face looked similar. He had herbs for such burns, but they were in his garret at the Plow and Anchor.

No, they weren't. He had sold them to pay for his passage to a better life. He no longer lived in a cramped garret above an inn.

He lived on a tiny raft in the middle of the sea.

He began to fear that he was losing touch with reality.

The stars had no allure for him that night.

Toward midnight, just as the Ghost Lord had reached his highest elevation, and his scepter had cleared the horizon, Yan saw a fin cutting through the water toward the raft. He scrambled to pull Peyto's arm from the water, but Peyto's arm wasn't in the water. The clerk was curled in a ball in the center of the raft.

Expecting the shark to be a delirium-inspired vision as well, Yan looked again to see if the fin was still there.

It was.

The fin slipped beneath the waves as it neared the raft. A moment later, something bumped the raft from beneath.

Yan curled himself into a ball. His stomach hurt, his throat ached as if he had been screaming for hours. He wanted to be elsewhere. Anywhere. What could he do? If he was small, he could hide and his father wouldn't find him. If he could hide, no one would hurt him. He retreated into darkness.

The sun brought a clear sky again on the third day.

It was the third day, wasn't it? He hadn't forgotten one, had he? Yan was distressingly unsure.

He was so thirsty.

Crawling to the edge of the hatch, he dipped his cupped hand into the sea. He moved quickly, lest a shark snatch his hand from his arm. The water sparkled in the sunlight. Inviting. Cool.

It burned his cracked lips and filled his mouth with the taste of salt.

Mocking laughter ripped the air around him.

Yan threw himself back from the edge of the raft, bumping into Peyto. The clerk groaned, a crackling, sickly sound. A splash made Yan turn, but he saw nothing. He turned back, afraid that something was sneaking up on him, and saw that he was right. Fins cut the water a dozen feet from the raft.

The sharks had returned.

Yan huddled against Peyto, making himself small. He hugged his knees close to his body and watched the sharks circle the raft.

And circle.

Waiting.

Waiting for him.

Without warning, one of the sharks hurled itself from the water. Its mouth opened and Yan saw the sharp, sharp teeth rimming the dark hole of its maw. Three yards of muscle and appetite rocketed toward him.

In mid-leap it transformed into a domarag, one of the striped dolphins of the Danteriff. Instead of dropping, jaws agape, onto him, the beast sailed over the raft. The water streaming from its sleek sides fell on Yan, searing him like boiling blood.

Yan wasn't fooled by the creature's trick.

Sharks weren't domarag. Sharks ate people.

The sharks circled the raft, mocking him. He lay down in the raft, too low to see the circling fins. But he couldn't escape the sharks. With his ear to the canvas, Yan could hear their laughter.

"Give us Peyto and you will be free," they called.

Yan shook his head.

"We will not eat you," they said.

He knew they lied. He had already saved Peyto from them once. They would not forgive him for that.

"Peyto's dead," they said.

"No," Yan croaked back. "Not yet."

"He's nothing but flesh. If you won't eat him, give him to us."

Yan twisted his head around to look at the clerk. He hadn't said anything coherent for more than a day. Certainly Peyto looked dead. His breathing, if he was breathing, was shallow and very slow. A dead man would only stink, stink like the stump at the end of Peyto's arm.

"Yes, he will stink if you keep him," the sharks said avidly. "Give him to us. We will relieve you of the problem. No more worry."

Yan reached over and felt Peyto's neck. He wasn't sure, but he thought that he felt a weak pulse.

"We will leave you alone if you give him to us."

"No."

"If you won't eat him, he's no good to you. Give him to us."

The thought of eating the clerk roused Yan's stomach to heaving. He doubled over in pain, alternately retching and gasping for air.

After a while, the sharks stopped calling to him.

Slowly, slowly, the desire to spit out his guts subsided. The sea became quiet and the sun slowly sank toward it. Yan wondered why he had felt so bothered to be alone before, adrift on the sea. He liked the quiet. He was glad the sharks had gone.

In a frightening moment of lucidity, he realized that he probably didn't have much time left.

Then the sea wasn't quiet anymore. It began to rattle and creak. Laughter welled out of the depths.

Yan forced himself up on one elbow.

The sharks had come back, in numbers beyond counting—at least a dozen. They were a squadron, a fleet, a flotilla, cruising before a great barge rowed by a single man.

Fisé's barge, it was.

There could be no doubt. Yan could see the broad dark hull, the plain coarse sail, the nets hung over the side. The Fisher of the Depths, the Netter of Men was coming for him. Yan could see Fisé coming forward from his place at the tiller of his barge. Coming forward to secure the hatch to his ship.

The godling Fisé was a lot less impressive than Yan would have thought. He looked like a scrawny old man, gnarled and bent by a lifetime of working the sea.

After lashing the raft to his barge, the Fisher of the Depths boarded Yan's humble and totally inadequate contrivance. The Netter of Men looked at the two weakened and sickly travelers huddled aboard and knelt beside Peyto. Yan saw Fisé turn his head away from the stench of Peyto's blackened stump. He felt sorry for the clerk. Poor Peyto. Rejected by the Fisher of Men. He would drift forever on the sea, but hadn't they already done that?

Fisé bent over Peyto, whispering as he did something to the gods-forsaken clerk. Yan's attention drifted away for a while, but returned in time to see Fisé draw a vast sword from his belt. The wicked eye of Horesh gleamed from the steel.

Peyto was to be cut away.

Yan looked at the clerk, sympathy filling his heart. He could not keep his eyes from fastening onto the darkness that infested the end of Peyto's arm, at the tendrils of corruption that crawled up from the stump over the elbow and past the new tourniquet as they sought to pass through Peyto's shoulder and into his torso. The tendrils sought the clerk's heart, a warm life place where they could curl up and a place they could corrupt and make as vile and loathsome as themselves.

Fisé brought the blade down on the stinking thing at the end of Peyto's arm. Peyto screamed and thrashed. Yan groaned, shutting his eyes against the rush of putrescence.

When he opened them again, Peyto was as he had been before, though no longer symmetrical, yet the darkness lessened. Fisé cast largesse upon the waters. The sharks patrolled the Fisher's gift and the spirits of the air, crying like lost souls, or perhaps like seabirds, descended upon Fisé's gift and fought over it.

No one fought over Yan. Everyone just wanted him to go away.

Fisé left, carrying Peyto in his arms.

Eons later, Yan felt the Fisher's strong arms around him. Fisé smelled of the sea and old fish. How appropriate. Yan was lifted into a spinning world of light and waves and laughing sharks.

He came to rest on a hard, lumpy surface. Fisé bent over him and opened his mouth, no doubt seeking the gift the wise dead always brought to the Fisher. Failing to find the missing gift, Fisé pawed Yan's clothes and rifled his pouch.

The only thing left to Yan that had any real value was his *claviarm*, and at last Fisé found that.

Yan watched, dispassionately. What was happening was happening to someone else. He was dead, wasn't he? The Fisher cut the thong and removed the *claviarm* from around Yan's neck. Holding the amulet at arm's length, Fisé said something to Yan, but he was too tired to respond.

*Can't the dead lie in peace?*

Yan watched Fisé throw his *claviarm* into the sea.

*Into the sea.*

*To the sea.*

*The sea.*

*Down into the depths. Far away and gone.*

*No more to be seen.*

*Like me.*

*Far away and gone.*

His trial—his life?—was over. Yan giggled to himself and went down into the sea of sleep, going far away into the darkness.

# 7

THE DARKNESS WAS COOL, soothing. There was no time in the darkness, just existence, yet Yan knew that there was time elsewhere, time and being. Slowly, imperceptibly, the dark no-place became a dark someplace. The space beyond his eyelids took on a substantial reality in the here and now.

He opened his eyes.

Above him, he saw thatch-covered, rough-hewn rafters. They smelled damp. Things hung suspended from the beams. There were bundles of dried fish, a skillet, a handful of pottery jugs, and scattered bunches of herbs, small bunches, smaller than those that had hung in his garret at the Plow and Anchor. In one corner a salted ham dangled, broad and solid, like a rapenar roosting among lesser birds. To his left there was a rough, hard earthen wall and to his right a smoky open space. Faint light from a fire pit gleamed red in the center of a dusty floor of packed earth. Fisé, looking like an old fisherman, squatted by the fire filling a mug by dipping a copper ladle into a crockery pot of steaming something.

If this was Fisé's palace, it was a poor place. Where were the fabled halls of pearl?

Even the bed upon which Yan lay was not a proper bed at all. It was simply a straw-stuffed tick. It was lumpy, but the straw smelled fresh.

Yan closed his eyes again. He felt safe here.

He slept.

He awoke to find a woman at his side. She was too young to be the old man's wife. At least his first wife. Yan wondered if she were indeed the fisherman's second wife as his own mother was his father's second wife, taken after the first had died in childbirth. This woman's broad-cheeked face was framed with twin, looped braids of thick red hair, and she was pleasant to look upon, although kept from prettiness by a strong chin. She seemed half-awake, as her eyelids spent more time down than up. That changed as she realized that he was looking at her, and he was treated to twin pools of startlingly clear blue water—her eyes. She smiled at him tentatively, then reached down for something on the floor.

She shushed him when he tried to speak.

"*Neight. Ythim anoee, deynaim'fokkal eil'anoee.*"

Yan didn't understand her words, but the spoon she pushed at him was unequivocal and the aroma rising from it was eloquent. Savory fish swimming in a porridge of winter oats. His mouth watered.

The fisherman appeared at her side and gruffly pushed the spoon aside.

"*Neight, Larra. Nei'ythim foss. Deynaim'fokkal ceyadd. Deynaim komharta caithir ceyadd.*" Staring down at Yan, he said, "*Fokkal'meigh glanne'a?*"

"I don't know what you're saying."

The old man nodded, then spoke in broken Empiric. "Understand me can?"

"Yes, as far as it goes. I might understand your own

tongue if you'd speak more slowly. It sounds familiar to me."

The old man held out a pitted sphere of iron. Rust had eaten ragged holes in, but it was still sound enough for ritual purposes. "*Deynaim komharta.* Make the sign, *Madiarounna.* Touch the iron."

Yan was not interested in superstition. "Where am I? Who are you?

"Touch it," the old man insisted.

Yan sighed. Obviously the old man wouldn't be satisfied until Yan proved that he could touch cold iron without ill effect. The old man almost flinched as Yan reached out, but controlled the reaction and held the sphere still. He watched suspiciously, almost fearfully, as Yan laid his hand on the iron. When nothing happened, the old man gave a curt nod and took the sphere back to the holder hammered into the door-frame of the hut. The woman sat quietly like a dutiful wife until the old man came back to the bedside and stared down at Yan.

"What name, *Madiarounna*?

"My name?"

The old man nodded. He also gestured to the woman, who again offered the spoon. Heedless of good manners, Yan took a spoonful into his mouth before answering. It was delicious.

"My name is Yan Tanafres," Yan said once he'd swallowed the first mouthful. The old man had seen Yan's *claviarm.* Since he knew Yan was a mage, Yan didn't mention his Art. If the woman held the common opinion of magicians, she might stop feeding him. He took and swallowed a second spoonful. "What's yours?"

"Gormen, *yasiach.* Fish-man." With a nod of his head, he indicated the woman. "Larra, daughter mine."

Larra smiled at Yan and he found himself surprisingly

relieved that the young woman was not the fisherman's wife. "You have a pretty smile."

"*Ya'kinniall.*"

The phrase sounded like "thank you" in Scothic, but Yan couldn't remember the words for "You're welcome," so he said it in Empiric.

She offered him more porridge, which he took eagerly. She continued to feed him for a while, stopping while he was still hungry. He almost protested, but realized that it was probably for the best. It had been some time since he had eaten and he shouldn't overdo. He needed the strength that the food would provide, and if he ate too much and vomited it up, the porridge wouldn't do him any good.

"Where's Peyto?"

"Peyto?"

"Peyto Lennuick. The man who was with me on the hatch."

"Ah. Your *chaelddur* is other place."

"*Chaelddur?*" The word didn't sound like any Scothic Yan knew.

The old man frowned. "Means friend-servant who travels with."

"I guess we were traveling together, but I wouldn't call him a friend and he wasn't *my* servant. Anyway, where is he?"

"*Basa'assait.*"

Another strange word. Did that mean dead? "I don't understand."

"*Basa'assait.* The sickness place."

"Then he is still alive?"

"Some. Maybe not."

Yan's addled thinking wasn't aided by the fisherman's limited command of Empiric. "What do you mean?"

"He need *V'Zurna'larai.* She come, maybe he live.

She no come, no live." The old man shrugged. "*Shuldai Morrigaeni.*"

V'Zurna was a lunar goddess associated with magic. Yan didn't know what a *larai* was, save that it was a person. The context indicated a person strongly associated with V'Zurna. While V'Zurna was acknowledged in the Triadic pantheon, she was of considerably less importance to those who followed the Art than Einthof, patron of knowledge in all forms. V'Zurna's worship came from an older, less enlightened time. Yan had heard that V'Zurna was stronger in Scothandir than in other parts of the Empire. This *V'Zurna'larai* might be a holy magician. If Peyto were in her hands, there might be cause to worry; there were whispers that some of V'Zurna's rites involved blood sacrifice.

"Well has anyone gone to get this *V'Zurna'larai*?"

"*Shuldai Morrigaeni.*"

Larra said something to Gormen. She spoke quickly, far too fast for Yan to follow, but many of her words sounded familiar, and he was sure now that they were speaking some sort of Scothic dialect. That meant he was on the mainland.

The old man shrugged and went away. The conversation was over.

Yan felt tired again. He wanted to find out more of where he was, but he wanted, no needed, to sleep as well. Larra sat by his side. She gave him something hot to drink, then began slathering some viscous substance onto his forehead and nose. A salve for his sunburn, if he smelled correctly. She moved on to his cheeks. Under her gentle touch he faded into sleep.

He awoke to the sound of screams, distant but piercing. For a moment he was back on the doomed *Mannar's Grace*, but then he remembered that the ship, her passengers, and her crew were all gone. All save for him and Peyto. He tried to rise and found he had no strength in his limbs. He didn't think that he should have been so weak; there must have been something in the drink Larra had given him.

He lay on the pallet and listened. The screamer sounded like a woman in great pain, but although his hosts stirred, they did not rush forth. It was as though they expected the caterwauling. Eventually, the screaming subsided, but Yan lay awake, remembering the screams from *Mannar's Grace.*

Those bleak memories became all too real as new screams rent the night. Screams that he recognized. Peyto's screams.

They were abruptly cut off.

*Basa'assait.*

Yan remembered more of his Scothic, realizing the word could be taken to mean more than the fisherman's "sickness place." It could mean "place where death might come."

Had death come for Peyto?

His hosts lay upon their pallets. They showed no concern, no surprise. Had they known this was to come? It seemed all too clear that they had. What was next? Was he to go to the *basa'assait* and be sacrificed in some heathen Scothic rite?

He did not want to think that their kindness to him had been merely the kindness shown to swine before the fall slaughtering. Most especially he did not want to think of Larra participating in such a scheme. But alone and helpless in the night, such fears were too real, too possible.

He shivered and almost wept. He had come so close to death and escaped. He wanted to live. Finally, mercifully, the drug took hold again and he slept.

He woke late in the afternoon. Neither of his hosts was present and he thought about getting out of bed, escaping, but found he didn't have the strength. The combination of the drug and his weakness from his ordeal left him as helpless as a newborn. He counted the things hanging from the rafters to pass the time and calm his mind. He found he recognized them all. Considering the uses to which each of the herbs could be put, he realized that none among them would have served to give the results of Larra's drink. He had begun to wonder what might be in some of the jugs when Gormen returned, laden with a tightly rolled net. Larra entered behind him, carrying a basket of reeds. As his hosts stowed their burdens, Yan spoke to them in halting Scothic.

"What happened last night?"

"Sifi became a full woman last night. Rulac has a son. Already the luck is good, *Madiarounna.*"

"A woman gave birth?" That would explain the first outburst. Yan wanted to believe it was so.

Larra nodded.

"Yes," Gormen said. "A good child. We are grateful."

Had it taken a sacrifice to assure that? "There were other screams."

Gormen and Larra exchanged glances before Gormen said, "*V'Zurna'larai* saw your friend."

"So she finally answered your call."

Gormen shook his head. "She is from the hills, and so she does not listen when we tell her of the *madiarounna.* She comes for to help Sifi. She says that since she comes anyway, she sees your friend. She says she does not let an animal suffer, so she helps an Imperial. She has a kind heart."

Yan was confused and relieved at the same time. "You called me *made-, madiarounna* when you first spoke to me. I don't know the word. What does it mean?"

"Mean? It means *madiarounna.* Don't know words for it in your tongue."

"Surely you can give me some idea."

"It's late. I go fishing in the morning. Time to sleep."

And that was all the old man would say. He banked the fire while Larra brought another drink and the bowl of salve. The smell of the drink was different from what she had brought him the night before, so he drank it. He needed the liquid. Larra smiled shyly when he tried to ask questions, shushed him, and told him to rest. Soon she finished her ministrations and put away the crockery. Gormen put out the lone lamp, and before long the hut was still.

The next day, Yan was awake before the fisherman left. He heard the old man speaking with other folk of the village. He couldn't see the visitors, and that helped, forcing him to concentrate on the words. He began to recognize the differences between the Scothic he knew and the pronunciation of the local dialect.

If he correctly understood what he was hearing, the locals were not happy to have him here. No one said why, but their questions centered around how well Yan and Peyto were doing and how soon they'd leave.

The only comforting thing in the conversations was the confirmation that Peyto was still alive. He had survived whatever caused him to scream in the night. The old clerk was a tenacious fellow, and Yan had to admire him for that.

Larra spent the day sitting outside the hut, weaving a basket. From time to time villagers passed by, and some stopped to speak to her. Yan found himself more able to follow the speech of his benefactors.

With Gormen away, Yan tried to get Larra to talk to him, offering to help her with her chores. She just laughed and told him to "sleep himself well." Unintentionally he acted on her advice.

He was awake for the evening meal, which was eaten in near-silence. Gormen and his daughter spoke little while they ate, reserving any conversation for after the meal. Yan tried to oblige their customs although it was hard. There were a number of things he wanted to ask the fisherman; he hoped the old man might be more forthcoming than his daughter.

As Gormen sat mending the net, Yan saw his chance to talk before him. He spoke in Scothic, trying to match his pronunciation to the local dialect.

"I wish to thank you again for rescuing Peyto and me from the sea."

Gormen looked up briefly from his work but said nothing.

"How did you find us?"

"The *domaeragi* found you. I just followed."

"*Domaeragi*?" That was a familiar word; did it mean the same as the Empiric word it sounded like? "The domarag? The dolphins led you to us?"

Gormen nodded. "Yes."

"How?"

The old man shrugged. "They swam, I followed."

"But why did you follow them?"

"They called. I am a man of the sea. I cannot ignore the sea trust. Some do, but they are not me. The sea trust is part of my family. My grandfather lived to sire my father only because of the *domaeragi*. They carried him from his foundered boat to safety in the shallows. No sea trust, no Gormen. When the *domaeragi* call, I listen."

"I don't understand this sea trust."

"You are not a man of the sea."

"But you are. Can you not tell me about it?"

"What I can tell, you will not understand."

"I understand a lot of arcane things."

Gormen's eyes slid sideways to regard Yan while his hands twisted in what was surely a sign of protection. "I know that you do."

"Of course you do. You threw my *claviarm* into the sea. Was that to repay the *domaeragi*?"

"One does not pay them. They have no need for money."

"Then why did you do it?"

"It is said that the dark ones can do no harm without their soul stones."

"I am not a dark one, nor was my *claviarm* a soul stone."

"I did not know."

"And you weren't willing to take the chance."

Gormen shrugged. The tension in the old man's shoulders told Yan that the old fisherman was not as indifferent as he wished to appear.

"Are you satisfied now?" Yan asked.

"You touched the iron."

For what it was worth, he had. "Would your *domaeragi* have led you to a dark one?"

"No."

"But you still don't think they made a wise choice, do you?"

"It is not for me to say. The luck has been good."

"So far."

"Yes." Gormen let the net slide into a pile at his feet. "It's late. Time to sleep."


Over the next few days, Yan spent more and more time out of bed. At first he just sat in the sun on a stool outside the hut, but before long he was helping Larra with the preparations for meals, caring for the small garden, and making small repairs to the hut. It was simple work, soothing work. And Larra was very appreciative.

Especially in the long afternoons when the village was quiet and Gormen away fishing.

She was an experienced and pleasant partner. Yan

found himself liking her more and more, although she was very careful never to show the least interest in him as a man while there were other villagers around. He understood that; these Scoths were very vocal in expressing their low opinion of Imperials. They seemed to care little if Yan overheard them. After a couple of days, he realized that the villagers thought more highly of magicians than they did of Imperial citizens, and they were no more fond of magicians than most people he had met.

Given such long-held hate, he was surprised that they had done anything to help him and Peyto, but they had. They had not even told their local lord of Yan's presence, fearing that the lord would kill Yan on sight.

"Laird Koyle is one proud who holds the old honor," Sednal, the headman of the village, told Yan in his fractured Empiric. "Whole clan like no Imperials. He like no Imperials muchly. He kill you."

Killing Yan would be an insult to the *domaeragi*, a spurning of their gift, and no one in the village wanted a part in that, for fear of the bad luck it would bring.

Perhaps there was good luck at work after all. He and Peyto had been rescued. They were both alive.

Of course, even though the clerk was on the mend, he'd never be the same. He had screamed because the *V'Zurna'larai* had amputated what was left of his left arm, stopping the spread of the corruption and saving the clerk's life. Though what kind of life would a one-handed clerk have? Yan shivered at the thought of trying to go through life with but one arm. Almost everything he did required two good hands. What sort of spell could be cast with only a single hand? How could he practice the Art?

But did the Art matter?

Yan had grown up in a small village and lived most

of his life with the Art being no more than a dream. He was once again in a small village where the Art had no part in people's lives. A small, quiet, peaceful place. Like the one he had grown up in. His village hadn't been a fishing village, true, but beyond the main source of the village's livelihood, they were much the same. Village life was a life he knew, and not a terrible life at that.

Here and now, he found himself slipping back into the rhythms. Here, he was free from the tyranny of his father. And he had Larra. Now, a simple life did not seem so bad.

# 8

"YOU SEEM PENSIVE TODAY," Peyto said. As usual, the clerk used Empiric; while he could read some Scothic, he could not speak it at all.

"A little bored is all," Yan replied.

They sat in the shade of the hornleaf tree. The sun shone down on the fields around them, nurturing to the growing plants but a bit warm for people more used to the chillier clime of Merom. The slight breeze was laden with the scents of field and distant forest. Breeze and shade made a pleasant island of coolness in the brightly lit landscape.

Spring had turned to summer.

"Boredom is a condition that I can appreciate." Peyto's right hand patted the empty sleeve hanging by his left side. The clerk seemed unaware of his gesture. "This rural life is so simple."

"Simple is not bad."

"I did not mean to say it was. But how much interest can it offer a scholar and mage like yourself?"

Yes, how much? Yan's eyes drifted across the field toward the cove and the small village nestled by it. He could see Larra working a new basket by the door of the cottage.

"Ah," Peyto said. "Some interest, certainly. And reciprocated, too."

"What do you mean?"

"It's my arm that's gone, not my eyes."

Having grown up in a small village, Yan should not have been surprised that the clerk knew of his trysts with Larra; news of a new liaison traveled quickly in a small community. Yan had thought that they had been discreet. Obviously not discreet enough, and if Peyto knew, the villagers knew as well. Gormen, too, most likely. No one had objected, so obviously no one found the pairing objectionable. Yan smiled. "She's a good woman. She's got a warm heart."

"And a warm bed."

Yan didn't like the clerk's tone. "Who are you to speak against us."

"No one, Master Tanafres. No one but a poor stranded citizen of the Coronal Empire, like yourself. I am no Scothic rube to be outraged by a foreigner, an actual Imperial citizen, taking advantage of a poor, innocent local girl."

"I'm not taking advantage of her," Yan protested, but Peyto's comment bothered him. Had some of the villagers expressed concern over his pairing with Larra after all? "Who says I'm taking advantage?"

"No one that I've heard, but then I don't speak the local dialect. I simply speak my own thoughts and observe what is obvious. Will she not think your attentions have sprung from no more than carnal concerns when you leave?"

"Who said I was leaving?"

"You don't belong here."

"I could."

Peyto looked away and sighed. For a while they sat

silently under the tree. Yan returned to the stitching
their conversation had interrupted. He threaded the
boar bristles through the last few awl holes, back-
stitched for a couple of holes to lock the thread in
place, then cut off the excess. He laid the lasted shoe
on the ground beside him; he would pull the shoe off
the last and set it to soak during the evening meal and
would turn it after they'd eaten. While Yan massaged
his thighs to ease the muscles cramped from holding
the last between his knees, Peyto spoke again.

"You intrigue me, Master Tanafres. How many more
rough hides will you turn to shoes to protect uneducated feet?"

"Shoemaking's an honest craft."

"You're not a shoemaker."

"I am here."

Peyto snorted derisively.

"I'm doing something no one else in the village is
skilled at," Yan said.

"You are capable of better."

"I'll get better with practice."

"I wasn't talking about shoemaking."

"I was." Yan was surprised by his defense of the
craft. He had hated shoemaking in his youth and on his
choosing day, in defiance of all expectations that he follow in his father's craft, he had petitioned Gan Tidoni
to take him as a student. But it wasn't the hard work of
the craft that he had fled; he was good at it and enjoyed
the feel of the leather and the satisfaction of a tight,
finely spaced stitch. Working with the leather here, he
was reminded of the pride to be had from a shoe well
made and of the regard a good craftsman received
from the community. The skill had come back quickly
to his idle fingers and with it had come the grudging
respect of a community that had little use for idlers.

"How can you find fault in my working at a craft?"

Yan asked. "You live on their charity. You take their food and sleep under their roof while returning them nothing but complaints about their being simple country folk."

"You mistake me, Master Tanafres. Horesh shines on Islander and Scoth alike, and He asks all to show charity to the unfortunate. But it is not a charity I take lightly. It sits uneasily on me, but I know no other solution to the dilemma of our exile in this culture-forsaken land. My, ahem, current condition would preclude effective manual labor, even were I spry enough for it. Thanks to Horesh, Mannar, and the Bright Lady that I lost my left arm and not my right, for once we return to civilized lands I will be able to support myself with no need for the charity you begrudge me here. I would earn my keep here if I could, but my skills are useless where there are no books nor accounts, and none who wish to read or write."

"You could teach them."

"Were I able to speak to them in their own tongue, I might teach; if any would come to learn from an Imperial. These folk seem to believe they have learned all they need from the Empire in the school of the sword."

"Only the rebellious need fear the Imperial forces."

"Only the rebellious, indeed." Peyto nodded, a wry expression on his face. "But this is far too fine a day to tempt gloom with talk of politics, past or present. On such a fine day, when Mannar sends her clouds to dance and flirt with her husband-father, I find that my thoughts turn to grand schemes of advancement and fulfillment, of making and doing. Do you not find it so, young magician?"

Yan held up the shoe he was working on. "I am making and doing, I need not dream about it."

"A trifle, though I think the lady—ah, your smile tells

132 ROBERT N. CHARRETTE

me it is the lady—will find it a pleasing trifle. Naetheless, I would have thought you would be more eager to complete your new *claviarm* than to make that which an ordinary man's skilled hands could make."

"I am in no hurry. This village reminds me of the one in which I grew up. I find it pleasant."

"Pleasanter than home?"

"Oh, yes."

"If you find this pastoral life so appealing, why bother with the *claviarm* at all? Why not make your life less difficult still and abandon it?"

"What do you mean?"

"It cannot be pleasant to argue with your lady friend?"

"How do you know about that?"

"It is a small village."

News of a disagreement within a household traveled faster than gossip concerning a new pairing of lovers. Larra did not care to see Yan at work remaking his *claviarm*; and when her attempts to distract him failed, she turned to shouting. Her harangues were long, and loud. They made clear her fears of magic and her hatred of its well-known ancient abusers, the dark mages of the distant past.

It seemed that the dark mages were better remembered—and more avidly hated—in Scothandir than in the rest of the Coronal Empire. Like so many other people, Larra could not seem to make a distinction between the ethical magic Yan had learned and the corrupted practices of those ancient magicians. Every time Yan tried to explain the differences, Larra would shut him out, complaining that he was trying to corrupt her and pointing out that, "Magic brings little favor from the gods." Once, she told him that he had been saved by the *domaeragi* so that he could give up magic, and he had laughed at her. They didn't share a bed for a week after that.

Although he had concluded that it was easier to just nod and go along with her tirades as though he believed her, he still worked on the *claviarm*. Not as often as he worked on shoes, helped around the cottage, or joined the villagers in the communal fields. The Art still drew him and he was not ready to abandon it totally for anyone, even Larra. A magician needed a *claviarm* to be effective. Yan might not need to be effective anymore, but that didn't matter. A *claviarm* let him perceive the magic, feel its power and flow, more easily; and that was something he was unwilling to give up. Even for Larra.

Was his desire to have the *claviarm* a sign that he was not content here? Maybe. He felt sure that Peyto would say it was, but for some reason he didn't fully comprehend, Yan didn't want to think so. He was happy here.

Wasn't he?

To shake off the doubts Peyto had raised, Yan gathered up his tools and his workpiece, stuffing them into his sack. He stood and offered a hand to Peyto.

"Come on, Master Lennuick. The sun will be touching the seaside hills by the time we've walked back to the village. There are still things to be done before supper."

"Ah, such a hectic life."

"It's better than the death the *baratani* offered us."

"In that I can find no fault."

The summer was long and slow, seeming to stretch on in the lazy way summer afternoons stretch on through the day. The small communal fields around the village slowly approached harvest. Soon the corbies and the grackles would come, first of the birds seeking to glean the fruits of the villagers' work before they could harvest the grain themselves.

Yan tipped the frame into the hole he had dug, letting the rough wood slide slowly through his hands. When the scarecrow's post hit bottom, he tilted the pole vertical and kicked dirt into the hole until the scarecrow stood upright on its own.

The scarecrow wore Yan's old coat, tattered and salt-stained. Using it for the scarecrow wasn't a loss; he hadn't worn it since Larra had completed the new tunic that now hung safely over the stump where they'd had their lunch. If his *claviarm* were done, he could have added a glamour that would have increased the effectiveness of the scarecrow, but without the amulet the effort to focus the magic was too much. He'd let the evil Imperial clothing serve to chase away the fierce Scothic birds.

Yan stepped back, wiping an arm across his sweaty brow, and Peyto offered him a dripping gourd cup. Gratefully, Yan swigged down the water.

"Fierce," Peyto suggested in Scothic.

"Frightened?"

"I'm not a bird egg."

"I think you mean you're not a 'bird.'"

He was handing the cup back to Peyto when he saw the man on the hill. The man sat astride one of the rough-coated Scothic ponies, his legs dangling nearly to the ground. He seemed very stocky—inhumanly so, even more so than a bregil—until Yan realized that he had a shield slung on his back. The shifting of the pony made the afternoon sunlight glint from the rider's shirt as he sat looking down into the valley.

Turning to see what Yan was staring at, Peyto squinted up the hill. The clerk's eyesight was worse than Yan's; he'd be able to make out little more than a silhouette. Peyto's face hardened into a frown.

"Baaliff called his messengers and sent them forth, shrieking, on wings of steel and fire," the clerk said in

Empiric. The words sounded like a quote, but Yan
didn't recognize the reference.

"What are you talking about?"

Peyto nodded toward the rider on the hill. "A bird
of ill omen, I fear. One who will not be frightened by
our new friend here."

A second rider joined the first, then a third.

"An ill sight indeed," Peyto said gravely.

"Do you think they're Laird Koyle's men?"

"Do you see a banner?"

"No."

"Unlikely then, isn't it?"

"What do you think they want?"

"Something that isn't theirs."

"You think they're reivers?"

"Reiving is something of a pastime among these
rurals, which makes one wonder why they complain so
much of the Imperial peace that has put an end to so
much of that travail. I suppose we get in their way."
Peyto sighed heavily. "Best run and warn the village,
boy. I'm too old to play Phaderades at the fire. Besides,
with my Scothic I'd probably tell them to come out in
their holiday dress."

Yan didn't like leaving the old man behind, but he
knew the village had to be warned. He started to run.

"Hide," he called back.

"Did you think I was going to fight them?"

Yan glanced back but he couldn't see the clerk. He
hoped the reivers wouldn't see him either.

Yan ran.

A handful of villagers were working on replacing the
thatch on Sednal's house. Too far away to be heard,
Yan waved as he ran. Someone on the rooftree spotted
him and waved back. Yan tried to point back toward
the hills where the raiders were and nearly stumbled.
Recovering, he gave up waving and ran harder.

"Reivers," he shouted as soon as he was near enough. To his gratification, the villagers reacted at once. The work party had scattered to their homes by the time he reached Sednal's house. Yan kept running down the road. With relief, Yan saw that warning had reached the village ahead of him. The first cottages he passed were shut and no one was to be seen. Dogs were barking and the geese down by the pond added to the bedlam. Despite the noise, Yan could hear hoof-beats growing louder.

He was nearing Rulac and Sifi's house, Gormen's was the next beyond that. He was almost there, but not near enough. He wouldn't be able to reach the cottage in time. The raiders would soon be topping the last rise. He vaulted over the fence into Sifi's garden, taking a fall as his foot tangled in the harness set out on the pole by the gate for him to find. He'd found it all right, but somehow he didn't think his promise to repair it would be fulfilled soon.

Yan crouched by the gate. The house was closed, like all the others. Rulac watched from the window, but he made no move to open the door and offer shelter to Yan. Not that Yan would have taken it; he wanted to be elsewhere. Through a chink in the wicker gate, Yan could look across the clearing that was the village's center. On the far side was Gormen's cottage. The door was closed and Larra's bucket of soaking reeds lay spilled on the doorstep, the puddle only beginning to seep into the ground. Larra was nowhere to be seen.

He hoped that meant she was hiding safely some-where.

He could walk across the village center to the cot-tage in less than a minute, run the distance even faster. But if Larra was inside and had barred the door, he would be left standing in the open, exposed to the reivers. The decision was taken away from him as a handful of raiders trotted their ponies into the open space. Half of them dismounted and, leaving one of their number to hold the animals, spread out toward the nearest buildings. The mounted raiders trotted off toward the village barn.

Only one of the reivers had kicked open a cottage door before a shout rose from the edge of the village. They halted, freezing for a moment like startled foxes before pelting back the way they had come. They slipped their arms through their shield straps as they ran for the ponies. The last of them had just mounted and drawn his weapons when another bunch of armed men galloped in. They looked a more ragtag bunch than the raiders, and their horses were already lathered from exertion. One of the newcomers wore a fancy helmet, and two had steel caps, but no other armor was in evidence. Most of the newcomers had shields, still slung on the men's backs where they wouldn't interfere with their horsemanship. One of the new arrivals carried a spear with a banner. Yan didn't recognize the insignia. He could only hope that these were Laird Koyle's men, come to defend the village.

Whoever the newcomers were, the raiders were not happy to see them. The reivers in the village's center turned their ponies toward the newcomers and set spur, swords waving and shouts of "Jonnagal!" springing from their lips. The newcomers responded with their own shout of "Koyle, Koyle!" Steel rang on steel as the riders engaged.

No casualties fell in the first passage. The two groups rode past each other and turned, ready to go at it again. The helmeted man pointed out the trio of raiders near the barn, and some of the newcomers broke off and headed for them. The Koyle partisans remaining in the village clearing charged the reivers again. With less distance to build up speed, the horses did not charge past

each other. The fight turned into a swirling melee of
prancing animals and shouting men. The weaponmen
paired off, and the battle became a series of individual
combats. Combatants sought every momentary advantage, backing off when pressed, only to return and push
hard when an opening appeared. Soon, the shifting skir-
mish left few of the battling men in the village center.

Only one of the newcomers remained, and he was
beset by two of the reivers. The lone man, the one with
the fancy helmet, roared insults at his opponents. His
high-combed burgonet glinted in the afternoon light as
his horse reared. That animal was of a larger-sized
bloodline and stood several hands taller than the
raiders' ponies. The extra height and mass of his mount
gave the man an advantage as the animals danced back
and forth under the urgings of men anxious to strike
with their swords. As Yan watched, advantage turned
to disadvantage and the animal's size proved its rider's
undoing. A stroke meant for the man came in low,
striking the saddle before glancing away to score a
bloody furrow along the horse's forequarter. Screaming,
the animal reared. The rider was caught in the midst of
an attempt to cut down his other opponent. Off-balance,
the man struggled to retain his seat, but a stirrup strap
parted and he was lost. He tumbled out of the saddle to
land hard on the ground. For a moment he lay still,
then he struggled to stand; but his uncoordinated
movements showed him to be dazed.

The man he had been trying to kill rode off after
other prey, but the one who had wounded the horse
clearly wanted to finish the job he had started. He
turned his pony around when he reached the edge of
the open space and came back, aiming to take the
thrown man on his sword side.

The helmeted man had lost his sword in the fall.
Dazed as he appeared to be, he was in perilous danger.

He would be cut down. The reiver closed, leaning forward in his saddle so that he could cut at the man on the ground with the twin advantages of his height and the pony's momentum.

Yan could not let a helpless man be cut down.

He was no swordsman—which was just as well, since he had no sword. He also had no desire to save the helmeted man by taking a sword blow meant for him. There was only one way Yan could possibly help the man.

Yan reached for the magic.

The strain was terrific. The mana flow was chaotic, disturbed by the emotions of the men who fought and the blood already spilled. He felt himself swaying, mentally and physically. His hand lashed out and grabbed the nearest thing, Rulac's ox harness, to steady himself and anchor him to the world.

With no time to waste, Yan pushed hard, diving for a deeper, calmer place, a place of magic familiar to him and far removed from the clash of armed men. He found it and wrapped himself in the mana.

Bathed in the magic, he reached out, feeling for something in harmony with the mana. He found the harness of the raider's pony, linked through similarity to the harness in Yan's hand. Leather to leather, beast harness to beast harness. Yan's mind encompassed the pony's tack in an instant. He found a place where the reiver had neglected to clean thoroughly. A tiny flaw in the leather, but a flaw nonetheless, a weak point. Yan took that minor flaw and expanded it, feeding the magic into it and making it more of itself, a larger flaw, a greater weakness.

While the rider charged down on the helmeted man, leather wilted as fibers aged prematurely and proved too weak for their job. The girth strap, stressed beyond its newly reduced strength, snapped. The raider and his

saddle pitched to a jumbled crash a mere yard from the
dazed man. Suddenly freed of the burden of man and
saddle, and maddened by the smell of blood, the pony
galloped off.

Two of the newcomers raced across the clearing in
pursuit of a trio of raiders. Yan reached out again. This
time it was a rein that rotted away, leaving a raider
unable to guide his animal. Freed of the insistent control of its rider, the pony turned in a new direction—an
unfortunate one for the rider. The leading pursuer
swung a sword into the man's side, doubling him over.
Horse bumped pony and the raider fell from his
mount. The pursuit continued beyond Yan's sight.

For the moment, the village center was clear of fighting. Yan stood, ready to run across, but sudden vertigo
and the sound of hoofbeats instilled caution in him. He
dropped back behind the fence as one of the newcomers, a big man in a sleeveless leather jerkin, rode into
the clearing. The man reined his horse in and leapt
from its back. With a glance at the fallen raider and the
saddle by his side, the big man ran to the helmeted
man and helped him to his feet. With the help of the
big man, the man Yan had saved unfastened the laces
of his helmet and tugged it off, revealing sweat-matted
red hair and a ruddy complexion. He gulped in several
deep breaths before saying, "Thanks, Enub. Where's
my sword?"

The big man, Enub, looked around. "Don't see it.
Must be around somewhere, though. Didn't see any of
them with it."

"If they've ... " He left the rest unsaid as another of
the newcomers, the one with the banner, rode back
into the clearing.

"They're running!"

"Good news, Aimuk. How many down?"

"None of ours." The man slammed the butt of his

spear into the ground, making it stand like a banner
pole, before dismounting. "Shammes got one over by
the barn. Makes three with the two here. The scuts running from us have got wounds to lick, too."

"Well done. Penn Jonnagal won't profit from this
day's work."

The weaponmen grinned at each other.

With the reivers on the run, the people of the village
began emerging from where they'd hidden. Yan saw
Larra emerge from Gormen's cottage and sighed with
relief. He stood again, swaying as his head pounded and
his vision dimmed. He leaned on the fence for support.
When his vision cleared, he was pleased to see her smiling at him from across the village center. She cast a worried glance at the armed men in the clearing and stayed
on her side. For the moment they each had to be satisfied
with knowing that the other had survived. Sednal and
Rulac came up beside Yan. The three of them exchanged
nods and smiles of relief. The attack was over.

The villagers stayed at the fringes of the clearing,
watching their rescuers, reluctant to get too close to
them. The rest of the band rode up, one of them leading the black horse. The redheaded man with the helmet found his sword and picked it up, checking it
carefully for damage. Aimuk bent over the saddle,
searching through the pockets on the cantle, while
Enub walked over to the first raider Yan had downed
and kicked him. The man groaned. "Prisoner," Enub
said. "I saw him charge, but I was too far away. Lucky
the man's girth failed when it did,"

"Koyle luck, eh? I must have cut it an earlier exchange with the scut."

"Nay, Laird," said Aimuk.

Slamming his sword into its sheath, the redheaded
man, who had to be Laird Koyle himself, advanced on
Aimuk. "What say you?"

"The leather, Laird. It's not cut, it's rotten." Aimuk held up the saddle girth and rubbed his thumb across the broken end, demonstrating the truth of his statement by crumbling off small bits of the leather. "Leather this rotten would not have withstood the ride here from Laird Jonnagal's steading. Something is strange here."

Not surprisingly, many of the villagers looked at Yan. They looked away just as quickly, but Laird Koyle noticed the byplay. Raising his arm, he pointed a stubby finger at Yan.

"Do you know something of this, man? Penn Jonnagal's weaponmen are not likely to neglect their gear."

Explaining the rotten leather would require Yan to admit that he had used magic, and Yan remembered that Gormen had said that Laird Koyle didn't like magicians. His head pounded, making it hard to think. He didn't want to say anything that would get him in trouble.

"Speak when the laird speaks to you," Enub said, stepping up to Yan with his hand raised to enforce his command with a cuff.

Sednal stepped between them, shaking his head. The weaponman frowned, obviously confused. Striking the headman of the village was a different proposition from striking a dirty young stranger.

Laird Koyle looked Yan over. "Are you a magician, then?"

"Yes."

"An Imperial spy, by the looks of him," Aimuk suggested.

"A spy would be bright enough to change his looks," Enub pointed out.

Koyle was direct. "Are you a spy, magician?"

"No," Yan replied just as directly.

"But you come from the Empire?"

"Yes."

Laird Koyle's mouth twitched back and forth while he thought about that. "You put me in a place I'd rather not be, magician. It's ill to be saved by magic, but it would be a greater ill to ignore the fact that you kept me from joining my ancestors. Honor demands that I grant you a boon for saving my life. But I warn you, don't think to take advantage of me. What will you have? Gold? Arms? Horses?"

"Horses, I think." Peyto had appeared from wherever he had been hiding. "That is to say, transportation and escort to a town with an Imperial garrison. A suitable reward, I would think."

"Who are you to claim a reward for the magician?" Koyle asked.

"His fellow traveler. A clerk, my lord. Peyto Lennuick by name. And a man who, like my friend the magician, only wishes to go home."

"He is a spy," Aimuk said sullenly.

"I'm not a spy," Peyto said testily.

"Nor am I." Yan was growing tired of the endless, groundless accusation. His head hurt and he was tired. He just wanted to go somewhere and lie down. "And I haven't said I want horses to go anywhere."

"You can't mean to throw away this chance," Peyto said incredulously.

"I didn't say I *didn't* want horses either."

"Do you know what you want, mage?" Koyle swung himself onto his horse and stared down at Yan. "I want your decision."

"Could you arrange safe passage to an Imperial garrison?"

"Aye," Koyle said quietly.

Aimuk spoke up. "I mislike it, Laird. They will scurry to their spymaster and we will have a swarm of Imperial wasps buzzing about in days. We'll lose the harvest."

"Such fears are unnecessary, Laird Koyle," Yan said. "I give you my word that I would have no business for the garrison beyond arranging passage back to the islands."

The soldier spit. "The word of a mage."

"The word of a man like yourself," Peyto asserted. Taking a step closer to Koyle, he said, "We did not come to this village of our own will. We were shipwrecked. We have no interest in your lordship's holdings here, save that we wish them prosperous. The people here have been kind to us by taking us in. How could we wish them ill?"

"You're Imperials," Aimuk said, as if any hostile or malicious intent was explained by their origin.

"Are you a wild dog, to bite the hand that feeds you?" Peyto asked. "Of course not. Neither are we."

"Lord Koyle," Yan said. "What need we do to convince you that neither Master Lennuick nor I is a spy?"

Lord Koyle appeared to consider his options. When the silence dragged on, Yan tried again.

"If you find a request for transportation beyond the bounds of your honor, say so, my lord. It was yourself that offered reward; I did what I did with no thought of reward. I really want nothing of your wealth. I used my magic to save you because you were a man in need. I didn't even know who you were at the time."

"You know now, magician."

"And given the attitude which you show Master Tanafres, he may be having second thoughts about having saved you," Peyto snapped.

The soldier raised his hand to Peyto, but lowered it as quickly when Yan put his own hand on the clerk's shoulder.

"I have no second thoughts." Yan looked into the stern face of the laird. "Were you to provide transportation, the escort you send can stay with us until we leave

your land. Surely you have those you could trust to
ensure that we offer no betrayal."

Koyle's eyes narrowed and his lips pursed. "Escort
and transportation to a garrison station. That's all you
want?"

Yan found himself saying, "That's all," and wondering
how he had come to accept Peyto's suggestion as his
own plan. If only he was thinking clearly. Laird Koyle
gave him no time to ponder.

"And you'll be gone from this land, nevermore to
come into my sight?"

Clearly, Koyle had reached a conclusion. It would
be dangerous to change his mind now. Yan inclined his
head. "If that be your wish, it shall be so. I shall under-
take never to return to these lands."

"And you, clerk?"

"I've no wish to come back here," Peyto answered
sincerely. "Name the oath you'd have me swear and I'll
swear it, if you will set us on our way."

Koyle smiled a tight, satisfied smile. He slapped his
hand against the pommel of his saddle and said,
"Done, then. You'll have horses and escort, but not
until Penn's lads are harried back to the moldering
piles of rocks from which they crawled."

"You hear that, Master Tanafres? We're going home."

Peyto was grinning from ear to ear, but over the
clerk's shoulder, Yan could see the grief-stricken look
on Larra's face.

# 9

LAIRD KOYLE'S RIDERS LEFT the village as soon as his footmen arrived. By then Gormen and the other fishermen had returned. The villagers stood in clumps, staring alternately at the departing weaponmen, the three footmen who remained behind, the two prisoners, and each other. What little talk went on was quiet and subdued. The main topic was the relief everyone felt that the raid had been countered so quickly. Soon after Laird Koyle's men passed out of sight, Sednal and the footmen hunkered down with the prisoners, asking after their clan lineages in order to set a ransom.

The excitement over, the villagers began to drift away to their homes. Hoping physical activity would help him forget his aching head, Yan helped Larra clean up the mess she'd left behind when she abandoned her basket weaving in order to hide. The throbbing inside his skull didn't stop, and every time he bent over he felt nauseated, so he soon stopped and sat down.

"Are you all right?" Larra asked.

"My skull is splitting." For a moment she looked

horrified, as though she thought he was speaking liter-
ally. "Just a bad headache from doing magic without a
*claviarm*. It will pass."

"It was good that you saved the laird. I'm very
proud of you. But your pain is a message from Horesh.
He sends you a sign that you should not be doing
magic."

"Horesh has nothing to do with my head," he
snapped. "If you'd let me finish my *claviarm*, I wouldn't
be having this problem."

Her mouth opened, but she didn't speak. Instead,
she whirled on her heels and vanished into the cottage.
Yan knew he should go after her and apologize, but he
didn't.

Later. Later he'd make it up to her.

He closed his eyes. The look on Larra's face when
he accepted Laird Koyle's deal of transportation from
the village came to him again. It was clear that she
assumed he'd leave her behind. He wanted to tell her
that he planned on taking her with him, but he knew
she would argue. She liked life here. Later he'd have to
deal with that matter as well, but he was not ready for
an argument.

He opened his eyes and stared at the small group,
prisoners and captors, sitting in a circle in the middle
of the village center. Yan's magic had made possible
the reivers' capture, so he felt something of a propri-
etary interest in their fates. He was still uneasy despite
Gormen's assurances as he departed that the men
would be ransomed back to their lord rather than exe-
cuted or imprisoned. Ransom seemed an odd fate for a
soldier involved in a raid against a neighbor. Had the
village been informed of open hostility between Koyle
and Jonnagal, Yan would have understood, but no
such declaration had been made. In the civilized parts
of the empire, honorable ransom would not have been

countenanced for villains participating a sneak raid.
For such ignoble deeds, the only justice was some
form of suitably ignominious punishment.

The faint scents of cooking drifted out of the cottage
and Yan's stomach flopped. He wouldn't be ready for
food for at least another decade. He stayed outside by
the door when Gormen called to him to come in and
eat, and continued to watch the weaponmen. One of
Sednal's children arrived with a bucket and a sack full
of wooden bowls and served all of the men. Everyone
seemed to be hungry. Food was not something Yan
found appealing at the moment. Finally, one of Koyle's
foot soldiers, by his studded jerkin the leader, got up
and started for the cottage.

More questions about his magic, Yan guessed.

Yan forced back the ache and smiled at the weaponman as he approached. The man smiled back.

"You Gormen?"

Surprised, and a little disappointed, Yan shook his
head and immediately regretted it.

"He around?"

Standing and stepping into the doorway, Yan called,
"Gormen. There's someone here to speak to you."

He stepped aside as the old fisherman came to the
door. Gormen squinted at the weaponman, frowning
slightly. Pointedly, he stepped outside rather than inviting the man into his cottage. Larra followed her father
out and tentatively slipped her arm around Yan's waist.
He returned the gesture and she settled in, clinging
silently to him.

"You Gormen?" the weaponman repeated to the
fisherman.

"Aye."

"I'm Yurmes, weaponman to Laird Koyle. It's on his
business that I speak to you." When Gormen accepted
the formal statement with a curt nod, Yurmes pointed a

thumb over his shoulder in the general direction of the
other weaponmen. "That man is named Timen. Says
he's of the Shelmun clan. Says he has relatives in these
lands and Sednal says those relatives was you."

"Shelmun?"

"So he says."

Gormen was quiet for a while, then said, "My daughter married a Shelmun."

"Daughter?" Yan was confused. Larra was here, a
widow. Her husband had been a local fisherman.

"Demisi," Larra whispered to him. "My elder sister."

"Demisi married a Shelmun in the Douganan's service, not the Jonnagal's," Gormen said.

"Douganan? That was three winters ago, before
Douganan and Laird Koyle had their row?"

"Three years ago, aye. Don't know nothing about
lairds' business. I'm just a fisherman."

"Yah," Yurmes said with a grin. "I remember now.
The laird had her married off to one of Laird Douganan's
weaponmen. Good party."

Gormen's frown grew deeper and Larra laid her
head against Yan's shoulder. In a moment he felt wet-
ness. Demisi's family didn't seem to have the same
fond memories of the occasion as the weaponman.

Yurmes either didn't notice or ignored their reaction. "You think they'll stand ransom?"

"He was in Douganan's service, not Jonnagal's."

"A Shelmun's a Shelmun," Yurmes said with a shrug.
"Douganan and Jonnagal are as tight as a virgin's—uh,
sorry—Those lairds have got no ill will toward each
other. Will your relations at least serve as go-betweens?"

"Don't know. We've not heard from Demisi since
before the last snows."

"It's unlike her to not send word," Larra added. She
was speaking to Yan, but the weaponman overheard her.

"Hunh. Might mean old Laird Douganan's going

hostile. Might mean he's just getting private again. Laird Koyle'll want to know either way. You know anything about that?"

Gormen shook his head. "Already said we ain't heard nothing from the hills."

"Maybe the prisoner knows something of what's happening there," Yan suggested.

"Won't say," Yurmes stated.

"Then perhaps he knows something of Demisi or her husband."

Gormen nodded and said to Yurmes, "Can I talk with him?"

The weaponman shrugged "Suppose so. He's given parole. I'd have brought him with me, but he was still eating."

The four of them trooped to the village center.

"Timen, this here's Gormen, father to a woman married into your clan. Closest you got to clansmen in this stead. Wants to talk to you."

Timen looked unhappy to see his best connection was an old fisherman. "So talk."

Gormen asked if the man knew his daughter or her husband, naming them. The fisherman tried describing them but Timen kept shaking his head. When Gormen reminded him of Laird Koyle's involvement, Timen finally said, "Goremmic, you say his name is? Aye, maybe I do know him. One of Laird Douganan's archers, is he?"

"Yes."

"I've not seen him in a double handful of months. He was with the lads serving Laird Jonnagal, but he went home after the harvest. Said he'd be back in the spring, but he didn't come. None of Laird Douganan's lads did, come to think on it."

"Didn't Laird Jonnagal send someone to investigate?" Yan asked.

"Nay." Timen tossed down his bowl. "Things have been quiet. No need."

"Are you saying it's been nearly a year since the laird communicated with his ally?" Yurmes asked.

"Maybe shouldn't tell you, but I don't think it really matters. Messenger rode in a week or so before midsummer with the spring taxes. Now if *they'd* not shown, Laird Jonnagal would have investigated quick enough. But the taxes were only a month late and that's a timely payment for one of the hill lords, though late for Douganan. He was always the first. Suppose he wanted to stay on Laird Jonnagal's good side, since he'd already found Koyle's bad one."

They talked more with Timen, and soon it became clear he had no knowledge of current events in Douganan's steading. Larra became more fretful. Leaving Gormen with the others, they returned to the cottage

As soon as they were behind the closed door, she said, "Something's wrong."

Yan tried to sound reassuring. "You don't know that. What could be wrong?"

"I don't know. I just feel that something *is* wrong." She paced away from him, stopping in the corner and hugging herself. Without looking at him, she spoke quietly. "Couldn't you use magic and find out?"

That was something new, asking him to do magic. How unfortunate that he had to disappoint her. "I don't have the equipment to do a proper scrying."

She spun and said harshly, "What kind of magician are you?"

He sighed. "A young one. Magic can't do everything and anything."

"But it's magic! And you're a magician!"

"We've been through this before," he said dispassionately, hoping to calm her. "No magician can do everything that is possible by magic, just as no crafts-man can know every craft."

"You don't seem to be able to do anything."

"I thought you didn't want me practicing magic."

She stamped her foot. "Don't throw it back on me! You used magic to save Laird Koyle. *He* was good enough for you to help."

"That's not—"

"It is! You were thinking of yourself, just like always. You always think of yourself. You never think about anyone else."

"Larra . . . " Yan took a step toward her.

"Don't take that tone. I saw. I watched you dicker with the laird like a common merchant. You thought yourself so clever. But I know. I know you didn't think about me when the laird offered you a chance to leave."

Guiltily, Yan thought how true her statement was. Claiming that his reaction to using magic without a *claviarm* had clouded his thoughts was not an excuse that she would accept. He was not sure it was one he could accept. Now that the chance to leave was offered, he didn't want to stay. But he didn't want to leave Larra behind, either.

"See," she accused. "You're thinking about yourself again."

"I'm not."

"You are."

There was no point in arguing. "All right, I was thinking about myself. That doesn't make me an ogre. Everybody thinks about himself."

"If you thought about other people, you'd use your magic to find out what happened to Demisi."

"You don't even know anything did."

"And you don't know it didn't."

"If something bad had happened, someone would have heard. Timen would have known."

She shook her head, helpless and confused. Tears appeared in her eyes. She let Yan take her in his arms, rocking in his embrace with the force of her sobs.

He didn't like to see her so upset, but he really didn't know what he could do. He couldn't answer her questions or allay her fears with the Art. But then, if he had learned one thing in his stay in the village, it was that he had other resources beyond the Art.

"Would it make you happy if I said I'd go to the Douganan steading?"

"Would you really go? It's a long way."

"Well, I don't know how to get there, but if I had a guide, I'd go."

"Oh, Yan." She kissed him fiercely. "I love you."

Her passion inspired him. "With the laird's horses, we both could go. You could see for yourself."

She pulled away from him, but he didn't let her go.

"It's too far," she protested. "I couldn't go. Who would look after Gormen?"

"Gormen can look after himself."

"Don't be foolish."

He wasn't the one being foolish. "You're saying you *won't* go."

"Can't go."

He tried to take her chin in his hand and make her look at him. She resisted. "Won't."

"Can't. Can't! *Can't!*" She pulled free of him. "You're a man and a mage. You can go where you please. Do what you please."

"So?"

"So, I'm only a woman."

"What's wrong with that?"

"You don't understand."

No, he didn't. "Larra?"

She didn't respond.

"I will go to the Douganan steading," he said.

She looked at him shyly. "You will?"

He nodded.

"You'll find out what happened to Demisi?"

Smiling in what he hoped was a soothing manner, he said, "I'm sure nothing's happened to her. You'll see."

"And you'll come back? You won't just send word."

"Yes, I'll come back."

She placed her hands on his shoulders and stared into his eyes. "Really?"

"Of course. I don't want to leave you."

"You really will come back?"

"I really will."

She hugged him hard, and before long something else was hard as well. They lay together, making love with a fierce passion. Afterward, Yan thought about trying to convince her once more to leave the village, but decided that he didn't want to upset her again. She nestled against him and he was happy to feel her soft breasts against him, her hand on his chest, and her breath in regular zephyrs upon his shoulder. Maybe he was wrong in trying to get her to leave. Maybe he was wrong in wanting to leave.


Two days later a banging on the cottage door interrupted Yan and Larra. Gormen had left before dawn to go fishing, leaving them the quiet early morning hours to enjoy each other.

"A moment, friend," Yan called, slipping on his shirt. Tugging on his pants, he was glad that he hadn't adopted the local fashion of hosen. The continued banging insisted that he take no time to don stockings or shoes. Placing himself to shield the still-dressing Larra, Yan opened the door.

Laird Koyle's men Enub and Aimuk stood there.

Behind them were five horses, three harnessed with a weaponman's gear and two with minimal tack and worn saddles. Enub snorted after looking Yan over. "Aren't you ready, magician?"

"Ready?"

"We'll be leaving now."

"Leaving?"

"Are ya sure this one's a magician, Enub?" Aimak asked. "He don't seem very bright."

"You're the one found the evidence," Enub said. To Yan he said, "Orman's off to get the other fellow. Soon as they're back, we're to take you over to Glaebur. We've got to be leaving now so we can get back across the pass at Bonkilly before the winter closes it."

"I can't leave now. I've got things to do here," Yan told him.

"Told ya he was wasn't very bright," Aimuk said.

Enub frowned. "You refusing the laird's reward?"

"No. I'm just saying that I can't accept it right now."

"Sounds like a refusal to me," Aimuk said.

"The laird's pretty touchy about his honor," Enub said. "He might take your refusal as an insult."

"It's not a refusal, so it's not an insult. If it's anything, it's simply a deferral. Surely your lord's honor can encompass that?"

"He knows his honor better than some Imperial magicker." Enub scratched his jaw. "What you want me to tell him?"

"Tell him that I have an errand to run first. For one of his folk. And since he offered horses as my reward, I'd take it kindly if I could use them for my journey."

"Douganan's steading?" Enub asked.

Enub's guess surprised Yan with its accuracy. But if the weaponman had spoken with Yurmes, which he undoubtedly had, such a conclusion was an obvious one. "Yes."

"Sounds like a spy's errand," Aimuk said.

"It's not," Yan said firmly. "Just tell Laird Koyle what I've said."

"I'll tell him," Enub said.

The two men left, taking all of the horses with them.

Yan spent the morning and the early part of the afternoon putting the finishing touches on his *claviarm*. If he was going journeying, he'd be happier with it done. He was glad that Larra was across the way helping Sifi with some chore. He didn't want an argument over it.

With the cottage quiet, it was easy to hear the hoofbeats of approaching horses. Yan slipped on the *claviarm* and was at the door and opening it before the knocking began. Enub and Aimuk eyed Yan suspiciously as Enub lowered the hand with which he was ready to pound on the door. The scene outside was much as it had been in the morning, save that Laird Koyle himself was there, sitting astride his great black horse.

"The laird says it's time to go," Enub said.

Yan stepped past the weaponmen and walked up to Laird Koyle. "Did your men misrepresent me, Laird Koyle?"

"They said you didn't understand."

"I think perhaps that it was they who didn't understand, my lord. I must visit Laird Douganan's steading before I leave your lands for good. It's a matter of . . . of honor. I'm sure you will understand that I must do this. I mean no disrespect to you or your generous offer of reward."

"You haven't got time."

Yan waved a hand at the fair blue sky. "The weather has been so mild that there is surely time enough."

"Are you so great a magician that you can make it so?"

"Weather magic is not my gift."

"Then you cannot delay. You must choose. You can have your escort of me and go to Glaebur, or you can go to the Douganan lands. There's not enough time before the snows for both."

"I must go to Laird Douganan's steading."

Koyle glowered down at Yan. His mount picked up his displeasure and danced away from Yan. The laird curbed it hard with a yank on the reins.

A rustle of cloth and harness announced the arrival of another party behind Yan. A glance showed it to be Peyto, dressed and packed for the road. The distressed expression on the clerk's face showed that he had heard the exchange between Yan and the laird. Upset, Peyto spoke in Empiric.

"Master Tanafres, you said yourself that you can't stop the snows. They'll come and we'll lose our best chance of getting back to civilization."

Enub poked Yan in the shoulder. "What'd he say?"

"He was urging me to accept the laird's offer."

"Yan!" Larra called as she ran across the clearing. She arrived breathless and looked him in the face.

"I know," he said. "Don't worry."

Looking up at Koyle, Yan said, "I gave my word to make this trip to Laird Douganan's lands before I knew you had a time limit on your gratitude, Laird Koyle. I must do this."

"Tanafres!" Peyto looked and sounded panicked.

Yan ignored him. It was easier than it might have been, owing to the fierce hug Larra was giving him. Peyto started to harangue Yan in Empiric.

"Silence," Koyle snarled. "Magician, your choice releases me. Take the horses for your journey, as you asked, as the recompense for your aid. Take them for your journey, and only for your journey. You go to the stead of one who is friend to my enemy, thus I want a surety that you will not join those who oppose me. My men will be here to take back my horses, waiting with your woman."

The not-so-subtle hint that Larra would be held hostage for his return was not lost on Yan. It was an unnecessary precaution on the lord's part, but Yan could understand why Koyle would take it. Yan didn't like it, but he understood how it would make sense to the suspicious lord. He also understood how it ruined his own plans. There was no way Larra would travel to Douganan's steading now; he would have no chance to convince her to keep traveling and not return to the village.

"Well, magician?"

Well? Not really. But there would be other chances. He inclined his head. "You are fair, laird."

"You heard. You all heard." Koyle looked at the gathered folks, accepting a nod of agreement from each. He looked at Yan with a hard smile. "My debt is paid, ingrate."

Koyle wrenched his horse's head around and rapped it in the flanks with his heels. The black reared slightly and then was off. The laird let it have its head. They raised dust, and scattered the geese by the pond as they went.

Peyto slammed his traveling sack onto the ground. "You're a fool, Tanafres."

Perhaps. But if so, he was a young fool and he had time enough to grow out of it. Time enough to grow into the impatience of age.

# 10

"THIS IS A FOOL'S ERRAND," Gormen said as he watched Yan pack his meager belongings into a traveling sack. Uncharacteristically, the fisherman had refrained from going to sea today.

"Larra's worried," Yan reminded him.

"Worry don't mean nothing. Larra ain't got the sight."

"You haven't heard from Demisi in over a year."

Gormen shrugged. "A woman leaves a house and goes to another. You don't hear from her after that, it's not trouble. It's the way of things. I expect Demisi was glad to be out of here. She never did like fish much. Probably happier being a weaponman's wife. 'Bout as much chance of being a widow, and the life's easier till then."

Yan didn't understand the old man's attitude. If Dancie had moved away and not been heard from, he would have worried. The thought raised a pang of guilt. It had been nearly as long since he'd had contact with his own family. "Don't you care about your daughter?"

"Raised her, didn't I?"

Yan's father had raised him, but Yan didn't think the man cared for him. "That's not an answer."

"You shoulda taken the laird's gift. Gone when you could."

"I had promised Larra."

"Hunh. A man oughta keep his promises, that's for sure. The gods don't have much use for a man who doesn't. You're doing what you said you'd do, and I gotta admire that." It was the closest thing to praise the old man had ever given Yan, but Gormen didn't leave Yan any time to bask in the sentiment. "Don't mean I think you're smart."

Yan had to laugh. "I like you too, old man."

Tying off his sack, Yan gathered the costrel of herbed water and pouch of dried travel food that Larra had laid out. He slung his burdens over his shoulder and opened the door. The horses were there, waiting.

"You might just take the laird's horses and keep going, you know," Gormen said from behind him.

"That's theft," Yan said without turning around. "Not all Imperials are born thieves, you know."

"Horses were what you wanted for saving the laird's life. By all rights, they's yours."

"Laird Koyle said he'd have men waiting to take the horses back when we return."

"If they're waiting here, they ain't chasing anybody heading for Glaebur."

"And what happens when they decide I'm not coming back?"

"That'd depend on who was here waiting with them. Me, I'd likely be fishing. Fall runs are coming on. Gets busy out there, so I'd need help. Man ain't got a partner or a son, daughter'll have to do."

Yan looked over his shoulder at Gormen and smiled. "You're a devious old man."

"I like you, too, magician," the fisherman replied straight-faced.

"You planning on explaining it all to Larra then?"

Gormen shrugged. "She'll get over it. She did before."

Before? Yan wondered if Gormen only meant Larra's late husband. He'd died, while Yan would still be alive. But then, the dead man had been married to Larra, and Yan had never exchanged vows with her; theirs was an arrangement of mutual consent and convenience. She certainly would get over Yan, but he wasn't ready to give her cause. He still had hopes of convincing her to go with him when he left.

Yan stepped through the doorway into the morning sunlight. The cottage had still been cool from the night, but the sun was warm. He might have stepped from one world into another.

"Larra and I said good-bye this morning. Say good-bye to her again for me."

Gormen nodded. "I will. Good journey to you, magician."

"I will bring you back word of Demisi."

"I don't expect you to."

"She does."

"She'll understand."

Maybe. Eventually. But not just yet. "I said I'd be back."

"You won't stay." Gormen's words weren't hostile, just a statement of fact. "Going's better done sooner than later."

"I've heard that the gods don't have much use for a man who doesn't keep his word."

Rebuked, Gormen said, "Travel well," and shut the door in Yan's face.

Yan stared at the door for a moment, then turned and started for the horses. As he did, he saw that they were attended; Peyto was tying a sack to the saddle of one of them. When Yan stepped up to him, the clerk gave him a broad grin.

"Good morrow to you, Master Tanafres."

"Good morrow, Master Lennuick. Here to see me off?"

"In a fashion. The broad ring is the best for securing the sack, but you'd better tie one to either side. The costrel should snug up nicely behind the cantle like my bottles. As soon as you're squared away, we can be off."

"We?"

"Certainly. I need to see something other than this miserable collection of huts. You didn't think I'd stay here among these Imperial-haters without the protection of a powerful wizard, did you?"

Yan was in no mood for jokes. "That horse was for my guide."

"*Our* guide has his own beast."

As if on cue, a smiling boy leading a pony emerged from behind the bigger horses. The animal had no saddle, just a blanket. Its bridle, however, was of fine leather, far finer workmanship than Yan had seen in the village. He recognized the bridle and reins as those of the man he had dumped to save Laird Koyle. Then he recognized the pony; it was that reiver's animal as well.

"This enterprising young lad is named Iaf. It seems he brought the beast in after it escaped from the reivers. Since none of the laird's men were around at the time, there was no one to whom he could report its recovery. Consequently, when the laird's men left without it, the village became the new owners with Iaf, as the finder, becoming principal caretaker. It also seems that young Iaf is the only one the village can spare who has been to the Douganan lands. Fortunate, is it not, that he also has a horse? One doesn't have to be a Preordainer to see the hand of the gods at work here."

"Please, sir." The boy's voice cracked as he spoke, hinting at the change soon to be permanent. "Mock not the gods."

"Don't be concerned, Iaf," Yan said. "Master Lennuick doesn't take the gods lightly, no matter how he talks."

Reassured, the boy nodded solemnly. He bounded onto his pony. Once mounted he smiled again. He did not seem the type to stay serious for long. Yan thought the boy would make a fine antidote to the usually somber Peyto.

With his gear secured to the saddle, there was no more reason for delay. They mounted and were off, walking their horses across the village center and down the track that led inland. Once past Sednal's house Iaf kicked his pony into a canter. Yan tried to follow, but found the gait of the horse too difficult. He nearly fell off. By pleading in the beast's ear, he managed to slow it back to a walk. Envious of Iaf's skill, Yan waited for Peyto to catch up, and then the two of them followed the exuberant boy at a sedate walk. Yan was glad that the clerk said nothing of Yan's aborted display of horsemanship.

At the crest of the hill upon which he had spotted the first reiver, Yan reined in. The village looked tiny from that vantage; a handful of cottages, a barn, a pond, and a few scattered fields by a narrow beach of shingle. Hardly the great city for which he had set out from Talinfad. He had found no fellowship of magicians here, and no opportunities to further his Art, but he had found other things. Were they better things?

"Come along," Peyto called from the base of the hill. "This trip was your idea. I'll not be wanting to have this high adventure without you."

Curiously reluctant, Yan turned his horse around and urged it down the hill. The three riders rode away from the village, Iaf in the lead.

The road was little more than a path winding through barren hills covered in gorse. An occasional gnarled gristlecone pine stood bold sentinel on one of the windswept crests, while other trees huddled in the more-protected hollows along the watercourses that threaded through the landscape. In front of them and to either side Yan could see distant mountains, their snowcapped peaks glinting in the sun. The tallest mountains lay ahead, and Douganan's steading was in a valley somewhere among those peaks.

They camped in a small meadow by a freshet of clear water. Yan watched Iaf cast a line into the water without success. On a whim he created a glamour on the boy's hook, one that he hoped would be attractive to the trout hiding among the rocks. He was surprisingly successful; Iaf caught enough of the small fish for the three to eat their fill. The boy banked the fire immediately after they ate and rolled up in his blanket. Though tired, Yan was not ready to sleep. Yan knew he was not the only one when Peyto spoke.

"You've finished your *claviarm*, I see."

Yan reached up and touched the amulet. "I thought it prudent."

"Prudent?" Yan imagined that he could see the curious expression on Peyto's face, and found that he actually could see the clerk's arched eyebrows and quirked mouth. His night vision was sharper now. "You weren't wearing it when you stopped those reivers. I thought a *claviarm* was the necessary key to work magic."

"A *claviarm* is like a key, and like a key, it is only a tool. Just as a thief, substituting skill and effort, can open a lock without the proper key, some magicians can do magic without a *claviarm*. Some practitioners are totally helpless without their *claviarms*, lacking the strength of will necessary to focus the magical energies, while other magicians can do minor magics. No one can perform a great magic without a *claviarm* and even the most trivial magics are, uh, difficult and sometimes unpredictable without the focus provided by a *claviarm*. Magic, like any craft, is easier with the proper tools."

"I'm surprised Larra let you finish it. She might like a certain magician, but she has no love for magic. Once she found you could still do magic without your amulet, I expect that her arguments lost a great deal of force."

Yan nodded. "She couldn't argue there was no good to magic after I saved the laird."

"Good? Yes, I expect she'd see it that way. These folk have little sense of real politics. Men like Koyle with their touchy honor and constant brawling are not fit rulers for a land. But even in thinking that you'd helped her and her village by saving Koyle, she still argued with you, didn't she?"

Remembering the heat of his last set-to with Larra and the nearness of the clerk's abode, Yan said, "You know that as well as I."

"Were I in your position, I might have sought domestic bliss, or at least tranquillity, by conforming to her wish; but you went ahead and remade your *claviarm*. You are so accommodating to her in other ways, and you've told me more times than I care to remember that you like living like a normal person. Why set yourself up to be different again? The village folk don't like different."

"I already am different. I'm not Scothic."

"Scoth. Imperial. Rolessdakkan. All are merin, all people. Even saü are people. Some would go so far as to say that bregil, despite all their physical differences, are people as well. But mages—mages are always different."

"Mages are people, too."

"Not everyone agrees with that."

"Well, it's true."

"Having come to know you, I'll not disagree. But there still remains an observable difference. Not everyone can do magic, even if he were given a *claviarm.*"

"A mage has to make his own *claviarm,*" Yan said automatically.

"Really?" Peyto looked surprised to hear it. After pondering a moment, he said, "I don't think that changes my thesis. If you let an ordinary person make a *claviarm,* he still wouldn't be able to do magic. Correct?"

"I suppose so."

"You know so. Mages may be people, but they *are* different. A *claviarm* is just a signpost, like the sign for an inn or a craftsman. You've hung your sign out again, telling people that you're different."

Had he? "I wasn't going to wear it like a sign."

"You wouldn't have to. Those folk in the village know that you're not one of them. You can't be, you know. You can never be one of them."

"You're talking like the kind of Imperial they believe you to be."

"Are you saying I'm lying?" Peyto asked mildly.

"I—no. No, I'm not. I just—"

"Just what?"

Yan didn't want to continue the discussion; he didn't like the thoughts he was having. "I just want to go to sleep."

To Yan's relief, Peyto acquiesced. The two of them lay down in their blankets, and shortly Yan heard the clerk slip into the rhythmic breathing of sleep. Yan lay awake for some time before he finally drifted off. He was still deep in sleep when Iaf shook him awake and remained muzzy-headed all morning.

The land about them grew wilder and more wooded. Yan saw plants and animals unfamiliar to him; he was

intrigued and it was difficult for him not to stop and
observe a strange animal or try to take a sample of a
unknown plant. About midday they reached a broader
path that Iaf called the highway. Though broader than
what they had been traveling, it was no different in
character. It would not have been more than a country
lane in the civilized parts of the empire. Peyto pointed
off to the west.

"That's the way to Glaebur. See the double peaks?
Bonkilly Pass is just to the left of them."

"How do you know that?" Yan asked.

"I asked Iaf."

Simple enough. "Did you ask the way to Douganan's
steading?"

"No."

"And why not? That's where we're going."

Peyto sighed. "I was hoping you'd be reasonable.
If we headed to Glaebur, no one but Iaf here would
know for quite a while. Koyle's bullies might not
even find out before we got to the town. Especially if
Iaf didn't go right back to the village." He smiled at
the boy. "You wouldn't mind gadding about out here
for a while and missing out on your chores, would
you?"

"Not at all, sir," the boy said cheerfully

Peyto smiled. "There, you see. We could be safely
quit of Koyle and this backwoods locale."

"The horses aren't ours," Yan said. "I told the laird
he could have them back."

"They're what you asked Koyle for. He didn't give
you an escort to go along, so you could count it even.
Or if your conscience won't let you do that, we could
sell them in Glaebur and have the money sent to him."

"Have you been talking to Gormen?"

"Pardon?" Peyto looked confused.

"Never mind."

Peyto wouldn't let it go. "You want to get back to civilization as much as I do."

As much as Peyto so obviously did? Yan didn't know about degree, but he did have to admit he missed city life. Compared to Scothandir, Talinfad seemed an urbane and sophisticated place. When looked at with honest eyes, even his own birth village compared favorably. But there were other considerations. "Larra wants to stay here in Scothandir."

"But you don't, lad. I can see it in your eyes."

"When we get back, I'll convince Larra to leave with us."

Peyto didn't look like he believed it. "What makes you think there'll be another opportunity to leave?"

"Which way to Douganan's steading?" Yan asked Iaf, effectively ending the conversation. The boy pointed east and Yan turned his horse's head in that direction.

They spent that night in a small village, no bigger than the one they had left. The place had no inn, so they spent the night in the communal barn with their horses, a quartet of oxen, and a bunch of milch cows and their calves. The folk were not unkindly, but neither were they friendly, especially once they'd heard Peyto's Empiric accent. The clerk's after-dinner conversation was mostly complaints, but at least he didn't press Yan to change his mind again.

Another day of travel put them well into the fringes of the mountains. The traveling was tougher, but Iaf and his pony showed remarkable energy. They often raced ahead or had to gallop to catch up after the boy had hared off to investigate some woodland sight or geologic quirk. Peyto talked little during the day, seeming to prefer saving his talk for after they had eaten and were settled around a fire that offered some relief from the chill night air.

"Perhaps tomorrow we should urge our beasts to a faster pace?"

"What's your hurry?" Yan asked. "I thought you wanted to see some sights."

"My hurry? Why, the same one that Koyle used for his excuse. Winter comes sooner in the mountains. I'd rather not be mewed up here for the winter. At least in the village, we were near the sea. If I can't have a town, I at least want the sea. These mountains are too . . . tall."

"We're not in the mountains yet, sir," Iaf said.

Peyto looked appalled and Yan laughed. "He's right, you know. These are just foothills, hardly what passes for mountains around here."

"They're tall enough for me," Peyto announced.

"Even the mountains here are children compared to the ranges on Merom." In Yan's memory white-crowned peaks reached higher toward the sky by far than those before them. "Now the Camnarian Range, those are mountains."

"I don't like them, either."

"Why so sour?" Yan asked.

"I don't want to be trapped here."

"You won't be. There hasn't been any sign of snow."

"Then what's that white stuff on the peaks?"

"It's snow all right, but permanent snow."

"I know that," Peyto snapped. "I just want to get on with this *errand*. Sooner there, sooner back."

"Sooner to sleep, sooner up," Yan said with a grin. "Sooner up, sooner there."

Peyto threw a handful of leaves at him, but they scattered harmlessly. Iaf looked stunned at first, but when he saw Yan laughing, the boy laughed as well. They bedded down soon after, and the morning chill came too soon for Yan.

As they followed the trail that only Iaf seemed to be able to see, Yan mused on the mildness of the weather.

"Why fear snow, Master Lennuick? Look at all the green around us. We seem to be riding into summer."

Peyto replied with a grunt. While Yan was finding himself more in tune with young Iaf's good humor, Peyto grew more worried in contrast.

"Look around you," the clerk said out of a long silence. "Where's your summer? Look to the peaks. We see more snow every day."

Yan looked. It was true, but then the mountains were higher every day. Every day was cooler as well, but that was only the elevation. The slopes of the mountains were covered in trees, still clad in their deep green leaves. Yan could see only the occasional glimmer of a golden aspen. Back home, the higher elevations would already be experiencing the first touch of winter, but these mountains seemed even less touched by the coming fall than the land around the village.

Yan didn't know this land. Though winter came early on Merom, that didn't mean it had to come early here; so he said, "You're worried over nothing."

"A snowbound winter in the mountains is not nothing."

"You should welcome the fine weather, since it makes for pleasant travel. And if it holds, we will get back sooner. And if it holds beyond that, we might be able to convince Laird Koyle to let us go to Glaebur after all. We could tell him that it's a sign that he should let us go."

"I don't think it's wise to try to fool Koyle."

"But it's all right to steal his horses?"

Peyto harrumphed, riding the rest of the day in silence.

With Iaf's assurances that they had little farther to

go, Yan no longer worried about the weather. This high up and still no snow on the ground meant it would take a truly severe storm to close the passes through which they traveled. Soon they would reach Douganan's steading, assure themselves of Demisi's continued well-being, and be on their way back to the village. They wouldn't spend the winter in the mountains. He was quite sure of that.

Two days later, Iaf pointed to a lightning-blasted aspen tree and said, "That's the sign. This is the trail that leads to Laird Douganan's steading. We're almost there."

Almost in distance, but not in effort. The trail steep-ened to a point where they had to dismount and lead the horses. The going was rough, but not impossible. Often they had to wait while Peyto rested. At such times, Iaf bounded ahead, whether out of sheer exuber-ance or to assure himself of the route, Yan never knew; but when the boy returned and they started off again he always seemed confident of their direction. Yan's woodcraft was too poor for him to be sure they were following a trail, so he relied on the boy.

By late afternoon they reached a level stretch and remounted the horses. The great mountains stood silent on either side of them, towering above in awesome majesty. They were tiny creatures, dwarfed to insignifi-cance by the stony giants around them. They might have been the only creatures in existence.

But they were clearly not the first to come this way.

Yan spotted dark hollows edged in half-burned sticks of wood, the remains of long-abandoned camp-fires. At the mouth of a hollow in the mountainside, he spotted a wicker fence, its gate open. They stopped to investigate. It proved to be no more than a shepherd's hole and goat pen, long disused.

The pass began to slope downward.

They came around a bend and were confronted with a wonderful vista. Below them lay a verdant valley ringed by tree-skirted mountains as tall or taller than the one they traversed. It was the gem in the heart of a dragon, the pearl in an oyster, and the insight at the end of a lesson—the unsuspected interior treasure hidden by the harsh exterior.

The valley was surprisingly large and flat, and its long axis was oriented east–west so that it was mostly free of the shadows of its protective mountains. The arduous ascent up the mountainside and the narrowness of the pass made the entrance easily defensible, securing the lush valley from unwanted attention. Yan could easily imagine how a person could find everything he needed here and dismiss the outside world, how tempting it could be to remain hidden in this solitude and let the rest of the world move on.

They were approaching from the west, coming through the only apparent pass into the valley. The trail led down the mountainside and disappeared into woods, one of the many stretches edging the open flat and gently rolling valley floor. The trail reappeared beyond the trees as a rutted dirt road and wound through fields of grain and other crops. Beyond the fields was the steading, a group of a dozen or so dwellings. The two largest structures in sight were a two-story longhouse and a rambling stone manor house with a tower at one end. Yan concluded that the latter had to be the residence of the lord of the valley. Who else would build his house so that it dominated the central area of the village? A small church stood on a knoll at the far end of the village, the orb atop its spire glinting golden in the sunlight. Beyond the church lay an orchard and beyond that a large barn, to judge from the shape of the roof visible over the treetops. To the north of the barn, by a broad pond, stood a mill, its wheel still.

Yan was puzzled; something was out-of-place, something seemed wrong. He scanned the valley again.

"There is no smoke rising," Peyto said.

"No people about either," Yan said.

"I like this not."

"The fields are untended," Iaf said. "See where they have let some animal tramp through the grain. What's wrong, Masters?"

"We don't know, Iaf. For now, I think you'd best stay by us."

"You're not intending to go down there, are you?" Peyto asked.

Yan nodded. He had promised to find out what had happened to Demisi, although that had been when he had thought the trip would be no more than a social call. Now that they had found Laird Douganan's steading, apparently abandoned, his obligation had not ceased. If anything, he was more obliged than ever to ride down and discover what had happened.

"There are no signs of destruction," Yan said. "I don't think there's any danger."

"What about plague?" Peyto asked.

"See the church spire? The priest hasn't veiled the orb as he would have if plague were loose."

"Maybe the priest was the first to die."

Yan hadn't thought of that. Still, they wouldn't be able to tell one way or the other from up here. Once on the valley floor, they'd surely see signs of plague before they exposed themselves to the contagion. They could retreat at the first evidence of sickness among the locals. "We won't take any chances."

As they started down, Yan noticed something he had missed in his earlier surveys of the valley. In the woods beyond the village, he spied a shape too regular to be natural. Calling upon the magic to strengthen his vision, Yan scrutinized it. It was an ancient tower of dark stone, crumbling and overgrown with rich green ivy that blended the tower's shape into the forest around it. Yan shivered despite the warm, summerlike air. Holding his enhanced vision tired him, so he let it lapse. His eyes felt gritty, as though he had been awake too long. He rubbed at them, but they still ached. Relief only came when the riders passed into the cool shadow provided by the woods.

The ride through the woods would have been pleasant if Yan had not been so apprehensive. His companions kept silent and the only sounds were those of the horses' hooves on the loam and the normal, ordinary sounds of the forest. Here among the trees nothing seemed wrong; everything seemed ordinary and normal.

Still, Yan slowly became convinced that something was most definitely out-of-place. He wasn't sure what, though. Worry about the obvious concerns was to be expected, but this was something else, something that nagged at him. It was sort of a mental tugging, that same odd sort of absence that seems not to be an absence at all while you're striving to remember something but can't quite recall what it is you're supposed to be remembering.

They emerged from the trees into the welcome warmth of the sunlight. The sights that came to their eyes stirred apprehension. The fields they passed were overgrown with weeds, the crops within them unready for harvest as if weakened and slowed in their growth by competition with the strangling weeds. This close to winter farmers should be concerned about their crops being in such a condition. Where were the farmers, that they should let their fields reach such a parlous state?

The first cottage they reached showed no black cloth warning of plague, but neither did anyone come out to greet them. Not even a barking dog. Everything was so still that it might have been a painting of a residence

rather than a real one. Yan started to dismount but
thought better of it when Peyto said, "Dead people do
not hang out plague warnings."

They moved on.

Riding into the village square, they halted by the
small central fountain. Here villagers would draw their
water, wash their clothes, and gather to gossip. In the
middle of an afternoon, someone should be present.
The riders and their horses were the only living beings
to be seen.

The horses strained to drink, but at Yan's suggestion
the riders held them back. He wasn't sure that the
water was safe, for all it looked clear and clean. The
saintly-looking bronze lady in the center of the fountain
smiled benignly at them, while the assorted grotesques
clustered around her feet leered at them. Some seemed
almost to dare them to drink.

Yan turned to Iaf. "Which house is Demisi's?"

"I dunna know," Iaf said.

"What do you mean, you don't know?" Peyto snapped.

Iaf looked sheepish. "I've never been here before,
sir."

"You said you knew the way. Were you lying to
me?" Peyto accused.

"Nay, sir. The way I knew, or mostly anyway. And
I'd been told the sign of the lightning tree. Like Master
Sednal said, it wasna hard after that."

"Einthof, look kindly on the ignorant," Peyto said.
"How were we supposed to find the woman?"

"Ask someone, I suppose," Yan said.

"That doesn't seem very likely now," Peyto said
harshly.

No, it didn't. Perhaps there would be records in the
laird's house. Yan turned his horse and walked it over
to the longhouse. The others followed.

"Well, I guess it wasn't plague after all," Peyto said.

The door of the longhouse hung at a crazy angle, its upper hinge ripped loose and its wood splintered and broken. Several windows were shattered and household goods lay scattered on the porch that ran the length of the front. Scorch marks, bullet holes, and weapon scars marred the woodwork and carvings.

# 11

YAN DISMOUNTED AND TIED the reins of his horse to one of the rings on the post outside the manor house.

"Are you going in?" Peyto asked.

"Plague doesn't fire guns and swing swords."

"Outlaws do, and they have no compunction about cutting down strangers."

"Were they still round about, I think we'd have had notice. As you say, they have no compunction about cutting down strangers. We're hardly the sort of party that would be feared by outlaws bold enough to attack Laird Douganan's own house. Still, you can wait here if you like."

Yan walked up the stone steps, stood on the broad porch, and stared at the carved arch. A defaced heraldic shield was centered above the doorway, but the image was too abused to be comprehensible. Behind him he could hear Peyto's shuffling dismount and Iaf's lighter scuffle as the boy rushed to help the clerk. Yan busied himself examining the damage to the main door.

"The lock was forced," he said as they joined him.

"But the ward bar was not in place. I don't think they were expecting trouble."

"A revolt?" Peyto suggested. "Perhaps the uncommunicative Demisi led a rebellion, seeking permission to visit her family."

Yan gave Peyto a frown, hoping the clerk would understand that he didn't appreciate such an ill-conceived attempt at humor.

"Well, I suppose the reasons don't really matter," Peyto said. "Whatever happened here is past and done. We are but spectators upon the ruin."

"I would like to know what happened."

Peyto had more to say, but Yan had stopped listening. He stepped through the doorway. The chamber beyond it was a large public hall. Over the fireplace on the far wall was a great shield painted with a double-peaked black mountain. Between the peaks a sun was rising, or setting. Seeing the complete arms, Yan realized that they were the same as those over the doorway. The Douganan arms, he supposed.

The room showed many more obvious signs of damage than the exterior of the building; paintings on the wall had been slashed, the furniture overturned, and the carpet tramped with mud and stained with blood. A crumpled suit of old armor lay in one corner, the fractured remains of its supporting stand sticking through gaps like bones. Its helmet was missing. Despite the open door, the disarrayed room showed almost no signs of weathering. How long ago had this happened?

"Come on, boy," Peyto called.

"Nay, sir. I'll not go in."

Iaf's response caused Yan to look back. The boy pointed to the empty fitting just inside the door. The bracket should have held an iron globe, according to ancient custom. Superstition held that touching the globe upon entering a house would ward off evil spirits; the custom was universal in the parts of Scothandir Yan had seen.

Iaf continued to refuse to enter. "I'll not walk in a house with no globe. Surely 'tis the house of a man in league with demons."

Hardly likely. If the owner of this house had been in league with demons, he wouldn't have allowed it to be assaulted with such mundane methods.

"Stay outside with the horses, then, and keep a look-out. We'll take a quick look around in here and join you shortly," Yan told the boy.

"We?" Peyto looked irked, but he followed Yan anyway. Yan suspected that the clerk was as curious as he was, but reluctant to admit it.

The ground floor was composed of the main hall, a kitchen and pantry suite, and a few smaller public rooms. All showed signs of violation, but none so thoroughly as the big hall. Toward the back of the building they found a circular stone staircase leading upward. Yan started up.

"You'll walk into a wall in the dark," Peyto said.

The clerk's warning reminded Yan that his vision was better than the clerk's. Yan called magelight into his hand and held the ball of wan green light above his head to light the way for Peyto. Together they climbed to the first landing.

"There's another level above," Yan said.

"Onward? Or will you poke around here first?"

"Here first, I think."

The second floor held living quarters and an office with a small scriptorium. The rooms were in a similar state to those on the first floor, but the looting had been more systematic. Things that had once had value were smashed, cut, or stained beyond worth. The steading's account books had been dumped on the floor and torched. Curiously, the fire had remained contained to the books.

"Barbarians," the clerk said looking at the pile of books with an appalled expression.

Yan hefted one of the books nearest him. Ash, fresh and light, sifted down as he lifted the book. The feel of the book stirred something in Yan's mind. Setting his mind in the proper frame, he looked at the book with his arcane senses and found the lingering effects of a spell. He didn't recognize the exact nature of the spell, but he could tell it was centered around negating effects connected with fire and water. Some poking showed that the pile of books had not burned well; intact volumes lay within a shell of charred and burned ones. If the spell on the ledgers was this effective in preserving books, it was a spell Yan wanted to learn.

Looking at the pile, Peyto shook his head sadly. "Only barbarians would burn books."

"Maybe it was just the laird's debtors seeking to wipe out their debts."

"Barbaric."

"The ledgers would contain a roll of the valley's tenants, would they not?"

"Standard practice," Peyto confirmed.

"Then we may learn where Demisi lived or if anything happened to her before this. . . whatever happened here."

"Most likely she was killed in the violence, or fled it."

"This damage is recent. She has not been heard from in nearly a year. Perhaps she died in childbirth or in an accident before the violence. Larra would want to know."

"And if we find such a notation in the accounts, you'll be satisfied enough to leave?"

"Such a notation would help."

"You didn't say you'd be satisfied."

"You look through the accounts, I'll take a look upstairs."

Peyto's insistence on an answer followed Yan up the stairway, but he ignored it. He knew Peyto wouldn't like the answer. The situation in the valley intrigued Yan, especially the total absence of people. If whoever had attacked the manor house was from outside, why hadn't they stayed to loot their spoils completely? If they had left, why hadn't the survivors returned to the village? It was unlikely that there would be *no* survivors, no matter how well organized a raid was. And if there *were* no survivors, where were the bodies? Reivers would hardly take the time to see that their victims received proper funeral rites.

Moreover, Laird Douganan had a mage in his service. The spell on the account books was proof of that. But no magic had been used in the defense of the manor house; such spells would have left a residue that Yan would have detected more easily than he had sensed the spell on the books. Also, none of the rooms on the second floor seemed to have belonged to a mage. None of the rooms seemed to be the laird's, either, and the third story was much smaller than the rest of the structure, too small to have many rooms. Was the laird or his lady the mage? Yan was curious to see what the laird's chambers looked like.

He found his way blocked by a barricade of furniture on the landing. Careful to be quiet, Yan clambered over the barrier. He nearly lost his balance when he stepped on something as he climbed down. A pistol. He picked it up and sniffed at it; the scent of gunpowder was heavy on it. It might have been fired today, but in the close air of the landing, it might as easily have been a week ago. He laid the pistol down again.

A closed door was the only way off the landing, so Yan spent some time listening for sounds on the other

side, but he heard none. Surprisingly, the door opened
to his touch and he entered the chamber beyond.
Windows in all four walls showed him that the upper
story was a single large room, and the heraldic shield
over the bed told him that he had come to the laird's
chamber. Aside from missing furniture used in the barricade, nothing seemed out-of-place. No raiders had
been here.

That was curious. Successful raiders would surely
have come back to loot the chamber. If the defense was
successful, why was the barricade still in place and why
hadn't the laird or his successor returned?

The bed and a pair of wardrobes were the only furniture remaining in the room. The bed, still made up
and tidy, seemed to offer little of interest, so Yan looked
into the wardrobes, finding only a man's clothes. Laird
Douganan, it seems, was unmarried.

He did not appear to be a magician, for there were no
books, no herbs and powders, and no tools. Frustrated at
losing the trail to the wizard who had protected the
books, Yan tried viewing the chamber with his magical
senses. Everything looked as ordinary as it had with his
mundane senses, until he turned his scrutiny to the
wardrobes.

The piece on his left was blurry to his sight; a ghostly
image overlay it slightly. Yan studied the images, looking for discrepancies, and found a piece of carving that
was angled differently on one. He touched the carving,
tentatively trying to slide or twist it. With a click, the
carving snapped into place. A soft soughing began
somewhere behind the wardrobe and it began to rotate
toward him. He stepped back out of its way.

A dark cavity was revealed behind the wardrobe.
Yan understood now what he had seen: the ghost
image was a residue of the normal position of the
wardrobe. Whoever had used this secret door last had

not completely closed it, leaving it not quite exactly where it always stood.

Yan stepped into the small space behind the wardrobe, careful not to step into the dark well beyond the stone lip. He looked down, but even his magesight couldn't penetrate the darkness very far. Iron rungs studded the far wall every foot or so as far as he could see.

An escape passage.

A niche in the wall held a small coffer, unlocked, and a sword belt with rapier and dagger, Yan opened the coffer and looked inside. Inside were a set of leather clothes suitable for traveling, a pistol, a pouch with shot and a powder horn, a sack of coins of both Imperial and local Scothic mintage, another sack with waybread and jerky, a ceramic costrel of water, and an empty box of dark, polished wood. The inside of the box smelled of herbs and resins. Curious.

The coffer was clearly a stash of emergency supplies, but whoever had opened the coffer hadn't bothered with anything other than the contents of the wooden box. Whoever had used this passage must not have been thinking of escaping. Or if they had been escaping, they were not thinking of going far.

Very curious.

Yan reached out across the well and gripped the uppermost rung in the wall. Taking a deep breath, he started down. The ladder took him down until he judged he was below ground level. The termination point was in a cramped, low-ceilinged chamber. A passage lined with damp stone led north and he followed it. It ended as it had began, in a small chamber with a ladder well leading upward. He climbed.

He emerged in a small shack twenty yards from the back of the manor house. Studying the tower to locate the position of the escape well, Yan walked around to the front, where he startled Iaf.

"It's all right, Iaf. It's just me."

"You gave me a fright, sir."

"Have you seen anyone?"

"No one, sir."

"We haven't seen anyone either. Well, keep a good watch."

Yan went back into the manor house. Rejoining Peyto, he told him of the escape passage and the lack of disturbance upstairs.

Peyto pointed at one of the account rolls. "Your Demisi is in there, listed as wife to one Goremmic. Goremmic was on the rolls as one of the laird's kept men. The notation was an assignment for upkeep in the longhouse accounts."

"What date?

Peyto grimaced. "The entry was dated to the Month of the Plow, mid-spring. Unfortunately, that was the most recent roll I found."

"We'll have to take a look in the longhouse."

At the longhouse, they found more evidence of fighting and destruction. In many places they found bloodstains. Some of the dark patches of rusty discoloration were too broad to be from a simple wound. Yan was sure that people had died on those spots.

The most significant thing Yan found in a small garden at one end of the longhouse. Herbs and vegetables had been grown there, and ornamental flowers had been nurtured as well. A row of pots lay smashed upon the ground, dirt and wilted flowers spreading out in fans from the shattered remains of their containers. One spray was crushed into the dirt. Yan bent over it and saw the imprint of a boot. The flowers had already been wilted when whoever walked this way had trodden upon them. Clearly, whoever it was had passed by after the fighting.

That someone might still be around.

When he pointed out his find to Peyto, the clerk said, "You look at the brushstrokes and miss the painting. What happened here is long over and done with."

"It doesn't make sense. All the damage seems recent, unweathered."

"So the raid happened yesterday, or last week. What's the difference? It's over and there's no one here anymore."

"But don't you see? That's part of what doesn't make sense. There is no one here, but people died here. Look around you. Sniff the air. Where are the bodies?"

Peyto scowled. "The outlaws took their wounded. The survivors took theirs, then fled."

"And no one died? With all the blood we've seen?"

"So, the survivors took care of them, too, before they fled."

"I've seen no evidence of a pyre. Isn't that what the Scoths do with their dead? Burn them?" Switching to Scothic from the Empiric in which he and Peyto had been conversing, Yan addressed Iaf. "Your custom is to burn the dead, isn't it?"

"We are gods-fearing folk, sir. Of course we burn our dead. It is the right they deserve."

"Well, they don't burn bodies everywhere, boy," Peyto said. He switched back to Empiric to continue his argument with Yan. "Maybe the folk of this village are more sophisticated. Didn't Sednal say the lord here was allied with Jonnagal. Jonnagal is opposed to Koyle, and may therefore be allied to the more sensible Scothic faction and in contact with Imperials. Something certainly rubbed off on him; he kept civilized records. Maybe he and his folk bury their dead here, like civilized people."

It was Yan's turn to frown. "I saw no cemetery by the church."

"Neither did I, but I wasn't looking for one either."

"We can resolve that question by going to see."

As they approached the church, Yan heard something move in the shadow of the building. He squinted, trying to see, but whatever it was had stopped or was gone. Iaf stood at Yan's side but Peyto kept on, stopping halfway up the rise of the church's hillock.

"Here are your bodies," he said, pointing.

In a hollow on the far side of the church lay a small plot enclosed by a low wall of stones. Grave markers stood in ordered rows. Most were small, plain obelisks, no more than a foot high, but one stood nearly a yard and was carved roughly into the shape of a dragon. That one stone was much more weathered than the rest, but most of the markers looked old compared to the half dozen near the opening in the fence. Each of those pale stones marked a fresh mound of earth. The clods of grass laid upon the mounds still showed raw, ragged scars of dirt at the edges. New graves.

Something moved at the edge of the orchard behind the church. But before Yan could focus on it, it had vanished. He had the distinct impression that he had seen a person but, standing so near the graveyard, he could not help but wonder if he had nearly seen a ghost. What he had seen might have been living, a fugitive villager or a laggard attacker, but it might have been his imagination supplying what he wanted to see: evidence that the valley was not totally deserted.

He chose to say nothing to his companions.

Yan stood looking down at the graveyard, pondering all he had seen, trying to make sense of it. He'd spent so much time on the *what* of what had happened, he had given little thought to the *why*. They had no evidence to suggest a reason for the violence that had occurred here. A survivor could tell them, though.

He turned to find his companions sitting at the edge

of the path to the church. They regarded him patiently.

"Let's take a look at the orchard," he suggested.

"It's growing dark," Peyto said, stating the obvious.
"If you want to waste more time poking around, we can
do it tomorrow, when there's light. We all need some
rest, and these old bones are tired of making the stars
their roof." Peyto waved an arm back toward the main
part of the village. "Surely among all those empty
houses, there's one with an intact bed."

They walked back to the horses and gathered their
blankets and sacks. Iaf balked when Peyto started to
enter a house carrying his burden. The boy snatched at
his arm.

"No, sir."

"Let go of me, boy," Peyto demanded.

"You canna mean to sleep in the house."

"Why not? It's better than being exposed to another
cold mountain night."

"No, sir. You canna."

"And why not?"

"Ghosts," the boy stammered. "The spirits of the village folk, sir. Surely they lie uneasy, dying thus by violence and without proper services. They will haunt
their houses. You canna sleep in one of the houses."

"What about a public building, Iaf?" Yan asked. "No
one lives in such a building, surely no ghost would
haunt such a place."

Iaf looked doubtful. "I dunna know."

"Well. You know that I am a mage. Mages know
something of spirits. Will you take my word that a
public building would be safe?"

Iaf eyed him suspiciously. "Are you saying that you
deal with ghosts, sir?"

"No," Yan replied. "I'm saying that I know something of their ways. That's all. I'm suggesting we stay in
the church. Hostile spirits will not come there."

"Aye, that's a grand idea, sir."

They tromped back up the hill toward the church, Iaf in the lead and a grumbling Peyto trailing. As they got closer, something looked odd to Yan about the church building. He was nearly bowled over when Iaf jumped back from the steps as though from a poisonous serpent. Looking where the boy was staring, Yan could see a dark stain half-obscured by the church door.

"What is it?" Peyto asked.

"Blood on the church steps," Yan replied.

Peyto sighed. "I suppose the spirits of murdered priests would be angered even more by strangers staying in their church."

"Aye, sir, I think they would," Iaf said.

"Thank you, Peyto," Yan said. Whether there actually were murdered priests or not, they'd never get Iaf into the church now. There were no other public buildings in the village. Actually there was one structure that might not affright the boy. "What about the communal barn? I've never heard of animal ghosts."

"Neither have I, sir. Nor would I have thought of them. You are a wise one."

"The barn?" Peyto groaned. "I wanted to sleep in a bed tonight."

"You still can. Iaf and I will stay in the barn. You need not stay with us."

Peyto looked back toward the village. In the dusk creeping across the valley the cottages looked like pale skulls, their windows empty eye sockets and their doorways open mouths.

"Straw's not so bad a bed," the clerk said as he strode past Yan.

On the way to the barn they had to pass the orchard. Not wishing to alarm his companions, Yan peered furtively into its gloomy aisles, searching for a glimpse of whatever he had seen before, but nothing stirred. The trees were alone in their domain, whispering to each other in a rustle of leaves.

The barn showed none of the signs of violence evidenced by other structures in the steading. It stood alone and closed in the gathering dark. Like the rest of the steading, it was enshrouded in quiet. Given all they had seen, Yan was not surprised that there were no animal sounds. He tugged at the door and found it stuck.

"Come on, Iaf, give me a hand here."

Together they heaved against the door, freeing it. The door swung wide and they hurried along with it, trying to keep it from banging against the wall.

Peyto gasped.

Yan spun, letting the door escape his control in neglect of caution. The clerk stood transfixed, staring into the barn. Yan looked.

An immense, bulbous shape filled the open space within the barn. It was banded with crisscrossed stripes and a long slender shape bulged beneath the greater mass. At first, the strange shape made no sense to Yan. Then the greater part of the form resolved itself into a gasbag hung with netting and the slender bulge into a boat-shaped gondola.

It was an airship.

A great black rapenar was painted on the side of the balloon. The bird's claws gripped a double-bitted ax and its broad wings swept up and out of sight around the curve of the gasbag. The crested head and open, screaming beak were very familiar. This was a ship belonging to the empire, perhaps even the Imperial Air Service.

Such craft were rare within the empire; to find one here was astonishing. If this was the raiders' transportation, the Scoths had rightly feared the involvement of Imperials. Suddenly Koyle's suspicion of any and all Imperials did not seem so farfetched and paranoid.

The wicker and arwood gondola looked empty, but the shadows were deep and the shapes within the gondola strange. Yan entered the barn to get a better look. Peyto followed, but Iaf stood wide-eyed in the doorway.

Was this ship abandoned, too, like the village?

Had it been brought here by Imperials, or Scoths?

Who had hidden it here?

Where was the crew?

The answer leapt upon him as men sprang from hiding places. They grabbed for Yan and Peyto. Two of them took hold of him. While Yan struggled, Peyto went down, swinging his one arm ineffectually. Yan pulled free of one of his attackers and staggered back, still in the grip of the other. He kicked out as the first, a small figure shorter than himself, tried to close again and was gratified to catch his assailant in the belly, sending him down gasping for breath. The man grappling with Yan swung him around by the arm, disorienting him. Another pair of hands grabbed him, pinioning his arms behind his back. As he was twisted around, he saw that Iaf had escaped the ambushers' first rush.

"Run, Iaf!"

One of the men hit Yan in the stomach and the air went out of him. He doubled over. Someone hit him hard behind the ear, slamming him down into the dirt.

"The boy! Grab the boy!" The voice was a woman's.

Booted feet rushed past Yan's face. He heard the sounds of a struggle and Iaf's cries for help. Yan was held helpless by a harsh grip, his cheek ground into the dirt floor. Suddenly Iaf's protests were muffled. A few moments later, the men returned, the tallest carrying a bound Iaf under one brawny arm. Yan couldn't see Peyto but he had no doubt the clerk had been overpowered.

They had all been caught.

# 12

"WHO ARE YOU? What are you doing here?"

It was the same woman's voice that had ordered Iaf's capture. How could the owner of that voice be responsible for the violence to him and his friends? Yan shook his aching head, but it still felt overstuffed. A hand grabbed his hair roughly and held his head up.

"Answer the captain," a man ordered.

The captain stood in front of Yan. From her size and the smear of dirt on the front of her leather coat, he recognized her as the "man" he had kicked. Like her companions, she wore leather clothing in the style of Imperial fliers. A helmet covered the upper part of her face like a half mask, her eyes indistinct behind lenses of glass set into the mask. Seeing her at rest and in the lanternlight, he had no trouble recognizing the curves under the flying leathers. Her chin was strong for a woman's, but her lips, pursed in a frown, spoiled the attractiveness of her visible features. Were she to smile, though . . . Yan wondered if the rest of her features were attractive as well.

A tug on his hair reminded him of the inappropriateness of his musings. "I said answer, dog."

Yan was jerked to one side and tried to throw out an arm to stop himself from falling, but he was bound. Pain lanced through his scalp until the man holding his hair released his grip. Yan collapsed to the floor. The man bent over him, gripped handfuls of Yan's tunic, and roughly heaved him back to his knees.

"Here, what's this?" Yan's *claviarm* had emerged from underneath the tunic "Look at this, Captain."

"Give it here, Kim." The hand she held out was slender, encased in a glove. The imperiousness of the gesture reminded Yan of another gloved hand, but where that one had worn a lady's embroidered silk, this one wore a soldier's buff leather.

Kim lifted the thong from Yan's neck and offered the amulet to his officer. The captain took the *claviarm* and held it up, turning it this way and that so that the brass disk glittered in the lanternlight. Yan wondered what was going through her head.

"You'd better tell us who you are," she said.

Grabbing Yan's hair again, Kim forced him to face the captain. Yan grunted with the pain, but his captor didn't seem to be inclined to ease off. Yan could do little physically and, under these conditions, nothing magically. He didn't like being treated this way, so he decided on a little mental retaliation.

"Your Scothic is quite poor, Captain," he said in Empiric. "Since you are an Imperial soldier, you should speak this language. Or is your command of the Empiric tongue as poor as your manners and treatment of Imperial citizens."

She took a half step back. "How did you know we're Imperials? Magic?"

"I saw the Imperial rapenar on your balloon—"

"In the dark?"

"It *is* magic," someone said. Kim cursed, while another flier behind the captain made the Triadic sign.

"I don't need magic to tell you're not a native speaker of Scothic," Yan said. "I could just listen to your voice. You have a noticeable accent."

The captain frowned at him. "You said you're an Imperial citizen, yet you're dressed like a Scoth and we didn't find any papers on you. Doesn't do much for your claim of citizenship. Anyone can learn a language. How do you come to speak Empiric so well?"

"It is the first language of everyone born in Oxhecar."

"Oxhecar?" She tilted her head and gave him a glimpse of dark eyes behind the glass. "That's on Viperhom, isn't it?"

"Why are we playing these games? I think you know very well it's a member of the Iron League of Merom."

"You've a good grasp of geography, but mages are scholars, aren't they? Assuming that you're telling the truth about where you come from, you're a long way from home. Why are you here?"

Yan sighed. "I'm tired of these games, Captain."

"This is not a game, Master Magician; if magician you are. I find myself in what I have to consider hostile territory, and I must be concerned for the safety of my ship and my crew. Were our positions reversed, I think you'd be as inclined to distrust me as I am you."

"I think not, Captain."

"Oh, really?" she said, grinning slightly. "You won't even give your name. What sort of honest man conceals his name?"

"You haven't told me yours, either."

"I have the advantage of position here. I am your captor, not your host. Besides, I'm not in the habit of giving my name to strange magicians."

Yan could see that she was not going to yield. Unfortunately, she was right, after a fashion.

"I am Yan Tanafres, magician. And I'm not lying to you, Captain. I was born in a village outside of Talinfad and apprenticed to Gan Hebrim Tidoni, magician to the court of Dochay Komat Junivall of Talinfad. My certification was approved by Bishop Colym Danashev himself."

"Odd credentials for a man dressed like a peasant and wandering the wild mountains of Scothandir."

Hearing it put that way, Yan had to agree. He understood how foolish his protestations. He was a stranger to her. His being a magician didn't have any bearing on the credibility of his story. "I suppose it doesn't sound very believable."

The captain nodded. She held up the *claviarm*. "This vouches for only the barest part of your claim. If it's really yours."

"It's mine."

"Can you prove it?"

"If you give it back to me."

"Not just yet, I think." She tucked it into her belt. "Suppose you try answering a few more of my questions. What brings a magician to this little valley in the middle of nowhere?"

"A promise to a friend."

"What sort of promise?"

"Nothing harmful to Imperial interests." Yan canted his head back to ease the strain as the man behind him increased the pressure slightly. "Captain, we could converse more easily if your man let go of me and untied my hands."

"Don't trust him, Captain."

"Ease off a little, Kim. He's not going anywhere." She squatted down and took her helmet off, shaking her head to free the braid previously wound around her head to fall down her back. Her nose was a little large for classic beauty, but her dark eyes were as attractive as promised. Those eyes sparkled with a fierce determination, a promise that she was no fragile woman to be trifled with. Yan told her about the shipwreck and the care he had been given by Gormen and Larra, and finally about his quest to discover what had happened to Gormen's daughter. When he finished, she looked at him solemnly. "Why should I believe you?"

"Because I'm telling the truth."

"I only have your word for that." She looked at him sharply. "I wonder if your friends will give me the same story. Why don't you think about it while I go talk to them?"

The fliers kept their captives separated from each other, so Yan heard nothing of the captain's interrogations of the others. He was surprised when she returned, carrying a water-stained envelope in her hand. Peyto and a flier, another woman, walked a step behind the captain.

"I have little enough left me from our ill-fated journey aboard that doomed ship, Captain," Peyto was saying. "You've seen that the documents prove me to be who I say I am. You are obligated to return them to me."

"If they're yours and not taken from the real Peyto Lennuick."

The clerk halted in his tracks, an expression of outrage on his face.

"I am not a criminal," he sputtered. "And I find the implication insulting. Your extreme distrust of the locals is misplaced when applied to me. I am not a Scoth; you can tell that simply by looking at me. And I am not now nor have I ever been a Scothic agent."

"The boy's Scothic, and you have said he belongs to your party," the captain pointed out.

"He was our guide."

"I see you have gotten the same story from Master Lennuick, Captain," Yan said. "Are you satisfied enough to at least have me untied?"

"For the moment," she gestured to Kim. "Untie him."

Kim hesitated. "Captain, that ain't smart. He's a mage."

"I'm no threat to you, soldier," Yan said.

The captain stared Yan in the eyes. "Will you swear to that, Yan Tanafres, magician?"

"Of course."

"And what about your acquaintances? Is your word good for them as well? Will you stand their parole?"

"I will take responsibility for their good behavior."

"Very well, then. Untie him, Kim."

As the flier started to loosen Yan's bonds, Yan asked, "And will you return my *claviarm*?"

"I think I will retain some options, Master Tanafres."

"Captain, we are not your enemies. We came here to find out what happened to the relative of my friend. Admittedly, both the friend and the missing relative are Scothic, but I assure you that my mission is in no way political."

"We are loyal citizens," Peyto interjected. "We just want to return to the islands."

"After we've done what we came here to do," Yan added. "We haven't come here to interfere with what you're doing, Captain."

She looked up quickly. "And what might that be?"

"I don't know, Captain, but I had assumed that you would."

"So had I," she said so softly that no one other than Yan seemed to hear. She thrust Peyto's papers back at him. "Penit," she said aloud to the female flier, "Go get Rom and the boy."

• • •

"You don't have any food?" The captain looked at once surprised and annoyed.

"Some trail rations," Yan replied. "We had been expecting to eat in the village tonight."

The fliers had little better, but soon the best was combined in a pot of water and a small fire lit to heat the various dried trail foods into a more palatable stew. The aroma brought all of the residents of the barn into a circle around the pot.

"Since we're all sharing our meal, I believe introductions are overdue. I'm Teletha Schonnegon, air captain in the Imperial Air Service. This is Kim Kamertrel, my sergeant. These others are Rom, Penit, Danel, and Bert, my crew."

The dinner conversation was dominated by the fliers, arguing in friendly fashion over the proper rigging of the balloon and the best ways to trim her ballast. There were more than a few crude jokes about the latter. Iaf, unable to follow the conversation in Empiric, just looked baffled and a little worried. After he finished his meal, he dropped off to sleep. The conversation turned away from technical matters and soon faltered.

"Penit, take the first watch at the door," Teletha ordered. "Danel, you've got the next."

Danel immediately excused himself from the circle around the fire, stopping at the airship to grab a blanket before disappearing into the darkness of the outer reaches of the barn. Other fliers drifted away from the fire and soon snores could be heard coming from different parts of the barn. Only Yan and Peyto, with Iaf sleeping against the clerk's thigh, and Teletha and her sergeant remained.

Teletha seemed more relaxed now. Yan decided that she might be more talkative. "So what are you doing here, Captain?"

"Eating bread and dried fish stew." She held up her tin mug. "Drinking wine."

"Seriously, Captain."

"I don't like to be serious over my meals, Master Tanafres."

"Well, if we're not being serious, call me Yan."

She ducked her head in acknowledgment of the courtesy. "I don't know where an air captain ranks relative to a magician, but I doubt it's higher. Yet your clothes say you're not so well-to-do either, so sharing familiarities shouldn't be too out of place. Call me Teletha." She leaned over conspiratorially. "But not in front of the crew.

"As you rightly concluded from our ship's markings, we are part of the Imperial forces in Scothandir, wherever the rest of them are."

"You're lost?"

Teletha shrugged and gave him a chagrined smile. "We were caught in a storm and had to run before it. We went as high as we could to avoid the mountains, and fortunately didn't get blown into them. Once we'd escaped the winds, we started looking around."

"I thought the army used balloons for battlefield observation," Peyto said worriedly. "Have the Scoths risen again?"

"Balloons are useful for many tasks," Teletha said. A trifle defensively, Yan thought. "As to the Scoths rising, no. At least not last we'd heard. There's unrest, but that's normal enough for this Horesh-spurned backwater."

Yan thought about Laird Koyle's reaction to the presence of Imperials. Had he been hiding something? For that matter, were Teletha and her crew hiding something? They'd been nearly as mistrustful.

"So what were you doing, Teletha?" he asked.

"Reconnaissance. We'd been doing a scout for *Goltianna* activity."

Peyto frowned, puzzled. "*Goltianna*? Kin of the lords?"

"More or less," Teletha said. "They're a faction dedicated to home rule for the Scoths. They can be murderous bastards."

"Do you think they're active here?"

"Who knows? Best not to take chances. There's only six of us."

Yan raised an eyebrow.

"Well, maybe eight," she conceded. "And before you say anything about the boy, remember that he's Scothic. That's enough for some people to hang him if he looked at them crosswise. I may not be so ready to condemn, but I'm not ready to trust either. Boys his age have killed good soldiers.

"Anyway, what we were doing is moot. The storm did some damage to the balloon as well as blowing us to Einthof knows where. We were looking for a place to put down and make repairs when we passed over this valley. It looked deserted, so we brought her in. When we got down below the peaks, I started to see that there'd been trouble here. I decided to get the ship under cover before investigating further. Can't have any *Goltianna* sneaking up on us while we're working on the ship.

"We'd just gotten the ship into the barn when Bert spotted you three coming down from the village. Your horses made it clear that you weren't local, but there was no way to know if you were friendly or not. We set up a little reception."

"So it was your man at the church?" Yan asked.

"You saw someone at the church?"

"Yes. At least I thought I did."

"You didn't say anything to me," Peyto said.

"I wasn't sure I'd seen anyone. I'm still not."

"Well," Teletha said. "If you did see somebody, he wasn't one of mine. We were too busy bringing in the ship to spare a hand to scout around. Bert just happened to be looking the right way when you cleared the trees."

If it wasn't one of Teletha's crew, who was it? Or was it anyone at all? Had Yan really seen someone? "Perhaps it was a local, then? Someone who can tell us what happened here, if we can convince him to come out and talk to us."

"Or it might have been one of the *Goltianna*," Peyto suggested.

"If there was only one, we shouldn't have any trouble. But if it was a scout for a larger band . . ." She looked at Yan. "I think we'd best combine our resources. I need to know if what happened here has anything to do with the *Goltianna*, or if it's anything my superiors need to know about. You want to find this Demisi. Perhaps we can help each other out, work together. Catch two fish in a single cast, as it were."

# 13

"CAPTAIN, CAPTAIN!"

Yan looked up when he heard the flier call. Penit, his escort, looked up as well. Yan couldn't tell where the call had come from, but Penit was looking toward the manor house, or rather, past it. Teletha emerged from the cottage she was investigating and shouted back, "What is it, Bert?"

"Something you ought to see over here."

She set off at a run. Yan started after her, but not so quickly, much to the obvious disgust of his escort. Still, they reached the site before anyone other than the air captain.

Bert stood over a corpse lying facedown in the loam and striped with stark tree shadows by the morning light. The dead man wore tattered Scothic finery and worn boots. A well-weathered hat lay beside his head. A pot, some combs, a half dozen spoons, and an assortment of other small portable goods lay strewn about him as if displayed by a seller with no sense of order. From those goods, and the heads of tools emerging from a sundered backpack, it was obvious that he had

been a tinker and a peddler. The slit purse lying beside
him said that he had been robbed.

Peyto, Iaf, and their escort, Rom, rounded the far
corner of the manor house as Yan and Penit drew up at
Teletha's side. Iaf raced in ahead of his companions.
Rom gave a look at the clerk and ran ahead as well.
The last two fliers reached the group as Peyto finally
hobbled up. For a moment, no one said anything,
everyone simply looked at the pathetic shape sprawled
just inside the verge of the woods. Peyto, last to arrive,
was the first to speak.

"Is he?"

Bert nodded, confirming for the others what Yan
had seen at once.

"How long?" Teletha asked.

Bert shrugged. "Hard to say. Since yesterday,
maybe. There's dew on him but not under him, so it
was afore dawn. The scavengers haven't found him, so
he can't have been dead too long. Day at most."

Teletha turned to Yan. "Something you want to tell
me?"

"If you mean to ask whether we had something to
do with this man's death, the answer is no."

She stepped up to the body and, grabbing the dead
man's hair, lifted his face so that those gathered could
see it. "You've never seen him before?"

"Not to remember."

"None of you have ever seen him before?" She
repeated the question in Scothic for Iaf's benefit. The
boy trembled under the attention. "Recognize him?"

Iaf looked to Peyto and Yan. The clerk didn't notice;
he was staring at the dead man. Yan nodded encourag-
ingly. The boy wet his lips and said, "It's Anpiam."

"Where do you know him from, boy?" Teletha asked.

"He comes to our village every year, usually just
before midsummer. He sells things, fixes them, too."

"Won't be doing that anymore," Kim said.

Teletha stood with her arms folded, but her apparently casual stance was belied by the tension Yan saw in her limbs and neck. Her hand was very near the butt of the pistol stuck in her belt. Keeping her eyes on Yan, she said, "Iaf, did this Anpiam visit your village this year?"

"Yes, dame. He arrived about the same time as Uhaer."

"Uhaer?"

"Another traveling man, dame. They had arguments."

"I remember now," Yan volunteered. "The two peddlers argued over who had the right to sell in the village. This one left before Uhaer. Said he was headed for the mountains."

"Convenient memory, Master Magician," Teletha observed.

"Not convenient at all. I didn't have much interest in peddlers at the time, Captain. Having been reminded, I recall something I thought unimportant. Surely you have done so yourself at times."

The right corner of her mouth quirked up, but she didn't say anything. Her eyes left Yan and roved over the man, then out and across his scattered goods. Yan looked them over as well. So many items. Traveling men depleted their stock as they traveled along their yearly routes, yet this man had little less than Yan recalled him carrying when he left the village.

"When I see this man here, I have to wonder," he said. "Such men rarely stay in one place long, especially during the summer. We saw few villages and steadings on our trip here. With so little to delay him, he should have been long gone from this valley."

"Must have found reason to stay," Bert said, moving his hand in front of himself in a suggestive fashion. "Made the wrong choice. She's never worth it if she has a jealous husband."

"Jealous men don't usually bother to rob their victims," Teletha said.

"Besides," Yan said, "the man was still in possession of a considerable stock of goods. For a traveling man, that's more reason to go than stay."

"So why was he here yesterday?" Teletha continued her examination of the body. She looked at the gory wound in the man's belly and the lesser one on his throat. Standing up, she looked around the debris of the man's trade. "At least we know none of you did him in."

Relieved to be free of Teletha's suspicion, but curious, Yan asked, "How's that?"

"He was killed with a sword and none of you have one. You would have had no reason to ditch the weapon either, since you didn't know we were here." She stared at the corpse a while longer, then nodded. "Caught by surprise with the gut thrust, and his throat was slashed to finish him. He was dead when he was robbed."

"But who, Captain?" Kim asked.

Yan was more interested in how Teletha had reached her conclusions. If her conclusions were based on deductive reasoning, she was shrewder than he thought, more intelligent than Yan would have expected a soldier to be. Despite his medical knowledge, he couldn't have guessed the order of the man's injuries, but then he'd had little practical experience with injuries of violence involving swords. Teletha, obviously, had such experience. He was impressed by her mental prowess, but he found himself a little frightened by her as well. It seemed wrong to him that a woman should be so familiar with violent death.

"We haven't seen sign of anyone all morning," Bert said. "Who could have done it if it wasn't this bunch?"

"*Sprith*," Iaf said.

"What?" Teletha asked

"Ghosts," Yan explained. "The boy believes the spirits of the dead villagers may still haunt this place."

"Ghosts don't use good steel. And they don't need money. This was done by a breathing soul."

"I agree, Captain." Yan said. "Which means that there is still a murderous someone hiding around here somewhere."

"Could be," Kim said in a curious voice.

Yan looked at the sergeant. The man was making a strange gesture, holding his hand close to his chest while pointing repeatedly at his right shoulder. Teletha nodded slightly, as if acknowledging some sort of signal. Abruptly she switched the conversation away from the murderer's whereabouts and back to the peddler and his goods. Talking louder than before, she speculated—unreasonably Yan thought—on what could be determined by the spread of the deceased peddler's stock. Kim added his own even farther-fetched suppositions. Yan's estimate of Teletha's intelligence began to slip. Until he noticed that she and her sergeant were working their way in the direction to which Kim had surreptitiously pointed.

The two fliers made a pretense of following some trail made by the peddler. Their progress took them across the open space between the woods and the manor house in an erratic path that brought them gradually closer to the shadows cast by the building. Without warning, Teletha dashed for the side of the manor house, shouting for someone to halt. Kim was only a step behind her. The long-legged sergeant soon outdistanced his officer and disappeared behind the building.

The other fliers started running after their leaders, leaving Yan, Iaf, and Peyto unguarded for the first time since their capture at the barn. Was this a ruse to see if they'd take the opportunity and attempt escape? Or

were the fliers in pursuit of someone real, perhaps the
lurker Yan thought he had seen on the previous day?

Iaf by his side, Yan trotted across the open space to
a point where they could watch the chase. Peyto followed more leisurely than necessitated by his older
bones. He had not been happy with all the poking
around, and the sudden hunt clearly upset him further.

"Did you see who they hared off after?" he asked.

Yan shook his head.

Peyto frowned. "One of the boy's ghosts maybe?"

"Slippery enough to be one," Yan said.

The fliers raced back and forth among the cottages.
Occasionally they would circle one, guarding it while
Teletha and Kim burst into it. Such tactics yielded no
success. Most often the two leaders emerged empty-
handed, but once a darting figure burst forth from a
back door as they entered by the front, barely eluding
the flier stationed to cover the door. The hunt went on.

To Yan's vague surprise, none of the fliers had drawn
weapons.

"The air captain wants whoever it is alive," Peyto
said, when Yan made this observation. "She's not
dumb, and she knows soldiers. Too easy to slip once
the weapons are out."

The pursuit went on for nearly an hour. Yan never
caught more than a glimpse of the lithe figure who was
the object of the hunt, but it was enough to assure him
that the fliers chased no spirit. The quarry couldn't out-
distance the fliers in the open and kept to closed areas,
where small size and maneuverability were advantages.
The runner was smaller than Teletha, shorter even than
Iaf; possibly a young boy.

When the fliers seemed to have lost their quarry,
Yan trotted up to Teletha.

"Captain, I might be able to help."

Panting for air, she gave him an evaluating stare. "And all I need to is give you back your magic toy."

"That would be necessary, yes."

"Well, we're not having much luck." She dug the *claviarm* out of her pouch, but did not surrender it immediately. "No tricks, now. Other than whatever you're planning to catch our rabbit, of course."

"I have given my parole, Captain. Do you wish my help or not?"

"Honestly, Master Magician, I'd rather do without it; but we're fliers, not Imperial couriers or hunters. Running through cottars' yards dodging tools and leaping fences is not what we do best, and I'm getting quite tired of it. I'd rather spend my time chasing answers than rabbits." Tossing him the amulet, she said, "Take your charm and do what you can."

Yan felt a shock as his fingers touched the cool metal. He nearly dropped the *claviarm*, but his fingers closed on the thong just before it slipped past them. He thought he had been prepared for the expected snap of his *claviarm's* return, but what he felt had been sharper than any he'd previously experienced. Gingerly, he placed the amulet around his neck, but no further shock ensued. Instead, his head felt clearer than it had for days, his senses sharp. So sharp that he felt something he would rather not have felt.

Out beyond the trees, there was . . . something. It was not exactly a presence, but he had the sense of life within it. It was oppressive and charged the air around them like unto a coming thunderstorm. He turned toward what seemed to be the source of the feeling and abruptly could no longer sense it. It was as though a window had been closed and the breeze through it cut off. He remembered the black tower he had seen upon entering the valley and shivered. He was facing in that direction now.

"I didn't give you back your toy so you could day-dream," Teletha said sharply.

Yan shook himself. "No, you didn't."

The lurker might know something about the tower or what resided there. Yan resolved to add his questions to whatever ones the captain posed. But first, the lurker had to be caught. Whispering to Teletha, he said, "Captain, I suggest you gather your men in one place, somewhere where they can easily block the exits. This lurker seems curious, drawn to the activities of strangers here in the valley. If we appear interested in something, we should bring the lurker to us."

"If you're right, that would hardly be magic. But this lurker is skittish too, she'll not come into our grasp just to find out what we're talking about."

"No, that'll be . . . Wait, you said *she*."

"Did I?"

"Yes."

Teletha shrugged. "Didn't mean anything by it. Could be a he as well as a she, I suppose."

Perhaps that was true, but something seemed right about the captain's apparently unconscious supposition.

"So just what kind of a magic trick are you planning on, Master Tanafres?" she asked.

"I'm not exactly sure. It'll depend on where we select to lay the trap."

The trap site turned out to be in the hall of the long-house, a large enough area that the lurker might feel she—or he, Yan reminded himself without conviction—might feel she had enough room to run and enough cover to approach closely. The dead peddler was brought in and laid in one corner, and his goods piled near the center. Everyone gathered near the goods. As Yan had directed, Teletha began to lead a discussion about the peddler's origin, using the goods as evidence. At first, the talk was intermittent; no one seemed comfortable with the situation. Peyto, frowning and sullen, held himself aloof from the discussion, forcing Teletha to do the work of goading the fliers to join in. They gave only grunts to her statements or short replies to her questions until she started making up stories about the possible origins of one or another of the peddler's items. Gradually, the fliers grew more interested, finding it an amusing game to add their own lies to the collection Teletha had started. Theirs were usually more lewd.

Yan let the talk flow over him. It was more important that he tune his senses to the building around them. He reached out first to the floor beneath him where it pressed against his buttocks and legs, then to the floor as a whole, then to the room, and finally beyond it. His consciousness expanded to fill the building, enfolding and identifying the glows of life within it. He noted them all, from the small specks of mice scrabbling in the walls to the larger beacons of the people gathered in the room with him.

The longhouse, too, he came to know from the boards and tiles of its roof through its rough-timbered frame, down past the old, rotted floor of the upper story to the beaten earth of its lower floor. He felt the coarseness of the building's plaster walls, the color of the paintings enlivening some of them, and the humidity of the root cellar. His goal was to be so attuned to the longhouse that he could feel it as if it were clothing upon his skin. At length, he succeeded.

He knew the shifting of the talkers as a twitch, a stirring of hair in a breeze. Mice scrambled along in their secret passages like insects pattering across his skin. The owl nesting in the eaves was a comfortable, barely noticeable presence like a pouch at his belt. When a new life crept into the longhouse, he was aware of its coming.

This new life was human life, and young, and

female; Teletha's supposition had been right. It moved
stealthily, doing little to disturb the house. Yan kept
silent, allowing it to approach. He followed it, and
when it turned away from the main chamber, he resisted the impulse to alert his companions. The intruder
moved up the stair to the upper floor. Yan felt the
floorboards sag under the weight, light enough to
impress but too light to raise protest from the ancient
boards.

The intruder stopped, nearly overhead.

Yan waited, but she came no closer. He extended
his senses, focusing on the part of the house in contact
with the intruder. He found a hole in one of the boards
upon which she knelt. A hole in that particularly rotted
board made an excellent spying point from which to
survey, and listen to, the chamber below.

But the board was what Yan needed as well.

He reached into its essence as he had with the
reiver's saddle cinch on the day he had saved Laird
Koyle. He eased the magic into the heart of the wood,
wrapping it around the rotted wood fibers, molding it
to the shape of the decay. Spreading the energy, he
brought the rest of the board and all of its neighbors
to the same state. With a rush of energy, he increased
the decomposition, robbing the wood of all structural
integrity.

Dust sifted down on the talkers, but before they
could react, the ceiling gave way with a crack. The
lurker crashed through in a cloud of rotted wood, grit,
and paint chips to fall directly on Rom. The flier went
down, surprised and stunned. Though equally surprised, the intruder recovered more quickly and started
to scramble away, but Penit leaned over and grabbed a
slim ankle. The intruder started to yell, her thin wails
clear through the deeper shouts of the fliers. Kicking
furiously, the lurker dislodged Penit's tenuous grip;

then Teletha was there, grabbing and holding a pair of small, flailing arms. The intruder knew herself caught and the struggling diminished, although the shrieking protests of the captive did not.

The fliers stood back, expressions of surprise on their faces, confusion clear in their auras. They had captured the spy and in doing so revealed their lurker to be a terrified child, barely coherent in her pleas for mercy.

"Let her go," Yan ordered as he shook off the trance. "She won't run now." In Scothic, he said to the girl, "Quiet," and when she shut her mouth in shock, "No one's going to hurt you if you behave. You won't run, will you?"

He got the barest shake of a head for an answer.

"She agrees. Let her go."

The fliers looked to Teletha for confirmation of the order, which she gave by relinquishing her own grip. The girl huddled on the floor, loomed over by the fliers.

"What's your name, girl," Teletha asked in her rough Scothic.

The girl just began to cry.

"I think you and your crew are scaring her," Yan said.

"You may be right." She reached for the girl's hand. "Come on, girl. We'll go for a walk."

The girl shied away from Teletha and grabbed Yan around the waist, panic-stricken.

"I think you may be scaring her, too. Perhaps if I talk to her alone?"

"I don't think so." The stern look on Teletha's face told Yan that she would not budge.

"Shall we do it together, then? Away from the rest of your men. That might be enough to calm her down."

"There's a room over there," Teletha said.

"Come along, child. You'll be safe," Yan said as he enfolded her in his arms and lifted her up. He was surprised to find her compliant, nestling into his embrace. Would that Teletha's trust were so easy to win. Yan continued murmuring reassurances to the girl as they walked to the room the captain indicated, a smaller space, most likely private sleeping quarters for a privileged weaponman and his spouse. Yan wondered if it might have been Demisi's.

Yan nodded toward the bed; Teletha gave him a scowl, but she straightened the disturbed bedding. Yan settled the girl on the bed, drying her tears and offering assurances for her safety. "Enough crying now. You're safe with us."

When her sniffling subsided, he decided to start with finding out who she was. "My name's Yan. This lady is Teletha. What's your name, child?"

The girl was clearly still frightened, but she seemed confused as well. Her hesitant movements signaled an ambivalence in her attitude toward the strangers. Yan suspected that the kindness he had shown her was unexpected. Welcome, but unexpected. "We won't hurt you," he told her. "We want to be your friends."

It took more assurances, a lot more assurances, and a bit of food and watered wine, but finally, the girl said, "I'm Jhezi."

"A fine name. And you're a fine girl. You live here, don't you?"

She nodded.

"Where are your mommy and daddy?" Teletha asked.

Small eyes went wide and the tip of Jhezi's tongue poked out between her lips. She quivered, frightened again and ready to bolt.

"It's all right, Jhezi. You don't have to talk about them," Yan said.

"Think they're dead?" Teletha asked in Empiric.

Yan was pleased to note that she had taken Jhezi's feelings into account. "Could be."

"Ask her about the laird."

Yan nodded. "Jhezi, do you know what happened to Laird Douganan? We'd like to talk to him."

"Gone."

"Gone where?"

"Away. He was afraid."

"He ran away?" She nodded. "What was he afraid of, Jhezi?"

She looked up at Teletha, then back to Yan. "You're not with them, are you?"

He didn't know who she meant, but the fear in the girl's voice told him that denial was his best course. "No, we're not. Would we be nice to you if we were?"

Jhezi looked unsure. "They were nice at first. Sort of."

Yan smiled. "We're not like them, Jhezi. We want to help you."

Jhezi seemed to have a sudden thought. "I canna give you money," she said, eyes darting back and forth between them.

"That doesn't matter," Yan told her. "We still want to help you."

"Really?"

"Really."

That seemed to be the key. Jhezi's reluctance melted away and she started talking excitedly.

"The money soldiers came. They were going to beat up the laird. He was afraid 'cause he didna have his weaponmen. They were all gone away. The laird hid in his house and the money soldiers said they'd burn everything if the laird didna come out so they could beat him up. That's what Mamma said, but I think they really wanted to kill him."

"They probably did want to, Jhezi. Did the laird come out? Did they kill him?"

"No, he ran away, but that was later. First he stayed in his house. He sent Master Shammes to talk to the money soldiers. Master Shammes said the laird would give the soldiers money to not kill the laird. He said the laird would make them his money soldiers and give them more than anybody else."

"And did the money soldiers take the laird's money?" Teletha asked.

Jhezi hesitated for a moment, looking to Yan for reassurance, then nodded.

"Bought them off," Teletha said in Empiric.

"Did I say something bad?" Jhezi asked.

Yan shook his head. "No, Jhezi. You're doing fine. The lady just wanted to know what happened next."

"Oh. Everything was okay. For a while. The big money soldier wasna a nice man."

"Their leader?" After Jhezi's nod Yan had to prompt her. "Do you know his name?"

"Uh-huh."

Normally Yan would have been annoyed by having to drag the information out, but it was clear that the child needed special handling. "What was the man's name, Jhezi?"

"Arham."

"Are Arham and his men still in the valley?"

"I dunna know."

"What about the other money soldiers, Jhezi. Were they like Arham?"

"Mamma called them brigands. They didna treat people nice. Nobody liked them. Except maybe for Mister Avery. He was nice. But Arham killed Mister Avery when he tried to keep Arham from taking Carlyn behind the barn. Things got worse after that."

"What do you mean?"

"The money soldiers argued a lot."

"With whom?"

Jhezi shrugged. "With the laird. With themselves. Nobody argued with Arham, though. Nobody 'cept the laird. One night, they had a big argument up at the laird's house. There was a fight."

"Who had a fight, Jhezi?"

"Everybody."

Clearly frightened by memories of violence, Jhezi wouldn't talk much for a while, answering their questions with nods or shakes of her head or not at all. Finally, as though making a definitive declaration, she said, "The laird went and hid in his house and the money soldiers ran around a lot. Everybody went and hid, well almost everybody. But I wilna talk about that."

"You don't have to talk about that, Jhezi," Yan told her.

"What happened to the laird?" Teletha asked.

Jhezi looked at Teletha for a long time. "Are you like them?"

Yan answered for her. "Captain Teletha is a good soldier. She's not a money soldier. You can trust her."

"I'd rather talk to you," Jhezi said.

"I'm not leaving," Teletha said in Empiric.

Yan nodded to her, then smiled at Jhezi. "Then talk to me. Pretend she isn't there."

"She wilna go away?"

"She wants to help as much as I do. We both need to know what happened if we're to help. Will you tell me what happened to Laird Douganan?"

"All right. Arham started yelling that he was gonna burn the laird's house down, but that was stupid. Everybody knows you canna burn stone. Then after a while they shouted a lot and all ran off into the woods. Some of them came back and did bad things."

"You don't have to tell us about that," Yan said quickly. "Where did everybody go after the money soldiers went away?"

"You're a nice man, but Mamma said I wasn't supposed to tell."

"In the forest," Teletha said in Empiric.

"Most likely," Yan replied.

"Should've come back by now," Teletha observed.

"Maybe." Switching back to Scothic he said, "Jhezi, when did all this happen?"

"I dunno."

"Think hard, Jhezi. Yesterday? The day before that? A week ago?"

"Not a week."

"More?"

"No."

"Are the people going to come back when they're sure that the money soldiers are really gone?"

"Uh-huh."

"Are you going to tell them that the money soldiers are all gone?"

"I want to. That's why I came back. I wanted to see if they were all gone. I didna see them, but I saw you. I didna know what to do."

"So you watched?"

"Uh-huh. I hope the bad men are all gone now. I wanna go back home."

"You can go back home soon, Jhezi."

"Good," she said decisively. "I wanna go to the fair."

"What fair is that?"

"Midsummer fair, silly. Everybody knows that."

Midsummer? Yan swallowed, feeling more than a bit queasy. It was autumn. What was going on?

He forced a smile. "I'm sure there'll be a fair."

"I hope so," Jhezi said. "I like the fair.

# 14

NEAR DUSK, YAN LET JHEZI slip away from his custody. She scampered off into the woods, confirming Yan's suspicions that her family was out there somewhere—or if not her family, someone with whom she felt safe, in any case. There remained some questions that he wanted to ask of the girl, or, better still, of some adult villagers, but he had other concerns at the moment.

It would be dark soon; the sun was slipping down past the mountains. The stars would soon be out.

The group had retreated to the barn for their evening meal. No one really wanted to stay in the village. The others were inside waiting for the stew to be ready. They were all hungry; it had been a long day. But Yan wasn't hungry, at least not for food.

He watched the sky, impatient for the dark.

At last, it came.

He watched the stars grow from faint points of light to full jewels. With a growing, fearful conviction, he watched the constellations form. At last it was dark enough and enough of the zodiac filled the sky that he could no longer convince himself that he might be mistaken.

There was the Serpent, nigh unto zenith. The Gate
wheeled close by. The Dragon. The Sickle. The Sword.
A double dozen of lesser shapes. The Ghost Lord, his
own sign, would be low on the horizon, but it was hidden from him by the surrounding mountains. Hidden,
too, on the other horizon, was the Sun Lord, the constel-
lation representing the incarnation of Horesh. Had
Horesh forsaken this valley?

He didn't know.

He did know one thing, though: he sat beneath a
summer sky, not an autumn one.

Somehow, in this valley, time was not what it
should be.

His mind flashed back to an inn at Crampton-by-
Drivvaner Stream, to a room where a withered mage
lay dying on a bed. Was this the great change Adain
had spoken of? Was the world slowing to a standstill?

He was staring up at the sky, lost in the dazzling, terrible glory, when Teletha emerged from the barn. He
knew she was staring at him, but he didn't see any
reason to turn his stare from the stars. The Dragon's
nose touched one of the peaks and he knew that he and
Teletha had held their tableau for some time.

Perhaps it would be better to think of things less
vast.

"Come to chide me again for losing Jhezi?"

She shook her head slightly and Yan noticed that
her hair was unbraided. Her locks were full, flowing
out to either side of her face and blocking the stars
behind her head. Yan saw her face as a strange, but
welcome, oval moon in a dark sky blessedly free of
traitor celestial bodies. Her smile was tentative, but as
welcome as her face, and her presence. When she
spoke, it was softly, her voice lacking the snap she used
when addressing her crew.

"Once should be enough." She stepped closer and

sat by his side. "Actually, I agree with what you did. Jhezi may or may not have relatives hiding out there, but even if she's been on her own since the trouble here, she's done well enough. Better she not be in the company of soldiers."

"Not a good life for a girl?"

"Not every girl."

There was such a wistful note in Teletha's voice that Yan wanted to ask, what about this girl by my side? Instead he asked, "Is there something bothering you?"

She chuckled nervously. "Is it that obvious?"

"Most people who come out on a starry night look up at the sky."

"Never thought of myself as most people," she said. Yan noted that, also unlike most people, she didn't raise her eyes to follow his gesture toward the heavens. She stared fixedly at the ground and asked, "You think she was crazy?"

"Jhezi? No. She believed what she told us, there was no deception in her."

"You know that as a mage?"

"As a mage."

She pressed the heels of her hands against her temples, grinding them there. "By Einthof's ordered beads, I hate magic."

"Then you've guessed."

She nodded. "That's why I didn't want to look at the stars. But you've been looking. Are they where they should be?"

Yan wasn't sure how to answer that question. Teletha seemed suddenly vulnerable and he feared that a simple, blunt answer might be too much for her. But then, he didn't really have a simple, blunt answer. All he had was a complex problem. "That depends on *when* it is."

"Vehr's sword!" Teletha swore angrily.

Her sudden oath brought three of her fliers running. Kim led the charge of sword-armed fliers; the sergeant had his pistol in hand as well. The lack of opponents brought them to a ragged halt, and they looked around, confused. Yan thought that Kim's pistol was pointed suspiciously close to him. Teletha calmed them down, assuring them that nothing was wrong. She tried to send them back inside, but they refused to go and she didn't make an issue of their disobedience.

Yan and Teletha's private conversation was over, and if he wanted more information, he'd have to ask for it in front of the fliers. Ah, well. The knowledge was more important than their fears.

"Teletha, you said that a storm blew you away from your mission and brought you here. When was that?"

She had jumped at his voice, but her answer was steady. "Storm ran us for a day and a night. Like I told you, we got here yesterday, just before you did. If you had arrived before we did, you'd have seen us in the air."

"We didn't see you, so I'd have to agree that you arrived before we entered the valley." Yan took a deep breath. "But what day was it?"

"What day?" Teletha turned wide eyes on him. "Oh, no. It can't be worse than I thought."

"What day?" Yan repeated.

"Third day of the Sickle," she said quietly, and Yan felt a chill run down his spine.

"On third Sickle, I was still on the coast, in the village."

"I didn't think the coast was so close."

"You're deliberately misunderstanding. That was two weeks ago."

Over the frightened murmurs of her crew she said, "But we've only been here for a little over a day."

"I know it seems that way to you, and that is bad

enough, but I fear that this phenomenon of slow time isn't happening just here."

"What do you mean?"

"In the village we came from everything seemed normal, but when Jonnagal's reivers came, they came expecting to loot the harvest. But we'd hadn't harvested yet. Our summer was not yet over."

"You're exaggerating," Peyto said. He and the others had joined them. "Blowing things out of proportion. Jonnagal's men came from farther north. Harvest is sooner in the north. There's no need to call upon magic to explain the raid."

"They didn't come from that much farther north. Besides, don't you think they know the timing of the seasons? You're the one who told me Scoths make a fine art of raiding."

Peyto shrugged. "So they started early. So what?"

"So what, indeed. Like you, I thought nothing of it at the time. I thought they had just started early, too. Now I don't think so. Remember the trip here? We kept heading up into the mountains and away from the level of the sea. As in northern realms, cold seasons come sooner to higher regions than lower ones. Yet we barely saw signs of the change of seasons. You were worried about snow, because of the date, but we saw no snow other than that which lies upon the mountains throughout the year. The fine weather seemed a good omen then."

"What exactly are you saying?" Teletha asked.

"I'm not saying anything *exactly*. Nothing about this is exact and that's part of the frustration. But I can't escape the conclusion that whatever is happening, it is particularly strong in this valley."

"Was the peddler involved in this magic?" Teletha asked.

Rom started to say, "I'd heard blood sacrifice—"

Yan cut him off. "I don't think he's a part of it. He just got caught in it like we did."

Peyto's voice was calm and level, but Yan detected an edge to it, as though the clerk were holding in some wild emotion. "You say he was caught like we were. If caught is what we are. Are you suggesting that he arrived in the valley sooner than we did?"

Yan nodded. "Much sooner."

"But you don't have any evidence."

"But I do."

"Then spit it out, man," Kim said, a near-hysterical note in his voice.

"You're a sergeant and in the flying service, which means you know something about navigation, right?"

"Yeah."

"Well, Sergeant. Just look up. Your answer's there."

Kim craned his neck back and looked at the stars. The rest of the fliers and Iaf did as well. Peyto steadfastly refused, staring instead at Yan. By doing so the clerk told Yan that he had guessed as Teletha had and, like her, did not want his senses to confirm what his mind had determined.

"Horesh shine on us," Kim said, his voice made tiny by awe. "That's a summer sky."

"Captain, let's go," Rom pleaded.

"Aye, Captain," Penit agreed. "We can fly the ship as is, if we don't go far."

"How far are you going to go?" Yan asked.

"Far enough to get out of this damned valley," Penit shouted at him.

"But how far?" Kim's voice was panicky. "How far is enough to escape?"

"How far, magician?" Rom demanded. "Where will we be safe?"

"I don't know."

The fliers didn't like his answer any more than they

liked the magic that they had stumbled into. Yan couldn't blame them; he didn't like the answer, either.

Teletha rejected suggestions that they leave at once, citing the difficulties of nighttime air travel and the still-unfinished repairs necessary for the craft. "We're all going to get some sleep and talk about this in the morning," she said. "We've fallen into a place where time isn't passing like it is back home. In some ways it's just like going on a campaign. We've lost a little time. That's all. Everything will still be there when we get back. Things will be a little different when we get back, but we're used to that. Show some courage!"

The fliers grumbled, but eventually they all went back inside. Iaf went with them, apparently happier in the company of soldiers than with a mage. Peyto didn't leave with the rest.

"You're sure about this magical effect, Master Tanafres?" the clerk asked.

"I'm sure it exists. Beyond that . . ." Yan shrugged.

"I'd pray to Lord Einthof to bring some order to this chaos, but I suspect that my prayers would not reach him in a timely fashion. Is this why we were saved from the *baratani* and the sea, to be cast into a timeless void, an eternity of barbaric Scothandir?"

"This is hardly the eternal moment," Yan said.

"From whose point of view?"

From whose, indeed? "Time is not frozen here. We are not trapped like insects in amber. The stars move, no slower than we are used to, but, I suspect, slower than elsewhere. We live. We breathe. We just aren't doing anything as fast as we used to. Relative to the rest of the world, that is."

"Are we helpless, then?" Peyto asked.

"The Church tells us no one is helpless while he has the favor of the gods," Yan said.

Peyto frowned. "Resorting to Church preaching? I thought better of you."

"Would you prefer a more philosophical commentary?"

"Generally."

"Well, the philosopher Lym Noracles says that whether a successful man is created by the touch of the gods, or the touch of the gods is made apparent by a successful man, the work still has to be done."

"That sounds as if you have something in mind." Peyto said, his expression lightening. He sounded almost hopeful, as if he had some confidence in Yan.

Yan wished he felt that way himself.

"I wish I did. But I fear that this magic is growing. Worse, I fear that no one other than those of us here in the valley have any chance of doing anything about it."

"What can anyone do?" Peyto asked. "You said yourself that you don't know what's going on. You don't even know if anything is actually *wrong.*"

The image of the black tower hung behind Yan's eyes. "Maybe there's something in the valley that will tell us."

"You won't leave this place, then," Peyto said accusingly.

"I would like to know more before we leave."

Peyto shook his head, frowning again. "A dnove is a great, nasty beast. It is larger than a bear and has far sharper teeth. If you wish to study it, you must watch it from afar, for if you get too close it will smell you, come for you, and eat you. You will learn much about its stomach, but you will never tell anyone what you have learned."

"We are not dealing with a dnove here," Yan said.

"We were not dealing with a dnove when the *baratani* attacked *Mannar's Grace* either. But they were as overwhelming and unbeatable as this magic. You were smart enough to run away then."

Then, there had been no choice. "I don't think this is a problem that can be run away from."

Peyto harrumphed. "Maybe you'll be more sensible in the morning."

Yan stayed outside when the clerk went into the barn. He wanted to watch the stars some more, in the hope that they might reveal something in their course. He watched them wheel through the bowl of the sky, but they suggested nothing, revealed nothing.

Teletha returned and sat quietly by his side. The Dragon's head was gone behind the mountains when she whispered to him.

"How much time has passed outside?"

"I don't know."

"I had hoped you'd have figured it out."

"I haven't."

"We'll have been reported lost."

"Surely. The storm will likely be blamed." All of them were lost to those they had left behind. How long had it been since word of the loss of *Mannar's Grace* had reached Talinfad? Bleakly he added, "Lost like a ship at sea."

They stared at the stars together in silence for a while.

"This is real magic, isn't it?" Teletha asked.

"How could it be anything else?"

She nodded solemnly. "Can you stop it?"

Yan wanted to laugh at the foolishness of the question, but he knew she wouldn't understand why he was laughing. He didn't want her to think he was laughing at her. "I don't even know what's causing it. Maybe if I knew something about the spells involved." He did laugh, then, a short sharp bark to mock his own foolishness. "But who am I fooling? This is an incredibly powerful magical effect, a spell of incredible scope. I'm not the prophet Sazarn or the magus Arkyn, I'm just a novice at the Art. This effect is totally beyond my knowledge."

Teletha sighed. "That's not encouraging."

"No, I suppose it isn't."

"I feel so helpless."

"I know." He tentatively reached his arm around her and laid his hand on her shoulder. She was warm, and shivering slightly. Yan didn't think she shivered because of the cool air. She didn't flinch at his touch, so he drew her closer. She nestled against him.

"I hate magic," she said.

And magicians? He hoped not. "How can you hate an abstract thing? Magic is only a process"

"So it's not magic that I hate. I hate what it can do to a person."

Fearful that she would make it personal, he asked, "What do you mean?"

"With magic, there's not much a person can do. It's there, but you can't change it. I had a friend once. He was in a revetment, a good one. It was proof against the enemy cannon, we knew that well enough by then. You were safe behind it as long as you didn't stick your head out. They had snipers, you see. He was a smart lad, a good soldier. He knew better than to stick his head out, but he died all the same. You see, they had more than cannon and snipers; they had a mage, too. That bastard got my friend and there wasn't anything we could do. When the magic got him, we had to just stand there and watch him kick like a gigged frog until he . . . died."

Her voice trailed almost to inaudibility.

"One man using magic for bad purposes doesn't make all magic bad."

"We got the bastard later," she said as if he hadn't spoken.

She was shivering harder, so he held her tighter. At

least she didn't seem to equate him with the killer mage. Finally, she stopped shaking.

"You can't do anything useful against magic," she said.

"You couldn't have stopped a sniper, either," he said softly.

"Sniper's got a gun. You can have a gun, too. It's even. It's you against him, fighting the same battle, the same way. It's different with magic. You can't hold magic, or see it, or touch it. But it can get you. Like then. Like now."

He wanted to give her hope, comfort her. "A mage can do something about magic."

"You said you couldn't."

"I said I didn't know what was going on, and I can't do much when I don't understand what's going on." He took a breath. This was it. "But I'm afraid we're going to have to try."

She shoved herself upright, breaking his embrace. "What?"

"I think that this spell which affects the flow of time might be spreading."

"I don't understand," she said, frowning.

"Neither do I. Completely. But when you put everything together a picture begins to emerge.

"If he kept a normal route, the peddler should have arrived well before we did, and well after the mercenaries attacked Laird Douganan. According to Jhezi, that attack happened less than a week ago. The peddler certainly did arrive after the attack, but near enough in time to be caught by somebody and killed. I think he may have run into one or more of the mercenaries. You concluded that he hadn't been dead for more than a day, meaning he died shortly before you and your fliers arrived. So we have a man who should have arrived two months ago arriving no more than two days ago. It might be coincidence, he could have stopped off somewhere, but we still have Jhezi waiting for midsummer fair.

"This valley exists in a time two months, or there-abouts, behind the proper seasons. Agreed?"

Teletha looked despairingly at the sky. "By Einthof's ordered beads, I can see no other explanation."

"There is no doubt that time is strange within the valley, but there's more to this situation than that. The peddler should have arrived no more than a couple of weeks after leaving our village. He left over two months ago by the time there, but arrived here less than two days ago. You saw the damage to the village. It's fresh, which accords with Jhezi's estimate of less than a week since the mercenaries attacked the laird.

"Let's look at who got here when. You and your fliers seem to have gotten here before we did. That makes sense since, as you say, we would have seen the balloon otherwise. Because you saw no one in the village when you flew in, I conclude that the peddler was already dead and his murderer or murderers had moved on. We surprised you in the barn on the same day you arrived, but by matching the date you say you arrived to the date we knew it to be, we got here about two weeks later than you did."

Teletha was shivering again, and once again she let him embrace her. "Two months. Two weeks. Two days. Is time compacting here?"

"That seems an apt description."

They were quiet for a while, holding each other beneath the strange stars and staring at the damning evidence of the timespell twinkling above them. Teletha was the first to look away.

"Where can such a spell have come from?"

"I have a suspicion," Yan said.

Teletha elbowed him. "Tell."

"Laird Douganan had a magician."

She frowned. "How do you know that?"

"There was a preserving spell on some of the steading's accounts. Someone had to put it in place."

"A preserving spell?"

"Definitely."

Teletha looked to be considering what Yan had said. "Maybe that's what's going on. Could this mage have cast some kind of gigantic preserving spell on the valley?"

It was an angle Yan hadn't considered. "For all I know, he may have, although I can't understand how it might have been done. Such a feat would take an incredible ability to channel arcane energy."

"But it could be done?"

Could it? In theory. "Maybe. But I don't really think—"

"And spells don't last forever." There was an edge of excitement in Teletha's tone.

"Basically, that's correct. A mage creates a conduit for arcane energy when he casts a spell, and the spell can continue as long as that conduit remains to channel energy into it."

"Then somewhere, someone is keeping this spell going."

"That seems likely," Yan agreed.

"Vehr's sword," she whispered almost inaudibly. "It's the darkest of magics."

"No," Yan said, affronted. "I don't think it's a dark magic at all."

"How can you say that?"

"I think I'd feel it, if it were a dark magic. This slow time in the valley is such a powerful effect that I would certainly feel the taint." Even as he spoke he remembered the feeling he'd had when she returned his *claviarm* to him and wondered if he *had* felt just such a taint. He almost retracted his statement.

"I think the Church would disagree with you," Teletha said.

"The Church doesn't understand the true nature of magic," Yan said automatically.

"You don't have to understand death to know a dead body when you see one. Can you deny that this spell is wrong?"

"Well, I—"

"It is wrong. It has to be. And it's dark, too. Anything that disturbs the order of nature as this spell has done has got to be a dark magic."

"Let's not rush to a wrong conclusion. There are certainly unusual effects and there may even be a less than beneficent intent, perhaps even an evil one, but that does not necessarily mean that the spell itself is a dark magic."

"You're playing with words," she accused.

"I'm trying to point out a specialized sort of difference."

"I'm sorry," she said. And she seemed to be. Her hostility had vanished as rapidly as it had appeared. "You would be the one to know."

"I *am* the expert here, after all."

"Yes, I guess you are," she said with a tentative smile.

The burdens of their situation seemed to fall away in the light of her smile, a sun to warm away the chill of their cold, dark night of worry. They were alone, he and she. That he was a mage and she a soldier didn't seem important.

He reached out, sliding his hand along her hair and onto her cheek. He applied pressure to turn her face to him. Slowly her eyes lifted to his. He leaned in closer, feeling her breath on his lips.

And she slapped his hand away.

"Who's taking liberties ungranted?"

Rocked more by this latest mercurial shift in her

mood than by the blow, Yan sat back, hands dropping to his sides. Teletha heaved herself to her feet and stalked off to the tree line. There she sat down, hugging her knees and staring into the dark woods.

Bad timing, Yan thought.

# 15

YAN SPENT THE REST OF THE NIGHT awake, but put off until morning doing anything magical. Waiting wasn't strictly necessary, but he felt uneasy about performing any magical operations within the valley during the hours of darkness. Despite his assurances that whatever had affected time in the valley was not a dark magic, he really wasn't so sure. This situation was not as simple as seeing a walking corpse and knowing that the dark magic of necromancy was at work. How was he to tell if this magic was dark? He had never personally encountered dark magic, never had the slightest contact with it—unless it was dark magic that he had felt coiled around the black tower.

Every magical text he had read about the dark magic and everything he had heard priests of the Church say was based on the belief that the dark magic was fundamentally different from the magic practiced today. Dark magic was a corruption of the natural order, a blight on the universe. Its practitioners had no code of ethics such as Gan Tidoni taught. If the magic Yan had learned were not different from the dark

magic, the Church could not approve the practice of
magic. So it stood to reason that if the dark magic *was*
different, and since it was different, it would feel different.
But as to what it would feel *like*, who could say? A man
couldn't know the taste of an apple without ever biting
into one or drinking its juice.

Could he?

The essence he'd felt in the direction of the tower
had certainly been *different*, but it hadn't seemed evil.
Therefore, it couldn't be a thing of dark magic—or at
least he didn't think it could.

Or was he just not recognizing the taint of dark
magic for what it was?

Hours of pondering failed to settle the question. The
only conclusion Yan reached was the one he had started
with, and with which he remained uncomfortable. He'd
have to investigate the tower; he'd have to touch the
magic that surrounded the place if he were to have any
hope of understanding it.

When dawn began to gray the sky, he knew that the
time had come. He needed answers. He would need
something more compelling than unformed fears, if he
was going to convince the fliers to go with him to the
tower. He didn't know what help they'd be, but he certainly didn't want to go into the forest alone.

He walked around behind the barn and up the slight
slope to the edge of the woods. Several trails led
beneath the trees, where night still held sway. He chose
one at random, hoping he wouldn't have to go far
before finding a suitable place. He didn't. Beside a
small brook, he found a clearing in which a rocky outcrop poked from the forest floor.

It would do.

He sat cross-legged on the ground cover, placing the
outcrop between himself and the tower. Scratching out
protective sigils and shapes in the loam, he readied the

site. He had to rely on his memory of the proper forms, trusting that the circle he made had all the necessary sigils to protect him, and that the pentacle he drew to focus his energies had the symbols for the proper correspondences in each of its six points. If he had his books, he could confirm his memory, but as it was, he had to be satisfied with what he had done. He entered the circle, closing and locking it with the sign of the Ghost Lord. Seating himself, he took out his *claviarm* and began concentrating on it. Fear and worry raced around his mind, threatening his ability to enter trance state successfully, but slowly, oh so slowly, he managed to calm his nervous mind. He dropped into light trance, then, following the flow of the magic, he went deeper.

Bit by bit he built the construct he needed for his search. The outcrop before him would symbolize the black tower, its dark stone rising from the earth as the tower's mass protruded from the forest. Reaching into his memory, he laid his image of the tower over the stone, merging the two, until—for his purposes—they were one.

The link snapped to life as the outcrop became the tower.

Swirling arcane energy wound around the symbolic tower construct in slow, slow spirals. The scent of the magic was utterly strange to Yan, but somehow not frightening. In the simplified image of his construct the magic was only a weak reflection. The dim image was not completely clear; Yan hoped he was not misreading it, misidentifying a dark taint as nothing more than an unfamiliar framing of arcane energy.

To know more he had to go deeper, using his construct as a link to the real tower. He let his consciousness drift free from his mortal shell, leaving his body to the protections of the circle he had drawn. He reached out to the outcropping.

As his astral consciousness touched the symbolic tower, he perceived a winding serpent of power, alive with active magic. The serpent twisted and contorted as it writhed away deeper into the forest. Shards of skin, dull and waxy, flaked off the shape to reveal brighter scales beneath. Other scales dulled and turned opaque, masking the bright colors briefly, before peeling away like the others. The effect rippled down the length of the apparition, wave following wave of alternating dullness and brightness.

Yan felt his own perception dull and darken. Frightened, he almost pulled back; but his perception cleared and he saw more sharply than before. The serpent was coiled around the tower, but it also stretched away into the forest. That was as it should be. The image of the magic partook in part of the nature of the magic; thus the construct was linked to the real. Connections based on like imagery were more tenuous than many other magical similarities, but they were real. Newly confident, he paced along beside the serpent of power, following it deeper into the forest.

He felt the strength of the swirling energies, and knew them to be more powerful than anything he had ever touched, stronger than any construct Gan Tidoni had made and certainly stronger than anything of his own creation. From moment to moment it seemed to grow stronger still. He thought at first that the apparent strengthening might simply be due to his closer approach to the source, but the increase was too rapid, too great. The spell was truly gaining strength. He no longer had any doubt that the distortion of time was increasing, spreading.

The tendril of magic led him directly to the black tower.

But it wasn't the tower he had seen when he entered the valley. This tower stood taller. It was cleaner, and it looked new. But it was ancient. The magic swirled around it like a whirlpool, the tendrils of energy vanishing down into its darkness.

Beneath the astral tower he could see the mundane tower. It looked like he remembered it, confirming his suspicion that it was the magical effect's locus in the mundane world. Forcing away his fear, Yan approached the dark monolith. He tried to pass within, but found his way barred by protections.

Wards left by Douganan's mage? The source was unimportant at the moment. He did not have the strength to force his astral self through the barrier. Any attempt to enter the tower would have to be made physically.

He retreated.

"It's here," he said, staggering into the circle of his companions as they sat at their breakfast. "At the black tower."

"What's here? What tower?" "Where have you been?" What are you talking about?" they asked in a cacophony of voices. Yan let them babble at him while he helped himself to a bowl of what was left of the morning porridge. The stuff was almost cool and full of burned bits where the meal had stuck to the pot. Not very palatable. But he was weak from his exertion and needed the sustenance. Scraping the bowl clean, he tossed it into the pile with the others.

"The source of the spell," he said. "It's at the black tower."

"Then let's leave it behind," Kim suggested

"No," Yan said. "Running's not the answer. We've got to stop it. It's growing."

"You're sure of that?" Teletha asked.

Yan nodded.

"If it's growing, it's a problem that we'd best look into," she said.

"Captain!" several of her crew simultaneously shouted in protest.

"Belay it!" she shouted back. "You've all taken oaths of obedience to your superiors. Right now that's me, and I say we need to find out more about this, this condition. I don't like it any more than you do. But if this condition is getting worse, there'll be a lot more trouble later. Better we do what we can to stop it now." She turned to Yan. "So where's this tower?"

"In the forest."

"We didn't see any tower when we came in," Kim said. "Can't miss a tower."

"I didn't see one either." Peyto had a very sour look on his face. He might have looked less unhappy if Yan had stabbed him in the back. "Is this some kind of magical thing?"

"The tower is real enough. It has magical protections, not the least of which is some sort of spell to hide it from notice. But such things are relatively minor magics. We have a bigger problem here, and I can't do any more to figure out what's going on without seeing the tower up close."

"But you *will* be able to do something once you do?" Penit asked.

"Like break the spell?" Bert asked.

"Maybe," Yan said.

"Maybe's not good enough," Rom complained.

"It's all we're likely to get," Teletha said. "You want him to lie to you and tell you everything's going to be all right? He'll do what he can, just like we have to do."

Yan felt a growing unease as they traveled through the trees, as though they were being watched. The mercenaries might still be out here, slowed in time because they were nearer to the tower. He had no evidence beyond Jhezi's statement that they had gone into the forest, but he had no reason to doubt the girl's word. More likely, the mercenaries had simply moved on once they determined that they were unlikely to gain anything more from the steading. He tried to believe that, but he remembered the unlooted upper floors of the manor house. They wouldn't have left without sacking those rooms. They still had to be within the valley. He began checking every tree to see if a lurker hid behind it.

The others seemed unaffected by his nervousness, but only because they were already stretched taut, fearful of the shadowy environment in which they found themselves. Prayers for protection from magic, evil, and unnatural beings were muttered on a regular basis. Danel broke the forest's stillness by firing his pistol.

"There's something out there."

"A fox," Peyto said sourly. "I saw it too."

"A fox? A fox!" Teletha started in on Danel with a scathing dressing-down for breaking discipline. From the tenor of her words it was clear to Yan that she, too, was worried the mercenaries might be out among the trees. The shot might have alerted them to the presence of the small group. Teletha didn't mention the ghosts or supernatural creatures that the other fliers seemed to be expecting. When Teletha finished, and Danel reloaded his weapon, they continued.

"Vehr's sword, there really is a tower," Teletha said when they reached the clearing in which it sat.

Had she doubted him?

The tower made Yan uncomfortable, but it positively seemed to terrify most of his companions. They remained in a tight clump at the edge of the trees. Only Peyto and

Teletha seemed willing to look upon the tower for
more than a moment at a time.

"A wizard's tower," Kim said, making the Triadic
sign. "May Horesh shine on us."

"*Sprithandir*," Iaf whispered.

Only a home of spirits if those spirits had been
called by the wizard. If it was a wizard's tower.
Whatever it was, Yan had never seen its like, either in
design or construction.

The glossy black stones of the cylindrical tower
loomed over them, blocking most of the sky. Those
stones were not like any Yan had seen in the valley or
the surrounding mountains. There was no mortar visible
between them, barely any seam between the blocks to
be seen. No one could climb the wall without a ladder,
or a rope attached somehow to the summit.

There were few windows and those were narrow
horizontal slits, a darker blackness in the stone. The
upper edge was jagged, either unfinished or broken
away. There was not enough debris around the tower's
base to account for the missing pieces.

A pile of gray granite stones formed into a makeshift
set of stairs leading to what had to be the entrance, a
circular opening barely more than a yard in diameter.
A door had once sealed that opening but it was there
no longer, the only sign of its previous existence a
twisted hinge leaning drunkenly away from the opening's edge. A log, roughly cut and trimmed, lay abandoned by the side of the crude steps. One of the log's
ends had been sharpened, the point now blunted and
splintered.

"A ram," Teletha said. "The mercs forced the tower."

"How do you know it was the mercenaries?" Yan
asked.

"Just guessing. They supposedly chased the laird
into the forest and I haven't seen any better place for

someone to try to hold out against armed men. They
must have caught him here. Wonder what happened to
his magician, though?"

Yan was wondering that himself. As at the manor
house, no magic had been used in the defense against
the mercenaries. If this was a wizard's tower, why
hadn't the wizard defended it?

Although he could not sense any remaining energies
of combat magic, he could not help feeling the tingle of
the power swirling around the tower. The energies
were strong. But even standing outside the tower,
touching its wall, he could not tell anything more of the
spell's nature.

"I must go inside," he said.

"You sure that's wise?" Teletha asked.

"No."

"Well, it's certainly not wise for all of us to go."

"It's not wise for any of us," Peyto said.

As soon as it was obvious that they intended to go
inside, Iaf took a step back into the forest. He shook his
head vigorously and shouted, "*Sprithandir! Neight!
Neight! Ayon caith'taym Sprithandir!*"

"Shut him up," Kim demanded.

"What he babbling about?" Rom asked.

"He doesn't want to go in," Yan said

"Smart boy," Peyto said.

"We ain't leaving him alone behind us," Rom said.

Iaf was trembling with the vehemence of his refusal
to enter the structure. Yan sympathized.

"Iaf can stay out here," Teletha said. "Bert, you stay
with him."

"Aye, Captain." Bert looked relieved.

Leaving Bert and Iaf behind, the rest of them
mounted the rough stairs. The group paused at the
threshold. All was silent within. Everyone, Yan included,
seemed reluctant to enter.

The interior was shadowed, the only source of illumination the open doorway. The unknown lay within. Yan could feel the weight of the magic on him, and wondered what the others might sense. Could they feel the magic, too, or were they just being cautious, unsure of showing their uncertainty about entering unfamiliar territory?

Teletha ended the stalemate and stepped inside

Immediately beyond the opening was a broad open chamber nearly devoid of furnishings. The missing door lay on the floor just inside the doorway. To one side of the door stood a cabinet, its door open to reveal a store of torches and candles.

"We'll have light anyway," Teletha said. "Help yourself."

Yan's magesight freed him of the need for artificial light, but he was glad he wouldn't have to use magelight for his companions to see. He didn't want the burden of maintaining a spell, no matter how minor. This place would demand all of his attention.

Once several of the fliers had lit torches, the others could see what Yan had already seen. Broad archways opened to their left and right, each led to ramps. One went up, one led downward. The ramps were the only exits from the room.

"Which first?" Teletha asked.

"Why not both, it'll be faster," Kim suggested.

"I don't think we should separate," Peyto said.

Yan nodded. "I think you're right. Up, then. There can't be more than one or two floors above us." But below were an unknown number.

Kim's nervous glances at the left-hand arch suggested that the sergeant had reached Yan's conclusion on his own.

The ramp took them to a landing, which Yan judged was at the top of the current structure. An archway

closed with fitted and mortared stones of gray granite
suggested that the ramp had once gone higher when
the tower itself had been taller. Now, though, the only
exit from the landing was through a ironbound wooden
door roughly inset in the glossy stone of the tower. No
light showed through the cracks, but Yan caught the
scent of herbs and chemicals from beyond the door.
The smell reminded him of the simpler days of his
apprenticeship to Gan Tidoni.

They had found the mage's workshop.

He stepped in front of Teletha as she reached for the
door handle. Though he had no desire to be a hero, he
was best equipped to deal with the door if the mage
had sealed it with magic or set a spell trigger within it.

"There may be a protective spell," he said as he
caught her hand. "Let me open it."

For a moment, she seemed ready to object, but she
just nodded and stepped out of his way.

His caution proved unnecessary, for the door was
not infused with any kind of magic; nor was it sealed in
a mundane fashion. It opened easily when he lifted the
latch.

The room occupied the entire upper story of the
tower. It was a workroom, a study, and a storeroom all
at once. Benches held arcane apparatus and several sets
of tools, each appropriate to a different craft. There was
even a small forge set next to the fireplace. Bundles of
skins, piles of wood and metal, and casks were piled all
along the walls, save for a small area occupied by a
scribe's table. Projecting from the wall on either side of
the table were shelves heavy with books, leather tubes,
and piles of both parchment and paper.

"I don't think those are account books," Peyto said
softly as he ran his eyes across the shelves.

Yan and Peyto went straight to the shelves, leaving
the fliers to poke around the room. The piles of books

and documents were disordered; not an uncommon condition in a busy workroom, but the total disarray suggested to Yan that the owner's last tour through them had been hurried.

Yan selected one of the more ancient-looking tomes, laying it reverently on the table. Undoing the hasps, he swung open the heavy leather-bound cover. He was not surprised to find that it was written in the old tongue; many volumes of such antiquity were. By the sigils and the formulae, he knew at once that the volume before him was a book of magic. He couldn't suppress the thought that the old tongue had been current in the time of the dark mages.

He checked more of the books and found that most of them were in the old tongue. Many had glosses in more recent languages, including Scothic. Indeed, the only hand common to all the books had made its entries in Scothic. Laird Douganan's mage, most likely.

The short passages he read made it clear that there was much magical information in those volumes, much that he didn't understand at all. He was amazed that there could be so much that was new to him. This library was only slightly larger than Gan Tidoni's, but he recognized so few of the works. What if these were books of dark magic? Still, he was intrigued. So many books, so much knowledge. Was the spell that compressed time hidden in these pages? Even if it weren't, what other secrets might the books contain? There was so much that could be learned from them.

Several of the volumes were written in a strange, sinuous script that Yan had never seen before. The letters—or were they pictographs?—were exotic, and the parchment leaves of those books were more fragile than those bearing words in the old tongue. He remembered histories with allusions to an ancient race that had ruled Aelwyn before man made it his dominion. Could these

books be relics of that long-lost race? And if they were,
what wonders lay within their pages?

Teletha poked him, forcing his attention away from
the fascinating books.

"Whoever used that ram didn't make it up here,"
she said.

He agreed. "That would seem to be true, Captain.
We're fortunate. I think we may find what we want here."

"A good soldier doesn't leave his flank uncovered. *I*
think we'd best check downstairs before you get involved
here."

"Why don't you all go on and leave us here?" Peyto
suggested.

"Weren't you the one that wanted us all to stay
together?" Teletha shot back.

Yan spoke before Peyto could. "The captain's right.
We had best make sure the tower is clear."

They returned to the entry floor and found it as they
had left it. Teletha went to the doorway to check on
Bert and Iaf, waving to them while the rest of the party
assembled at the top of the ramp. When the captain
rejoined them, they headed down. The ramp's spi-
ral seemed to grow wider, suggesting that they were
headed for a chamber larger than the one they had left
behind. The changing arc made it difficult to estimate
distance, but Yan thought they had made at least two
complete revolutions before they reached a landing.
He reckoned that they were well below the surface of
the outside earth by that time.

An archway opened onto darkness. Directly opposite them, seemingly far away, a faint glow showed the
shape of another arch. Yan stood still, staring in
amazed incomprehension at the walls of the chamber.
The others passed by him and entered the chamber.
When the torches cast light on the walls, they stopped
and stared as well.

The glossy black stone of the tower was here hidden beneath a layer of plaster, smoothing the surfaces and rounding the edges where wall met floor. Sinuous glyphs, arcane symbols, and sigils of power and protection had been painted onto the walls. It seemed as though no part of the surface had been left unadorned. More of the sinuous glyphs had been incised into the plaster; they were only visible, even to Yan, when light played over the surface of the wall.

"This looks like the stuff in some of those books upstairs," Peyto said, tracing one of the carved symbols with a finger.

Yan thought so, too. He also thought he recognized the intent in the arrangement here. He walked to the center of the chamber to be sure. When he saw the scuffed chalk lines, the half-effaced sigils and pentacle, he knew.

"This is a ritual-working chamber," he announced.

"Dark magic?" Teletha asked for them all.

"Not a magic I know," Yan admitted.

"All right, be difficult. What kind of ritual?"

"I haven't the faintest idea."

"Wonderful."

Kim stood by the arch opposite the one through which they entered. "Captain, look here."

Beyond the arch was another ramp, slanting down into deep darkness, but the flickering light of Kim's torch glittered on something a dozen feet down that stretched across the width and height of the passageway. Teletha pushed past her sergeant, taking the torch from him as she did. Little more than a sword-length away from the obstruction, she stopped and raised the torch above her head.

"It reflects light like a mirror, but it seems more like ice. I can see some distance into it. What is it?"

Yan knew the construct's nature at a look. "It's a ward. A powerful one."

"Is it dangerous?"

"Possibly."

Peering into the ward, Teletha cocked her head. Holding the torch high, she stepped to one side, then the other. "I think I see something on the other side."

"What?"

"I'm not sure. I think it's a couple of men."

Yan joined her and peered into the barrier. Below them, almost out of sight because of the curve of the ramp, was another landing. On that landing stood two men, a spilled torch on the floor at their feet. The men were standing still, as if frozen in place. The two were lit strangely with a steady light as though the flame of the torch were held in mid-flicker.

"There are men down there," Yan confirmed.

"They're not moving," Teletha said softly. "The spell?"

"I think so."

The sword of one man was slanted down toward the floor and the tip of the other's blade almost touched it. They might have been an illustration in a fencing manual. Obviously, time beyond the ward was slower still—if not at a complete standstill.

Expecting to be blasted instantly, Yan laid his palm against the ward.

Nothing happened.

He pressed slightly and watched his hand sink into the glow. He didn't let it go more than a fraction of an inch, but it took all of his strength to pull his hand back. His palm tingled.

He was breathing hard, frightened by what he had done, but he had learned what he wanted to know. By the feel of the energies, he knew that the ward partook of the same energies that were suffusing the valley, compressing the time. It was connected to the spell. Furthermore, his touch revealed that the ward was permeable. Matter could pass through from the side on which they stood. But most importantly, his contact with the ward had told him that somewhere on the other side of the barrier lay the heart of the spell.

"We've got to go through," he said.

"You're crazy," Teletha told him.

She might be right. But what choice did they have? Dark magic or not, this spell was wrong. The nature of the world was being warped. Someone had to do something about it.

"Perhaps I am crazy. Is it crazy to want things to be the way they are supposed to be?" he asked.

"Most people wouldn't say so," she replied.

"This spell has changed the valley, and wrapped us into its magic as well. The spell grows stronger. Can you stand idly by and let this go on?"

"No," she said quietly. "But what can we do?"

"I'm not sure. But I am sure of one thing. The only way to understand this spell, to end it, is to find its heart; and *that* lies on the other side of the ward."

Teletha's eyes were bleak as she stared at the ward.

# 16

"TIME IS THE ISSUE," YAN BEGAN, addressing the others in the ritual chamber.

"Not very funny," Peyto said, interrupting.

"I didn't intend it to be. The more contact I have with this magic, the more concerned I grow. This spell is gathering strength. Soon it may be irreversible."

"How do you know that it's reversible now?" Teletha asked.

"I don't, but I have to believe that it is. I am sure, however, that it is incomplete, for it is still gathering power."

"Then the mage is still alive down there," Teletha said.

"That would seem likely."

"What about those two guys down there? They dead or something?" Penit asked.

"Something, rather than dead. I believe that time passes very slowly beyond the barrier, so slowly that we cannot see it. The torch down there does not flicker, the flames do not move."

"The first useful effect of this magic," Peyto mused.

"With such a constant light indoors, a scholar's life would be vastly improved."

"Steady like the sun," Teletha said.

"But it is not sunlight," Yan pointed out.

"True enough," Rom said. "Horesh has no part in this."

"Can Horesh have forsaken us?" Penit asked.

"Let's hope not," Peyto said.

"If light like the sun's can exist within the spell, then maybe it's not a dark magic," Teletha said.

"It's dark magic all right," Danel snarled. "Just look at the scribbling on these walls. Twisted and warped. The mark of evil is plain to see."

"Aye," Rom agreed. "It's demon work."

"I think we should just leave," Kim said.

Yan shook his head in frustration. "We can't just leave. The spell must be stopped."

"So go ahead and do it, magic man," Kim said.

"I need to reach the heart of the spell."

"Like I said, go ahead." Kim smiled coldly. "We'll watch."

"I *will* go alone if I have to," Yan said, hoping it wouldn't come to that. "One of the two men on the landing down there wore a badge that looked like Laird Douganan's arms. I think it very likely that the other one is a renegade mercenary. I also think it likely that they are still fighting—but so very slowly that we, on this side of the ward, cannot comprehend because we are moving in a different flow of time. If those two are indeed still fighting, the conflict between the laird and Arham may still be unconcluded down there. Were I to go alone, I might be killed before I could find the heart of the spell."

"Well, if they're still fighting down there, let them fight, I say," Kim declared. "Let them settle it."

"And how long will that take?" Yan asked him.

"Don't matter to me," the sergeant replied.

"It ought to. How long has your airship gone without reporting in?"

"Dunno." He shrugged. "Captain?"

Teletha didn't look at the wall. "Too long."

"It will be longer still if you turn your back on this. As time passes here, it is passing faster outside the valley."

"Time passes anyway, Master Tanafres," Teletha said.

"I meant that in a more dangerous sense, Captain. The spell is growing stronger. I fear that it is just plain growing. We spoke of the time compression effect and found that an awful enough concept. Consider what might come to pass if the range of the spell grows. You put not just yourselves at risk by ignoring this threat. What about the empire? You all swore an oath to defend the empire when you took the emperor's coin."

Teletha folded her arms across her chest. "This is magic."

"Yes, it is. Serious magic. Dangerous magic. Magic that might grow to be a threat to the whole empire."

"It might not," she said.

"Can you take that chance?"

"We only have your word that the spell is growing."

"That's not entirely true. You have seen the stars, and you are no fool. You know that this magic is more powerful than it was."

"I don't *know* that."

Neither did Yan, actually. He had his feelings and his suppositions, all unsupported, but he couldn't see any other conclusion. "But you fear it as much as I do."

Teletha stared into Yan's eyes, seemingly searching for something. Finally she looked away. Yan didn't know if she had found what she sought.

"All right," she said. "We'll go."

"Captain!" Kim shouted.

"Mutiny, Master Kamertrel?"

"No, Captain," he replied, but his tone made it clear that he was unhappy with her decision.

"All right, then," Yan said with relief. He started back for the ramp, only to have Teletha grab him by the arm.

"One moment, Master Tanafres. You may have led the decision-making, but I'll lead the expedition."

"I don't think that's wise, Captain. I'm best equipped to deal with the ward."

"You thought yourself best equipped to deal with the door upstairs, too, and that didn't need more than a hand on the handle. Here, we know there's magic, but I watched you touch it and survive, so it can't be all that bad; and if it is bad, better one of us soldiers find out. You're our only magician, we can't afford to risk you that way. If there's a problem in crossing the barrier, we need you alive and functional to deal with it."

"Then let one of your crew go first," he said, sudden fear for her safety taking surprising control of him.

She looked at him as if he were a snake. "I'll not ask any of my crew to do what I won't do."

He cringed at the contempt in her voice. Hoping to redeem himself in her eyes, he said, "I only meant to suggest that your command expertise might be as valuable as my magical knowledge, if the factions are still fighting on the other side."

"Kim's a good officer. You won't be losing much."

He didn't agree. He was worried about losing more than an air captain. His respect for Teletha's sharp mind had grown. She was more in command of herself than many men he had met, and he found that attractive. And she had courage to go with her intellect. Unfortunately so. He found her decision to risk herself unsettling, and he grew more disturbed when he real-

ized that there was something more to her decision
than a leader's concern for her crew.

"You *want* to go first, even without knowing what
will happen to you," he said.

She looked at him out of the corner of her eyes and
smiled. "Do I look crazy?"

There was a gleam, an eagerness, in her eyes, but
not the sort he could ascribe to insanity. For a heart-
beat, he thought that she might want to die rather than
face this strange problem of time, that she was being
suicidally reckless. The moment passed. Her stance
spoke of confidence, her attitude of conviction. She
might be afraid, but she was not one to lie down before
fear. But there was still that gleam in her eyes.

"It's the risk, isn't it?" he asked.

"I'm a soldier of the empire. As I recall, you yourself pointed out that investigating this mess is my job,"
she said. She brushed past him, effectively ending the
discussion.

He followed her down the ramp and the fliers crowded after him. Teletha stopped two steps before the barrier and looked at it contemplatively for a moment.
Taking her pistol in her left hand, she drew her sword
with her right, raising the blade to her lips.

"Vehr, guard a soldier," she said, and kissed it.

She stepped into the ward.

Yan felt the magic swell, a sensation similar to what
he had felt when he touched the ward; and though
secondhand, it made his skin tingle. The ward was
admitting her, engulfing her, and the energy flowed
past her like a breeze from a suddenly opened window on a winter night.

Then she was past the perimeter of the ward.

Yan watched, anxiously. Teletha's image was vaguely
distorted; he might have been watching her through a
window of cheap glass. At first she seemed to be moving

at almost normal speed, a wary soldier moving slowly and cautiously down the ramp. But gradually her movements became slower than caution might demand. With each step, she moved more slowly. Each step took longer and longer to complete. Less than a dozen steps past the barrier, she slowed to a stop, frozen into apparent immobility.

The fliers cursed by an assortment of martial gods and saints. Rom turned to run back up the ramp and blundered into Peyto. Rom struggled to get past the clerk. Before he could, Yan grabbed the flier by the shirtsleeve.

"Where do you think you're going?" he asked.

"Let me go!" Rom bellowed.

"So you can run? So you can desert your captain?"

"I ain't gonna die a statue," the man babbled.

"She's not dead," Yan told him. "But she could well die if you won't help her."

The flat of a sword touched Yan's wrist. He turned his head, letting his gaze travel along the blade and up into the eyes of the man holding the sword. Kim Kamertrel's face was locked in an expression of rigid calm as he said tonelessly, "Let him go, magician. No one can fight magic like this."

"We can try," Yan protested.

"Let him go," Kim repeated, turning the blade so that the edge rested against Yan's flesh.

Yan released his grip and Rom tumbled backward to sit down hard on the ramp. The man's face twitched as he stared venomously at Yan. But rather than pull a weapon, Rom picked himself up and ran up the incline, disappearing into the ritual chamber.

"There's nothing we can do here," Kim said.

The fliers nodded to each other. Kim sheathed his sword and started up the stairs. The other fliers filed up after him. Peyto looked at Yan with an expression that seemed to say, "What now?"

Yan wondered himself. How could they give up? Teletha was unharmed—at least Yan believed her to be. She had simply fallen under the sway of the more powerful magical environment on the other side of the barrier. Was the fliers' fear of magic so great? Teletha had placed her own safety behind that of her crew and this was how they repaid her loyalty.

Loyalty went two ways.

Yan took the last two steps and stood by the barrier, then turned to face the departing fliers.

"Go ahead, leave. You are, after all, brave Imperial soldiers. Much more courageous than ordinary citizens."

Kim looked over his shoulder contemptuously. "You don't know what you're talking about. You may be a mage, but you're still just a squall."

*Just a what?* "A squall?"

"An unblooded civilian," Peyto told him.

Yan didn't like the contempt the sergeant had put into the word, but he realized that he could use that contempt against the man. "I may be a squall, but I'm not such a coward as to abandon Captain Schonnegon."

Kamertrel halted, his back stiff, but he didn't turn around. Penit and Danel looked nervously at each other.

"What are you waiting for?" Yan called. "I'm sure you've got soldierly things to do. Leave the rescue of the captain to us squalls."

"What do you mean *us*," Peyto whispered. "You're always assuming that—"

"Shut up," Yan told him. Louder, he said, "If you fix the airship, you can run away faster. Nobody will know but us squalls. Well, nobody else but Captain Schonnegon."

Kim turned slowly. "If you weren't a mage . . . "

"What *I* am doesn't matter. We're talking about

what *you* are. What are you, Sergeant Kim Kamertrel? Are you a soldier? Are you a loyal man?"

"What you think don't matter, squall," Kim snapped.

"What about what Captain Schonnegon thinks?"

"She's gone."

"Only if you abandon her."

The sergeant's eyes narrowed and Yan wondered if he had pushed the man too far. There was one way to find out. "Are you going to abandon Captain Schonnegon?"

"Do you swear she's still alive in there?" Kim asked.

"I will call any god you name to witness that I believe so."

"By Horesh's all-seeing eye and by Vehr's sword of justice?"

"By Horesh's eye and Vehr's sword."

"And if we go through this magic wall, you can stop the spell?"

"I don't know that. But if we *don't* go through, there is no way to stop it."

Kim considered Yan's words for a moment, then drew a deep breath and let it out slowly. "Penit, Danel, I won't order you."

"I'm with you, Kim," Danel said.

"I don't like it, Kim," Penit said. "But I guess we ought to try and save the captain."

"That's it, then." Kim led the two fliers back down the ramp. "Let's get on with it, mage, before we all change our minds."

"You've made the right decision, Sergeant Kamertrel."

"Stuff it, squall." Kim drew his pistol. "You're so anxious, you go first."

It was no less than Yan had expected. He gave the fliers what he hoped was a confident smile and faced the barrier. Calming his mind, he tried to attune his senses to the magic of the ward. Passing through it might give him some information about the spell.

He stepped forward.

Time flowed around him, shifting as he crossed the boundary of the ward and filling his ears with a rushing sound. There was a flare of light from no source at all, and then his vision darkened until his eyes were full of swirling stars, as if all the nights that the valley had missed were compressed within the ward, unleashed at last to fill his head. He felt light-headed, vertiginous. He thought he might fall and tumble all the way down, falling forever, although forever still and motionless to those who were behind him.

Then the pressure eased and he was through the worst of it.

The light took on a more normal cast, then flickered, once, then again like a slow blink. A few yards below him, Teletha began to move, slowly continuing her progress. Intent on the tableau on the landing below, she seemed unaware that he was following her.

But the tableau was no longer a tableau. The frozen men were moving, but even more slowly than Teletha. The one with his sword pointed toward the floor, the laird's man, shifted his blade over, continuing in his block. The blades touched as the mercenary's sword slid forward. Sound grated on Yan's ears, at first slow and dull, then faster and sharper, rising in pitch as the action below sped up.

The mercenary's sword tip was past the weapon-man's blade, slithering forward and reaching for his guts. The parry was too slow, and the blade slid home under the weaponman's ribs. He gasped as the steel entered his body. Tugging his sword free, the merce-nary recovered from his lunge and returned to guard.

His caution was unnecessary, for his thrust had won the fight. The weaponman's sword fell from his hand as he clutched his side. He whimpered as he twisted slowly to the floor. As the man went down, the mercenary stepped forward and slashed his blade across the man's throat.

For a moment, Yan saw the dead peddler's body superimposed upon that of the dying weaponman.

For the first time, the mercenary seemed to notice that there was someone on the ramp. He looked up, eyes widening in surprise. His gaze swept past Yan and he took a step back, mouth flapping open. He stood still for only a moment before turning and pelting away.

Teletha started after him.

"Teletha, wait!" Yan called. The others would be slow to pass through the barrier, if they came at all. More than before, it was imperative that they stay together. Who could know what strangeness to time there might be here within the ward?

"He'll get away," she said, continuing down the ramp.

"Where can he go?"

Teletha looked back over her shoulder, frowning, but to Yan's relief she stopped. She waited for him, and when he stood by her side, she asked, "Where's Rom?"

Yan didn't want to tell.

"Run off," Peyto said. "Seems he doesn't have the courage of a squall."

Teletha frowned. "What happened?"

"It took a few minutes to gather the courage necessary to come through," Yan told her.

"I'll hear the whole story some other time," she said. "Just the six of us, then?"

"Six lost souls," Kim said from above them. He was standing by the barrier. Raising his fist, the sergeant slammed it against the ward. At the spot where his fist struck the barrier, the ward pulsed with opaque light. The ward tolled like a bell, ringing out Yan's fears.

"We can't get back," Kim wailed. "You've doomed us, magician!"

Eyes narrowed in suspicion, Teletha turned to Yan. "A one-way trip?"

"That is the nature of time," Yan said.

"You knew," she accused.

"I guessed."

"Then we're committed to finding the heart of the spell if we're ever to see daylight again."

"Seems that way."

"You'd best be able to hold up your end, magician. I don't like the idea of wandering down here until Horesh decides to take the world into His bosom again."

# 17

THE RAMPWAY OPENED ON a chamber with six squat arches spaced around the perimeter. There were no furnishings, but neither were the walls covered with painted and incised plaster like the chamber above. Here the glossy black stone lay bare. The floor, though made of the same material, was not glossy, but scuffed and gouged; it must have seen much traffic in ancient times.

Yan, Peyto, and the fliers left the stairs and spread out across the floor. Teletha sent one of her men to watch the arch through which she had seen the mercenary killer flee.

"What now?" Teletha asked.

"Follow the killer?" Peyto suggested as he wandered toward one of the arches. Not the one the killer had used.

"He was a swordsman, not a mage. We're here to find the source of the spell," Yan said.

"Bet the scut is heading back to the rest of his band," Penit said.

"Could be," Kim agreed. "Any idea how many of them there are?"

"More than us, I'd guess," Teletha said. "We can't afford to split up."

"I don't think we should anyway," Yan said.

"And what's *your* reason?" Teletha asked.

"We're within the ward now, and we don't know how time flows in here. Someone separated from the group may find himself separated in time as well."

"Wonderful." Teletha looked worried. "At least we agree on something: we stay together. But if that merc is headed back to his chums, we may be in for trouble."

"He's got a lead on us, but from what the magician says, that may not matter," Kim said.

"Or it may. We can't know."

"The spell's heart is our objective here," Yan pointed out.

Teletha countered, "One we'll never reach if we get ourselves ambushed by the mercs."

Yan frowned in frustration. Fear of ambush was why he wanted the fliers to accompany him in the first place. Why did she have to use that to make her point, especially when she was usurping his place as leader. Here within the ward, he was the expert. "We don't even know they're down here."

"I think that killer's good enough evidence," Teletha said evenly. "More solid than some of what you're feeding us about this spell business. We trusted your instincts in coming down here. Trust me a little in taking care of us while we're here."

"All right."

"Cheer up, Master Tanafres. Maybe the mercs have already found the heart of the spell for you. That swordsman may lead us right to it."

Teletha called the group together and led them through the arch taken by the fleeing man. They found themselves in a long, rectangular chamber, almost a corridor. Its far end was beyond the range of their torches until they had advanced a few yards.

"Except for the door on the far end, it looks like the other two I checked," Peyto announced.

"You went into some of the other rooms?" Yan asked.

"I had to do something while you all were arguing about which way to go."

"You might have—"

"I didn't." Peyto smiled smugly. "So, is my being here evidence against your theory of different time in this place, or was it just luck that I didn't walk into one of the rooms and come out a hundred years later?"

"I hope it's evidence against such a theory," Teletha said.

"Even if that means the killer has a good lead on us, and will tell his comrades that we are here?" Peyto asked.

"Even so."

The killer was obviously no longer in the chamber, and the half-open door at the far end was the only means of egress. The door, like the one to the work-shop, had been added after the construction of the black stone walls, presumably by later occupants. The door led to a huge gallery excavated from living rock, not the black stone.

The gallery stretched away into darkness both ahead of them and above their heads. Columns of unexcavated stone made the pillars of a colonnade that ran in a row on either side of the gallery. The outer walls of the chamber stood almost a double handful of feet beyond the rows of pillars. Spaced at regular intervals along the walls were dark, arched openings. Yan tried to see into the openings but, even with his magesight, he couldn't see anything from where he stood by the doorway.

"The scut might have gone straight on, or he might have gone through any one of those doorways," Teletha whispered to him.

"We'd better investigate. We shouldn't leave him behind us."

"You're learning."

The first archway led to a small chamber, hewn from the rock. Here the stone had been cut more carefully and brought to a finer finish than in the gallery. The walls, floor, and low ceiling had been smoothed, then plastered over, and the plaster painted with scenes of martial strife. In the center of the chamber stood a stone sarcophagus. The lid was carved in the likeness of a man in full armor of an archaic style. The effigy held a spear and bore a shield incised with the Douganan arms.

Teletha looked down at the shield, then at Yan. "The ancestral crypt?"

He thought it likely and said so. The next dozen alcoves were sarcophagi chambers as well, and Yan felt that Teletha's hypothesis was well confirmed. Near the end of the gallery they found a larger chamber that was clearly a mortuary. Long, narrow niches were cut into the walls, and the resulting shelves were covered with piles of old bones. Skulls stared at them, grinning with the humor only appreciated by the dead. They had to be careful not to tread on the bones scattered on the floor.

Beyond the mortuary lay a last burial chamber, only half the size of the others and unfinished. The workface that made up the far wall had a ragged opening in it roughly the size of a doorway. The long-gone workers had broken into another space. Even before they entered, Yan could seen the now-familiar glint of the glossy black stone.

Teletha had Kim hold his torch closer to the opening. She spent some time scrutinizing the other side before squeezing through the opening. Yan and Kim followed, but the three of them almost filled the small room. They had to move on to the next chamber before the others could follow.

The area beyond the workface was linked by the black stone to the tower, but its construction was different. Repetitive geometric patterns ran in decorative strips along the tops and bottoms of the walls. The archways were less squat, and some of them had doors of dark, thick wood. Most likely, this place was built by the same culture as had built the tower, but its purpose seemed different. The difference between a castle and a manor? Or a prison and town? Without knowing more about those who had done the building, Yan could only guess.

For what seemed to be the better part of an hour, they wandered a warren of rooms, chambers, corridors, and halls. Some of the doors wouldn't open, although Yan could detect no magic holding them closed. Other chambers had windows, not slits like the tower, but actual windows. Or they would have been had they looked out on something other than stone and dirt. Such rooms seemed buried.

The fliers grew more jittery the longer the explorations went on. Yan did, too. The killer, and his comrades, could be anywhere down here, waiting around the next corner or hiding in the next chamber. But the tension of possible ambush was only a part of the group's anxiety. The air was close and still, and the only noise they heard was what they made themselves. Even more than the darkness beyond the torchlight, each of those windows on the earth was a reminder that they were under the ground, trapped by a barrier they could not cross. In effect, buried alive.

And Yan had led them here.

Were they never to find their way out?

Yan was very conscious of the sidelong glances the fliers gave him when they thought he wasn't aware. There was venom in those stares. Accusation. Reproach. What did they want of him? He was as trapped as they.

And no closer to finding what he sought.

He considered trying a trance to locate the spell but
was afraid that using magic might rouse the fears of one
of the fliers to a dangerous level. In trance, he'd be
helpless; he didn't want to leave his body to the tender
mercies of fear-crazed persons who thought him the
author of their problems. Peyto understood that Yan
was doing all he could, but the clerk wouldn't be able
to stop an armed soldier. Teletha would almost certainly
defend him, but here in the uncertain and threatening
darkness, her control over her crew was eroding. Would
she put her life on the line to save him? He wasn't ready
to find out.

They continued their wandering. At length they
found a broad sloping space that ended in a natural
rock wall. A portico of carved black columns surrounded an opening in the rock face. The carving on the
stone was the sinuous writing they had seen in the
books and in the ritual chamber.

"Is this it?" Peyto asked.

Could it be? Yan didn't sense any magic. "I don't
think so."

"We'd better take a look," Teletha said.

The opening led to a narrow and twisting cave. After
ten yards or so it broadened into a natural cavern.
Rock spikes thick as a man's arm hung from the ceiling
and jutted up from the floor, occasionally meeting to
form pillars. The torchlight, flickering now in a slight
breeze, reflected in shards of light from small pools of
water. The floor was uneven and the group began to
spread out. There seemed to be no clear path and too
many ways the killer—had he come this way—might
have gone.

Yan was lagging behind the group, mulling over the
situation, when from up ahead Danel whispered, "I
think I hear something."

At least he didn't shoot at it this time.

"Where?" Teletha motioned everyone to stop. "What is it?"

"People, maybe. Off that way."

"Pull the torches back here," Teletha ordered.

"There it is again. That way."

Yan could see Danel pointing. He tapped Teletha on the shoulder and directed her attention in the direction the flier was indicating.

The light, steadier than a torch but not as steady as magelight, grew stronger. The walls of the cavern began to sparkle as light caught and reflected from bits of mineral in the stone.

"Snuff the torches," Teletha ordered.

To Yan's surprise, her fliers obeyed, surrendering themselves to the darkness. With their own light gone, the only illumination was that which approached, but that approaching light, faint though it was, allowed the watchers to see what it shone upon.

Teletha squinted through the gloom. "They're armed, whoever they are. Douganan's men or the mercs?"

"We could ask," Yan said.

"I don't want to go looking for trouble," she said.

"You may not have to go. They're coming closer."

"Still, they may not have seen us yet."

The casual manner of the approaching group suggested that they remained unaware of the fliers' presence. Yan watched as the others emerged one by one from behind a wide column of stone. There were ten of them, nine men and a bregil. By their equipment, he judged them to be soldiers, and by the mismatched nature of that equipment, he concluded that they were the mercenaries. There were a half dozen lanterns among them. The man who had killed the weaponman held one of them. The tall man near the front carried himself like a leader; he would be Arham.

"The mercenaries," he whispered.

"If they see us, get the lanterns first," Teletha whispered to Kim. "If we get them all, back off. I'd rather not push a fight against long odds."

The sergeant nodded, then slipped away to tell the others. Teletha drew her pistol, checking the wheel lock to ensure it was wound and ready.

"Arham," the bregil barked. "There's someone here."

The bregil was looking directly at the rocky outcropping behind which Yan and Teletha sheltered. They had been discovered.

"Now!" Teletha shouted, rising and firing.

The other fliers discharged their weapons in a ragged volley. The reports of the pistols were ear-shatteringly loud in the cavern, echoing like a hundred peals of thunder. Three of the lantern carriers dropped, their lanterns hitting the ground and going out. But three remained to provide enough light to fight by.

Before the echoes died away, the fliers attacked. The startled mercenaries shouted and began unsheathing their weapons. They faced every which way, clearly unsure of the direction of attack.

"Keep the lanterns safe," Arham called. He grabbed one of the bearers and tugged him closer, scanning the darkness around him. "Don't fight unless you have to. There can't be more than half a dozen of them."

Danel lunged from behind a rock pillar, nearly skewering one of the lantern holders. Grinning evilly, the bregil put himself between Danel and the man. The bregil put his back to the light, holding sword and dagger before him; another blade, gripped by his tail, winked in the lanternlight as he swished it around near the floor. The flier went into guard, sword well out in front of him as he squinted at the shifting shadow that was the bregil. For his part, the bregil seemed to have no difficulty seeing Danel. He struck at the flier, slipping past his guard and cutting him along the thigh. Penit came to Danel's aid, but the bregil continued pressing, holding both fliers on the defensive.

Teletha engaged Arham and their swords sparked in the gloom. Kim traded cuts and thrusts with another of the brigands. He was soon sorely beset as the last mercenary unburdened by a lantern joined the fray. At the edge of the fight, Yan watched one of the lanternmen discover Peyto and, disdaining to use a blade on a one-armed man, double the clerk over by punching him in the stomach with his sword hilt. A second blow to the back sent Peyto to the floor.

The fight was not going well. Unaided, the fliers would lose.

There were no leather straps to burst here, no floor to collapse. What could he use?

Danel went down, but Penit rained blows on the bregil, preventing him from finishing off her comrade.

Teletha was being forced back by Arham.

Kim was scrambling away from three of the mercs. One of the lanternmen had ignored Arham's orders and joined the melee

There wasn't much time left.

Yan's eyes fell on the torches they had brought.

He grabbed one in each hand and leapt to his feet, calling fire to relight them. Raising them over his head, he summoned the magic, sent it into the flame, and let it burst forth in a flash of light. The torches showered him with sparks as they sputtered and flamed, but the cavern filled with light.

"Magic!" the bregil howled, shielding his eyes against the illumination.

Yan created an image of a firesphere and sent the crackling, flaring globe floating toward the mercenaries. It was just an illusion and could do them no harm, but they didn't know that.

"Back! Watch for the mage!" Arham yelled. "Back off!"

Yan sent another globe of illusory fire toward the mercenaries. This one he exploded in a shower of sparks when it appeared to hit one of the stone spikes hanging from the cavern's roof. One of the lanternmen dropped his lantern

"He'll fry us," he wailed. "We can't fight magic like that."

"Press them," Teletha called with false bravado. She charged forward. "Don't let them escape."

Swords pointed to the ceiling and empty hands were raised above heads as Arham led the mercenaries in shouting, "Our oath! Our oath! By Baaliff, Vehr, and V'Narra, we give our oath!"

The fliers hesitated, putting Teletha out ahead. Yan feared that the mercenaries would fall upon her en masse; their behavior in the valley had not shown them to be honorable sorts. No guilded mercenary would go back on his oath, but these were not that sort of mercenary; they might find the lone air captain too tempting a target.

"Drop your weapons," she ordered.

Arham seemed to be counting heads among his adversaries. Slowly, he smiled. That smile vanished when Yan sent another illusory firesphere hissing over their heads. Two of the brigands let go of their weapons.

Arham gave them a disgusted look before dropping his sword. The rest of his men followed his lead. Yan saw that while the bregil had dropped his sword and dagger, he retained his tail blade. He was about to warn Teletha when she said, "*All* of them. That means you, bregil."

She was sharp.

The bregil snarled and laid the weapon on the floor.

"Penit, gather the weapons. Danel, take one of the lanterns and see if you can get the others going again. I want enough light to watch these dogs."

Yan expected Arham to show some concern for his fallen men, but the mercenary leader's first question was, "All right, where is he?"

"Who?"

The mercenary leader didn't answer. Instead, he squinted in the bad light, trying to get a look at Yan. When Danel got another lantern lit, the light revealed Yan to the mercenary leader. "You're not Gornal," he said.

"Gornal?" Yan didn't know the name.

"Laird Gornal Douganan. Who are you that you don't know him?"

"I'm Yan Tanafres, magician, and this is—"

"An air captain of the Imperial Air Service," Arham interrupted.

"—Teletha Schonnegon. As you noted, an air captain."

"I was wondering how old Gornal had managed to get Imperials to do his fighting. Hadn't figured how he could've stashed them down here either, but I can see I was on the wrong trail. You're not working for him, are you?"

Yan ignored his question and asked one of his own. "Why did you think I was Gornal?"

Arham shrugged. "I thought he was the only mage around here."

"Laird Douganan is a mage?" This was news.

"Surprised, hunh?" Arham laughed. "You're definitely not from around here."

"No, we're not. But we've seen what you did to the village."

Arham snorted. "What *we* did? Look here, Master Magician. Gornal was trying to double-cross us. I called him on it and he tried to raise his folk against us. We did what we had to do."

"So you attempted to kill him?"

"Tried to teach him a lesson."

"A lesson that included innocent people?"

"Listen, Master Magician. Real life ain't all cozy like your books. There ain't nobody innocent."

"You won't even deny you killed them."

"We did what we had to do. Gornal pulled a double cross, but the stupid git didn't have his weaponmen around, didn't have his spook stuff with him, and he thought he could scare us with a bunch of squalls. When we showed him just how stupid he was, he ran away. We almost caught him, but he got into this thrice-damned tower. Had to cut down a tree and make a ram to get in." Arham laughed, obviously warming to his tale-telling. "Thought we was going to die when we did bust in. There was the biggest, nastiest dnove you ever seen slavering at us. The lads didn't want to go in, but I had a suspicion. Dnoves don't like to go against bunches of men, but this one stood its ground. I would have thought it'd charge; that's the way dnoves deal with what they don't like. But this one just stood and howled like a devil.

"I got suspicious, so I put a foot of good steel in its face and it just sort of sank into the floor. The thrice-damned thing wasn't really there. I took its going through the floor as a sign, like a whipped dog running to its master, and brought the lads down the stairs. I was right, too. Old Gornal had some kind of fancy magic show going on."

"You interrupted a ritual." Yan was aghast; the interruption of a ritual usually resulted in some unpredictable part of the magic having effect.

"Sure did." Arham sounded pleased. "Broke it up right quick. As soon as Gornal saw us coming, he ran down here. We weren't going to let him get away, so we followed him. Been looking for him since."

"He's still alive then," Teletha said.

"Must be. We ain't found him. Caught a couple of his servants, though, and took care of them."

Like the man on the landing? How many others had these dogs killed? Yan didn't like Arham's attitude, but he had to wonder if the man hadn't done some good in the midst of his crimes. If Laird Douganan was responsible for the spell, and if Arham and his mercenaries had disrupted Douganan's ritual, perhaps the spell was not properly completed. What might have happened had Gornal completed the ritual? Yan shuddered.

Whether it sprang from a completed ritual or not, the magic had to be dealt with. The more information Yan had about its effects, the better he could deal with it. He especially wanted to know about the time distortion on this side of the ward.

"Arham, how long have you been down here?"

"I don't know. Hard to tell without the sun." He turned to the bregil. "What do you think, Horm?"

"Couple hours," Horm grunted.

The bregil's response was casually given. Did they have any idea of what was happening? "And when did you enter the tower?"

"You got ear problems?" Arham asked insolently. "Like Horm, said, a couple hours ago."

"What day?"

"You're asking awful strange questions."

"We are all in an awfully strange situation, Master Arham. Humor my curiosity and tell me what day it is."

The mercenary leader gave Yan a distrustful look, then he shrugged. "Don't know the date. Couple of days before midsummer. That's when Gornal was gonna get us. At the fair."

"Outside the valley, midsummer is long past."

"You're a liar," Arham said. The other mercenaries were less aggressive; they looked fearful.

Yan went on to tell them what he understood of the effect of Laird Douganan's magic. By the time he fin-

ished, most of the mercenaries were clearly terrified.
Arham and the bregil only got angry.

Arham spoke earnestly. "Well, Master Tanafres, you
can count on us. We'll help you get that bastard son of
a poxed whore. Man can't be allowed to pervert nature
like that and get away with it."

"We have to find the heart of the spell first," Yan
told him. He didn't want to trust the man's sudden
nobility, but dispelling the magic came first. To accom-
plish that, Yan would take whatever help was offered.
"What's back the way you were?"

"More caves. They go deeper and get wetter, but
there's nobody down there."

"You're sure?"

"Horm did the scouting. Ask him."

"Mage didn't go that way," Horm said without prompt-
ing.

"You're sure?" Yan asked.

"I wouldn't question the word of a bregil about cave
stuff," Arham said affably. "Fortunately, Horm here is a
patient sort. Real forgiving."

"What about the black stone rooms?" Teletha asked.

"Ain't checked them out too careful. There's lotsa
them. Like it was a whole town buried down here. We
saw the worm writing on the door to this place and figured Gornal had rabbited this way. Thought he might be
setting up some more magic and didn't want to give him
time to come up with something realer than his dnove."

"A reasonable conclusion from unreasonable men,"
Peyto said. "I suggest that we return to the stone rooms
and continue searching."

It was really the only strategy. Yan turned to Arham.
"If you give us your parole, we will return your weapons
and you can help us try to end this magic."

"If it'll get us out of this, we'll swear to anything,"
Arham said. Several of the mercenaries agreed.

"I don't like this," Teletha said.

"Don't worry, Captain," Arham said. "We're on your side in this. You can trust us."

The two leaders locked stares. Teletha was the first to break away. "All right. We'll take your parole."

"Consider it given." Arham held out his hand and smiled.

Teletha took Arham's weapon from Penit and handed it back to the man. She didn't smile. Penit passed weapons back to the other mercenaries and when all were rearmed, the combined group made its way back to the entrance to the cavern and out into the black stone maze.

Time, unknowable in its quantity, passed as they searched. They saw no sign of Laird Gornal Douganan or any of his servants. At last they came to a unique feature of the warren, a stairway leading downward. The stairs were broad and shallow and made uncomfortable walking. Before they reached the foot Yan discerned a faint glimmering, an echo of the ward they had encountered in the tower. Like the ward, this magical effect shimmered with a faint hint of green and echoed with familiar resonances. Here, then, was what he was looking for. At once eager and reluctant, he led the group down the stairway, stopping at the shimmering wall of energy.

"Not another one-way trip?" Kim asked sourly.

Yan extended a hand. He felt a tingle of power but none of the cloying stickiness of the ward. This was part of the spell, but not a barrier as the other wall of energy had been.

"No," he said. "This one is different."

He walked through the curtain of energy without any of the concern he had felt in breaching the ward. They could follow if they would.

On the other side of the energy wall was a small, flat

area about ten feet long and a bit narrower. Twin
grooves were incised into the floor and spheres of black
stone lay in those slots. The grooves led to a great cube
of black stone. Beyond the cube lay an opening lit with
steady green light.

As Yan stepped up to the opening, he saw a chamber beyond, its wall curving upward and away from
him in either direction. The wall merged imperceptibly
with the domed ceiling. The surface on which he stood
made a walkway that ran around the perimeter of the
chamber. That walkway was narrow and lacked a railing, letting him see that the chamber opened to a similar dome shape below him. Though the block cut off
his view of the whole chamber, he felt sure that it was a
gigantic sphere. The curvature of the walls suggested
that it was on the order of fifteen yards across.

As he started around it, he saw that the cube was not
exactly a cube after all. Its inner surface was concave,
curved with a radius matching that of the chamber
walls. If the block were rolled back to seal the chamber, its inner surface would be continuous with the rest
of the chamber's boundary, forming a complete globe.
It was magnificent, the most perfect ritual chamber he
could conceive of.

He rounded the block. The perimeter walkway included a two-yard-wide tongue that reached out to the center
of the chamber. He saw no supports for that black
catwalk. What marvelous engineering! But for all the
magnificence of the chamber's architecture, what lay in
its center was more wonderful still.

Six globes of energy, each a couple of yards in diameter, floated above the catwalk without any apparent
means of support. A man might walk beneath the sphere
directly over the walkway and reach up and touch it.
The six globes made a ring, its open center above the
end of the catwalk. The spheres were of a full rich green

rather than the hint of color shown by the ward and the energy wall. Within each of them was a dark shape.

He walked out on the catwalk to get a closer look, ignoring the voices behind him urging caution. He stared at the nearest globe, trying to see what was inside.

It was a creature of some sort.

The thing was black, its skin leathery. It had two legs, two arms, and a tail, but it was no bregil. The tail was much thicker and did not have a flexible gripping surface. The legs were oddly jointed, more like those of a bird than a man or bregil. Unlike a bird, the foot had four claws, the fourth positioned on the inside of the foot; it wouldn't touch the ground when the being stood. The arms were jointed in human fashion and ended in hands with five fingers, but with two opposing three, unlike the four fingers and thumb arrangement shared by humans and bregil. The neck was long and sinuous, supporting a narrow, wedge-shaped head that looked halfway between that of a serpent and one of the river lizards of Merom's coastal plains.

The creatures seemed to be asleep, though he could not say how he knew. Certainly he could not see them breathe. But then, if they were behind another layer of the timespell, he could not expect to.

Were these creatures representatives of the ancient beings who had built this place? Were they the builders themselves? If so, they might be the very ones who had written the books in Laird Douganan's workshop. It was hard to accept. Could they really be living, breathing—or so he presumed—representatives of the prehuman race of man's legends.

They might be something else—something that dark mages might have summoned to do their bidding. Something like demons.

Whatever they were, they were fascinating.

As was the magic woven around them. Yan tried to

understand the swirls in the arcane energy, to assess the importance of the eddies and currents. He sensed the control that underlay this edifice of magic and admired the skill with which it had been constructed. It was a work of art as well as a work of the Art. He sensed a flaw in the interplay of energies, a subtle twist or shift in the flow. The dissonance was like that of a piece of art which had been repaired after some damage, a piece repaired by a craftsmen of lesser skill than the original artist. There was something so human about the flaw. Still, he tried to ignore the dissonance, preferring to contemplate the elegance and beauty of the woven magic.

"Tanafres! Tanafres!"

Someone was calling him. He knew that he should answer, but the magic was so appealing, so fascinating. He had never seen anything like it. Nothing Gan Tidoni had ever shown him could compare to it. Its power and depth, its sheer sophistication, were overwhelming. He didn't want to leave it.

"Yan!"

Outside, they were getting insistent, beginning to abuse his body by slapping his face. Reluctantly, he backed away from the magic. He found Teletha staring worriedly into his face.

"You've been staring at those things for nearly an hour."

"Have I?"

"Yes," Peyto said slowly. "Didn't you realize?"

"I suppose so."

"Is he always like this after using magic?" Teletha asked the clerk.

"How in the name of Einthof should I know?"

Yan knew that they didn't understand, so he told them.

"This is it. Before us is the juncture of seasons unspent, ages untold, and eons beyond mortal knowledge. It is a well of time, the heart of the magic we seek."

# 18

"LISTEN TO HIM BABBLE," Danel said. "How do we know the demons haven't taken him for their own?"

Yan was still confused by the dissolution of his link with the potent magic englobing the beings. The magic was immensely powerful and strange, but it didn't feel demonic. At least, he didn't think so.

"What demons?" he asked.

"Those black ones," Danel said, pointing at the creatures entombed in their globes of magic.

Yan almost laughed. "They're not demons."

"See! They *have* taken him."

"Don't be a fool, Airman," Arham said contemptuously. "There are no demons anymore."

"Even if there were, this is an unlikely manifestation," Peyto said authoritatively. "Where the chronicles speak of demons, they speak of a variety of shapes, no two alike. These creatures are very much of a type, identical for all I can see."

Yan was taken aback by the clerk's statement. Chronicles of the dark times were rare in the extreme, and the Church forbade the preservation of any with specific details concerning the demon servants of the dark mages. Yan wanted to ask where Peyto had come by such knowledge, but this was not the time. Instead he said, "Danel, whatever those creatures may be, they are as mortal as you or I."

"Mortal maybe, but they're not like me," Teletha said very quietly. Aloud, she said, "So what have you learned, Master Tanafres? Can you end this spell?"

"There is much that I do not yet understand, but I have made a beginning in comprehending the matter. The astral resonances of the globes surrounding these creatures are born of the same energies as the ward. Or at least very similar energies. The magic enfolding these creatures holds them lifeless yet living in a magic of time. Still, there are both subtle and blatant differences between the magic I can touch so easily here and the hints that I detected before. The time distortion that we have experienced is not exactly a part of the magic holding these creatures away from the normal passage of time."

"What do you mean, 'not exactly'?" Teletha asked.

"The energies I sensed in the ward and in the barrier at the entrance to this chamber are different, as if shaped by another hand," Yan replied

"Gornal," Arham said.

Laird Douganan? That didn't seem likely. If the man had possessed significant magical skills, would he have been chased away from his home by Arham's brigands? But then, Yan himself didn't have effective spells to deal with physical violence; perhaps the laird had a similar limitation. Unfortunately, Arham and his men were the only ones with any idea of the laird's skills, and they were not trained to tell the difference among trickery, illusion, and real magic. He had proven that with his own illusion. "Dealing with this sort of magic would have taken a very knowledgeable and powerful mage."

"He was," Arham said. "Or so he always claimed."

"Yet he could only raise an illusion to defend himself." Teletha shook her head. "Doesn't seem likely that he could raise such a great magic as this. Should we be considering the possibility of another mage, Master Tanafres?"

"Perhaps Laird Douganan found the secret in his books," Peyto suggested.

Now, that made sense. If that was where Gornal found the spell, given time and access to the books, Yan could figure out how the spell had been accomplished. Then he could work out the formulae necessary to defuse the magic. All he had to do was—curse himself as an idiot! The books were still in the workroom on the other side of the ward. Why hadn't he thought of them before they crossed the ward? How could he have been so stupid?

Yan sat down on the catwalk and dropped his head into his hands.

"Did I say something wrong?" Peyto asked.

Teletha, unsurprisingly, was the first to figure it out. "The books are the key, and they're where we can't get them."

"Yes," Yan moaned.

"Are you saying you've dragged us down here and now you can't do anything to save us? That we're trapped down here forever?" Kim's voice cracked on the last word. Hand reaching for his sword hilt, he took a step toward Yan.

Teletha slid between them, stilling Kim with a touch on his sword arm. "This is not good, Kim."

"Captain, he—"

"He's caught just like we are."

"Your captain's right, Sergeant," Arham said. "We're all trapped down here. But I'll tell you something: we're not stuck here forever. Even *I* know a spell can't last forever."

Most spells didn't, anyway, but what about this one? Yan's eyes drifted to the black creatures curled within their spheres of power. How long had *that* spell survived?

"What are you suggesting, Arham?" Teletha asked

"I'm not suggesting anything. But I'm saying that I ain't never yet met a spell that outlasted the mage who cast it."

"But we don't know who cast it," she pointed out.

Arham snorted. "Don't we?"

"*You* may be sure," Yan said. "But I'm not."

Arham turned on Yan. "Use your magic, magician. Find Gornal and you'll know I'm right."

"I'm not a finder," Yan said.

"Then we'll hunt him down without your help," Arham said. "Once we've got him, we can get this over with quick enough."

"Gornal's been successfully avoiding you long enough to make me sure that you won't find him down here unless he wants you to," Teletha said. "Whether or not he's responsible for the magic, it's clear he knows his way around down here."

"Maybe we haven't found him because we haven't looked hard enough. But with your crew we should be able to flush the old bastard out. Once we do, we'll be done with this soon enough."

"We didn't come down here to help you in your murders."

"Murders! I told you the old bastard double-crossed–"

"And *I* told *you* that we're here to unravel the magic."

"For that we need Gornal."

"Master Tanafres doesn't agree with you."

"Him? He's more worthless than Gornal. I'm surprised he knows how to wipe his arse."

"Don't know that he does," Horm put in.

"Stay out of it, Horm," Arham warned. "This is between me and the captain." He turned to smile at

Teletha. "Let's be reasonable. We both want the same thing, Captain. We can work something out. We're both soldiers, you know, we've got a lot in common. Magicians and soldiers get along like sea and earth; things may be fine for a while, but it'll be war sooner or later. Your pet magician here ain't got no more thought for you than some dumb animal he'd put in a cage and pour potions down. Right now you may be sweet on the git, but–"

"But nothing, mister. I've had enough of your talk," Teletha shouted. She turned her back on Arham and Yan could see that her face was red, but she looked more embarrassed than angry. Behind her Yan could see fury on Arham's face; clearly he didn't like the way Teletha treated him. Teletha controlled her own emotion and her voice was almost normal when she spoke again. "Master Tanafres, what can you do about this spell? I want to be back where the air is clean."

Yan felt uncomfortable when all eyes turned to him. He swallowed hard. "I could try to unbind the spell from the energies that power it. Without a channel of power, a spell is no more useful than an unloaded pistol."

"What are you waiting for?"

Yan hesitated. "It's not an easy procedure."

"See, I told you he's useless," Arham said. "Next he'll be telling us that it won't be his fault if he fails."

"Shut up," Teletha snapped. "Master Tanafres, can you or can you not undo the spell?"

"I can try, but I have to tell you that I can't guarantee the procedure will work. I'm not very experienced, and I've never dealt with magic this powerful. If I had Laird Douganan's books, I would know more and be better equipped to handle this magic."

"Well, you don't have the books; and experienced

or not, you're the only magician we have. You'll just have to do your best. We're all counting on you."

Yan didn't want everyone counting on him. Having so many lives depending on him was frightening. He wasn't ready for this. He was about to tell Teletha that when he looked into her eyes. There was honest faith there. He felt that she really did believe he would do his best, and that she would not criticize him if he failed. She believed in him.

Gan Tidoni's words came back to him. "Faith is fuel to the will, and will is the heart of all magic." Teletha's belief in him restored a measure of his confidence. Maybe he could unlock this spell, after all. He'd have to try; he couldn't let her down.

He looked up at the dark, curled forms. They seemed so serene, so quiet. Yet even without calling upon his full magical senses, he could feel the power enwrapping them; power exotic and strange, and so very, very strong. As he contemplated what he was about to attempt, the doubt rose again, threatening to overwhelm his renewed conviction. The energy release from a failure to disconnect the spell from its power channel could be enormous, probably enough to destroy him. He had enough experience dissipating the backlash from the miscasting of simple spells, that such a result was unlikely. Possible, but unlikely; though if it did happen, it would be disastrous for everyone here. He might simply die of his failure, leaving the others stranded within the ward. In the worst case, the uncontrolled release of the energies coiled in the magic would create a firestorm that would burn everyone to a cinder.

But there was a subtler, more private danger here as well. One that was much more likely, since he had already nearly become lost in the rapturous wonder of the ancient magic. If he fell into such a state again, he might simply lose himself until his body died of neglect. And the others would eventually die as well.

Relying on Teletha's understanding, he quietly spoke his fear. "If I'm to avoid getting lost the way I did the last time I touched the spell, I'll need an anchor."

"We didn't bring our airboat's anchor with us, Master Tanafres," Teletha said wryly. "Or hadn't you noticed?"

"I didn't mean that kind of anchor. I meant a spirit anchor, a person whom I can use to provide a steady link to this plane and hold me tied to it, the way an anchor holds a ship."

"You're not witching me," Arham said vehemently.

That was fine with Yan, he wouldn't want to rely on the mercenary leader anyway. The worried and fearful glances exchanged among the fliers and the mercenaries showed that they felt much the same way as Arham about participating in the magic.

"Well, I suppose I could do it. I've always wondered what it would be like to do magic," Peyto said.

"I appreciate it, Master Lennuick, but I'm afraid you don't qualify," Yan said.

"Need another mage, do you?"

"No. In fact, a person who is not a magician is superior for this function. My problem is that the ritual I know requires that I hold hands with the anchor."

Peyto glanced down at his empty sleeve. "Won't one do?"

Yan couldn't look the clerk in the eyes as he said, "Not with the ritual I know."

Peyto harrumphed, but mercifully said nothing.

"Will I do, Master Tanafres?" Teletha asked.

"I thought you didn't want anything to do with magic?"

"That's not unusual in this bunch," she said with a weak, fleeting smile. She swallowed hard. "However,

I'm the commander, and the rest of these folks are my responsibility. I'm your anchor." Smiling another faint, tentative smile, she added, "Unless your ritual doesn't work with women."

"That's not a worry," he said. "Come, sit in front of me."

When she settled herself facing him, he held out his hands. She did not take them immediately, but sat wiping her palms on her trousers. He waited. When she was ready, she reached out to him. Her hands were harder, more callused, than he expected, but they were warm and alive in his.

"It's all right," he began soothingly. "Forget anything that you find uncomfortable. You are just sitting here with me. There is nothing to fear." He hoped. "We are sitting here, here in the world you have always known.

"Think about that world.

"It is your world, my world, our world.

"We live in it every day, you and I.

"We are a part of it every day, you and I."

Her eyes began to drift closed. Yan continued to speak, drawing her deeper into the trance. Her breathing settled into a deep, steady rhythm and he wrapped himself in her growing calm and the solidity of her presence. He found it comforting in the embrace of her spirit, but he knew he couldn't stay. He had work to do.

He opened his mind to the astral.

The magic blossomed around them in a marvelous and frightening swirl of contained power. Yan reached out to tentatively touch the energies around him. The shock thrilled him and frightened him; the power with the spell was so great. He tried to feel the shape of the color, the texture of sound of the magic surging around him. It was so much more than he had ever experienced.

There were two methods to unravel another mage's spell. The first took raw power, sundering the link by forcing a break, the way an ax parts a rope. That could not be his method here. The other required knowing the spell, or learning it by contact with its manifestation, and insinuating one's own will into the pathways of the magic until one could find a weak point, a flaw in the weaving that one could exploit.

Touching the spell, Yan saw the link from the ward to the energies surging about the englobed creatures. He saw the thread that ran past the barrier of the ward to the ritual chamber. That thread was a thread of origin, now drifting apart from the pressures of time. He caught a brief impression of the desperate, and desperately ill-trained, man who had cast a ritual spell that he had not fully understood and set in motion the magic that had ensnared everyone gathered here in this ancient ritual chamber, and everyone in the valley as well.

Arham was right: Laird Gornal Douganan was a mage, powerful but barely trained. The spell Gornal had wrought was complicated, in its own fashion. Certainly it was greater than anything Yan had ever attempted. But compared to the artistry of the underlying magics upon which it had drawn, Gornal's spell was crude, unsophisticated, and hasty, a mere veneer made by a poor craftsman overlying the work of masters incredibly more skilled than he.

Yan was distracted by the intense beauty of more ancient magic. He wished he could show Teletha the wonder of it, but even linked with him, she would not be able to see those auras. He could try to describe them, but he knew he wouldn't have the words.

Thinking about her made him more aware of his connection to her. With his earthly eyes he could see her sitting before him, a reminder of his mortality and his place in the world. With his spirit he felt her as a sense of purpose, a reminder of what he was supposed to be doing. In that way, she was almost a drag on his spirit. But then, as an anchor, that was her function: to bind his spirit to the ordinary world, the world where magic was visible only in the most banal ways.

With his awakened awareness of the earthly world, he realized that the others would be worrying by now, afraid he had fallen into the spell and taken Teletha with him. He decided to tell them something of what he had learned, but to return to his body and speak would disrupt the delicate harmonies he had achieved with the spell. He didn't want to have to rebuild them upon returning to the astral. So he drew on his link to Teletha, his anchor, and spoke to them with her voice.

"I am Yan Tanafres speaking to you through Tele-Captain Schonnegon. A human, quite likely Laird Douganan, is responsible for the effects we have been experiencing, but it is not entirely his magic. He has woven his spells around this greater magic before us. The energies coursing through the time compression spell are not those of a human mage, but they are being used by a human mage. The deeper magic is still a mystery to me, but I may be able to affect the lesser. It will be dangerous, but I don't see any other choice."

"Let the captain go," Kim requested, almost pleading.

"I'm all right, Kim. He's not hurting me," Teletha said of her own volition.

Yan was surprised. Most untrained personalities were submerged in the link.

*Sorry to disappoint you,* she said to him.

*I'm not disappointed. But I was serious, it will be dangerous. It might be wise if we broke the link.*

*Will you be able to get back without it?*

*I don't know. Probably.*

*I don't understand how I know, but you are not being*

*honest.* She seemed more puzzled than surprised. *You don't think you'll get back at all.*

She was right, of course, but he didn't want to endanger her as well.

*You're worried about me.* Now, she was surprised. *The problem's the same one we had before we crossed the ward. You're the only magician we've got, and we cannot afford to lose you.*

Her statement was honest, as far as it went. The sense he got of her emotions thrilled him, but now was not the time to explore such hints. He hoped that there would be another time.

*Be my anchor, then. I will try to keep you safe.*

*Do what you have to do and get the job done. Don't worry about me.*

*I will worry.*

*As will I.*

*I—*

*Need to get on with it.*

She was right, of course.

Reluctant to leave her, but eager to touch the magic again, Yan reached out with his mind. He probed the spells, feeling out their boundaries and tracing them down to their roots. Each contact with the older magic rocked him with the muted suggestion of power and magic beyond his imaginings. He wanted to be able to cast spells of such beauty, to make magics of that complexity. Each touch brought him more in tune with the ancient magic, closer to understanding. If he understood it, he could control it. All that power would be his. Was this how Sazarn had felt when the demon Yawymti tempted him on the mountain?

Yan teetered on the edge of a precipice of power, before him a magic fashioned to hold back time. He knew it for a shield, a bulwark against the threat of a world marching on in an unacceptable way. A shout drew Yan back from visions of ancient robed mages immersed in a ritual magic of world-shaking power. The shout, human, all too human like him, smashed the vision. His understanding shattered into glittering shards that shredded the otherness he had touched and blew his insight away on the astral winds. He tumbled back into his body and the words of the shout became clear.

"Leave them alone!"

The new arrival was wild-eyed and tousled of hair, as if he had just been woken from sleep. His clothes were of fine stuff, and would have identified him as Laird Gornal Douganan even without the repeating heraldic pattern that trimmed his overrobe. The pattern was echoed on the tabard worn by the mousy servant behind him.

Fliers and mercenaries stood shocked by the sudden appearance of the long-sought laird. Gornal Douganan strode through their ranks unmolested.

"Finally come out of hiding," Arham drawled as Douganan strode toward him.

Eyes fixed on Yan, the laird ignored the mercenary until Arham stepped into his way, blocking him from the catwalk. Douganan tried to move around the mercenary, but Arham sidestepped, blocking him again. Horm grabbed the servant, preventing him from interfering.

"Get out of my way," Douganan ordered Arham. "You have no idea what he's tampering with!"

"You don't give me orders anymore," Arham said coldly.

"Don't be a fool, Arham. This matter is beyond your understanding. Let me pass."

"Excuse me, your lordship." Arham stepped to one side, but in doing so drew his dagger. When Laird Douganan started past him, the mercenary struck, burying his blade to the hilt in Douganan's back.

Douganan's eyes went wide and his mouth worked, but no sound issued forth. Slowly, he put one hand to his chest like an orator about to begin a speech. Instead of speaking, he struggled to draw a breath. He took a step forward and half turned. Those staring eyes slid sideways and met Arham's predatory gaze. Douganan's free hand rose, finger pointing in a quivering, accusatory gesture, then his knees buckled and he fell onto them, hard. He remained upright for a moment before falling face first to the walkway.

"You shouldn't have killed him," Yan protested.

Arham just smiled.

"Kill the mage, kill the spell. No quicker way to do it. We don't need your magic after all."

"Maybe so," Teletha said groggily. "But you didn't have to stab him in the back."

"The justice of the poets, Captain. Just giving him back what he gave me."

Arham kicked the body over the edge. It struck the curving lower wall of the chamber with a meaty smack and continued on, rolling to the low point of the sphere. Douganan's head lay at an angle which left no doubt that his neck was broken. Sightless eyes stared up at Yan.

"He might have been able to tell us how to end the spell safely," Yan said.

"Don't matter anymore," Arham said. "We can leave now. Let's go, lads."

"What about this?" Horm said, tugging on the tabard of the servant he held.

"Bring him along. He might know where Douganan hid his gold."

"Captain," Kim said tentatively.

"We're going too, Kim. Come on, Yan," Teletha said. "I can't let that man go back to the surface unescorted. My ship's still up there. Besides, you don't want to stay down here by yourself."

How did she know what he wanted to do? Yan
looked over his shoulder. The creatures in their energy
globes still hung in the center of the chamber. That
much, at least, had not changed. Yan could still feel
echoes of the ancient magic. If there was a change in
Douganan's spell, the greater brilliance of the older
magic masked it.

"Captain, will you be leaving immediately for the
empire?" Peyto asked.

Eyes on the departing mercenaries, Teletha responded, "First things first, Master Lennuick."

She led her crew after the mercenaries. Peyto looked
beseechingly at Yan. He seemed to be waiting for
something. When Yan nodded, Peyto grinned in relief
and started to leave the spherical chamber.

Yan looked around. There was so much more to
learn here. But Teletha was right: first things first. Yan
did want to know if Douganan's death had really lowered the ward. He caught up with the others on the
ramp to Douganan's ritual chamber.

"By Baaliff's balls, what's this?" Arham exclaimed.

"Vehr save us, it's still there," Kim moaned.

Arham stood at the ward. When his tentative touch
yielded nothing, he struck the barrier with his fist, making it ring like a bell. Horm snarled at the sound, then
recovered himself. Eyes aglitter, the bregil glanced
around, apparently ready to attack anyone who men-
tioned his reaction. Arham kicked the barrier, then
kicked it again and again, raising a tolling of futility.

The spell had not failed.

It was worse than before. The ward's barrier was
nearly at the edge of the ritual chamber, several yards
higher than it had when they had passed it some
unknown time ago. The magic was not only still func-
tioning, it was spreading.

# 19

"IT IS AS I FEARED: WHATEVER Douganan did, he linked it too well to the magic encasing the creatures."

Arham spun on Yan. "So they're the source of our problem."

Yan didn't like the way the man leapt to conclusions. He was too quick to solve his problems with blades. "Well, not the source, I think. That was Douganan."

"But they are why the barrier blocks us?" Peyto asked.

"The barrier is an artifact of Douganan's spells," Yan said.

"But he's dead," Peyto said. "Didn't you agree that without the mage who cast a spell, the spell would have no power? Why isn't the barrier gone?"

"Douganan didn't have the mastery of magic necessary to complete his spells on his own. In some way I don't understand, he must have linked his ritual to the magic surrounding the creatures, and drawn on that ancient magic for energy. Rather than using his own will to drive the transfer of arcane energy, he stole energy from the ancient spell."

"And because that spell still exists, Douganan's spell not only still exists, but thrives," Teletha said.

Yan nodded. "I'm afraid so."

"So why are *those* spells still around? If the magic is ancient, the mages who cast such spells must surely be dead."

"There are ways to empower a spell beyond the life of the caster. It's difficult, and expensive in effort and materials, but it is possible."

"That has been done here?" Peyto asked.

"I don't think so," Yan replied.

"Then why do the spells still function, Master Tanafres?" Teletha asked, frustration in her voice.

"I think because those creatures are mages."

Arham grinned evilly. "That makes it easy. You said they were mortal; they can die as easily as Gornal." He turned to his men. "Come on, lads. We're going back there and carve us some sleeping lizards."

Yan's demands that they stop went unheeded. Even Teletha and her fliers charged off, leaving Yan and Peyto alone at the ward barrier.

"We've got to stop them," Yan said.

"There you go with the 'we' again," Peyto said. "Why do we have to stop them? If it works, I'm all for it."

"If you agree with them why are you still here?"

"I'm not a young man anymore. I've had enough excitement, and killing, for today." He sat on the ramp. "Why do you think they should be stopped? If the barrier's still here, the spell must be as well. I thought you wanted the spell ended."

"I do."

"Then maybe *you* ought to be helping them."

"They don't know what they're doing."

"If you have a better way, use it. If not, well . . . They are frightened people, Yan. They fear this magic. I don't think they'll take kindly to your getting in the way."

"I can't let them just kill those creatures."

"Why not? Isn't it them or us?"

"Are you just going to sit here?"

"Yes."

Yan couldn't. He raced after the soldiers. He racked his brains as he ran, but he couldn't find a solution. When Yan reached the chamber, Arham was pointing at one of the spheres. "Ab, give that one a taste of steel."

"Right."

Ab stared at the huddled form for a moment, perhaps deciding where to strike. His body extended and his arm snapped out, driving his blade before it. Light exploded when the tip of the sword touched the boundary of the globe. He froze in place, extended in his lunge. Green lightnings crackled to life and scampered down the blade, over the hilt, and onto him. At the touch of those energies, Ab's back arched and his mouth opened in a soundless scream.

The lightnings vanished as quickly as they had come, leaving behind a charred corpse holding a pitted and blackened sword. The body crumpled to the catwalk.

"Vehr shield us," Kim whispered.

For a long time no one said anything. Yan walked up beside Teletha. She raised bleak and frightened eyes to his. He had no words of comfort.

"That doesn't seem to have worked," Arham observed.

"I could try again to unravel the spell," Yan said.

"Then why don't you?" Arham yelled.

"It's dangerous. I'd—"

"*It's dangerous*," Arham said mockingly. "It's always something. I don't know. I don't understand. If I had this, if I had that. You've got yourself, magic man, and you're worthless."

Arham's taunts struck home. It was Yan's fault that Douganan's books were still upstairs. How could he have been so stupid as to leave them there? He should have realized that they would be crucial to understanding the spell. He'd been too eager to get to the heart of the matter, always he was too eager. He'd been sloppy in his thinking. What good was a mage who had sloppy thoughts?

What good? What good at all?

"There may be another way to get these things," Teletha said, pulling her pistol from her belt.

She had given up hope in Yan as well, fallen prey to Arham's bloody solution. Was there really no other course?

"How can you?" he asked.

She looked at him with apologetic eyes.

"You had your chance and it didn't work. This magic is beyond you, Yan. You shouldn't take it personally. No one is the master of all of his craft. There's always someone a little faster, a little stronger. Someone who knows a trick that you don't. Accept that. You have to do what you can to survive. Arham's is the only practical solution."

She gave him a chance to say something, but he didn't have anything to say.

Teletha took aim at the farthest globe and fired. Yan involuntarily closed his eyes as the roar of the shot rang in his ears. He started as if poked with a stick, but no one had touched him; it had been a jolt from the magic. He opened his eyes and looked at Teletha's target, expecting to see the creature writhing in its death agonies. To his surprise, the creature floated as serenely as it had before, curled up in peaceful slumber. The ball of Teletha's shot was suspended in the air just within the boundary of the creature's globe of power.

"Maybe you will have to try again after all, Master Tanafres," Teletha said.

Yan looked at the floating pistol ball and at the charred corpse. There was more to the magic than he had sensed, defenses he hadn't known existed. If the ancient magicians had protected themselves against physical threats, they had doubtless guarded against arcane threats as well. His mastery was nothing compared to theirs. His will, driven by his desperation to survive, might allow him to overcome those elegant magics through sheer power, but what was his will compared to the six wills—the six trained wills—of unknown but obviously immense resources?

"I can't," he said.

"Can't or won't?" Teletha asked.

"I cannot challenge that magic directly and hope to win. Those creatures are too well protected."

"Then we're lost," Kim said.

"Unless we can figure out some way to kill these black bastards," Arham said. "What I'd give for a cannon."

Horm made a guttural remark in a language unknown to Yan, but Arham laughed harshly. Teletha huddled with her despondent fliers, while Arham and his brigands held their own discussion. They sought some way to strike the creatures and kill them without exposing anyone to the dangerous magic. Yan didn't think they'd find a way: anything held by a man would provide a conduit for the magic to fry the wielder, and anything short of Arham's nonexistent cannon could not overwhelm the magical shield.

Yan considered his own options. He could try to disrupt the magic flow; but then he'd end up like Ab, dead. Douganan had found a way to utilize the ancient magic safely. No doubt the secret was written in his books, but they were still in the tower. Even were they here, the secret might be in the ones Yan couldn't read, the ones in the script of these ancient beings. No doubt Douganan had learned some of that script. With time . . .

With time, indeed.

Time seemed to be all they had. Plenty of time to think. Plenty of time to argue. Plenty of time to despair. The touch of Teletha's hand on his arm shook him free of such paralyzing thoughts.

"Master Tanafres, didn't you say that the things in those globes are mortal?"

"Yes."

"Well, everything mortal has to breathe, doesn't it? They do breathe?"

"They do, although they do so too slowly for us to see."

She nodded eagerly. "I don't really care how fast they're doing it. What matters is that they are breathing. They need air as much as we do."

"Unquestionably." What was the point?

"So air must pass through their protections. And if air will pass, smoke should pass as well, since it goes where air goes."

"Smoke?"

"Aye, smoke. I've seen bodies pulled from fires as dead as their burned comrades, yet they showed no touch of the flames nor mark of violence. I would guess that somehow the smoke killed them."

"Yes," Yan said, remembering one particular failed experiment of Gan Tidoni's. "A room may be so full of smoke that the smoke seems to take the place of the very air itself, leaving one coughing and unable to breathe."

"Even in a drift of smoke from a fire one can find oneself unable to breathe."

"Just so. I'd guess that where there is smoke, it takes the place of air."

"Preventing a person from breathing," she finished for him. "If we set a fire, the smoke from it would fill the upper part of the chamber. It would be a lot like filling an airship's balloon. And once this chamber is full of smoke, those things up there will have to breathe smoke instead of air."

"But we have nothing to burn to make such a volume of smoke," Yan pointed out.

"You have no magic for that, either?"

He looked away to escape her disappointed eyes.

Again she touched him on the arm. "I did not mean to offend."

"You didn't. It's just that . . . Never mind. I'm sorry I can't help."

"Well, I'm sorry, too, but I shouldn't have expected it. I've always thought magic was unreliable. All you've done is confirm the workings of the world for me. When the gods are busy elsewhere, you've only got yourself to rely on."

He wanted to tell her that she was wrong, but he didn't have an argument beyond his emotional denial. He knew she wouldn't accept that. "You've only got yourself to rely on," she had said. Well, he had thought he needed no one other than himself, and look where it had gotten him. It had gotten all of them trapped down here. He and Peyto, Teletha and her fliers, Arham and his brigands, even Douganan's wretched servant. They were all trapped together, not separately. All of them.

All?

Yan looked at Douganan's servant huddled under Horm's watchful eye. The man was old, and Yan remembered that he limped when he walked. Such a man could not run fast or scramble nimbly away from searching brigands. So where had he and his master been since they had crossed the ward? They could not have crossed back without leaving an astral sign, which

Yan would have read while examining the ward. Could Douganan have had another workroom down here? One which might have the secrets they needed to unlock the ward?

"Come on," Yan said to Teletha as he stalked off to confront the servant.

"What's your name, man?" he asked as the old man looked up with frightened eyes.

"I'm just a servant, sir. I've done nothing."

"I asked your name."

"Capurmes, if it please you, sir," the old man quavered.

"Capurmes, where were you and Laird Douganan hiding?"

The man shivered.

"You need not fear betraying your master, Capurmes. He's well beyond betrayal now."

"You think he knows a way out?" Teletha asked.

"Not directly," Yan said. "But Douganan might have had another workroom hidden down here."

"More magic stuff?" she asked.

"Let's hope so."

"Let's not," she said. "I'd rather just have a nice ordinary back door."

Not a promising hope; it probably wouldn't be useful if it existed. The ward would block it as well. He turned to the servant. "Well, Capurmes? Will you show us where you hid?"

The man hesitated and Horm cuffed him.

"Talk," the bregil growled.

"Horm will get very upset if you don't talk," Arham added.

Cowering, Capurmes addressed Yan. "Please, sir, don't let him hurt me. I'll show you."

"Show all of us," Horm said.

Capurmes looked to Yan. The man was clearly terrified of the bregil.

"He won't hurt you if you show us," Yan assured him.

"All of us," Horm repeated.

"All of us," Yan agreed.

"I knew there had to be a way out," Arham said gleefully.

"Don't be so sure," Yan said.

"If you like it here, you can stay. The rest of us are getting out. Aren't we, lads." Arham's men shouted their agreement. Kim and Danel shouted with them. Arham grinned at Yan. "Now if you don't mind, we're putting this old turd to work."

Urged on by Arham and Horm, Capurmes led them to a room Yan recognized as one they had searched before, one of those with windows opening on earth. The servant went to the window and pressed with both hands against the packed dirt, causing it to swing away from him. Light, bright and warm as dawn, flooded into the room from beyond.

Yan's companions' hopes of escape were dashed when they saw that the illumination came from lanterns hung on pillars in the chamber beyond the concealed doorway. Yan's own hopes were dashed when he saw what lay in the room. It was full of bales and boxes, and piles of wood. There were no books, no writing desk, no workbench. Gornal and his servant had hidden in a secret storeroom.

Arham's men spread out in an immediate search for another exit. The fliers joined in, leaving Teletha and Yan alone with Capurmes. Yan spoke softly to the old servant.

"And there is no other exit?"

"None that I know of, sir."

The servant did not seem to be lying. They had reached another dead end. He turned to Teletha to apologize for raising her hopes and found her gazing around the storeroom with a faint smile on her face.

"What is it?" he asked.

"We've got our way out," she said.

"But there is no way out, dame," Capurmes whined.

"He's not lying," Yan said.

"Not your way out, Master Tanafres. Mine. This stuff will burn."

Yan stood near the opening of the creatures' ritual chamber, and watched the smoke rise from the pile of material filling the lower part of the sphere. He had used magic to kindle the flames, ensuring that the fire was widespread, the better to fill the chamber with smoke faster; but he wished he weren't participating in this act. Still, it was the safest solution.

The smoke gathered near the roof of the chamber, first in lazy tendrils, then in larger and larger clouds. The air became thick, and several of the brigands started coughing. Within the thickening atmosphere Yan could see the glowing spheres although the shapes within them were little more than silhouettes. Some of the fliers started to cough.

"We'll die of our own remedy if we stay here," Teletha said.

Strangely reluctant to leave, Yan nodded.

They retreated to the top of the stairs, but soon even the air there began to be displaced by smoke as well.

"The cavern?" Teletha didn't sound sure.

"Why not the ward?" Yan suggested. "That's the point of all this. We may as well be there if it goes down."

"When it goes down," she said, trying to sound confident, but failing.

Peyto was waiting for them at the ward. Teletha explained their plan to the clerk, and he nodded at each significant point. "Clever, if it works."

Clever indeed.

Yan touched the ward barrier. It was as strong as ever. Pricking his finger with his belt knife, he daubed a drop of his blood against the barrier. It hung in midair, prevented from falling by the spell's suspension of time. Linked through his blood, he could feel the barrier like a nagging, half-remembered thought at the back of his mind. He sat on the ramp, back against the glossy black wall, confident that they had a long wait ahead of them.

The others settled in as well. Time passed. How much? Who could know? Certainly more outside the ward than inside. At length, they drifted off to sleep. Danel's cough was the first sign that the smoke had come.

"The smoke's rising up the well," Arham said.

"We should go down," Horm said.

But the smoke looked even thicker below them. No one seemed to want to act on Horm's advice. Even Horm seemed reluctant to descend. Kim beat at the barrier until he collapsed in a fit of coughing.

"Put out the torches and lanterns and lie down," Teletha ordered. "Stay low to the stairs."

Frightened people followed her orders, lying close together on the ramp. Yan thought they already looked like corpses, slaughtered like deer at the end of a huntsman's drive.

He started coughing.

Their time was running out.

He looked up at the drop of his blood on the ward; then blinked, thinking the smoke was fouling his vision. Had it moved?

He wiped at his eyes and looked again.

Yes, it was lower than it had been.

Yan shifted into trance, tracing the ward, feeling the surface of the magic until he satisfied himself that the ward was weakening. Down below, the creatures must at last be feeling the effects of the smoke. Down there, those incredibly ancient beings were dying, and their special magic going with them.

But they were not dying fast enough.

While Yan had been testing the barrier, the smoke had grown thicker. Penit, Danel, and all of the brigands were down, no longer coughing. So was Peyto. Teletha coughed weakly at irregular intervals, and Kim lay curled at the foot of the barrier, alternating sobs with hacking coughs.

At this rate, they would die before the creatures did.

Yan reached out to touch the ward barrier.

It still stood.

He gathered his strength and threw it at the ward. He tried to beat it down with his own need to survive, but he could not get a grip on it. Still, he felt it give under his pressure as it had not before. The ward was weaker, but still too strong for him.

He tried again, inserting a tendril of power into a gap he found between Douganan's shaping and the power underlying the spell. He was flung back at once. The backlash rippled out of the astral and into the earthly plane, but he managed to dissipate the energy. The effort set him to coughing. He felt as though his lungs were filled with fire. Breathing as shallowly as he could, he calmed himself, trying to ready himself for a last effort, for he knew his body could not survive much longer.

If he failed this time, he would fail them all. It might already be too late. Perhaps the world would not miss Arham and his brigands, but what about the fliers? They had not asked to come here, they were innocents, undeserving of the death they faced. If Yan failed, Peyto would never again see the civilization he longed for, his escape from the *baratani* and the sharks would be made a mockery. But most distressing, if Yan failed,

he would fail Teletha, magic-hating Teletha, who had
put herself in his hands, who had faced the magic, to
save those for whom she was responsible.

But who had led them all down here? Who had convinced them to cross the ward?

Yan knew only too well who was really responsible.

The ancient magic might tear his mind to shreds or
char his body to a cinder, but he had to try. Not just for
himself, but for them. For Teletha.

*Teletha.*

He didn't know if he spoke aloud, but she moaned
and reached out, groping for him with her hand. She
touched his leg. As her hand patted searchingly along
his thigh, he felt the heat of her touch through his
hosen with each fleeting contact. Then her touch was
gone, only to return on the arm he reached toward her.
Her hand slipped into his and he knew that some small
part of the bond they had forged when she was his spirit
anchor remained.

He felt her strength, her will to survive, and he knew
he could not fail her. He forced his will into the ward.
Power battered his mind, ripping at his defenses, but he
did not yield. The last bits of Douganan's spells shredded away, but they had done their work too well; they
had twisted the power stolen from the ancient mages
and now that power remained locked in the form
which Douganan had set upon it. The ward stood, a
wall still.

Yan found that intolerable.

He grappled with the ancient magic, throwing his
whole strength against it, ready to pit his will against
that of the six ancient mages.

But he could not find them.

Only an echo of brilliant minds clouded, extin-
guished, and gone.

He swam through those echoes, searching. At last he

found a presence, a power behind the magic. It moved
sluggishly at his touch. Though weakened unto death,
one of the ancient wizards still lived. For a single blind-
ing instant, Yan occupied the same space as that mind,
and he screamed in pain. Visions assaulted him. Sights,
sounds, smells ran riot through his mind. He was elsewhere, living another life. His tail bothered him. But he
had no tail! Howling, he fought against the chaos assail-
ing him. This was not his life, not him. He was a man,
not a—a—

It was gone.

Yan's head rang with a single alien thought, words
that were not words. A sense of relief. A question.

*Is it time, brother?*

A single drop of blood splashed onto his hand.

His blood.

He fell into cool and sweet darkness, where fire did
not burn in a man's mind, and strange beings no longer
walked on two legs, tails held proudly high as they
called to the stars and walked the ways of magic.
Huddled within himself, he felt sensations, disturbances
affecting his body. He knew he should find them
important, but they were so distant. They might even
be happening to someone else. But, no. They were
happening to him. Yan Tanafres. A magician?

Somewhere else Teletha's hands were upon him.
The rough surface of a ramp scraped along the exposed
parts of his skin. Cold, fresh air blew across his face.

Then a last sensation: a warm body draped across
his.

Teletha.

# 20

YAN CAME BACK TO THE EARTHLY plane to find his hands bound behind his back. Sitting up with difficulty, he found one of the brigands grinning at him, no doubt amused by his struggles.

Yan started to ask a question, but Horm stepped up to him and cuffed him with a backhanded slap. The blow toppled Yan and nearly sent him back into the darkness.

"You talk when we tell you to talk," the bregil said.

When his head stopped spinning, Yan struggled upright again. That, it seemed, hadn't been forbidden, and it allowed him to get a better look around.

He didn't like what he saw.

They were in Douganan's ritual chamber. For a moment the sinuous writing on the walls seemed almost comprehensible, but the moment passed and Yan was as puzzled as to its meaning as ever. The air in the chamber was tainted with the smell of smoke. He couldn't tell if it just hung in the air, or if it rose from their own smoke-saturated persons.

Yan saw that Horm and the grinning man weren't

the only ones about. Two more of Arham's brigands and Arham himself were present. Yan didn't see the man who had killed Douganan's weaponman just inside the ward. In addition to their own weapons, the mercenaries now carried pistols that Yan had last seen in the hands of the fliers. One of the brigands had appropriated Penit's helmet and was adjusting the padding to fit his head.

The fliers themselves lay in a row near the wall, bound as he was. Kim was awake, staring venomously at any brigand who passed before him, but the others seemed still unconscious. The bandage on Danel's leg was redder, as if his wound had opened. From where he sat, Yan couldn't tell if Danel or Penit still breathed, and his head was too muddled for him to check their auras. He hoped they weren't dead.

Where were the others?

A cough behind him made him turn his head. He saw Peyto sitting there, hunched over with his one hand tied to his ankles. The clerk looked like he'd just bitten into a sour fruit.

To avoid Peyto's glare, Yan turned his attention to Arham, who crouched over Teletha, staring intently at her. When she groaned and tried to roll over, the mercenary leader smiled. He waited until she opened her eyes and looked at him before he spoke.

"Ah, Captain. I'd begun to despair of you rejoining us."

"Untie me," she said in a hoarse voice.

"All in good time, Captain. It seems your luck is better than mine. All of *your* crew survived the smoke."

Yan was fiercely glad to hear that. It would only be justice if the killer had died on the other side of the ward.

"Obviously my luck isn't all good," Teletha said to Arham. "You woke up first."

"The gods smile on those ready to improve their own lot," Arham said.

"What do you want?" she asked.

Arham looked her up and down before replying. "You ask after something beyond the obvious, of course."

She glared at him. From the stiffness in his own facial muscles, Yan realized that he was glaring as well. A glance at his nearby captor revealed the man grinning wider still. Yan forced himself to relax.

Arham trailed a finger down the line of buttons closing Teletha's buff coat. "Why, what would I want other than your airship?"

"You can't fly it." Yan was amazed that Teletha's voice stayed steady when Arham's finger passed below her belt and across her crotch.

"I know that, but I find myself in need of the airship," Arham said. "You see, while you were asleep, I sent the lads out to do a little scouting. It seems that the thrice-cursed peasants of this village have stolen our horses while we were down there trying to roast ourselves. Without horses, I have two choices: I can walk out of here, or I can fly. I've hated walking since I marched with Count Raldry the year he kicked the rebels out of Oric. Horm doesn't mind walking, but me and the rest of the lads are cavalrymen at heart. We all prefer to ride where we are going. So we need your airship. And since I can't fly it, I need someone who can."

"If it's not to a *Goltianna* stronghold, I might agree to take you there," Teletha said. "But you have to untie me now."

"You're in no position to make demands, Captain. But if it makes you feel better, I wasn't planning on going native and joining with those doomed rebels. I think I'll be little more welcome than you Imperials around here now, so I was thinking more of heading across to the Megeed. A man can carve his own fortune there, especially if he has a starting stake. Your airship will fetch a fine price there, more than enough to rehorse all the lads and arm them well."

Teletha spit at his feet. "You'll not sell my ship."

"Control your temper, Captain. That ship is mine now, and if you're not more reasonable, I might just decide to sell you and your crew as well. There's always a market for healthy slaves in the Megeed, especially female ones."

Teletha seemed to think about that for a while. "You'll let us go if we fly you where you want to go?"

"As long as you treat me fair, I'll treat you fair. I'm a reasonable man," Arham said with a smile.

"Your word? By Vehr's sword?"

"Of course, Captain. You have my word. You fly us to the Megeed, and I'll let you and your crew go."

"But you keep the ship."

"Yes. I keep the ship. Old Gornal hid his wealth too well. I need to realize something from this venture. You understand, of course."

"I understand very well." She looked down at the ground. "I agree to your terms."

"See, I knew you could be reasonable. Horm, cut her free." The bregil moved to comply, but Arham stopped him with a gesture. "One moment, though. You wanted my parole when we surrendered to you down below. I think I should have yours now. Will you swear by Vehr's sword to give me your honorable parole?"

"I already agreed to your terms."

"Come now, Captain. Your parole, or you stay bound."

Teletha remained silent for so long that Yan thought she had refused Arham's offer. Arham began to tap his fist against his dagger scabbard in irritation. When Teletha spoke, her voice was very small. Yan doubted that Peyto, situated as he was behind Yan, could hear her.

"May Vehr's sword find my heart should I take arms against you or yours for so long as you hold to our bargain."

"And your crew?"

"They will do as I tell them."

"Very good. That wasn't so hard, was it?" Arham nodded and Horm cut Teletha's bonds.

Teletha lay where she was, chafing at her wrists to restore feeling to her hands. Yan watched her and Kim exchange glances, then nods. She looked at Yan and he gave a smile to let her know he was all right. She nodded. Arham brought her a cup of water.

"How many will your craft carry?" he asked.

"The ship took some damage coming in over the mountains," Teletha said.

"I have confidence that you will fix it. Answer my question."

Teletha drained off the cup before answering. "She's a six-placer, but she'll carry ten if you don't need speed."

"Ten? Then I fear that even with our losses, we have some extra baggage. Let's see. There's Horm and I, Ean, Worton, and Ars. That's five. You, of course. Your sergeant and the two fliers are three more to make nine. We have picked up some loot, more than a man's weight, I'm afraid. So we can't take anybody else at all. You were hoping not to leave your mage friend behind?"

Teletha shrugged, and Yan's heart sank.

Arham chuckled. "Well, Horm, she doesn't want him, so I guess you get to play with him after all. And kill the clerk, too, while you're at it."

Teletha spoke up. "You don't understand, Arham. I just meant that you're wrong."

"Don't play games with me, Captain. Gornal Douganan

tried that, and you know what happened to him. The mage stays. In the ground, so he doesn't tell any awkward tales."

"The mage goes."

"You've got nothing to bargain with." With a leer, he added, "Well, there is *one* thing."

"You're not stupid enough to kill the mage."

"What do you mean?" Arham asked suspiciously.

"The mountain winds are tricky. We'll need the mage. His magic is part of what makes the balloon work. It's part of what makes it move. Also, he can summon the wind we need to clear the peaks."

Yan knew she was lying and expected Arham to pick it up at once. The mercenary leader surprised him by saying, "So that's why you had him along. All right, he goes, but someone else stays."

In a grave, Yan thought. Would she sacrifice one of her crew for him? This time it was Teletha's turn to surprise him.

"Not necessary," she said. "If the mage works hard, we can lift another two."

"Two?"

"Your loot and the clerk. The mage will need his assistant."

Arham frowned at her. "You'd better not be lying. Horm doesn't like being cheated out of his games."

"Save the threats. Let's get on with it."

Arham was agreeable to that; despite his bluster it was clear he wanted to be away. The brigands wasted no time in marching everyone out of the tower and back to the barn. They even pitched in to drag the airship out of the building. It proved an awkward process, since the balloon was sagging, partially deflated. Arham looked worried.

"What's wrong with it? It looks dead."

"Just tired," Teletha said. "Like a man gets after he's

had his fun. As I said, we've got some work to do before she's ready to fly."

Teletha started to climb aboard, giving orders to her crew as she did. Arham grabbed her arm.

"I don't think I like this arrangement, Captain. Let your crew do the work. You and me and the mage will sit right here and watch. Horm will see that your crew works hard at their jobs."

"There aren't enough hands," she protested.

"My lads will help."

"Do they know how to run the shroud lines through the weather cams? Or rig the balloon for storm watch? Or set the anchor to hold the ship in place when the balloon reaches full inflation?"

"Of course not, but I'll bet your sergeant does. He can direct the work."

"You want me to sit here while Kim does all that?"

"Quite right, Captain."

Teletha frowned, then she sighed. "You heard him, Kim. Follow my orders."

"But Captain," Kim protested.

"Do it!"

"Aye, Captain."

"You've a good snap to your commands, Captain," Arham said, apparently in honest admiration.

Teletha ignored the compliment, turning her back on Arham and finding a place to sit under a shady tree. Yan joined her, and in the moment he shielded her face from Arham, she winked at him.

It was surely a signal. But for what?

Arham sat with them and the three of them watched as the others worked on the airship. Kim directed the setting of the anchor first, making sure that it was well hammered in. After spending nearly an hour directing Penit and two of the brigands as they climbed about the floppy and sluggishly churning balloon, Kim was

finally satisfied with the new set of the rigging. He took
time out for a brief argument with Peyto, ending the
discussion by dragging the clerk over to the fire basket
amidships and leaving him to tend the fire Kim started
there. While the others worked, Peyto continued to
look at the rigging and shake his head. No one paid
attention to him, however; they were working too hard.
Danel, his injured leg consigning him to less strenuous
work and, therefore, to helping the clerk, could regular-
ly be heard cutting off the clerk's questions and telling
Peyto to be quiet. Working together, the fliers and the
mercenaries removed both twinblades at the craft's
stern and straightened the end of the crankshaft. They
replaced and secured the twinblades in half the time it
had taken to remove them. Kim climbed aboard and
gave the crankshaft a few tentative turns to satisfy himself that it was turning true before giving Teletha a
thumbs-up sign. Above the boat-shaped hull the huge
balloon floated, straining against its rigging.

"It looks much better now," Arham commented.
Yan heard what might have been awe in the mercenary's
voice, but it might as easily have been greed.

"Like a man," Teletha said. "Big and eager at the
start of a ride."

Arham laughed loudly. "Let's hope this one has staying
power."

The mercenary leader ordered their gear and loot
brought aboard. When Teletha complained of the volume, suggesting that Yan would be overloaded, Arham
ordered some of the fliers' gear dumped, saying, "We
don't want to tire him out too early."

Horm and the brigand wearing Penit's helmet were
busy stowing stuff in the bow while Teletha went
through the airship assigning stations. Yan and Peyto
she put just aft of the fire basket "as usual." Arham
assigned them a guard.

"Worton, keep your eye on the mage. Kill him if he tries anything that's not what he should be doing."

"How will I know?" Worton asked.

"Use your judgment," Arham told him. "He's useful, not necessary."

Yan expected the brigand to draw his pistol, but Worton unsheathed his dagger instead. Thumbing the edge, the mercenary stepped around behind Yan. Grabbing one of Yan's arms, Worton twisted it behind Yan's back before putting the blade to his throat. "Didn't like magic before this. Like it less now. Understand, magician? You don't want to give me cause. Me, I'd like the chance to slit your throat."

Teletha set Kim to tending the fire and asked for the last mercenary to aid him.

"What's wrong with the other two?" Arham asked. "Or the clerk? He helped before."

"He's got to help the mage now. I need Danel and Penit as deckhands. There isn't time to teach your boys all they need to know. Any idiot can tend a fire."

"Such a way with words. Are we almost ready to leave, then?

"Almost," Teletha said. She led him back to the wheel and started checking its linkages. Arham bent over her as she worked, watching everything she did.

"I'm not rigging it to break," she said, sounding annoyed.

"I didn't think you were. If the ship crashed, you'd suffer as much as me."

"Well, if you trust me, get out of the way."

"I just want to know how to sail this thing," Arham said, almost apologetically. "If I like it, I might not sell it to some Megeed baron after all. Maybe I could hire out to some of them. There'd be good pay for a good crew, especially one with an experienced captain."

"That an offer?"

"Are you interested?"

Teletha hesitated, as if she might actually be considering the matter. She had been warming up to Arham. Could she seriously be considering joining up with the brigand?

"Let's get you out of here before we make any decisions like that. You might not like flying." She opened a hamper and took out a mass of straps and cords. "Ever work as a marine?"

"Hate the water."

"Me, too. Well, even if you've never sailed, she's not too hard to handle. You want to learn, best thing is to do. Man like you'll want to be at the wheel."

"I thought that would be your station."

"I'll take it if you want, but it won't be hard taking her up here. You could get the feel of her."

"Why are you doing this?"

"You said you might keep her. I'd rather see her in a soldier's hands than in the paws of some Megeed robber baron who'd run her into trees the first time up."

"Hah," Arham laughed. "I knew there was more to you than could be bound by an Imperial lackey's oath."

"Right," she said. "Stand here. Put this on."

"What is it" Arham asked suspiciously.

"Safety harness. Keeps you from falling out if the ship rocks. It's a long way down if you haven't got wings." Once he'd gotten it on, she said, "Let me check the straps."

Teletha cinched the buckles tight, slipping the loose ends of the straps around the buckles and securing them in their own knots. She took the trailing lines and lashed them onto cleats at Arham's feet with large, bulky knots. Splicing their long, loose ends together, she casually tossed the result over the crankshaft.

"Penit," she called. "Toss me the ratlines."

Penit looked at her questioningly. Teletha pointed at what she wanted. "That one and that one. Just toss them over here."

When Teletha started to secure them onto Arham's harness, he asked, "What are those?"

"Control lines. They'll let you feel the balloon. This way you'll know when you've got good lift."

"I haven't done this before. How will I know?" Arham was beginning to sound eager.

"You'll know. You'll feel it."

"How soon before we're ready?"

"We're ready now if your lads have gotten everything aboard."

"All aboard," Horm responded. The bregil hunkered down in the bow and shut his eyes. He, at least, showed no desire to be airborne.

"Stand by the shroud cleats," Teletha ordered.

Penit, who had been talking with Danel ran at once to obey. Danel, favoring his wounded leg, was slower. When they were at their stations, Teletha gave the next order.

"Bring up the flame in the fire basket."

Ars followed Kim's lead in adding wood to the basket.

"Mage, are you ready?" Teletha called. "I don't want this gondola staying behind if you're not ready."

Yan cleared his throat and said to the brigand behind him. "I'll need my hand free and a little leeway from the dagger if I'm to spell properly."

"Blade's sharp and I'm fast. It ain't gonna be far away," Worton warned him.

Yan knew that only too well. He hoped he understood what Teletha was doing. "Ready," he called.

"All ready then," Teletha said. "Ean, or whatever your name is, stand by the anchor line and start hauling when you get the lift order." She waited until the mercenary in the bow had his hands on the line, then turned to Arham. "All right, Arham, it's your show. Hands on the wheel, though, need to keep her steady as she lifts. Got to be ready for ground gusts."

Arham stuck his pistol into his belt, careful to place the grip away from Teletha. "So what's the order?"

"To lift? 'Away the balloon.'"

"Away the balloon," Arham shouted.

Penit and Danel hauled on their lines, then released them, letting the lines play through the weather cams. The pulleys squealed and the hull began to rock, lifting slightly from the ground and bumping down again. Urging Ars on, Kim stoked the fire, while Ean hauled ineffectually on the anchor line.

"It's stuck," he called.

"Keep hauling," Teletha shouted back as she stepped back behind Arham.

Yan could see the mercenary leader grinning in anticipation of his first flight.

"I can feel it!" Arham's grin got wider. "I can feel the balloon rising."

"Good," Teletha said, slipping her hand around to Arham's left and snatching the pistol from his belt.

"What are you doing?"

"Saying good-bye, Arham." She lifted the line she had placed on the crankshaft and yanked. Her bulky knots dissolved, leaving Arham with nothing securing him to the deck of the airship. The mercenary began to rise.

As his feet left the deck, he started screaming.

Yan sensed Worton's attention waver and slammed his head back into the man's face. He felt Worton's nose crunch against the back of his skull. The dagger blade rose before his eyes. Yan ducked his head past it and, cupping his right hand with his left, he drove his elbow back into the brigand's gut. Worton grunted, and went down.

Arham's grip on the wheel was not enough to hold him against the lift of the balloon. Trailing lines, he rose above the airship's hull, which remained firmly on its landing runners.

Kim slammed his arwood log across the fire basket and into the face of his surprised helper. The brigand howled. Kim stepped around the basket frame and pounced on him. The two went down in a struggling heap.

Ean had abandoned the anchor line and stood staring at Arham as the brigand leader rose higher into the sky. Horm exploded from the bow and came to an abrupt a stop, staring at the pistol Teletha pointed at him.

"I'm waiting," she said with a grin.

Yan and Peyto disarmed the moaning Worton, Peyto taking the pistol and helping to cover the two mercenaries in the bow. Kim emerged bloodied but victorious from his scuffle by the fire basket.

Overhead, Arham's screams were diminishing with distance.

"You've lost your balloon," Yan said to Teletha.

"She'd never have made it over the mountains with this load."

Yan raised his eyebrow. "Not even with the mage working hard?"

"Mage? I didn't know magic had anything to do with flying."

"Neither did Arham," Yan said.

She smiled wickedly. "That was the important part."

Teletha began to laugh. After a moment, Yan joined her.

# EPILOGUE

THE BALLOON CARRYING ARHAM away might as well have been a signal rocket, for Jhezi arrived within the hour. The fliers were still debating what to do with their prisoners. Yan spoke briefly with the young girl, telling her that the prisoners were the last of Arham's brigands, and that she and the other villagers were safe now. Jhezi disappeared back into the woods and soon returned with a pair of grim-visaged villagers. They in turn spoke with Yan and returned to the woods. Before the sunset, the first family, Jhezi's, returned to the village, carrying what goods they had taken to their refuge in the woods and driving livestock before them.

A violent storm blew through the valley that night. Rain and snow alternated with hail and sleet, all driven under high winds. It was as though the world was trying to compress into a single storm all the weather the valley had missed by remaining in its magical isolation.

It took several days before all of the scattered villagers could be convinced to return. During that time Yan and the fliers questioned the returnees, to little effect. Few villagers knew more than their own story

and those were drearily familiar; each family, terrified
of the mercenaries, had hidden in the forest. When the
mercenaries had disappeared in the direction of the
tower, the local folk had hurriedly buried their dead,
taken what they could, and fled again to the woods to
wait out the reign of terror. None had taken much note
of his neighbors, living or dead.

Bert and Iaf, who had been left outside the tower,
were not among those who returned. Neither was Rom,
the flier who had fled rather than pass the ward barrier.
None of the villagers had seen them or the animals
Yan, Peyto, and Iaf had ridden in on. Yan hoped they
had not fallen afoul of the scouts Arham had sent out
after they escaped the timespell, but no one reported
any bodies or signs of violence.

Among the last to return was one Shay Miller. He
had been the one with the presence of mind to turn the
livestock out of the barn so that the brigands would not
slaughter the beasts. He was also the one who answered
the question Yan had asked of all the villagers. Shay
had been the last one to see Demisi alive, and had
buried her mutilated body himself.

With Laird Gornal Douganan dead, no one ruled in
the valley. Calling upon her authority as an Imperial
officer, Teletha appointed a council from among the
villagers and charged them with the responsibility of
maintaining peace and justice in the valley until the
Emperor approved Laird Douganan's successor. They
complained, Shay loudest among them, that she was
not their lord and could not force such responsibility
upon them. Their cries lessened when she remanded
the prisoners to their justice.

While the council members debated the most appropriate fate for the brigands, Yan found himself thinking
about leaving the valley. Teletha joined him and he
soon learned that he was not the only one.

"How much time do you think passed out there?" she asked.

"There's no way of knowing. We'll have to go and see."

"Will it be the same world out there?"

"No. But then it never is the same world, from day to day."

"And I thought you had learned something."

"What do you mean?"

She chuckled at his perplexed frown. "I thought you had learned to talk more straightforwardly. Instead of using all that mystical, 'you figure it out' kind of street-corner-prophet talk."

"I'm sorry."

"Don't be. I expect it's too much to ask you to turn around so quickly. After all, you've been a mage for . . . how many years has it been?"

Yan looked up at the sky and the mountains around them, newly clad in a dusting of snow. Had it only been in the spring that he had received his *claviarm*? So short and so long a time.

"It'll be one year in the spring," he responded shyly.

"One?"

Yan felt his cheeks heat. He feared his answer had destroyed any respect she might have held for him.

"No wonder you have so little effective magic," she said, confirming his fear.

"I really am quite skilled in ritual," he protested.

"Really? Then why do you sound as though you don't expect me to believe you?"

Yan almost said *because I don't*, but decided that such a response was too much of an opening to his inner self. He had been open enough already. He just shrugged.

"You've done quite well then, for an initiate," Teletha said. "With your help, we've survived brigands and dreadful magic. Time is restored to its normal passage and the countryside has returned to its proper season. Some would call such deeds great. I suspect the empire will offer a generous thanks, once the Emperor learns of the magical threat you dispersed here."

"*We* dispersed here."

"As someone once pointed out, it's part of my job." She seemed to ponder for a moment. "Still, there might be a reward in it at that. Will you accompany us back to my commander?"

Yan thought about Larra and his promise, an uncomfortable thought standing here next to Teletha.

"I may not have authority to reward you," she said. "But I can tell you that the Coronal Empire has places for clear thinkers, even if they are mages. I could get you an introduction to my superiors, a chance to show them what you can do. Colonel Jessidern has connections in the court."

That was the dream Yan had left Talinfad for. So why was he hesitating? "I'll think about."

"You'd better think yes," Peyto said as he joined them. The clerk had an annoying habit of butting into Yan's conversations when he was least wanted. This time was perhaps an exception. Peyto's continual desire to leave Scothandir might deflect Teletha. At the very least, it would pull the conversation to safer, more familiar ground.

"I'm a mage, not a courtier," Yan said.

"You're an idiot if you think you'll be content staying in this backwater," Peyto said.

"Direct," Teletha commented.

"Necessary, Captain. This lad doesn't respond well to subtlety." Peyto smiled at her. "What exactly are your plans, Captain?"

"I've got to get back to my commander."

"And how are you planning on doing that? The balloon is gone."

"That Shay, whether you think it bright or foolish, was bold enough to take the mercenaries' horses into the woods. I've already told him that I'm requisitioning them in the name of the empire. He took my chit, but he wasn't happy about it. There are enough horses for you two as well."

"A generous offer, Captain. I sure that both of us—"

"I've got to go back to the village," Yan said.

Peyto sighed, and gave Teletha a long-suffering look.

"This was a fishing village," Teletha said. "Do ships call there often?"

"Not while we were mewed there," Peyto said.

"As Peyto says, ships do not call there. However, on the way to the village we will cross the road to Glaebur. There'll be ships there, though none may be wanting to leave this late in the season."

"We'll get there first and worry about ships later," Teletha said. "We could ride together until then, companions on the road. It might be best if we rode with you all the way to the village. These lands are turbulent."

"I don't think you need worry about us," Yan said.

"Don't be rude, Master Tanafres," Peyto said, smiling. "I think the captain's offer is a generous one that we should not decline."

*Why? So the two of you can work on me together?* "There's little to see in the village, Captain. You'd be wasting your time. Best you go straight on to Glaebur."

"Still, I think I would like to meet the fisherman who pulled you two from the sea," Teletha said.

"Actually, he rescued us from a raft," Yan said.

"Whatever," Teletha said with a dismissive shrug. "It's settled, we'll ride together to the village and then on to Glaebur."

"An excellent solution," Peyto said. "It occurs to me, Captain, that if we are riding, you will have to abandon your airship's hull."

Sadness settled on Teletha's face. "We'll salvage what we can and pack it out on the horses. The rest we'll burn. Standing orders."

Peyto shook his head. "What a waste."

"Orders can be that way," she said. She visibly took hold of herself. "This overland trip will be interesting. We may even be able to make it useful to the empire as well; we can show the Scoths that the empire isn't completely populated by ogres."

"It'll be a difficult journey back if we don't get started soon," Peyto said cheerfully.

Yan saw no reason to be cheerful. The journey was going to be difficult whenever they left.


"What is so important in that village?" Teletha asked as they started the horses down the trail through the woods.

"An unfulfilled promise," Yan replied. More than one, actually, but only one seemed fit for discussion with Teletha. "I have to tell Larra and her family about Demisi."

"Larra?"

"The, uh, friend I told you about. The one who asked me to come here."

"Hunh."

They bounced along in silence for a while.

Thinking about Larra made Yan uncomfortable His reexposure to things magical had made it clear to him that, whatever else he was, he was still a mage. Magic would always be a part of his life. And Larra, with her antipathy for things magical, would never be a mage's woman.

He didn't know what lay ahead. He had thought that he could convince Larra to leave the village, to go with him to the islands, to Sharhumrin, but now he felt that

such a plan was only a dream. He couldn't ask Larra to
leave her life to follow him. Well, he could, but whom
would that serve? She would never be happy with his
magic, she would never understand. How could she?
He was not sure *he* understood the needs pulling at
him.

But he had come to realize that his needs wouldn't
be fulfilled in a fisherman's hut in a tiny village in the
wilds of Scothandir. He had Gornal Douganan's books
now, a treasure trove of magical lore, and just possibly
an invitation to damnation.

He had choices to make.

Since Gan Tidoni had first shown him how to touch
the magic, Yan had desired to know more, to learn
more, to understand more. Douganan's books held so
much. Too much for Yan to ignore. Far too many
secrets. And he'd need more than the resources of a
backwater fishing village to unlock those secrets.

And that, he realized, was one choice already made.
He just had to live with the results of the decision.

That's all.

Such a little thing.

Time had passed during his stay in the valley, perhaps a lot. Yan wondered if Larra had forgotten about
him and found someone to take his place. He hoped
so; it would be easier for both of them that way.

But what if she hadn't? Could he make her understand that it would be better for her, for both of them, if
she stayed behind when he left? He tried to think of
what he'd say to her, but every path seemed to lead to
confusion, and he knew that his mind wasn't as settled
as he had thought. He began to dread seeing Larra
again.

As they cleared the last trees, a chill breeze blew
down from the pass, raising shivers.

"Mannar's breath," Peyto commented. "The Sky

Queen warns us of the end of a fall we never saw, thanks to Laird Douganan's magic."

"Would that Mannar brought us the end of magic," Kim said.

"Magic is a part of the world," Yan said.

Teletha sighed. "A part we can do without. Magic almost destroyed time as we know it."

"A unintentional effect," he said.

"Still, it's nasty stuff," she said. "The world would be better off without it."

"We would all be dead without my magic," Yan pointed out.

"It was magic that caused the danger in the first place," she shot back.

"Magic is neither good nor bad," Yan said stubbornly.

"Don't let a churchman hear you say that, he'll revoke your license."

"What I mean is that it was the magician at fault, not the magic itself."

"So maybe we need to be rid of magicians," she said with a laugh.

Hurt by her comment, Yan drew himself up haughtily. "I'm a magician."

"And you didn't stop the spell. Nay, take no offense, for I meant none. But magic was not needed to stop this runaway magic, just natural laws well applied. Don't you see, Yan, the natural world, without magic, is stronger in the long run. Magic's had its run."

Teletha's word's called up the echo of an ancient voice in Yan's mind. *Is it time, brother?* Time? Or the end of a time? While Yan listened to the echo in his head, Teletha continued speaking.

"The seasons will turn as they must. And we will go through them, as we must."

Might not the world be turning as Teletha suggested? Gan Tidoni had been telling Yan for years that magic was not what it once was. Under the tower, they had faced a problem born of magic; and as she said, Yan hadn't stopped the spell with magic, but Teletha's scientific reasoning had managed to do it. Could magic's time be passing?

Was this the change that Adain had foreseen? "The wheel of the universe turns," he had said. Were they on the verge of a new season, a season without magic? And what place did a mage have in a world without magic?

Time would tell.

"Better save your thinking for later," Teletha suggested. "Unless I'm mistaken, those clouds are carrying more snow, and we've got to get out of the hills."

They urged the horses to a faster pace.

# ☷ HarperPrism

## WELCOME TO A WONDROUS NEW WORLD OF FANTASY!
### Here are your tickets to the adventures of a lifetime . . .

⊕

### THE HEDGE OF MIST by Patricia Kennealy-Morrison

The final novel in Kennealy-Morrison's *Tales Of Arthur* trilogy from her highly-acclaimed science-fantasy series, *The Keltiad*. This Arthurian cycle takes place on the double-ringed planet of Keltia, weaving together epic fantasy, romance, and science fiction. Here is the story of how Arthur found his way to the land where he still lingers, and how the bard Taliesin returned to his legendary home, called Earth. ($22.00 Hardcover)

⊕

### THE DRAGON AND THE UNICORN by A. A. Attanasio

The bestselling author of *Radix* and *Wyvern* pens a tale rich in myth and magic as the legendary romance of Uther Pendragon, king of the Britons, and Ygrane, queen of the Celts, sets the stage for the coming of Arthur. ($16.00 Trade Paperback)

⊕

### ARTHUR, KING
### by Dennis Lee Anderson

This thrilling time-travel fantasy adventure brings King Arthur to the rescue at England's darkest hour: World War II's Battle of Britain. Arthur's greatest enemy, his bastard son Mordred, has stolen Merlin's book and used it to flee to the far future. Now all Camelot is at risk unless Arthur can recover the sword. ($4.99 Paperback)

⊕

### HUNTER OF THE LIGHT by Risa Aratyr

In this story of Eirinn, Ireland's alternate past, the white elk that appears on Eirinn's shores must die or the balance of Light and Dark will be destroyed. Blackthorn has been chosen for the critical task—but he is unaware that a renegade wizard seeks to usurp the Hunt and betray Eirinn to the Shadow's King. ($5.99 Paperback)